# PAM WEAVER
# Goodnight Sweetheart

Published by AVON
A division of HarperCollins*Publishers* Ltd
1 London Bridge Street
London SE1 9GF

www.harpercollins.co.uk

A Paperback Original 2020

First published in Great Britain by HarperCollins*Publishers* 2020

Copyright © Pam Weaver 2020

Pam Weaver asserts the moral right to be identified as the author of this work.

A catalogue copy of this book is available from the British Library.

ISBN: 978-0-00-836619-3 (UK)
ISBN: 978-0-00-841076-6 (US/CA)

Typeset in Minion by Palimpsest Book Production Limited, Falkirk, Stirlingshire
Printed and bound in UK by CPI Group (UK) Ltd, Croydon CR0 4YY

This book is dedicated to the GI father I never knew.

# One

Ten-year-old Frankie Sherwood pulled her skirts over her bare legs and tucked her feet under her body. She was an attractive child with clear blue eyes and blonde hair. Although small for her age, what she lacked in height she made up for in her personality. A bright and determined girl, she always did her best. Pressing herself into the tree trunk, she felt the long grass swish back and surround her – but was she hidden enough? Her heart was racing. This was so exciting.

As she looked back the way she had come, Frankie saw her friend Jenny Ruddock standing to attention behind a tree. She would be easy to find. Doreen Toms had jumped into a ditch so she was well hidden. Further down in the more open space, Frankie's mother was still counting. 'Nine, ten, eleven . . .'

The long bramble branch Frankie had lifted in order to tuck herself right into the hollow of the tree flopped back down. That was a bit of luck. Now she was completely enclosed behind the green leaves and its blackberries, but all the same, she breathed in to make herself even smaller.

Frankie grinned to herself. What a wonderful birthday she was having. For a start, it was a beautiful day. The late summer sun was warm. A bee flew by making a soft humming noise.

1

Somewhere in the open space, a bird sang and in the far distance, a dog, probably out for a walk with its owner, barked happily. Frankie loved it up here on Hillbarn with its wide open spaces surrounded by trees and bushes. Mummy had told her that long ago the Worthing Rotary Club had given the land to the Corporation for the local football club who had created five football pitches. The rest of the land was for the locals but she and mummy might not be able to walk around much longer because there was talk of creating a golf course. Thank goodness it hadn't happened yet. The other reason why she was happy was because Mrs Ruddock had helped mummy to carry some picnic food in a big bag along with a grey blanket.

Frankie liked Mrs Ruddock. She was about the same age as mummy but she didn't go out to work. Mrs Ruddock did a lot of swimming in the sea. The family had a beach chalet near Splash Point in Worthing and in the summer she asked Frankie if she would like to come so that Jenny had someone to play with. That was fun and it didn't even matter if it rained.

Mrs Toms, on the other hand, didn't join in anything much but mummy said not to say anything probably because Mrs Toms didn't have a lot of money. Frankie felt sorry about that, but Mrs Toms wasn't a very nice lady. When they were carrying the things for the picnic, Mrs Toms said she was nobody's skivvy and would only carry the flasks and the lemonade. They had set down the blanket and enjoyed fish paste sandwiches and egg and salad cream sandwiches together. Then, while the three girls ran around, the mums spent a pleasant hour relaxing in the sunshine. When Frankie and her friends grew bored, they had left the other mums on the blanket having a chin-wag, while Frankie's mum joined them in a game of hide and seek.

'Nineteen, twenty, twenty-one . . .'

Frankie couldn't resist moving the bramble branch over a

bit. Now she could see her mother. She stood with her back to them, her head up and her hands covering her eyes.

'Twenty-six, twenty-seven . . .'

Frankie felt a surge of love and pride. An attractive thirty-four-year-old, Moira Sherwood worked hard to keep a roof over their heads. As a dressmaker she was hugely popular and as a result she was busy, busy, busy. Sometimes it felt as though people were coming to the house for fittings all day long. And why not? Moira could turn her hand to anything: wedding dresses, dresses for bridesmaids, even school uniforms; there was always a half-finished garment either on the dressmaker's dummy or hanging from the picture rail. Sometimes she altered men's clothing as well – a trouser leg which was too long or a jacket sleeve which needed to be invisibly mended. She didn't always charge them for it. If they were down on their luck or something she'd say, 'Pay me when you can.' Mummy never minded helping people out, although Doreen said her mum said it wasn't seemly. Frankie had no idea what that meant but it didn't sound very nice to say it. Mummy often worked long into the night to get an order ready and when that happened, she didn't have time to play games or to tell Frankie one of the lovely stories about her colourful life. But today was different. When they'd got up that morning, mummy said whatever needed to be done could jolly well wait. Today was September 3rd, Frankie's tenth birthday. Today was the day she went into double figures and that made it extra special.

'Thirty-nine, forty . . .'

Even though mummy was so busy, Frankie had a happy childhood. She was surrounded by people she loved and all mummy's clients were nice to her. All except young Mr Knight. Old Mr Knight had been their landlord and years ago he'd been daddy's teacher in school. Frankie would have liked to have known a little more about her father but she didn't like to ask.

Daddy had died in 1925 when Frankie was just over a year old. Mummy said he'd got a weak chest and he'd caught the noo-moan-ea. Mummy had loved him very much and she always said he'd adored Frankie, but Frankie couldn't even remember him. Sometimes when mummy talked about daddy, she would shut herself away afterwards, and have a little cry, so Frankie kept her thoughts to herself. And now she would never even know about daddy's school days because, earlier this year, old Mr Knight had died and young Mr Knight had taken over.

'Forty-nine, fifty,' her mother called, 'I'm coming, ready or not.'

Frankie shivered with excitement and squeezed her eyes tightly shut. After a few seconds she could hear her mother's footsteps coming closer. She held her breath. Perhaps the hiding place she'd chosen wasn't so good after all. A wave of disappointment surged through her at the thought and although she stayed perfectly still, she quite expected her mother to tap her on the shoulder at any moment.

'I see you, Jenny,' her mother called and Frankie heard Jenny groan as she emerged from behind the tree. Frankie held her breath again as her mother's footsteps came right up to her, but then to her utter joy, her mother moved on!

'Frankie,' she called, 'where are you? And I can't think where Doreen is hiding. She must be somewhere around here.'

On the picnic blanket, the other mums chatted. Every now and then, snatches of conversation drifted towards Frankie. It was all a bit boring: the price of coal and how difficult it was to get it at summer prices and Mr Ruddock's boil which kept him away from his chemist shop for three days.

'I've asked Mrs Sherwood to make Jenny some gym slips for school,' said Mrs Ruddock. 'She's very good.'

'I don't want my Doreen to have anything home-made,' Mrs Toms said sniffily.

Frankie struggled not to giggle as she saw her mother walking on up towards the top of the lane where the fabulous views of the Downs spread out for miles. Hillbarn was on the outskirts of Worthing, in an area north of the village of Broadwater and surrounded by farm land. In days gone by, the village had been a focal point for Easter Fairs and a June Fair when people came from miles around. Broadwater Green itself had been the home of cricket since the beginning of the eighteenth century and somebody called W.G. Grace, who was, apparently, very famous a long time ago, had played there. Frankie had learned all that at school, and men still played cricket on the green.

A moment later, her mother must have turned back because Frankie heard her say, 'Ah, there you are, pickle! How clever you are. I was looking everywhere.'

She lifted the bramble branch and Frankie stood up. 'The only one I can't find is Doreen,' said Moira. Frankie and Jenny looked at each other and grinned. Moira began to search once more. 'I see you,' said Moira at last and Doreen emerged from the ditch. 'I hope you haven't got wet.'

Fortunately the ditch was bone dry and once mummy had brushed the dirt from Doreen's knees, she was fine. Frankie's friends ran back towards the picnic blanket where Mrs Ruddock was blowing smoke rings with her cigarette. Sitting a little apart, Mrs Toms watched her with pursed lips. A little later, they heard her scolding her daughter for hiding in the dirty ditch.

Before they went back to the others, Moira gave her daughter a hug and then said, 'Just look at all those blackberries. Quick, Frankie, go back and ask the other mummies to bring the empty tin I used for the sandwiches. We must pick some while we're up here. It would be a shame to miss out on an apple and blackberry pie.'

Everyone, except Mrs Toms and Doreen, spent the next twenty minutes or so picking the luscious blackberries. Some were as big as a penny and as far as Frankie was concerned, very few of the ones she'd picked ended up in the tin. Doreen wasn't allowed any because her mother said you didn't know what animal had been sniffing around them and it wasn't healthy.

'I had no idea there were so many up here,' said Mrs Ruddock. 'My mother-in-law is coming tomorrow for Sunday lunch. I shall get Mrs Brown to make a blackberry fool.' Mrs Brown was her cleaning lady.

The girls were soon bored. The brambles scratched their arms and most of the berries were too high for them to reach. After a while they gave up and chased butterflies or picked wild flowers instead. All too soon, their mothers were saying it was time to go and they all trooped back to Frankie's place, where her mother promised to make a pot of tea while Frankie opened her presents.

Doreen Toms had given her a magic painting book. 'You only need to make your brush wet,' Mrs Toms explained. 'As soon as the water touches it, the colours come through.'

Frankie leafed through the pages of the book. It seemed very babyish.

'I had one like that for Christmas,' Doreen remarked and her mother flashed her a dark look. Doreen didn't seem to notice because she added, 'but I lost it.'

Doreen was almost jolted out of her chair by her mother's elbow.

'What do you say?' Moira reminded her daughter as she passed the cups of tea around.

'Thank you,' Frankie said dutifully.

As Moira sat with her own cup she rubbed her arm.

'Are you in pain?' Mrs Ruddock asked, concerned.

Moira shook her head. 'Bit achy, that's all. Probably all that reaching up for those blackberries.'

Jenny's present was a hair slide with little green rhinestones on it. She also gave Frankie three different pieces of coloured ribbon for her hair. Frankie smiled. 'Ooh, thank you,' she said, holding up the red ribbon.

'That will go perfectly with the jumper Aunt Bet sent in the post,' her mother remarked.

'Thank you,' said Frankie, holding still for her mother to fasten the hair slide.

It was then that mummy handed Frankie a shoe box tied with pink ribbon. 'And this is from me,' she said.

Frankie's eyes lit up. Her friends stared enviously as she slid the ribbon carefully from the box and lifted the lid. Inside was a doll. Not just any old doll but a beautiful dolly dressed in an exquisite pale blue satin dress. As Frankie lifted it from the box, she heard a collective gasp.

'Oh, Moira,' said Mrs Ruddock. 'Did you dress it yourself? It's gorgeous.'

Rubbing the top of her left arm again, Moira gave them a nod. 'I've been saving the material for ages.'

Everyone knew nothing was wasted as far as Moira Sherwood was concerned. Her clients bought the material for their garments and once it had been cut and sewn, any pieces left over, big or small, went into a pillowcase Moira kept hanging on the door for the purpose. From those same pieces she would make baby clothes for the new born, cot quilts, pram covers, even the odd patchwork cushion cover. This doll was exceptional. The women could see the love which had gone into every stitch. Frankie lifted her skirts to reveal some pale pink pantaloons (bridesmaid's material), a silk petticoat (from an alteration of an evening dress into a cocktail dress), a pale blue satin skirt (from the nightdress of someone's wedding trousseau), a white broderie anglaise blouse with blue ribbon on the cuffs and a ruffle at the neck (made from bits which had been in the pillowcase for so long that Moira had forgotten where they came from), and, finally, a neatly embroidered waistcoat with tiny glass buttons down the front. Frankie held her up to her face and kissed the doll's lips. She had fallen in love with her the minute she'd set eyes on her. She was so beautiful. 'She's my Russian princess.'

Everyone glanced admiringly at Moira but she only had eyes for her daughter. 'I thought you would say that,' she smiled.

'Russian princess?' Mrs Ruddock repeated.

'Frankie loves to hear the story of the time I made an ensemble for the Princess Alexeievna,' said Moira, the exotic name slipping easily off her tongue.

'What, a princess came here? To Worthing?' Mrs Toms asked breathlessly.

'No,' said Moira with a chuckle. 'It was a long time ago when I was working in London. She came to the dressmaker where I trained.'

'Are you sure she was a real princess?' said Mrs Ruddock.

Moira nodded. 'Not only that, but she was very beautiful as well. She still is. I saw her picture in a magazine not so long ago. Of course, she's married now, to a Baron von somebody-or-other. Bit of a come-down, I suppose, but considering what happened to the rest of the Russian royal family soon after she arrived in this country, I guess you could say she got off lightly.'

Everyone was spell-bound. Frankie ran her fingers over the dolly's skirt, the waistcoat and the tiny little buttons, wondering if some of the older materials could have belonged to the Russian princess. The doll's straw hat was decorated with tiny pieces of wax fruit. Could that have been hers? No, now she thought about it, she recalled seeing the same fruit on a pretty jewellery case her mother made for someone's twenty-first birthday. Apparently the client was going to fill the case with family heirlooms: a string of pearls which belonged to the girl's grandmother, a ring belonging to an old aunt, and some earrings her mother had worn on her wedding day. Right there and then, Frankie made up her mind that this dolly would be her family heirloom. She would play with it, of course, but she would be very, very careful.

'Tell them about when the bad man came for the princess, Mummy,' Frankie said, looking up at her mother.

'I'm sure nobody wants to hear about that,' her mother said, pouring herself another cup of tea.

'Oh, please do,' Mrs Ruddock interrupted. 'Go on, Moira. This is fascinating.'

'I don't hold with them foreigners,' Mrs Toms said. She might not have been as well off as the others but that didn't stop her from being a sour-faced woman not averse to expressing her opinions, no matter how abrasive they might be. 'It's not right, them helping themselves to what's ours.'

'It wasn't like that.' Moira blew out her cheeks and put her fist to her chest.

'You all right, love?' interrupted Mrs Ruddock. 'You look a bit pale.'

'Touch of indigestion, that's all,' Moira said dismissively.

'While the princess was in the fitting room,' Frankie began, her eyes glistening with excitement. 'A man in a great big fur hat came to the shop. As soon as the princess heard his voice she was very scared, wasn't she, Mummy? They had to hide her in a big basket.'

The two women gave Moira a quizzical look.

Moira went on. 'Like I said, it was a long time ago. The Princess Natalia Alexeievna wanted a wedding trousseau. When she came to the workshop, the only clothes she had were what she stood up in.'

'I can't believe that,' Mrs Toms remarked. 'I always thought people like them were rolling in it.'

'I read somewhere,' said Mrs Ruddock, 'that when they lined that Czar Nicholas and his family against the wall and shot them, the bullets ricocheted from their bodices because of the precious stones hidden inside the seams. It was a regular blood bath, so I'm told.'

Doreen let out an audible gasp.

'Do you mind,' Mrs Toms scolded. 'Remember the children.'

Quick to apologise, Mrs Ruddock blushed. 'Sorry.'

'I don't know why you feel sorry for them,' said Mrs Toms. 'They treat their people like dirt and they're full of superstition and devil worship.'

'Come, come,' said Moira. 'I'm sure it wasn't as bad as that.'

'So did your princess have precious stones in her bodice?' Mrs Ruddock asked.

Moira looked away, as if the truth was being dragged reluctantly from her, then nodded. 'Not only diamonds and freshwater pearls but an emerald or two as well. It was my job to unpick the seams without spoiling her clothes.'

'Go on,' Mrs Ruddock gasped incredulously.

'The workshop was in London near a rough area they called Little Russia,' said Moira. 'And this Bolshevik burst through the front of the shop demanding to know where the princess was. We were all terrified. Even Madam said he looked very frightening.'

'Did someone go for the police?' Mrs Toms asked.

Moira let out a hollow laugh. 'You'd be lucky to find one. It was so bad around there that the police had to walk around in twos. Anyway, like Frankie said, I shoved her into the big linen basket and we all covered her over with material.'

With a look of horror on her face, Mrs Toms clutched at her throat.

'The other girls distracted him while I wheeled the princess down to the boiler room in the basement,' Moira went on. 'We left her under the covers, praying to her favourite saint.'

Mrs Toms tutted disapprovingly.

'Sounds like something out of a book,' said Mrs Ruddock.

Moira smiled mysteriously.

Mrs Ruddock's eyes widened. 'But did she survive?'

'Oh yes,' Moira said. 'Soon after that, she set sail for New York on the Cunard ship *Berengaria*. I went down to Southampton to wave her off.'

'I hope she gave you something for saving her life,' Mrs Ruddock remarked.

Moira shrugged absent-mindedly and looked down at her fingernails. 'Why should she? I only did what anyone else would do.'

'How disappointing,' said Mrs Ruddock. 'You know, when you first came to Broadwater, I heard a rumour that you'd got a stash of jewellery hidden somewhere.'

'Did you really?' Moira teased.

'You could have easily kept a diamond or two,' said Mrs Toms. 'Who would know?'

Moira looked her straight in the eye. 'I would know, Mrs Toms,' she said tetchily. 'I'll have you know, I'm an honest woman.' Embarrassed, Mrs Toms looked away. 'Besides,' Moira went on in a more relaxed tone, 'the princess knew exactly how many she'd got. We'd helped her count them.'

'I still think she should have given you something,' Mrs Ruddock said stoutly.

'Well, she did offer me a job in America,' said Moira. Glancing at Mrs Toms she added, 'and she did give me a little box of something to steer me in the right direction in the future.' Her gaze drifted towards the mantelpiece.

'America!' cried Mrs Ruddock. 'Why on earth didn't you go? If someone offered me a job in America I'd be off like a shot.'

Mrs Toms didn't seem impressed. 'That box looks like a set

of tarot cards. You should throw them away,' she said, nodding at the mantelpiece. 'I wouldn't want them in my house.'

'Perhaps under different circumstances I might have gone to America,' said Moira, 'but by that time I'd promised to marry Frankie's father.' She gazed lovingly at her daughter. 'I had made my choice and I have no regrets.'

'You two had to wait a long time to get married, didn't you?' Mrs Ruddock observed.

'Her father and I had to wait until I was twenty-one,' said Moira. 'That was two years after the war. Besides, Ernie was injured in the trenches. He was a sick man. He needed time to recover.'

Mrs Ruddock pulled a face. 'Mustard gas?'

Moira nodded. 'He was in a sanatorium for most of the first three years of our marriage.'

Mrs Ruddock looked away. 'Poor devil.'

'See? What did I tell you? You should have got rid of those tarot cards,' Mrs Toms said staring at the mantelpiece again. 'Witchcraft and divination are the sins of Jezebel.'

The door suddenly burst open. 'Good God,' a man's voice boomed. 'Haven't you hens finished clucking yet?'

Frankie jumped out of her skin and at that point the party broke up. Nobody bothered to ask who the man was. They all knew young Mr Knight and they knew he was Moira's landlord. If Mrs Toms and Mrs Ruddock wondered why he'd walked in uninvited and in such an over-familiar manner, they kept their thoughts to themselves.

Mrs Ruddock rose to her feet. Young Mr Knight belched loudly and sat in her chair, making himself very much at home as he helped himself to a piece of cake and pulled an empty cup towards him.

Mrs Toms looked down her nose. 'You disgusting man. You ought to be ashamed of yourself.'

Mr Knight's lip curled as he put up two fingers. Mrs Toms rose to her feet with a horrified look on her face. 'Doreen, get your coat. We're leaving right this minute.'

Frankie didn't like young Mr Knight. He was loud, and brash, and sometimes he frightened her. He didn't seem to have a proper job so he'd taken to turning up whenever he liked. Frankie had seen him walking around the street with a little red book. When he stood near a wall with one foot up behind him, people would sidle up to him shiftily and give him money. Then he'd write something in the little red book. One time when she'd been watching him, a policeman came around the corner. Young Mr Knight stood up straight and began hurrying away but not before he'd snarled at Frankie, 'And you can keep your big fat trap shut.'

By now Frankie's friends had put on their coats or cardigans and her mother, tight-lipped and pink with embarrassment, had said her goodbyes. When everyone was gone young Mr Knight poured himself a cup of tea from the pot. 'This is cold,' he complained.

Moira glanced at Frankie. 'I think it's bedtime, darling,' she said softly.

Frankie began a half-hearted protest but in truth she was very tired and she didn't want to stay up if young Mr Knight was there. She kissed her mother goodnight and took her dolly with her. Later, as she lay in bed with the princess doll on the chair beside her, Frankie could hear raised voices downstairs.

'You had no right to burst in like that.'

'I'll go where I please.'

'This is my home and you should treat me with respect.'

'Ah, ah,' said Mr Knight in a scolding tone. 'This is my house. *My house*,' he continued, his voice becoming more strident. 'You only pay the rent.' There was a short silence, then he said in a softer tone, 'Come on, Moira. I don't want to quarrel with you. Be nice to me.'

Frankie heard the chair legs scrape on the kitchen floorboards.

'Don't you touch me!' her mother exclaimed. 'What me and my Ernie had was something special. I'm not interested in anyone else, least of all you.'

Alarmed, Frankie sat up in bed.

'Come on, woman. What's the matter with you?' Mr Knight said. 'He's been dead for years. You must be gagging for it by now.'

'How dare you!' her mother snapped. 'And I shan't tell you again; keep your filthy hands to yourself.'

There was the sound of a scuffle but it was the sound of a slap which brought Frankie to the rail at the top of the landing. Her heart was pounding and dolly trembled in her arms.

'Get out,' her mother gasped. 'Get out before I take the poker to you.'

'There's no need to get on your high horse,' Mr Knight was saying. 'We could come to some sort of arrangement, you know. How about you say yes and I reduce the rent?'

'Clear off, I tell you,' her mother spat. 'Go on. Take the rent money and get out of here.'

Frankie heard the sound of coins being spilled on the kitchen table.

'Perhaps I could come back sometime and look for that Russian egg of yours.'

'Don't be ridiculous,' her mother snapped.

'All right, Moira,' said Mr Knight. 'Keep your hair on, but I'm telling you, if you say no next week, you and that kid of yours better start looking for somewhere else to live.'

Frankie heard a squeak as the kitchen door opened. 'Just one little yes,' Mr Knight said. 'That's all it will take.'

The door banged shut and Frankie heard her mother say, 'And hell will freeze over first.'

*

The new school term began on September 5th. While she was getting ready, Frankie couldn't help noticing how pale her mother still looked. Of course, she was also still her usual efficient self. While Frankie washed herself in the scullery, Moira made the beds and tidied the room. While Frankie got dressed, her mother made herself some sandwiches for lunch (Frankie had school dinners) and as Frankie ate her breakfast, she sat beside her at the table with a cup of strong tea. The princess doll sat opposite them.

'So,' her mother asked, 'do you still like your dolly?'

Frankie nodded happily. 'She's the bestest dolly in the world.'

'Best,' her mother corrected. 'Not bestest, just best. What are you going to call her?'

Frankie shrugged. 'Princess something.'

Moira ran her fingers through her daughter's pretty blond curls. 'And why not,' she said. 'After all, I made that bodice from the bits my Russian princess left behind. That blue suede was from the leftovers of a skirt and the buttons came off a blouse she asked me to alter. Someone had given it to her but it was far too long and she was so tiny.'

Frankie's jaw dropped. So she had been right. Some of the material *had* belonged to the Russian princess. When she got down from the table, Frankie touched the doll's clothes lovingly.

'Right,' said Moira, clapping her hands, 'off to school and don't dawdle on the way home.'

Taking one last look at the doll sitting on the cosy chair by the range, Frankie and her mother hugged each other at the door and Moira kissed her cheek. Frankie ran up the path but stopped by the gate and ran back. Wrapping her arms around her mother's waist she said, 'This was my best birthday ever.' As she hurried towards the gate, she turned and saw her mother standing in the doorway waving. Frankie waved back and called over her shoulder, 'And thanks again for my dolly.'

Moira had plenty to be getting on with. She had taken the day off on Saturday to celebrate Frankie's birthday, and been glad to do it, but now she had some serious catching up to do. Moira hadn't said anything to her daughter but over the past few days she hadn't been feeling too well. Nothing she could put her finger on, but she kept coming over all weak and she just couldn't seem to shake this wretched indigestion.

The doctor's wife was coming this afternoon for the last fitting of her cocktail dress. She was a good customer – happy to spend a small fortune on both material and Moira's skill in order to maintain her reputation for being the best dressed woman in Worthing – but before that, Moira made a start on some alterations on new garments which had been bought by customers in Bentall's. She had been thrilled to land the job as their resident seamstress. The alterations were simple enough: a couple of inches off a hem, a sleeve which needed shortening and a waist band on a skirt which had to be let out a little. These had become her bread and butter jobs. Today she had three things to alter – a nightdress which was too long, a curtain to shorten, and some buttons to move on a coat because the wearer had put on weight. She worked quickly but every now and then her left arm ached and she had to stop to give it a rub.

She worked steadily until lunchtime, when she stopped to stretch her legs with a walk around the garden and to eat her sandwiches. She lifted her arms about her head a few times to ease the dull ache in her chest after sitting hunched over her work for so long. After she'd had a cup of tea, she put the doctor's wife's dress on the tailor's dummy and settled down again with her sewing but she was soon interrupted by a sharp knock on the door. She glanced up at the clock. Was that her customer? No, it was too early for her. She said she'd come by after she'd finished a game of golf.

When Moira opened the door, she let out a gasp of surprise. 'Oh, it's you!' Her visitor hovered on the step until she said, 'I never expected you to come so soon.' And stepping aside, she let her visitor in.

*

It was hard to concentrate on her lessons. More than once, Frankie's mind drifted back to Hillbarn and the picnic she'd enjoyed on her birthday. In her imagination she could feel the sun on her back while the bees were humming around the blackberries. They'd eaten the ones they'd picked on Saturday for lunch on Sunday and they'd gone back for some more in the evening. Those blackberries were in a large bowl on the draining board and her mother had said she would make a blackberry and apple pie for their tea. Frankie was looking forward to it.

In the morning, Frankie and her class had to practise their best writing. Miss Smith had written *'The quick brown fox jumped over the lazy dog'* at the top of the page in her writing book and she had to copy the beautiful copperplate hand. It was quite hard work even if she did have three horizontal lines on the page to aid her. As she concentrated with her tongue sticking out of the side of her mouth, Frankie was thinking of her dolly. What should she call her? What did mummy say the princess was called? She'd heard the name umpteen times but she still couldn't quite get her tongue around it. 'Alexy Vena' or something like that. She'd have to ask mummy to say it again when she got home.

They had PE after break and Frankie did ten star jumps. She sat with Jenny at the dinner table but Doreen was monitor so she sat at the other end of the form. It was mutton stew. Frankie didn't much care for mutton stew. You often had big lumps of slimy mutton fat and of course you had to eat everything on your plate or you got into trouble. Getting it down was slow going and not very enjoyable but they had semolina and strawberry jam for pudding. She didn't mind that, especially the jam.

In the playground, Doreen seemed a bit stand-offish. Frankie didn't understand why but then someone told her it was because Doreen's mum didn't like Mrs Sherwood's fancy man. Frankie didn't understand what that meant but she could tell that Doreen and her mum weren't being very nice and it upset her that her friend had stopped talking to her.

They did sums in the afternoon and then Mr Bawden read a book to the class. He began with *The Adventures of Tom Sawyer*, an exciting story about a boy and his adventures in America. Frankie held her breath as Mr Bawden read the bit where Tom and his friend, Huckleberry Finn, see Injun Joe murder Dr Robinson in the graveyard. Then, terrified that Injun Joe might do them harm, Tom and Huck swear a blood oath not to tell. The class had heard it all before but it didn't dampen their enthusiasm for a 'ripping yarn', as Mr Bawden called it.

Remembering her promise, Frankie didn't dawdle on the way home, but as she turned into her road there was a St John Ambulance outside her gate. She broke into a run just as Mrs Dickenson, their next-door neighbour, came out of Frankie's house. Frankie tried to dodge past her but Mrs Dickenson stopped her from going indoors.

'It's no good going in there, dear,' she said. 'You come along with me.'

'Why?' Frankie gasped. 'What's happened? Where's my mummy?'

Two men in blue uniforms came out of the front door. One of them glanced at Mrs Dickenson. 'Is this her?'

Mrs Dickenson nodded.

'You get the stretcher, Charlie,' he went on. 'I'll deal with this.' He came towards Frankie and bent down. 'Now then, little girl,' he said with a fixed smile which was a little scary, 'you mustn't cry. Your mummy wouldn't like that, see? You have to be brave. So do what the nice lady says and go over to her house.'

'But I live *here*!' Frankie cried. 'This is where I live with my mummy.'

'That's as may be,' the man said a little more firmly, 'but you have to stay away until the police come.'

Frankie stared at him in horror. Police? What on earth was he talking about? Pushing against the man's leg, she struggled to get past him. 'Mummy, Mummy!'

'No good shouting like that,' said the man curtly. 'She can't hear you no more.'

Frankie looked up at him helplessly.

'Your mother is dead,' he said quietly.

# Two

**North Farm, Sussex, 1933**

The hours since she'd left school and come home became a blur. Frankie had watched the ambulance take her mother away but she couldn't actually see her. Moira was covered right over with a red blanket. As soon as she had gone, Mrs Dickenson made Frankie come away from the window. Neighbours came and went, all speaking in hushed tones. They'd say something to Mrs Dickenson then turn their heads to look at Frankie. Invariably they would give her a wide smile and say something like 'You'll be all right, dear,' or 'Keep your pecker up.'

Frankie said nothing, not even when she heard them whispering. 'Does she know? Does she understand?' Frankie frowned to herself. Of course she knew. She understood perfectly. Mummy was dead, or gone to be with Jesus, or in heaven with the angels, depending on who was talking to her. She understood but it was hard to take in. Just this morning, when she and her mother had waved goodbye, she'd never said she was going to see Jesus.

Nobody actually told her why her mother had died but she heard their whispers.

'They say it was her heart.'

'Mrs Ruddock said she kept rubbing her arm all the time

when they were up on Hillbarn for the kiddie's birthday on Saturday. '

'I heard she complained of indigestion.'

Then they would all shake their heads and smile at Frankie again. 'Poor little mite.'

Shortly after, a policeman arrived. 'Who found Mrs Sherwood?' he said getting out his notebook and licking the end of his pencil.

'Me,' said Mrs Dickenson. 'I could hear somebody banging about,' she went on, closing the kitchen door slightly but not enough to stop Frankie hearing what she was saying. 'Scared me out of me wits. Then somebody slammed the back door and I went round. Poor Mrs Sherwood was sitting in the chair with a tea towel over her head and someone had gone through her things.'

'Who?'

'I've no idea but whoever it was must have been looking for something,' Mrs Dickenson went on. 'I heard her having a row with somebody earlier on.'

The door whined open and the policeman looked at Frankie, giving her a kindly smile.

\*

Eventually a woman from the Welfare turned up and began trying to find Frankie a place to stay. Apparently Mrs Dickenson couldn't take her in. 'I've got three strapping lads and my old mum in the place already,' she said stoutly. Miss Paine, Frankie's next-door neighbour on the other side, didn't want her either. 'I'm an unmarried woman,' she'd protested. 'I can't have a child living in my house. What would the neighbours think?' The fact that the neighbours already knew who Frankie was and what had happened seemed to be lost on her. And all the while,

Frankie sat quietly in Mrs Dickenson's little sitting room, swallowing the huge lump in her throat and trying not to burst into tears.

In the end, they sent a message to Frankie's Aunt Bet, her mother's sister, who lived only a couple of miles away, and a little later her case was packed. The woman from the Welfare walked her up to North Farm and her uncle opened the door and invited them in. When Aunt Bet came in, the two women exchanged a few words at the door and Aunt Bet ushered Frankie upstairs.

The room itself had been hastily prepared and although she'd been to Aunt Bet's farm loads of times, this was the first time she'd ever been upstairs.

'Come on, lovey,' her aunt said. 'I've made up the bed for you and you can put your dolly on the chair right beside you.'

She was a plain woman with a round face and mousey-coloured hair, cut short and permed. She was a little on the plump side (her wrap-over apron was straining over her middle) and she had strong-looking arms.

Gently taking Frankie's coat from her shoulders, she lifted the child's small suitcase onto the bed. Frankie could see by her face that Aunt Bet had been crying. Her eyes were red-rimmed. When the Welfare woman knocked at the farm door, even Uncle Lawrence, or, Lorry, as everyone called him, had red eyes. Frankie still hadn't shed a tear but her chest felt as if she had a brick inside it and her head pounded. *You mustn't cry*, the man had said. *Your mum wouldn't like it.*

Frankie put her princess doll on the chair just as Aunt Bet suggested, but she didn't look the same as before and she couldn't sit up properly. Aunt Bet lifted her skirts and let out a strangled cry. 'Oh dear, dear, how on earth did that happen?' The doll had a large gash across her middle. A large amount of stuffing had been removed and not all of it had been put back. Fortunately the clothes were intact. As she tried to re-arrange

22

her, Frankie let a little gulp of anguish slip from between her lips. Her hands were trembling. 'Somebody cut my dolly,' she said, her eyes glassy with unshed tears.

'There, there, lovey,' said Aunt Bet, coming over to give her a hug. 'While you're in bed I'll have a go at mending her. She'll be as right as ninepence in the morning.'

'My mummy made her for my birthday,' Frankie said.

Aunt Bet squeezed her shoulder. 'I know she did, lovey. She showed her to me last week.'

They shared a wobbly smile. 'She was a very clever lady, your mum,' said Aunt Bet, dabbing her eyes again.

They unpacked Frankie's case and put her things in the drawers. Until now, the bedroom had belonged to Frankie's cousin, Alan. He was motorbike mad so the walls were covered in pictures of motorbikes and their riders. A pair of grubby boots hung by their laces from the mirror on the dressing table. As Aunt Bet took them down she said, 'We'll soon get rid of all this stuff and then you can make the room your own.'

'Am I going to stay here forever?'

Aunt Bet turned her back, quite forgetting that Frankie could see her anguished reflection in the mirror. 'Yes, dear.'

Her face was a picture of misery. It was obvious that she was struggling not to cry again. Frankie's heart flipped. Judging by her aunt's expression, Aunt Bet didn't really want her here. 'I'm sorry,' Frankie blurted out. 'They told me I had to come.'

Her aunt turned around suddenly. 'Oh, lovey,' she blurted out as she pulled Frankie into her arms. 'I didn't mean it to sound like that. Of course I want you here. We all want you. Uncle Lorry, Alan and Ronald, we're so glad you've come. It's just that I feel so sad about your mum, that's all.'

Later, as Frankie lay between the crisp white sheets, she stared at the empty chair beside the bed and wondered what her life would be like now. Aunt Bet said she didn't have to go to school

23

the next day but, in truth, Frankie would have liked to go. She'd miss her friend Jenny. She hoped Doreen might talk to her again. She turned over in bed but she couldn't sleep. If only mummy was here to kiss her goodnight.

Downstairs everyone had gathered around the kitchen table. They had eaten their supper, although Frankie had only picked at hers, and now they were relaxing over a cup of tea. Lorry had laced Bet's tea with a little brandy. He was a man of few words but he was thoughtful and kind. There was a box of papers belonging to his sister-in-law in the middle of the table. Ever since they'd had the news, they'd been living an absolute nightmare. When the police turned up on the doorstep, they'd said Moira was dead and Frankie couldn't be left on her own. They'd asked the neighbours to take her in but nobody could. Thank God somebody remembered Bet and Lorry. Of course there was no hesitation. It was only right that Frankie should come and live with them and Bet had settled the girl in Alan's room. At sixteen, he wasn't too happy about bunking in with his younger brother, Ronald, but it couldn't be helped and he'd accepted the situation with good grace. As for Ronald, he was the sort to get on with whatever happened in life. As soon as he got home from school he'd moved his things to one side of the small bedroom to make room for his older brother and now it looked as if it had always been that way.

The policeman had explained that someone had obviously been in the property looking for something, and there was every possibility that whoever it was might come back. Lorry was advised that as next of kin, he and Bet should get over there and retrieve anything of value. Of course, Bet couldn't go – she had to stay with Frankie – so he and Alan had gone over to grab a few things, planning to collect the rest of Moira's stuff later on. They found that some of the drawers had been disturbed and the cupboards had been left open. The only real damage was to Frankie's new doll. Whoever had been in the property had ripped it open with a knife. It was the only thing the little girl had asked for when she was told she had to come to North Farm.

Having cleared the supper table, Bet reached for her sewing box.

'Do you know how Auntie Moira died, Mum?' asked Ronald.

'The Welfare lady said it was a heart attack,' said his mother.

'I don't understand it,' said Lorry. He was a small man, stockily built. He still wore his moustache in the style of Lord Kitchener; something which he'd grown as a young man, although it was now flecked with grey and tobacco stained. 'She seemed well enough, didn't she?'

'Obviously not,' Bet said tartly.

'If someone was with her when it happened,' said Alan, 'why didn't they get help?'

'Nobody said she was still alive when whoever it was was in there,' said his father, 'did they?'

His mother looked alarmed. 'I hope not. Moira was the salt of the earth.'

Alan shook his head. 'What could they have been looking for?' He was a tall lad, much taller than his father. Legs right up to his armpits, as his mother would say, and good-looking to boot. A keen motorbike rider, he had been working with his father since he'd left school at fourteen.

His mother blew her nose and stuffed her already damp handkerchief back up her sleeve. 'No idea. It's not as if Moira had any money. She may have worked all the hours God gave but she lived hand to mouth.' She pushed the stuffing back inside the doll angrily and began adding some torn up pieces of rag before sewing the two halves together.

'People were always saying daft things about your sister,' Lorry observed. 'All that stuff about the Russians.'

'That was just a stupid yarn she made up to amuse Frankie,' said Bet. 'You know Moira. She was great one for story-telling.'

'People said she had a secret stash of jewellery,' said Alan.

'A Fabergé egg, I heard,' said Ronald. He leaned over and pulled up his school socks with an exaggerated sigh. He was a disappointed boy. He had asked his mother – no, begged her – to be allowed to wear long trousers now that he was thirteen, but still she said no.

Bet frowned disapprovingly. 'Utterly ridiculous!' she retorted. 'Do you really think Auntie Moira would be living in two rooms in Broadwater if she had something as expensive as a Fabergé egg?'

'Load of tommyrot, if you ask me,' his father interjected.

Ronald put his hands up in mock surrender. 'All right, all right, I'm only saying.'

His mother was immediately repentant. 'Sorry, son. I'm on edge, that's all.'

'So is Frankie going to live here for good?' asked Ronald, rubbing his ear.

'Of course she is,' said Bet. 'Where else could she go? We're the only family she's got.' She glanced up at her son. 'You got ear ache again?'

Ronald nodded. Ever since he was a child he'd suffered from ear ache and whenever he got a cold he would go deaf. The doctor said he'd got narrow Eustachian tubes which were easily blocked.

'Well, you'd better put those drops in your ear before it gets any worse,' she said.

Sidney Knight had got the fright of his life when he'd found Moira. Ignoring her protest of Saturday that he should knock first and wait to be invited in, he had let himself into her rooms with his key. She'd be annoyed with him, of course, but he didn't care. He liked her best when she was roused.

She was sitting in the chair with her back to the door. He said her name but she didn't move. She must have nodded off, he told himself as he crept up to her. He came round the chair slowly. Her legs were slightly apart and one of her shoes wasn't on her foot properly. Her skirt had ridden up slightly on one side, and looking at her shapely leg, he licked his lips in anticipation of what might be to come. He lifted the hem gently, so as not to disturb her sleeping, and put his hand onto the top of her thigh, in between her stocking top and her panties.

'Moira,' he said hoarsely, as he looked into her face.

Her eyes were not quite closed and her skin was pale. There was a blue hue around her mouth and she was completely still. He jumped away from her like a scalded cat. Was she dead? She couldn't be. Her leg had still been warm when he'd touched it. He looked again. She wasn't breathing. He stared at her chest. *Was* she breathing? He looked around for a mirror. There was a toy mirror next to a peasant doll on the chair. He put it under her nose and waited. The glass remained unchanged. Oh God, she was dead. He took several steps backwards and stared at her again. He'd never seen a dead body before. When his father died they'd wanted him to look at the body in the funeral parlour but he'd refused. He hadn't seen the old man in a month or more and he wanted to keep it that way. His last memory was of the row they'd had. 'Stay away from that race track, Sidney,' his father had bellowed. 'Gambling is a mug's game.'

He suddenly shuddered. Even though he knew Moira was dead, she looked as if she were asleep. He turned away. Oh Moira, we could have had some good times together, he thought. I've never wanted a woman like I wanted you. What did you have to go and die for!

He supposed he should tell someone. The kid would be home from school soon. He should say something before then.

His eye gravitated towards the dresser where Moira's purse rested in a blue plate. A moment later, he was stuffing coins into his back pocket. There wasn't much in the purse. Maybe she had money somewhere else. He had found the rent book in a drawer and pocketed the half crown between the pages. That led to a search of the other drawers. He'd have to be quick. He didn't want to be caught rifling through her things.

She was still looking at him through half-closed eyes. It unnerved him so he put a tea towel over her face and carried on searching. The Post Office Savings Book was in a tin right at the top of the dresser. There were two postal orders folded inside. One was for twenty pounds and the other for twenty-eight pounds. There was a further fifteen pounds deposited in the account. He gasped. So the gossips were right. The woman did have money. She glanced back at the body. 'What were you up to, you dirty cow?' he spat. 'You wouldn't let me touch you, would you, but you were obviously getting it from somewhere.'

It was then that he'd noticed a man's hat had fallen between the chair and the small table beside it. His blood boiled. So she did have some fancy man. Now that he was annoyed, his search became more frantic, more untidy and at the end of it, he was even more frustrated and angry. There was no more money and he couldn't see anything of any real value. In a temper, he threw a kitchen chair onto the floor and pushed the mannequin wearing a dress over.

When he heard the sound of the next-door neighbour moving around, it brought him to his senses. As a landlord no one would have the right to challenge his being there; but he would be in trouble if they realised he was the one who had turned the place over. He was just about to leave when he saw a shadow on the glass of the door.

*

Back home he was a disappointed man. It upset him to think of what had happened but it wasn't his fault. He'd only turned up because he wanted to get her alone. He'd been so sure she'd have been more willing if the kid wasn't around. He hadn't expected her to have a fancy man. True, he'd had a good snoop around to look for anything of value but he'd been cut short by the arrival of the other bloke and one thing led to another. He hadn't meant for it to happen. He was upset. It was an accident. His stomach was churning. That's why, to cheer himself up, he'd put the cash on a horse in the three-thirty at Goodwood on the way home. But it really wasn't his day. He'd lost the lot but fortunately, the money in the Post Office Savings Book and the two postal orders were still in his possession. They were both made out to M Sherwood. How the hell could he get his hands on it? There was one thing he could do – he could try and get the rent off her relatives when they came to get her stuff. He could show them the empty rent book. They weren't to know he'd already had it. He smiled to himself. He was, if nothing else, bloody clever.

\*

When she went round to Moira's place the next day, Bet looked around with a sinking feeling in her stomach. The reports were right. Someone had been in here going through her sister's things. It made her feel uncomfortable, edgy. Moira's usually neat and tidy rooms were far from the way she would have left them.

Lorry was shaking his head. 'It's a bloody disgrace, isn't it?'

They'd come with a couple of suitcases and a few shopping bags. The police had suggested that they collect what they could as soon as possible. 'You don't want every old Tom, Dick and Harry going in there and helping themselves,' the constable had said.

They planned to take everything back to the farm and sort it out from there. Anything which could be sold would be sold.

'We'll get a Post Office Savings Book and put the money in there for Frankie,' said Bet.

'Moira would have liked that,' Lorry said gruffly as he tried to hide his emotions.

'I don't want her to know yet,' said Bet. 'She can have it later on.'

'What, when she leaves school?'

Bet shook her head. 'I think we should wait until she leaves our place, whether she gets married first or gets a job living away. It will help set her up.'

Lorry nodded grimly.

They packed up what they could. Household items which would be useful for Bet went into one case. The contents of the food cabinet – including the left-over birthday cake – went into a large shopping bag. Bet shed a tear when she saw it. Moira's clothes and her few personal possessions were packed into the suitcase and Frankie's things went into the other case. The only thing she couldn't find was the little brass box, the one which Moira kept on the mantelpiece. Bet had never actually seen inside but apparently some grateful customer had given her the box before she was married, and Moira kept it beside the clock. She mentioned it to Lorry.

'Why take that?' he asked. 'There was nothing of value inside, was there?'

Bet shook her head. 'Not as far as I know.' It was real puzzle.

With regards to the furniture, Bet had given first refusal to the neighbours so by the time Lorry put everything that was left onto the tractor trailer, the rooms were almost bare. After that, he went back to the farm with the promise to come and fetch her at tea time, while Bet spent the next hour cleaning the rooms, readying them for the next tenant. Everything was fine until she opened the oven door and found a beautiful looking pastry tart waiting to be cooked. Putting it onto the draining board, Bet clamped her hands over her mouth for a few moments as her grief overwhelmed her.

Mr Knight, the landlord, turned up just before Lorry came back and told Bet her sister owed him two weeks' rent. As they hadn't been able to find any money put by, Lorry coughed up the ten bob as soon as he walked in the door. Before she locked the doors for the last time, Bet stood for a while by the window, looking out onto the garden where only the pegs danced on the washing line. Outside in the road, Lorry tooted the horn and for a fleeting moment, Bet thought she heard the sound of laughter – Moira's laughter. She didn't turn around. Bet knew the room was empty. Her sister – her fun-loving, clever, story-telling kid sister – was gone. Gone forever.

'I promise you, darlin', she whispered, her voice thick with emotion, 'we will do the best we can by your girl.' Bet turned to face the empty room and took in a deep breath. 'Bye, Moira, my dear. Rest in peace.'

# Three

When Frankie had opened her eyes that first morning in North Farm, the doll was back in the chair. Closer examination revealed that she had been stitched together and she had a large bandage around her middle. When she came into her room, Aunt Bet smiled. 'The "doctor" left a little jar of dolly mixtures which I put on the chair. His instruction is that you should eat two sweets three times a day until they are all gone,' she said.

Once she was up and dressed, Frankie sat in the chair with the dolly in her lap. The princess doll didn't feel quite as robust as she had done when her mother gave it to her, but it was comforting to hold her. Somehow it brought mummy closer. There were still no tears but Frankie had that empty feeling inside her tummy and the pain in her chest felt like a lead weight. It was a strange feeling and she hated it. She wanted mummy back. She wanted her to wave goodbye to the angels and Jesus and come home, but she knew in her heart of hearts it was never going to happen.

Aunt Bet filled the larder with mummy's food and the left-over cake. The pie went into the oven for their tea and all the while she fussed over Frankie, giving her special treats. She let Frankie feed the chickens and Uncle Lorry and Alan gave her little jobs around the yard. Ronald had gone to school. He was supposed to leave at Christmas; although he would have liked the opportunity to further his education, he had to go to work.

Despite being called North Farm, the place Aunt Bet and Uncle Lorry called home was really a smallholding. They kept chickens, duck and a few geese. There were a couple of glasshouses where they grew mainly tomatoes and cucumbers. The whole of this part of Sussex was still a grower's paradise. Before the Great War it had been the main source of occupation, but the staggering losses on the battlefields of Europe meant that the workforce had been seriously depleted. Many nurseries lay derelict but quite a few plodded on and why not? Worthing was famed for its tomatoes, cucumbers and grapes. Next door, on Lyon's Farm, they grew tomatoes and chrysanthemums. At the height of both seasons, lorry loads of produce left for the station twice a day to take it to the market in Covent Garden, London. North Farm had a much smaller yield and mostly supplied local traders.

Both Frankie's cousins were keen bikers. They had their own machines and they spent hours breaking them down and rebuilding them. At weekends they held races on a muddy track on a piece of ground which was no longer fit for growing. Ronald asked her if she would like to come and watch but Frankie preferred to stay inside and watch from the safety of the kitchen window.

There was an inquest, of course. Aunt Bet went and came back telling the family, though not Frankie, that Moira had indeed died of natural causes. 'It was a heart attack,' Bet told her family at the table. 'She'd been unwell since the weekend. The two mums who went to Frankie's birthday picnic said she'd complained of chest pains.'

'So why didn't she do something about it?' Lorry asked.

'I suppose she thought it would pass.'

Lorry and the boys fell silent.

'Did they say anything about the state of her place?' Lorry wanted to know.

'The police say it's an ongoing investigation,' said Bet. 'They seem convinced she was already gone when whoever it was went through her things.'

'How can they be sure that whoever it was hadn't left the poor woman to die while he rifled through her stuff?' Lorry retorted.

'I keep wondering that too,' said Bet, pinching the end of her nose with her handkerchief. 'The coroner asked me if anything was missing but as far as I know, it was only that little brass box she kept on the mantelpiece.'

Lorry shook his head in disbelief. 'So nobody saw who came to the house?'

'Mrs Dickenson talked about a foreign-looking man knocking on the door,' Bet went on.

'That'd be the landlord,' said Alan.

'Surely Mrs Dickenson would know the difference between a foreigner and Mr Knight?' his father said. 'Anyway, she owed him two weeks rent.'

'As it happens,' Bet interrupted, 'I don't think she did. Mrs Dickenson said she paid regular as clockwork on a Saturday. Always did.'

Lorry pursed his lips. 'So what you're telling me is that cheating bastard, excuse my French, had me over?'

His wife nodded.

'So who was the foreign-looking man?' Ronald asked.

Bet shrugged. 'Miss Paine saw him too. She said he was wearing a funny shirt with buttons on the side but no collar. Apparently he knocked on the door twice.'

'Twice?' Lorry echoed.

'Mrs Dickenson saw him at lunch time and then a bit later on. About half past two.'

Everyone seemed puzzled.

'I don't think we should tell Frankie any of this.'

'I agree,' said Lorry, 'but I wish I could get my hands on the lousy bugger.' He leaned over the table and squeezed his wife's hand. 'Have they released the body?'

Bet nodded.

'Good,' said Lorry. 'It's time we put that poor lass in the ground.'

Bet glanced up at the ceiling. 'Do you think we should take Frankie to the funeral?'

Lorry frowned, unsure. 'People don't usually take nippers to funerals, do they?'

'She's a bit young, Mum,' said Alan. He was going out with his mates so he was busy combing Brylcreem through his hair as he stood in front of the mirror by the sink.

'In that case,' said Bet, considering the matter settled, 'I'll ask Mrs Mac to invite her to her cottage for a couple of hours that day.'

Her husband nodded.

'You know, I'm worried about Frankie,' Bet went on. 'Have any of you ever seen her cry?'

Her husband and both sons seemed slightly bemused by her remark but they shook their heads.

'Neither have I,' said Bet. 'Considering how close she and her mother were it's not right. She shouldn't be keeping it all in like that.'

'Have a word with Doctor Rutherford,' said Lorry. 'He'll know what to do.'

*

It was arranged that Frankie would go to school in Sompting starting from next week. Everyone agreed that it was within walking distance and it would give her a completely fresh start.

As soon as Frankie had gone outside with Lorry, Bet took the opportunity to sort through the cases she'd brought back from Moira's place. She had a small blue case of her own on the top of her wardrobe. It was one she had bought in Woolworth's years before when Lorry's mother had to go into hospital. When she died, it seemed too good to throw out so, even though it was small, she'd kept it. She got it down and put the few personal things belonging to Moira inside. They wouldn't mean a lot to a little girl right now but when she was older, Frankie would appreciate having them. Moira's jewellery for instance. There was nothing of value and she only had a couple of brooches and a necklace or two but because they had belonged to her mother, Bet was sure that in due time Frankie would treasure them. She also put in her mother's diary. It was only a record of her clients but might bring back a few memories. The children's books she'd put beside Frankie's bed but she decided that a dark blue and gilt book called *The Russian Princess* looked too good for a child to play with. Bet leafed through it and would have read a few lines, but she was interrupted by the grocery boy calling up the stairs.

'Hey-up, missus. Copeland's delivery.'

'Coming,' she called. Throwing the book into the case, she heaved it onto the wardrobe and hurried down to the kitchen.

# *Four*

Doctor Rutherford was unambiguous in his opinion. 'If, as you say, the child was devoted to her mother, it's imperative that you encourage her to grieve.'

'But what can I do?' Bet said helplessly. 'She simply won't cry. She just holds everything in.'

'Talk to her,' the doctor said curtly. 'Tell her what a wonderful person her mother was. Reopen her memories.'

Bet nodded miserably. Did he really think she hadn't already tried that?

'Is she wetting the bed?'

'Oh no, nothing like that,' Bet said quickly.

'Will you take her to her mother's funeral?'

Bet shook her head. 'We thought it best not to.'

There was a short pause then Doctor Rutherford said in a kindlier tone, 'I understand that it will be very painful for you to talk about your sister all the time, but I can't stress enough the importance of helping your niece to release her emotions. Is she back at school?'

'I thought it best to keep her at home for a bit.'

'Send her back tomorrow,' said the doctor, picking up his pen and scribbling something onto the brown card in front of him. 'Talk to her teacher.'

Bet felt dismissed. 'Yes, doctor,' she said, picking up her handbag from beside the chair. 'Thank you.' She rose to her feet.

He carried on scribbling. 'Send the next patient in as you go. Good morning, Mrs Cavendish.'

Back home, Lorry was more sympathetic. 'He's right, I suppose.' They were in the kitchen at lunch time. He and their son Alan had come in for a bite to eat. Ronald was at school and Frankie was outside, sitting on the old tree stump, with the chickens scratching all around.

'She hardly ate a thing,' said Bet, scraping Frankie's half-eaten sandwich into the pig bin. 'If she carries on like this she'll be losing weight.'

'You're doing your best, Mum,' said Alan. 'She'll come round.'

'But she's got no interest in anything,' Bet said desperately. 'It's like she's gone inside herself and shut the door.'

Lorry put his arm around his wife's shoulders. 'We'll get there,' he said optimistically.

When Lorry and Alan went back to work, Aunt Bet called Frankie indoors. 'Today is my baking day,' she began cheerfully, 'and I could do with some help.' She went on to say that she planned to make a couple of pies. 'My boys have big appetites.'

She planned to make a pie for tonight's tea time and one for the next day. She decided against mentioning that Moira's funeral was tomorrow. On the day they buried her mother, Frankie would be at school until four and Mrs Mac had promised to meet her so she wouldn't have to walk back on her own. When Bet dropped Frankie off in the morning it would give her a chance to speak to her teacher, Miss Smith, and put her in the picture.

While Aunt Bet made the pastry and lined the pie dish, Frankie was given the job of peeling and cutting up the carrots, onions and potatoes. As soon as they were busy, Bet began to talk about Moira. 'We've got some lovely memories of your mum, haven't we?'

No reaction.

'Do you remember that Christmas when your Uncle Lorry came home a bit tipsy and dropped the goose on the kitchen floor? I was so cross with him but your mum laughed so much I saw the funny side of it too and it wasn't long before we were all laughing.'

Frankie's expression hadn't changed.

'What do you remember about your mum?' Bet asked.

Frankie only shrugged.

Oh dear, this was like wading through treacle.

'Mrs Ruddock told me she played hide and seek with you when you went up to Hillbarn for your birthday.'

Stony-faced, Frankie pushed some chopped up carrots into the saucepan.

'She said you all picked blackberries.'

The girl was ignoring her and carried on as if she was quite alone in the room. Bet looked away. This wasn't working. She pushed the diced lamb into the frying pan to seal in the juices before putting it into the pie dish. The meat sizzled as it hit the fat. Frankie put some chopped onion onto the work surface beside her aunt.

'Thank you, dear.'

A delicious smell filled the kitchen.

'Everybody loved your mum,' said Bet, her voice growing thicker. She paused for a second or two before adding harshly, 'but that's because they didn't know her like I did.'

Behind her Bet heard Frankie falter in her rhythmic chopping.

Bet took a deep breath. 'See, I remember the stuff she did as a child. She was jealous of me. Did you know that?' She could see Frankie's reflection in the shaving mirror Lorry had hung next to the window to get the best light. The child had stopped working and stood stiffly to attention, her face a mask of horror. Hating herself for doing this, Bet carried on, 'Did you know she tore my school dress? Deliberately too, but I got the blame for it. Our mother sent me to bed with no tea.'

Without looking at Frankie, Bet tipped the sealed meat and lightly fried onions into the pastry case then turned back again. 'She just couldn't bear it because I had pretty hair. She used to pull my plaits all the time.'

Glancing in the mirror again, Bet could see Frankie was staring at her back. 'I bet she never told you she took the laces out of my best shoes and hid them,' she said coldly. 'I had to go to church with my shoes tied up with string. Imagine that. Everybody laughed at me. It was awful and she wasn't even sorry.'

Frankie's chin was beginning to wobble. Bet sucked in her lip anxiously. This was tearing her apart and it might not even work but Bet carried on regardless. 'She was selfish too, your mum. She persuaded people not to talk to me and she told me our father liked her best. She said she was his favourite.'

Frankie jumped to her feet.

'Had enough?' said Bet turning around with an innocent smile.

'It's not true,' Frankie shouted angrily. 'My mummy wasn't like that.' Her eyes were bright with tears but they remained unshed.

Bet chewed the side of her mouth. Her every instinct told her to reach out and hug the child, to comfort her in her pain, but she hadn't actually cried yet. She had the feeling Frankie still had enough strength to gulp down the need to release her grief and carry on as before so she drew herself up to her full height and said, 'Oh, you haven't heard the half of it, my girl. Did I ever tell you about . . .'

The door banged behind her as Frankie ran from the room. Lorry was coming in and stepped aside just in time to miss the little hurricane charging outside. 'What the . . .?'

Bet had her eyes closed and was gripping the edge of the sink. 'Is she crying? Is she crying?'

Her husband nodded. 'I think so.'

They both looked out of the window. Frankie was standing by the big gate in the yard. They could see her shoulders heaving vigorously so they knew she was sobbing. It looked as if a dam had burst. 'I must go to her,' Bet said brokenly.

Lorry gripped her arm. 'Not for a minute, love,' he said quietly. 'Let her have a good cry first.'

His wife wiped her own eyes and blew her nose into her handkerchief. 'I only did it by saying horrible things about her mum. I feel dreadful now.'

'What on earth did you say?' said Lorry.

'I told her all the awful things I did to Moira when we were children,' said Bet. 'We were five years apart, you see, and I was so jealous of her when she was little. She had pretty hair and Father spoiled her something rotten. I told Frankie it was the other way round.'

Lorry gathered her into his arms. 'You only did what you had to, love,' he said as she wept on his shoulder.

They heard the door leading to the yard open and Alan came in. 'You all right, Mum?'

His parents sprang apart and Bet busied herself filling the kettle. Their son sat himself down at the table.

'Your mother's upset because we had to make the nipper cry,' Lorry said gruffly. 'She was bottling everything in and the doc said it wasn't good for her.'

Their son moved to the window and looked out. 'Well, will you look at that!' he exclaimed.

They both joined him. A chicken stood on the gate post beside Frankie pecking at her hair, not viciously but gently, like a kiss. She was a beautiful bird, with burnt orange coloured glossy feathers and an intelligent look. The smallholding was home to three varieties of chicken, the dark grey and white flecked Sussex, the black Australorp and a few like this one, a Rhode Island Red. Frankie's shoulders stopped moving and she reached out to stroke its back. The chicken didn't move away but made a soft warbling sound as she came closer.

'Well, I'll be damned,' said Lorry.

Frankie had taken the bird down from the gate post and was sitting on the tree stump with it in her lap.

'She's a beautiful bird,' said Bet, 'and she must have flown up there herself.'

'I've never seen any of the others on that post,' Alan agreed. 'It's quite high up. She couldn't have jumped up there . . . could she?'

'I must have missed that one when I clipped all of their flight feathers,' said Lorry. 'I'll do it now.'

'No,' said Bet, grabbing his forearm as she watched the child stroking the bird's back. 'Don't do that.'

Lorry gave her a quizzical look.

'Apart from her doll, that bird is the only thing I've seen Frankie relate to since she came here,' said Bet.

Bet waited a few more minutes and then went out into the yard. Frankie didn't look up as she came towards her but Bet saw her back stiffen. It made her feel awful. The chicken gave an indignant squawk as she pushed her aside to sit next to her niece. Frankie lifted her arm as if to wipe her tears and snot with her sleeve but Bet held a clean handkerchief in front of her. She waited until the child had cleaned her face.

'All those horrible things I said about your mum,' Bet said gently. 'They weren't true.'

Frankie turned to her, swollen-eyed.

'It was me,' Bet went on, the shame and guilt from all those years ago finally coming out. 'I was the one who was jealous.

I took the laces out of her shoes, and I was the one who tore your mum's dress, not the other way around.'

Frankie frowned, clearly puzzled.

'I'm sorry, sweetheart,' Bet went on miserably, 'but the doctor said it wasn't good for you to keep it all in. He said I had to make you cry and this was the only way I could think of.'

'The man said I mustn't cry,' said Frankie.

'Man? What man?'

Frankie told her about the St John Ambulance man. 'He said mummy wouldn't want me to make a fuss.'

'Oh, sweetheart,' said Bet, her voice breaking. 'I don't think he meant it quite like that.'

Her aunt put her arm around Frankie's shoulders and the little girl rested her head on her chest. 'Of course you can cry. It's perfectly natural to cry because your poor mummy died.'

They stayed like that for some time, each lost in her own thoughts and mourning the enormity of their loss until Frankie said, 'Did you know my mummy once knew a real Russian princess?'

Bet had heard the story many times but as she smiled down at her niece she said, 'Did she really? When was that then?'

Frankie blew her nose. 'Well, it was a very long time ago, before I was even born . . .'

# Five

'But you promised!'

Frankie Sherwood stood with her hands on her hips, her legs akimbo and a thunderous look on her face. Her cousin Alan was doing his best to ignore her as he struggled to replace the light bulb in the front of his motorbike.

Not quite fifteen, Frankie had lived with her cousins for almost five years. It had taken a while to get used to the change in lifestyle but now she embraced it fully. From the moment Aunt Bet and Uncle Lorry saw the affinity she had with the only flying chicken in the coop, Frankie had been put in charge of the hens. She made it her business to know all about them and their egg production, making it into a serious business. Frankie's hens were very productive. Some of her best layers gave her as many as two hundred and fifty eggs a year. If for some reason a hen's egg laying dropped, she would give her special attention for a while but if all else failed, that chicken would be a candidate for the next Sunday roast. However, Frankie's pet chicken, which she'd called Loopy-Lu, was still around. Now five years old, she was hale and hearty and a good layer. She was a good looker too. Her feathers were a lovely russet red and she had a keen eye. Frankie's chicken had always

44

been the independent sort, refusing to go into the hen house at night with the others. Loopy-Lu preferred to roost on one of the upper branches of the tree and Uncle Lorry reckoned she could live for anything up to eight years providing she kept out of the way of foxes.

As time went by, Frankie grew closer to her cousins and they became more like brothers and sister. Normally boys didn't mix very much with girls but Ronald and Alan included her in the things they did. After a while, Frankie lowered her guard and grew more relaxed. She learned a lot about motorbikes. The lads loved all things mechanical and eventually Frankie was captivated by their passion for riding. At first she watched them as they tinkered with and repaired their machines, but after a few months she wanted to do more. Alan let her check the battery and change the oil, making sure the filters were clean. Soon she was cleaning carburettors, taking off the rear wheel, and removing the drum cover to check the brakes by herself. Before long, she could strip a machine down, clean it and put it back together again – no trouble at all. Uncle Lorry said she was a natural.

A little after her thirteenth birthday, she'd managed to persuade the boys to let her have a go on one of Uncle Lorry's old bikes. They'd waited until Aunt Bet and Uncle Lorry had gone out because they were all pretty sure Aunt Bet would never allow it. The bike was a bit clapped out but they'd got it going and she'd sat on the saddle with the engine firing under her for the first time. It was magic.

'Take her right round the path and up the hill,' said Alan. 'Remember to open the throttle when you go up and keep your speed up.'

Frankie had been so excited. Ronald and Alan stood either side of the bike to hold her steady. After a couple of false starts when she stalled the engine, she was off. It was great on the flat but then she had to tackle the incline. Nervous, she took the rise too slowly. The minute she made contact with rough ground, she knew she didn't have enough speed to go on. She'd tried to rectify the situation but she already knew it was far too late. She was going to fall. When it happened, it was in slow motion, like a moment in a Marx Brothers movie or something from a Will Hay film. The bike leaned heavily to the right and Frankie felt her bottom slide from the saddle as it tilted over, ever so slowly. Holding the handlebars tight, she'd managed to get her right foot down and push herself away from the heavy machine, but she couldn't get a firm foothold. Staggering in an ungainly way, her legs being forced apart by the mud, she'd let out a loud squeal. The next moment, she'd hit the ground. Fortunately, it wasn't on the hard packed soil but on a patch of squidgy mud, which softened the blow. The bike was on its side and she'd been relieved that she wasn't trapped underneath or hurt.

She'd tried to stand but her feet squelched in the mud and she went down again. Frankie tried a second time but the same thing happened. As she went down a third time she saw Alan running up the hill towards her. Ronald was still by the barn, laughing his head off.

'Here, let me give you a hand,' Alan cried.

He held his arm out but as Frankie grabbed his hand, his feet slithered apart and he fell beside her.

'I'm sorry,' she spluttered.

By then Ronald was beside himself. Alan frowned, but seeing the state they were both in, he began to laugh. After a moment or two, Frankie began to laugh as well and before long, they were all helpless. Eventually Alan managed to crawl on his hands and knees towards a small grass verge and finally found his feet. Frankie did the same.

'That was the funniest thing I ever saw,' Ronald said.

Now, almost a year later, Frankie had proved herself to be an accomplished rider, even managing to impress her aunt and uncle. But she was confined to the farm. Frankie's one desire was to race but it was well-nigh impossible to find a meeting where girls were allowed to take part. The meeting this Saturday was no exception. Alan had just told her she couldn't go.

'You let me do all that work on the bike,' Frankie said crossly, 'and now you refuse to let me ride. It's not fair!'

Alan shrugged. 'It's not me. It's the system. Rules is rules.'

'I don't see why we have to stick to the rules when they are so stupid,' Frankie fumed. 'I bet you're only saying that because you don't want to be beaten by a girl.'

Her cousin chuckled. 'Are you serious? A tiddler like you beat the men? Don't be daft.'

Frankie's eyes blazed. Alan stood up, his heavily Brylcreemed hair glistening. 'Look, I'm sorry,' he said in a more conciliatory tone. 'I can't do anything about it, Frankie. Girls aren't allowed.'

Turning on her heel, Frankie stomped off.

The Sussex Trials brought bike riders from all over the county and had become quite an event. A couple of years ago, Uncle Lorry had cleared a patch of ground by the boundary line with Lyon's Farm and they'd cordoned it off as a car park. The route Alan and Ronald – and lately, Frankie – had used had been refined and recreated into a proper race track. A couple of chaps who had converted an old caravan into a mobile kitchen had asked him if they could make teas and sandwiches for the punters and Uncle Lorry was happy to let them do it, especially when he could charge them a small fee. With the growing numbers of people turning up for race meetings, the track was proving to be a nice little earner and it took far less graft to keep it going than a day working on the smallholding. Aunt Bet sold eggs at the door and when extra produce was available from the vegetable patch, she bagged up anything spare. She was getting a bit of a reputation with her honey from the beehives and apples from the orchard as well as gooseberries, redcurrants and raspberries when they were in season.

Of course, Frankie had ridden the course many times, but never in a competitive race. Kick-starting was a bit of a problem. At only five foot one inch, her short legs meant that Frankie found it hard to get enough power behind her thrust to get the bike started. Never one to be beaten, she soon discovered that if she put the other foot onto a box or a bit of higher ground, she could put more force into it and bring the lever down quicker.

'Why the grumpy face?' said Aunt Bet as she walked in the door with a basket full of eggs.

'They won't let me ride on Bank Holiday Monday,' Frankie said bitterly. 'It's so unfair. Just because I'm a girl.'

Her aunt shook her head sympathetically. 'I know, but they don't call it a scramble for nothing. Those competitors are very ruthless.'

'But I'm just as good as the boys,' said Frankie, 'and I don't need wrapping up in cotton wool.'

'You may be right,' Aunt Bet said sagely, 'but until people realise that, nobody's going to give you the benefit of the doubt.'

Frankie smiled to herself. Now *that* was food for thought.

# Six

Frankie's friend Barbara was waiting for her when she got off the bus outside the church in Worthing. They'd been friends ever since Frankie changed schools soon after her mother died. She'd lost contact with the girls who came to her birthday picnic on Hillbarn almost five years ago. She missed Jenny Ruddock a bit but she hardly ever thought of the other girls from her old school. It was as if they were part of a whole different life. Of course she remembered her mother and there were still times when her grief and loss would overwhelm her for a while. When that happened, Frankie would either shut herself in her room for a bit or take a walk with Loopy-Lu. The silly old chicken seemed to sense when she was upset and tagged along to give her a friendly peck or a sympathetic crow.

There was still so much she didn't understand. They had told her that her mother had had a heart attack that was so cata-strophic she had died almost immediately – but why had someone gone through all of her stuff? There was a hint that it might have been something to do with her knowing a Russian princess, but anyone could see her mother didn't have many personal posses-sions, let alone anything valuable. Frankie had her own suspicions. There was talk of a foreign gentleman being seen at the house but she'd always blamed Mr Knight. When he'd turned up on her birthday and broken up the party, her mother had said:

'What my Ernie and I had was something special.' For years she'd thought that was significant, but now that she was older she realised it was nothing to do with owning a piece of jewellery. Her mother was trying to stop Mr Knight turning up whenever he wanted to and making advances. But he never listened and he could have come back to search for something.

There wasn't a lot left from her old life. Aunt Bet and Uncle Lorry had cleared up the mess the intruder had left behind in the rooms which had been her home with her mother, and they brought back a few bits and pieces. There was no money. Whoever searched the place had taken the rent money and the little Frankie knew her mother had put by for a rainy day. The doctor's wife claimed her dress but she said she'd paid in advance, and although Frankie heard Aunt Bet telling Uncle Lorry she didn't believe it, there was no proof to say otherwise. Aunt Bet took her mum's leftover material to her WI meeting and some of the ladies used it to make baby dresses and pretty nightdress cases which went into their weekly sale to raise funds for needy causes. 'At least it did somebody some good,' Aunt Bet had said dryly.

Now, Frankie waved to her friend and crossed the road. Barbara was a fun-loving girl. She was quite a bit taller than Frankie and she fancied herself as very mature. Her mother had just bought her daughter her first brassiere and Barbara was very conscious of her burgeoning breasts. She was beginning to notice boys as well, especially Frankie's cousin Alan. Frankie was pleased about that. It would come in handy as part of the plan.

The girls linked arms and headed for the Rivoli cinema where the beautiful Margaret Lockwood was starring in *The Lady Vanishes*. Barbara was full of a flirtation she'd just had with a boy on the bus so it was a while before Frankie could get a word in edgeways.

'Listen, Barbara,' she began, 'There's something I want you to do for me. Would you come to the race meeting on Saturday?'

Barbara pulled a face. 'Not really. It's so muddy. I'll ruin my shoes.'

'Can't you wear wellingtons?'

'Wellingtons!' Barbara squeaked. 'Don't be silly! "A lady has to look elegant at all times",' she said, quoting Miss Rose, their Home Craft and Deportment teacher at school.

Frankie sighed. 'It's really important,' she insisted.

Something in her voice must have convinced Barbara because she listened without interrupting as Frankie explained the situation. As they arrived outside the cinema and joined the queue, Barbara seemed hesitant and Frankie's enthusiasm dipped when she saw the expression on her friend's face.

'Will your cousin Alan be there?'

'He's the one I want you to distract,' said Frankie, getting a florin out of her purse for the cinema ticket.

Barbara swung her shoulders back so that the outline of her new bra under her jumper showed its full effect. 'All right,' she cooed. 'You're on.'

*

August Bank Holiday Monday was warm and sunny, even though it had rained all week. As a result, the track was muddy and rutted. Uncle Lorry and the boys had spent the morning marking out the course with posts and white tape so that by the time the officials from the Sussex Dirt Bike Trials Association arrived at around noon, everything was as it should be. The race meeting itself was due to begin at two.

Bet was alone in her kitchen doing the washing up. Lorry and the boys had come in to grab a hot drink and a bite to eat and she'd taken the opportunity to prepare a shepherd's pie for tea. In a minute she would take a chair down by the farm gate to sell some eggs, tomatoes, cucumbers and a few bags containing the first crop of plums.

People started gathering at the trials just before one and made their way to the best viewpoints. A few hung around the start and some preferred the finishing line, but the majority trudged up the hill towards the grassy knoll with a line of trees beyond. From here, the views of the Sussex countryside were spectacular. Most spectators came prepared with sandwiches in a rucksack but some, who had probably already had their meal, relied on the mobile caravan and its cups of tea.

As Bet wiped the last plate, she glanced out of the kitchen window and something caught her eye. Frankie was walking towards the race track with a small suitcase in her hand. For a split second, Bet thought it might be the blue case full of her mother's belongings, but as she leaned towards the window pane she could see that this suitcase was brown.

Frankie glanced nervously over her left shoulder and then her right. Bet pulled herself back from the window. It was then that she noticed Barbara running up towards Frankie. Bet frowned. What were they up to? The two girls had a brief exchange, then parted. Barbara headed towards the temporary shelter where the competitors gathered with their machines. Young riders from all over the county had descended on the farm and it was here that they registered and tied their entry numbers around their waists. Frankie, still carrying her suitcase, walked towards the toilet tent. Bet tut-tutted and dried her hands on the tea towel. If those girls made a nuisance of themselves there would be trouble.

Barbara was a bit scared that she'd give the game away while she got Frankie's registration done but it turned out to be quite easy. All the riders queued behind a small trestle table. The officials on the other side of the table checked the name of the competitor against a list on a clipboard. One did the paperwork whilst the other handed out the race numbers, which were on a sort of bib that went on the rider's back and tied around his waist at the front. All she had to do was say the name of the competitor and hand over the race fee.

By the time she'd reached the table, Barbara's heart was in her mouth. Supposing they could see through the excuse she and Frankie had dreamt up? Supposing the officials frog-marched her away? Supposing they called the police? She was shaking like a leaf and her face flamed as she held out the papers.

The man behind the table looked her up and down and gave her a broad smile. 'You're a sight for sore eyes,' he said. 'I hope you're not planning to race.'

Barbara shook her head. Behind her she could hear muffled laughter. Just as she'd practised with Frankie, Barbara leaned forward and whispered something in his ear. The official rustled some papers and struggled not to smile. She watched him check the names on his clipboard and put a cross beside one of them. Then his colleague gave Barbara the number forty-six and she moved away from the table. She hadn't gone very far before she heard the man say, 'Poor blighter sent his sister 'cos he's so bloody nervous he's stuck in the bog.' His comment was followed by a gale of masculine laughter.

Having made sure no one was looking, Frankie locked herself in one of the temporary toilets. It was only a wooden bench over a large hole and even at this early stage of the meeting it didn't smell very pleasant. She put her suitcase over the gap and opened it up. It didn't take long to change. She put her all-in-ones on over her overalls and tucked all of her blond hair into the leather cap. Pulling her scarf over her nose, she fastened the flaps firmly under her chin. Her new regulation

53

pudding bowl helmet fitted over the top. She heard a slight sound on the other side of the door and Barbara whispered her name. Frankie opened the door and Barbara held up her registration papers and her number.

With her entry papers in her top pocket, Frankie pulled on her eye goggles. Not even her own aunt would recognise her now. She darted round the back of the toilets to where she'd parked her bike under a piece of canvas tarpaulin. Putting one foot on the suitcase, she kick-started the engine. Now she had reached the most dangerous part. Whatever she did, she had to keep the engine going. If she stalled she'd be out of the race and if anyone realised she was a woman, she'd be banned under the stupid 'no girls allowed' rule. As she passed the place where the officials sat at their tables, she saw her friend making eyes at Alan. Good old Barbara. She was doing a grand job.

# Seven

Frankie took it steady getting to the start line. She knew if she went too fast she might draw attention to herself and if she went too slowly, she could wobble and fall sideways. There were about twenty or so riders in this race, the high-pitched whine of the engines now and then changing into a spluttering roar as men revved the throttles of their bikes. Frankie kept her head bent towards her chest. Her heart was in her mouth. It was imperative to keep her engine running. There was no way she could kick-start again without her foot on the suitcase and the minute Alan saw what she was doing, he would know it was her. After what seemed like an age, the green flag went down and they were off.

Lower down the field, Barbara was enjoying herself now. Having given Frankie her papers and race number, she had embarked on the next stage of the plan which was far more enjoyable: distracting Alan while Frankie made her way to the starting line. She found him with a small group of bikers admiring someone's machine. When she said his name, he raised an eyebrow.

'Barbara, what are you doing here?'

Barbara lowered her eyes in the same coquettish way she had seen the beautiful Jean Harlow do in her last film, *Saratoga*.

'I came to see the races.'

'No,' said Alan, 'I meant what are you doing here? This part is reserved for competitors and their machines.'

Barbara pretended to be horrified. 'Oh my! I am so sorry.' She looked about her. 'I'm so confused,' she said helplessly. Out of the corner of her eye she could see Frankie in the line of riders making their way up the hill from the starting line. 'Oh dear, dear. There's white tape everywhere,' Barbara wailed. 'Which way do I go?'

Alan wiped his hands with a greasy-looking cloth and threw it onto the saddle. 'Why don't I show you?' Behind them both, his mates sniggered.

'Oh, would you?' Barbara purred happily. 'That would be wonderful.'

*

Frankie's inexperience of racing became apparent almost straight away. As the faster riders took off, she was left floundering in a shower of mud, exhaust fumes and small stones. Her goggles protected her eyes but she was looking at the track through a brown smear. For a few frantic seconds she wobbled furiously but as luck would have it, she corrected the bike and held it steady while she hastily wiped her lenses with the palm of her gloved hand.

The first part of the track was up a steep incline. Frankie found herself leaning slightly forward in the saddle as she followed the pack. She knew the course like the back of her hand and negotiated the dry patch on the other side of the hill carefully.

With deep muddy furrows in front of her, Frankie put her legs out to balance herself but she didn't actually touch down. Under the rules of the Association, a foot on the ground meant a penalty point.

Having caught up with the rest of the pack, she was beginning to enjoy herself. What with the whine of the engines, the smell of petrol, the taste of dirt in her mouth and – most of all – the speed, it was all so exhilarating. As she burst out of a small wooded area, she could see the start/finish line again. Hurrah! She'd done one lap; only nine more to go.

Down by the gate, Bet had almost sold out. People streamed by even though the race meeting had already started. She craned her neck as they came out of the woods but she didn't recognise any of the riders. She did, however, spot Frankie's friend Barbara with her son Alan. Alan had his arm draped around the girl's shoulders. Barbara was gazing up at him. Bet frowned. What on earth was the boy thinking about? Barbara might be nearly a year older than Frankie but she was still scarcely more than a child. She'd have to have a word with Alan. Thank goodness Frankie was more sensible. She sighed. The school leaving age was fourteen and although Frankie wouldn't be returning when term time started, she still didn't have a job. It couldn't be allowed to continue. The girl had to pay her own way in life. The time for messing around was over. There was nothing for it; Bet would have to take matters into her own hands.

As it turned out, barely half the field had managed to stay the course. Frankie waited by the side of the track for the results but she didn't take her leather cap or the scarf off. The adjudicators totted up the points and everyone held their breath. First place Dick Manning, second place Keith Purcell, third place John Wilson, fourth place M. Clark. Frankie grinned. That was her. M. Clark was her mother's maiden name; Moira Clark. She saw her cousin turn his head sharply but it was when she took off her goggles and her leather skull cap that the trouble began.

There was an audible gasp from the crowd when Frankie tossed her head and rubbed her fingers vigorously through her hair.

'But he's a woman!'

'Who said a woman could ride in this competition? This is a man's sport.'

Alan was the first by her side. 'What the hell do you think you are doing?' he hissed.

'Well, I didn't quite manage first,' Frankie quipped, 'but fourth place isn't too bad for a beginner, is it?'

'You may have been fourth in positioning, young lady,' one of the adjudicators called out, 'but on points you were second.'

'You can't do that. She cheated.'

'I did not cheat!' Frankie said indignantly.

'Yes, you did. You're a girl.'

'Frankie, for goodness' sake go home,' Alan snapped.

'Why?' Frankie, hand on her hip, demanded to know.

'You should be disqualified,' someone else shouted. 'It's not fair, changing the rules like that. This is no place for women.'

'But she's not even a woman,' someone else observed. 'She's only a silly school kid.'

The shouting grew louder and tensions were running high. The general consensus among the organisers was that if they allowed the result to stand, they would have a riot on their hands. At the end of a heated argument, Frankie found herself disqualified on the basis that she was not quite fifteen and of the female sex.

'You'd better go back to the house,' Alan said, steering her away.

Snatching her arm back and fuming inside, Frankie knew it was hopeless. She walked away with as much dignity as she could muster.

Ten minutes later, she and Barbara were back in the bike

shed near the house. Frankie stamped her foot. 'I don't believe it,' she said crossly. 'How could they do this to me?'

'It does seem a little unfair,' Barbara agreed.

'A *bit* unfair,' Frankie raged on. 'It's more than that. I came second in that race fair and square.'

They heard the chickens scatter as Aunt Bet came across the yard. As soon as she saw her face, Frankie knew she was in for a ticking off. Aunt Bet came into the shed all guns blazing. Barbara bid a hasty retreat.

'How could you?' Aunt Bet spat. 'Embarrassing Uncle Lorry like that . . . and don't interrupt me . . . against the rules. . . I haven't finished yet . . . can't always have what you want, my girl . . .'

Frankie gave up trying to explain and sat on a straw bale, staring at the ground in front of her while her aunt vented her spleen. Ten minutes later, her aunt left and the light level fell as someone else stood in the doorway. It was Uncle Lorry. Frankie's heart sank. Was he going to be cross with her too?

'Well, that was a turn-up for the books, wasn't it?' he said.

Frankie rose to her feet. Whilst she didn't regret what she'd done, she felt uncomfortable because the last thing she'd wanted was to upset her uncle. 'Look, Uncle Lorry, I'm really sorry if I embarrassed you . . .'

She didn't get to finish the sentence because he hurried towards her and gave her a rough hug. 'I never thought a little pipsqueak like you had it in her. Well done, my lass.'

As he released her, Frankie blinked. 'You're not angry?'

'Angry? Why should I be?'

Frankie lowered her gaze. 'Aunt Bet said I'd embarrassed you.'

'Stuff and nonsense,' he said with a dismissive wave of his hand. 'I'm far too proud of you for that. You leave your Aunt Bet to me.'

# *Eight*

First thing on Tuesday morning, Aunt Bet took Frankie into Worthing. She told her she'd been talking to an egg customer who had mentioned a Saturday job with a view to a permanent position going in a florist along Montague Street. In Aunt Bet's opinion it would be an ideal situation and for once Frankie agreed with her. Of all the suggestions she'd been presented with, this was the best so far. Frankie hadn't got a clue what type of job she wanted but the usual girly jobs such as working in a shop or becoming a hairdresser didn't appeal to her. Aunt Bet had come up with a few suggestions. She might like to be a waitress or become a shop assistant. Not really. Frankie preferred to be outdoors. She had been tempted for about five minutes by the thought of getting a job with Worthing Borough Council Parks and Gardens but that turned out to be mostly seasonal work and once again, no girls were allowed. As a florist she would be stuck indoors but at least she would be working with something organic.

The florist was half way along the street. Frankie was shown to the back of the shop where two girls were making up bouquets. They looked so amazing that Frankie immediately felt out of her depth. How would she manage to arrange flowers like that when there wasn't an artistic bone in her body?

'Of course,' said Mrs Waite, the owner, 'we shall have to train you to do the arrangements, but we'll take it one step at a time. You will begin with simple tasks.'

At the end of the interview, Aunt Bet and Mrs Waite shook hands and it was agreed that Frankie would start next week. It was only as they walked away that Frankie realised that her new job would seriously curtail her dream of ever becoming a dirt bike rider if she ever did find a race meeting open to girls. Because of the strict Sunday Trading Laws, all the meetings were held on Saturday and she'd just agreed to a six-day week with a half day off on Monday.

*

Frankie couldn't wait to tell Barbara about her new job but soon after they arrived at the cinema, her cousin Alan joined them. There was little conversation as they waited in the queue. Alan and Barbara only seemed to have eyes for each other and Frankie felt miffed. Even more annoyingly, Alan bought Barbara's ticket but left Frankie to get her own. When they reached the stalls, Alan sat between them so there was no chance to talk at all before the film started. It was a good film, but Frankie was the only one watching it. At the end, after they'd all stood for the National Anthem, Frankie glared at Alan and Barbara. 'You needn't think I'm going to play gooseberry again.'

Barbara looked contrite but her cousin just grinned.

*

Frankie's first day in the job at the florist's was exhausting. As the junior, Frankie was given the most menial of tasks. She wasn't allowed to do any arrangements, of course, but she had to keep the workshop clean and tidy. That meant frequently sweeping the floor and putting bits of stalk and fallen petals into a special bin. This was collected at the end of the day by the owner's father for his compost heap. She made cups of tea for the girls doing the flowers and she was expected to run errands.

Frankie was amazed at the skill of the florists. In less than an hour, they could transform a humble gathering of flowers into a beautiful bouquet fit for a queen. Before the end of her first week, Frankie became aware of the pressures under which they worked. One consignment of flowers arrived in the shop but because the driver had lost his way, they had been in a hot van for far too long and were already wilting. As the blooms were needed for a wedding, everybody was in a flat spin. Another time, a customer complained about her bouquet. That called for diplomacy. There was nothing wrong with the blooms but Mrs Waite had to placate the customer in case she told her friends not to come to the shop.

On her third day Frankie was taken away from her usual jobs. Another girl who usually worked as a junior was ill. Her job was to make deliveries on a large bike with a basket on the front. It not only helped her get from place to place but it was a great way of advertising the skill of Mrs Waite's florists. Frankie was asked to take her place until she got back. Making deliveries turned out to be the best part of the job. Mrs Waite would give Frankie a green slip with the customer's address on it. Of course, she had to be careful that she didn't disturb the arrangement in the basket but it gave her an opportunity to bike around the town and sometimes up the driveways of some really impressive houses. Frankie learned to be polite to the customers, even those who were being awkward or picky.

The arrangements she carried were so imaginative: a dish garden with desert cacti or a shopping basket with a beautiful display of summer roses held in jam jars inside the basket. Mrs Waite stressed that she should remind the customer to keep filling the jam jars with water, particularly before putting it in the centre of the table. The most attractive of all was Mrs Waite's speciality called 'Flowers of the Sea'. She had spent hours creating artificial blooms from sea shells for the central part of an arrangement.

By the end of her first week, Frankie had acquitted herself well and Mrs Waite told her she had a job for life. Frankie was pleased but in her heart of hearts that was the last thing she wanted. She was looking for something else; she didn't know what, but something a bit more challenging. She was paid twenty-five shillings which was considered a good wage. Out of that she was expected to give Aunt Bet a pound for her keep. That left her with five bob for herself, so when Barbara, who had just started work in Woolworth's, suggested going to a dance in the Assembly Rooms, Frankie was quite keen. 'But what about Alan?'

'He's off to a race meeting somewhere in Surrey,' said Barbara, and Frankie remembered the conversation at the tea table a couple of days ago when Alan told his parents he was going to take part in the Bagshot Heath scramble.

Entry to the dance hall cost one and six and they planned to buy a drink in the interval, so Frankie could just about afford it.

As it turned out, they didn't have to buy their own drinks. Barbara met a young lad called Norman on the dance floor so he and his mate bought the girls a round. Barbara and her new friend seemed to be getting on like a house on fire but Frankie felt self-conscious being with Norman's friend. It was obvious that he had little interest in Frankie and she was too embarrassed to ask him any questions, so it was an awkward evening.

*

Monday found her back at the shop sweeping the floors as the other junior was back from sick leave. Frankie could hardly believe her eyes when she walked in.

'Doreen!'

It was Doreen Toms. The last time Frankie had seen her old friend was when she was ten years old. She had become a rather plain-looking girl. Her hair was straight and pulled back from her face with a Kirby grip, and she wore rather dowdy clothes. She smiled shyly when she saw Frankie but said nothing.

'How lovely to see you,' Frankie burbled. 'When they told me you were called Doreen, I never dreamed it was you. How long have you worked here?'

'Not long.'

'I only started last week,' Frankie went on. 'This is my first job.'

'There are two deliveries this morning,' Mrs Waite interrupted as she handed Doreen two green slips.

'My mother says,' Doreen said, her voice still thick with cold, 'can I stay indoors this week?' She coughed noisily.

Mrs Waite looked annoyed. 'If you can't do the work . . .' she began.

'I don't mind going out, Mrs Waite,' Frankie interrupted.

Her employer glared at her.

'Just until Doreen is better,' Frankie added quickly.

Mrs Waite pursed her lips and sniffed loudly. 'Oh very well. Just for this week but I really can't have my employees telling me what they will or will not do.'

As she handed Frankie the green slips, Doreen mouthed a 'thank you' behind the older woman's back.

# Nine

Their days at the florist shop were so busy that it was hard to find a time to talk. For a while, Frankie and Doreen seemed like passing ships in the night. There wasn't even time for a chat after work. Doreen's mother came to meet her and always seemed anxious for her daughter to get home. Frankie was left watching them head for the bus stop. Poor Doreen. She'd always seemed timid and shy, sort of on the outside looking in, even when the girls in the florist made a cup of tea or there was a lull in the work. It was little wonder with such a harridan for a mother. Mrs Toms hadn't exactly been very nice at the picnic as Frankie recalled, although her own mother had made no comment at the time. In fact Frankie had never heard her mother say anything bad about anyone.

Before long they were taking Christmas orders and Frankie surprised herself by settling down in the job. She knew she wouldn't stay at the florist's forever, but for now she was content to stay for at least a year to get a good reference. The work was varied and she was learning all the time.

'Cut your blooms to different lengths,' Mrs Waite told her. 'Taller flowers in the middle and the shorter stems on the outside. That way your bouquet looks fuller.'

Doreen developed a flair for making terrariums. Mrs Waite

taught her how to plant orchids and ferns in a little soil at the bottom of a goldfish bowl. The trick was to peg them down with hair pins. Everybody else's terrarium looked good. Doreen's was always sensational and whenever her efforts were on display, they always sold first.

Occasionally the two girls worked side by side on the bench. That was the only time they had a conversation.

'Where did you go after . . .?' Doreen hesitated.

'After my mother died?' Frankie said. 'I went to live with my aunt; mum's sister.'

'Were you happy?'

'Oh yes,' said Frankie. 'I still am. In fact I sometimes forget that I'm not part of the immediate family.'

Doreen gave her a wan smile.

'My cousins, Alan and Ronald, are motorbike mad,' Frankie went on. 'They taught me how to ride.'

Doreen's eyebrows shot up. 'You actually ride a motorbike?'

Frankie nodded. 'I love it. I took part in a race a few weeks ago but I can't do it again because I'm a girl. Besides, most of the big races are on Saturdays. There are a couple of circuits where they race on Sundays though.' She paused and looked at her friend. 'Why not come along sometime?'

'Mother wouldn't like it,' said Doreen, her voice flat. 'We always go to the hall on Sundays.'

'That's lovely, Doreen,' Mrs Wait interrupted as she looked over her shoulder. 'Frankie, finish up here and come through to the office. I've got a couple of deliveries for you.'

'Yes, Mrs Waite,' said Frankie, and, scraping the bits into the bin, she added to her friend, 'Fancy coming to the pictures with me on Saturday?'

Doreen shook her head. 'I'm not allowed,' she said.

'Why ever not?' Frankie gasped. 'It's a good picture. It's not an "X" or anything.'

'My mother considers the cinema to be a den of iniquity,' said Doreen dully. 'She says it's the devil's playground.'

Frankie blinked in surprise. 'What on earth does she think goes on in there?'

Doreen shrugged. 'I don't know but I can't come.'

'It's only the pictures,' Frankie muttered as she headed for the office.

*

Alan was becoming quite well known on the motor scramble circuit. He hadn't been placed at the Donnington course but he had come in third at Bagshot Heath.

Frankie could only look on enviously. She still tinkered with the bikes in her spare time, little that there was, and her knowledge of the machines had advanced enormously.

In the run up to Christmas, Frankie had her own money for the first time in her life. She bought a tin of boiled sweets for the girls at work to share. She also found some really good presents for the family. She'd saved hard and managed to get a lovely little oil dispenser for Alan, some handkerchiefs for Uncle Lorry, a fountain pen for Ronald (good old Woolworth's), and a new torch for Aunt Bet – her old one was knackered even if it did have new batteries. It was very satisfying to be able to get them something she'd bought using her own money. They had been wonderful to her and Frankie would never forget it. The holiday season brought with it a few fond memories of her mother which were not without tears. It was five years since she'd been gone and Frankie still missed her.

Aunt Bet was making some Sussex Plum Heavies, always popular with her boys. She'd served them up so often she could almost make them without looking but a movement down by the old bike shed distracted her. Bet could hardly believe her own eyes. There was her son Alan with that Barbara Vickers again. Alan had her pinned to the wall of the shed with his hand inside Barbara's coat and judging by the way the girl was gyrating, it wasn't around her waist. The pair began kissing passionately. Bet frowned crossly. Hadn't she warned her son about that girl just a month or so back? The little madam. She'd always thought that girl was trouble. Did she have no shame? Alan was virtually eating her. The way she led the boys on, she'd be having a baby before long.

'Well, not with my son, you won't,' Bet muttered.

On the Friday before Christmas, Doreen and Frankie were both given time off. All the orders had been done and Mrs Waite said there was no point in hanging around in case another customer came into the shop. 'Besides,' she continued, 'tomorrow will be very busy with husbands doing their last-minute shopping, so off you go and enjoy yourselves.'

'You know, it's at times like this that I miss my mother the most,' said Frankie as they strolled down Montague Street. 'We used to come into Worthing occasionally to do some window shopping.'

'I remember her so well,' Doreen said. 'She was really kind to me and I loved her stories.'

Frankie smiled. 'She certainly had an eventful life.'

'I particularly liked the story about the day she fought off that Russian and saved the princess,' Doreen went on.

'I liked that one too,' said Frankie.

'Do you still have that beautiful doll she made you?'

'She sits by my bed,' said Frankie with a sigh. 'You know, my mother was so full of life that for ages I struggled to believe she had gone.' She paused, adding, 'And I blamed myself.'

Doreen raised her eyebrows. 'Why would you do that?'

Frankie shrugged. 'I suppose I thought I might have saved her if I'd got home from school earlier.'

'But she didn't take her own life, did she?' Doreen gasped.

'No,' said Frankie.

They had wandered into Woolworth's. Doreen squeezed Frankie's arm. 'People said she'd been dead a long time before Mrs Dickenson found her.'

'I heard that too,' Frankie agreed. She was standing at the lipstick counter. She had two colours but she only wore lipstick when she went to the pictures or the Saturday dance with Barbara. Frankie twisted the end of a Max Factor lipstick to reveal a bright and luscious red. Perhaps she should wear lipstick every day? It was about time she started behaving like a young woman now that she was working. 'What do you think of this colour?'

'It's lovely,' Doreen said absent-mindedly.

'It's called Carmine,' said Frankie, but Doreen wasn't really listening.

'You know you weren't the only one who blamed herself about your mother,' Doreen said quietly. 'I used to worry that her heart attack was all my mother's fault.'

For a moment, Frankie froze. 'What do you mean?'

'Oh Frankie, the day she died, they had the most fearful row.' Doreen's face was the picture of misery and Frankie could see tears standing in her eyes. 'All my mother wanted to do was to save you.'

'You're scaring me,' said Frankie. 'Save me from what?'

'Don't you remember?' Doreen went on. 'The tarot cards in that little tin on the mantelpiece.'

'And what do you think you are doing here, young lady?' A harsh and angry voice interrupted them, making them both jump.

Doreen visibly trembled as her mother pushed herself between them. She leaned towards her daughter and hissed in her ear. 'I hope you're not thinking of painting your mouth like a common Jezebel.'

'Actually I was the one looking at lipsticks,' said Frankie. Her gaze went to Mrs Toms' shabby coat pulled tightly around her middle with the buttons straining. She had no hat but her hand-knitted scarf was over her head and tied under her chin.

'Oh, I might have guessed you had something to do with it,' Mrs Toms sneered, her steely grey eyes fixed on Frankie. 'Don't I always say, corruption breeds corruption.'

'Doreen wasn't doing anything wrong,' Frankie insisted.

'Why aren't you at work?' Mrs Toms demanded of her daughter.

Doreen seemed to have shrunk a couple of feet. Her face was ashen and she stared at her feet like a naughty little girl. Frankie could have sworn she was trembling too.

'Mrs Waite gave us the rest of the afternoon off,' Frankie blurted out, 'so I suggested . . .'

'Is everything all right?' The shop assistant had joined them.

'Everything will be perfectly all right,' Mrs Toms retorted, 'as soon as my daughter and I are out of this palace of sin.' She snatched at her daughter's arm. 'Come along, my girl. We're going.'

Frankie stared after Doreen and her mother, feeling quite sorry for them. They must be very poor. Mrs Toms' shoes were so worn down they went right over as she walked. When the pair reached the door, Frankie turned back to the shop assistant.

'What was all that about?' the girl asked.

Frankie shrugged. She felt surprisingly upset. Replacing the lipstick, she turned to go.

The shop assistant sniffed loudly and walked away muttering, 'Nutty as a fruit cake.'

Doreen didn't come to work the next day, nor the day they went back to work after Christmas. Mrs Waite contacted her and Mrs Toms said her daughter had left the shop and would not return. Frankie was both sad and curious. Poor Doreen. Fancy having an old battle-axe like that for a mother; and what did Doreen mean when she said her mother and Mrs Toms had had a row about the tarot cards? What were tarot cards anyway?

Back at the farm, Aunt Bet had bided her time until she and Alan were alone with little chance of interruption. They were both in the scullery; he was cleaning his best shoes and she was folding the washing ready to iron.

'Looks to me like you're quite keen on that Barbara Vickers,' she said, willing herself to sound casual.

Her son pulled a face. 'She's all right, I suppose.'

'That's a matter of opinion,' Bet said coldly.

He turned his head to look at her. 'What's that supposed to mean?' His voice had an edge to it.

'When you get to my age,' said Bet, 'you learn how to take stock of people and that girl is trouble with a capital "T". She's the type who can trap a boy into marriage and . . .'

Alan snorted. 'You needn't worry on that score, mum. I've no intention of marrying Barbara Vickers.'

'Well, see to it that you give her no reason to expect it,' said Bet, sweeping out of the room.

# *Ten*

There was nothing on at the pictures so Barbara suggested that she and Frankie go to the matinee variety show at the pier pavilion. Over the past year, the two girls had fallen into a sort of routine. They often met on a Wednesday night to go to the pictures and on a Saturday they went to a show in the afternoon or to a dance in the evening. Today they had managed to get good seats and the show was enjoyable. Frankie particularly liked the glittering costumes of the dancing girls. The comedian Cyril Fletcher recited some very funny poems and Dorothy Ward led everybody in the theatre in some community singing. The lead singer of the show was an up-and-coming name (or so the compère told the audience) – Conrad Merriman. Good-looking with deep-set eyes and black hair, Conrad was everybody's idea of tall dark and handsome and when he smiled he had a long dimple on his cheek. Frankie didn't like him that much but Barbara thought he was wonderful. After the show Barbara insisted they go to the stage door and she was amply rewarded when Conrad Merriman emerged.

'Can I have your autograph?' said Barbara, rushing towards him.

'Of course, darling,' he simpered and, giving her a kiss on her cheek, he signed her programme then looked up, expecting Frankie to want the same treatment. Embarrassed, Frankie handed him her programme and he signed it.

'A few of us are going onto the pier for some ice cream,' he said. 'Would you care to join us?'

Barbara was overjoyed so they joined in. There were several in the group including some of the dancing girls and another comedian called Stainless Steven. They all went to the kiosk and bought their cones, then everyone strolled along the wooden planks towards the other pavilion at the end of the pier. Conrad slipped his arm around Barbara's waist and pulled her close.

'Put her down, darling,' someone said. 'You don't know where she's been.'

'She's too young to have been anywhere,' said another voice and everyone laughed.

Barbara wasn't too happy with that remark, but she was delighted when Conrad kissed her cheek again and said, 'I think she's absolutely gorgeous, aren't you, darling?'

Frankie struck up a conversation with one of the dancing girls, Lily, who said she was from York. 'I love it here,' she said. 'I've got a booking for the whole season.'

'You looked beautiful on the stage,' Frankie said. 'I loved the top hat routine.'

Lily did a few steps just for her and they both laughed. Halfway along the pier, there was a photo booth. You could stand in behind a wooden frame with Tarzan, Jane and a monkey picture on it. The faces had been cut out so day trippers were invited to stick their heads through the holes and pose for a picture. Conrad stood behind the Tarzan cut out and invited Barbara to join him as Jane. Frankie was encouraged to bend down low and put her head through the monkey hole. While the photographer snapped away, Frankie was startled to feel Conrad's hand wandering over her bottom. She stood up smartly.

'Just one more,' said the photographer but Frankie was already walking away.

*

A day or two later, they were sitting at the dinner table when Alan told his parents about meeting Mr Jarvis, Durrant's promoter. 'He's going to take me on next year for the Isle of Man TT.'

Uncle Lorry was bursting with excitement. 'Dear Lord alive, you'll be up there with all the best riders. What an experience, lad.'

'No,' said Aunt Bet. 'Alan, you can't go. It's too dangerous.'

'Now then, Bet love,' Uncle Lorry began.

'Don't you "Now then, Bet love" me!' she snapped and she banged a plate down in front of him. 'You know Percy Pritlove was killed there last year.'

'You can't stop me, Mum,' said Alan shaking the HP sauce onto his dinner. 'I'm old enough to make my own decisions.'

'This is a chance of a lifetime, Bet,' Lorry protested mildly. 'You can't say no just because you're afraid he might get hurt.'

Frankie could tell her aunt was upset but she didn't say anything. As soon as the men went back outside and Aunt Bet stood up to put the plates in the sink, Frankie came and put her arm around her shoulders. 'He's a really good rider,' she said. 'He thinks things through and he doesn't take stupid risks. That's why he's been chosen.'

Aunt Bet nodded. 'I suppose you're right,' she said. 'And your uncle's right as well. I'm just being silly. I know he's a grown man but he's still my boy.'

The two women shared a hug. 'And just look at you,' said Aunt Bet suddenly holding her at arm's length. 'Soon to be sixteen and quite the young lady already.' Frankie gave her a half smile. 'What?' said Aunt Bet. 'What is it?'

'Now you'll think I'm being silly,' said Frankie, sitting back down at the table.

'Let me be the judge of that,' said her aunt.

All the time she'd lived with them, they'd never really talked about her mother. The grief they'd both felt, they'd kept it private. It wasn't a deliberate decision, it just happened to be that way. Frankie knew any one of them would have listened if she'd needed to talk but she'd slipped into the habit of managing on her own.

Frankie took a deep breath. 'Before she left the shop, Doreen told me her mother had taken something from my house. Something belonging to my mother – tarot cards.'

Aunt Bet seemed surprised. 'I can't imagine your mother having tarot cards,' she said. 'I was the one who worried about the future and superstitions. I got it from your gran, I suppose. Your mother was different. She was very much a no-nonsense sort of person.'

Frankie frowned. 'What are tarot cards anyway?'

'They're supposed to be a guide for living,' said Aunt Bet. 'People use them to find out what's going to happen in the future.'

After hearing that, Frankie had to agree that her aunt was probably right. Her mother had had no time for what she called mumbo-jumbo, such as predicting the future.

'Anyway, why would Doreen's mother take something that didn't belong to her?' said Aunt Bet. 'I thought she was religious.'

'She is,' said Frankie.

'Then what was she doing stealing Moira's things?'

'Doreen seemed to think she was trying to save me.'

Aunt Bet frowned and shook her head slowly.

'I often think about the things my mother had,' Frankie said wistfully. 'I remember some playing cards and a white cat that used to be on the mantelpiece.' She smiled. 'She always told me not to touch it but when she wasn't looking, I used to stroke it.'

Aunt Bet laid her hand gently over the top of Frankie's. 'Stay there, ducks,' she said. 'I want to show you something.'

Her aunt hurried upstairs and came back down a few minutes later with a little suitcase. As she seldom dusted up high, the case was covered with a thick layer of grime. She found a damp cloth and a moment or two later, she put the case in front of Frankie.

'I wasn't sure when to give you this,' she said. 'I was going to wait until you left home or when you got married but I think now is the right time.'

Frankie looked up. 'I've never seen this before.'

'The case is mine,' said Aunt Bet. 'But the things inside belonged to your mother and now they belong to you. You may want to keep some, you may want to get rid of some, it's up to you.' She smiled. 'I'm going to leave you now,' she went on. 'The men won't be back until tea time and judging by the things in that case, you'll be a little while. Take your time. I've got plenty to do upstairs.'

Taking her box of dusters and cleaning things, she left the room and the door clicked shut. Frankie stared at the lid of the case for some time before she found the courage to open it. The first thing she noticed was the smell. She couldn't define it, but somehow or other it was exclusive to her old home. Five years of being shut up on the top of the wardrobe hadn't taken it away. A mixture of Lily of the Valley (her mother's favourite soap) and blackberries; the smell of silks and other materials she used for her dressmaking. It was all there. Perhaps it was only her imagination but it made Frankie's heart flutter and brought a lump to her throat. She stared at the contents.

A few official papers rested on the top. Frankie turned them over but didn't examine them closely. They included her mother's marriage certificate and Frankie's birth certificate. She spotted a little pink card which said 'congratulations on the birth of your daughter'. Next she found a black-edged card announcing her father's death and a misshapen lump of baked clay – a pot Frankie had made at school. Her mother had kept it on the mantelpiece and used it to store her long tapers for lighting the fire. Frankie smiled, recalling her mother's reaction when she'd presented it to her. 'Oh, Frankie, it's beautiful! How clever you are.' Well, it wasn't beautiful and she wasn't one bit clever. It was hideous, but the love in her mother's voice had told her something very different on the day she'd brought it home. Frankie's eyes smarted.

Next she found a bundle of letters tied with blue ribbon. It would take a while to read them but a glance at the back of the one of the envelopes told her they had been written by her father. It was stamped 'Somerley House, Ellingham, Ringwood, Hants,' the convalescent home where her father had started his road to recovery. She remembered her mother once telling her that they had transferred him from there to Cecil's Red Cross Hospital, Chappell Croft in West Worthing just before they'd married.

Laying the letters down, she picked up the white cat, only now that she looked at it more closely she could see it wasn't a cat at all. It was an exquisitely carved ivory lioness. Where on earth had her mother got that from?

Frankie found a few more things which were meaningless to her but obviously had been treasures to her mother: a broken watch, a few bits of jewellery, two grainy photographs, one of her mother with a young man and another of her mother standing on her own in front of a large house.

Frankie heard a footfall behind her and looked up to see her aunt standing beside her.

77

'All right, my dear?' she asked anxiously. She held out a folded handkerchief and shook it open. Frankie hadn't even been aware that she was crying. She wiped her wet cheeks and blew her nose, then holding up the photograph she said, 'Who is that man standing next to my mother?'

'Why, that's your father,' said Aunt Bet sitting down beside her, 'before he went to war.'

Frankie looked more closely. He was a handsome man, no more than twenty, with thick wavy hair. He stood close to her mother but not actually touching. 'I never saw a picture of him before,' she said quietly. 'What was he like?'

Aunt Bet smiled. 'I liked him a lot. Before the war he was funny and a bit of a practical joker. He enjoyed singing too.'

'Go on,' said Frankie sensing there was more to come.

Her aunt took the photograph in her hands. 'They used to ride on a tandem. Went all over the place.' She chuckled. 'I remember him telling us that one day they went to see his auntie and uncle. His uncle was famous for his home-made wine and your mother and father had a couple of glasses. When they left, your dad reckoned they did five miles in about fifteen minutes before they both fell off the bike and into a hedge.'

Frankie smiled, imagining the scene. 'Why didn't Mum have any photographs of him after he came back from the war?'

Aunt Bet seemed embarrassed and made to leave the table. 'No, tell me,' Frankie insisted.

Aunt Bet laid her hand on Frankie's arm. 'He was so terribly injured,' she said quietly. 'His poor face was . . .' She faltered, her eyes brimming with tears. 'But your mother never stopped loving him. She didn't seem to notice how dreadful he looked but she didn't want any photographs. She wanted us to remember him as he was.'

'She never told me,' said Frankie. 'What happened to his face anyway?'

Aunt Bet seemed reluctant to say any more but eventually she put her hand to the side of her face in a sweeping gesture. 'All of this side of his face was shot away,' she said simply. 'The shell fragment didn't hit any vital organs or an artery but your poor father was left with only half a face.'

Frankie was stunned. 'But Mum said he was gassed,' she protested.

'Well, she wouldn't want you to know about his face, would she?' said Aunt Bet. 'You were only a child. She didn't want you to be upset.'

Frankie turned back to the case. There wasn't a lot left inside but she began to empty everything out and put it onto the table.

'They bought that silly ornament when they were on their honeymoon,' said Aunt Bet holding up a china boot with 'A present from Weymouth' on it.

Frankie lifted an upside-down book from the very bottom of the case. When she turned it over, she took in her breath sharply. Aunt Bet had got up from the table and was making a fresh pot of tea. Frankie quickly leafed through the pages. It was a children's book, beautifully illustrated on every page. She didn't need to read the story. She knew it off by heart. A Russian princess comes into a dress shop. A fearsome-looking man with a knife follows her in and it's obvious that he has evil intent. To save the princess, the shop assistants bundle the princess into a big wicker basket and cover her with clothes.

Frankie stared at the pages in bewilderment. She felt angry, confused and disappointed. She had loved that story and had grown up believing it to be true. 'Tell me again,' she would beg her mother and her mother had repeated it word for word as if it had really happened. Frankie had been so proud of her mother, just a chit of a girl, as she would say, standing up to that man. Her mother was her hero, courageous and brave.

People often said it sounded like something from a story book. Frankie had never believed them, but it was true, wasn't it? Her mother had pretended to be something she wasn't and Frankie had grown up believing a lie, a great big fat lie. Tears pricked her eyes. She felt sick, shaky and faint.

Aunt Bet put a cup of tea in front of her. 'There you are, duck,' she said.

Frankie looked up at her. 'It wasn't true, was it,' she said brokenly, 'about the Russian? She made it all up.' Slamming the book shut, Frankie threw it back into the suitcase before running up the stairs to her room.

# Eleven

**Broadwater, Sussex, September 1939**

*'In this grave hour, perhaps the most fateful in our history . . .'*

Frankie willed herself to concentrate. It was six o'clock and they were gathered around the wireless. The King's speech made for uncomfortable listening but not because of its content. It was well known that the King had a terrible stammer and that he found making speeches purgatory itself so they listened with dread that he might suddenly falter and have to abandon his speech altogether.

*'For the second time in the lives of most of us,'* his Majesty continued, *'we are at war. Over and over again we have tried to find a peaceful way out of the differences between ourselves and those who are now our enemies; but it has been in vain . . .'*

Frankie looked around the room. They had already got used to the idea that the country was at war when Mr Chamberlain's earlier broadcast had spelled out the gravity of the situation. If she survived this war, she would be sure to tell her children and grandchildren what it had been like. The whole family was there listening to the King, plus Mrs Mac and few of their near neighbours who didn't have a wireless of their own; she supposed that they were all as concerned as she was.

*'. . . I now call my people at home, and my peoples across the*

seas, who will make our cause their own. I ask them to stand calm and firm and united in this time of trial. The task will be hard. There may be dark days ahead . . . with God's help, we shall prevail.'

When the national anthem began, it was with a sense of relief that everybody in Aunt Bet's kitchen rose to their feet.

'Not one stutter,' murmured Mrs Mac as the anthem died away and they all sat again. 'Well done, your Majesty.'

That raised a wry smile to everyone's lips.

Frankie got up and went outside. She needed time to think. As soon as she appeared dear old Loopy-Lu hurried towards her. She wasn't so agile anymore and couldn't move as quickly as she once did but even at seven years old, she was a force to be reckoned with in the henhouse. Frankie absent-mindedly picked her up and made her way to the bike barn. She stood in the doorway breathing in the smell of engine oil and looked around at the machines which meant so much to her. There was talk of all public meetings being closed down for the duration of the war.

And what of the rest of her life? Would she ever meet a boy and fall in love? Several lads had asked her out and she occasionally went to the pictures with somebody or to a dance but there had never been anyone special. Just lately, what with all this talk of war and Hitler, she'd been thinking a lot about her mother again. Oh, why did she have to die like that? She'd taken a walk around to their old place and looked over the fence. Whoever lived there now had let the pretty little garden go and the windows were badly in need of a clean. She didn't stay long. That horrible Sidney Knight opened the door and shouted at her.

Barbara had stopped coming to the farm and although nothing was said, Alan didn't take her out any more. Not that Barbara seemed to care. She was too busy enjoying life. As far as Frankie knew she was still with Conrad, who had stayed for the whole summer season in the Pavilion Theatre.

Frankie couldn't stand him. Conrad was nowhere near as wonderful as Barbara seemed to think he was. She couldn't forget that day when they had their picture taken on the pier, how he had his arm around Barbara's waist while at the same time he was touching Frankie's bottom in an over-familiar way. He'd even tried to make a date with Frankie when Barbara went to the ladies' room and he was always flirting with other girls in the company.

Frankie had tried to talk to her friend about it but she was having none of it.

'How dare you!' she'd shrieked. 'I don't believe you. You're just jealous, that's what it is.'

'Oh, Barbara,' said Frankie, 'you know I wouldn't say this if it wasn't true. He kisses everyone in sight.'

'That's the way they are in show business,' Barbara had said haughtily. 'It doesn't mean anything.'

A tetchy silence had descended between them.

'Anyway, what about Norman Miles?' Frankie eventually asked. 'He seemed like a nice chap.'

'Norman is boring,' Barbara said dismissively. 'Conrad is going places. You mark my word, he'll be the star of the show before long.'

Frankie had signed inwardly. Yes, and pigs might fly, she'd thought to herself. She was upset that she and Barbara had fallen out, but what could she do? Conrad was a cad but Barbara just couldn't see it. All she could do was hope and pray that her friend would come to her senses before she got hurt.

Although the rift with Barbara was upsetting, now that the country was at war, Frankie supposed her little business would flounder as well. She had a nice little side line doing repairs or souping up old bikes to make them faster, but now that war had been declared, she supposed all that would change. Who would have time to take a ride out into the country on his motorbike and sidecar if there was a war on? No more race meetings; no more scrambles. Would she ever get to ride in competitions? She sat on the chair by the bench and stroked the hen with a heavy heart.

A footfall in the doorway made her turn her head. It was Alan.

'I'm joining up,' he said dully.

Frankie nodded. 'I thought you might.'

'Mum won't like it,' he said. 'She'll be upset when I tell her so I want you to help her.'

'Of course,' said Frankie. 'Once she's got used to the idea, she'll be all right.'

He nodded curtly and turned away. 'Bloody Hitler.'

She watched him go and sighed. So this was it. She was just sixteen years old and once again her life had changed forever.

# Twelve

Sidney Knight sat at the kitchen table with his head in his hands. War. What was he going to do now? There had been talk at the racetracks that if war came, the racing calendar would be suspended. For Sidney, nothing could be worse.

That girl had been here. He'd seen her standing by the fence and looking up at the house. He'd had to duck behind the curtain in case she saw him. All grown up she was and quite a looker too. How old was she now? Fifteen, sixteen? It was then that he'd realised that it was six years almost to the day that her mother had died. She had her mother's look about her; the way she stood, the way she held her head; got her hair too. But what was she doing back here, for goodness' sake? He saw her reach her hand over the fence and pull a branch towards her and held his breath as she bent to smell a rose. All at once he felt angry. Marching to his front door, he pulled it open and stood on the doorstep. 'What you doing, you nosey little tike?' he demanded. 'Leave that alone!'

She'd blanched. 'I'm sorry,' she said, her eyes filling with tears. 'I didn't mean anything, Mr Knight. I'm sorry.'

'Then bugger off and don't come back,' he'd snapped.

She'd thrown him a hurt look and started to run. Back in the house he'd sworn out loud and kicked the hall stand. Everything was going bloody wrong these days. The horses hadn't been good to him. He was running out of assets, having sold his father's house a couple of years ago to pay off his gambling debts. The Post Office money orders had stopped coming. He'd backed a sure fire horse at the Doncaster meeting but it had come in last but one. Now the bank account was almost empty. He'd thought about letting out the top floor rooms but he couldn't risk a tenant snooping around up there. He hadn't been upstairs since the day she'd died. The terrible smell and the mould on the walls had lingered for a lot longer than he'd thought possible. It had even filtered into the rooms he used downstairs. Of course, it hadn't helped having a broken gutter which let in the rain. He supposed he should have seen to it when he'd got the money from his father's place but he didn't want builders in the house. Besides, there was this filly running in the Derby. And now that bloody girl was back smelling his roses. Grabbing a pair of scissors from the kitchen, he went back outside and hacked the bush down as best he could.

His temper gone, he sighed. War. No race meetings and what was even more dreadful, men of his age were being conscripted into the army. He couldn't go to war. He wasn't the type. What did he care about bloody Hitler? All he wanted in life was a few bob to put each way on a horse. Was that too much to ask for?

# *Thirteen*

**Broadwater, Sussex, October 1939**

Posters went up at the railway station, the Old Town Hall and on hoardings throughout the community. The only illustration was a picture of the crown of King George VI over the words: *Your courage, your cheerfulness, your resolution will bring us victory.*

For the next few months, life carried on as normal. After the initial panic that the Germans would be pouring up the beaches before the end of September, everyone breathed a sigh of relief when it hadn't happened and settled down. The British Expeditionary Force had been sent to France as early as September 4th and were guarding the Belgium–France border. Surprisingly, Aunt Bet had accepted Alan's decision to join up without protest, and he was at present doing his ten-week training in the Royal Army Ordinance Corp workshops in Chilwell, Nottingham. Ronald had gone to the recruiting offices as well but had been turned down on account of his hearing loss. He was a bit disappointed but in his usual stoic manner he put it behind him and joined the Local Defence Volunteers instead.

True to her word, Frankie made sure she spent as much time with Aunt Bet as she could and the two of them enjoyed some pleasant outings and doing things together in the house.

Preparations for an invasion carried on apace. Worthing's beaches were closed and heavy concrete blocks were positioned all along the seafront. Underground shelters were dug in Steyne Gardens and another was opened opposite the clinic in Stoke Abbott Road. Everybody knew the country really was at war when a gun placement appeared at Splash Point. All British citizens had to carry the gas masks issued earlier in the year but people still hoped that they would never need to be used. Aunt Bet had made some black-out curtains and council workmen spent their time painting black and white paint onto the kerb stones to make them easier to see in the dark.

Aunt Bet and her branch of the Women's Institute were immediately immersed in making chutney and helping to organise tea parties and country walks for some of the twelve thousand evacuees sent to the Worthing area from London. When they'd arrived in town, they'd each been given a brown carrier bag containing enough food for two days and Aunt Bet had been part of the preparation for that too.

Frankie felt at a loose end. Too young to join any of the uniformed forces, she still wanted to 'do her bit'. The local Red Cross and St John Ambulance had joined forces and were offering First Aid courses. There was no age limit so Frankie volunteered. The course was held in a room adjoining Worthing hospital. There were sixteen people from all walks of life and a wide age range but the leader, Mrs Kerridge, soon put everyone at ease. After they'd given their personal details, each applicant was given a little booklet and they spent their first evening learning how to stop a severe bleed by pressing a clean handkerchief on the wound to act as a 'plug'. Then, using each other as guinea pigs, they practised bandaging the wound and putting on a sling. Frankie's partner was called Margery. She was a lot older than Frankie but they got on really well. Mrs Kerridge was very complimentary about Frankie's reef knot but a little less impressed with Margery's granny knot which sent her companion into a fit of the giggles.

On her third evening at the Red Cross, Frankie was hailed as she pushed her bicycle out of the hospital grounds. It was Doreen Toms.

'What are you doing here?' Frankie asked as the two girls embraced.

'Visiting my mother,' said Doreen. 'She's on ward three.'

'Nothing serious, I hope,' said Frankie.

Doreen gave her awkward smile. 'Actually she has cancer. She's dying.'

Frankie gasped. 'Oh, Doreen, I'm so sorry. Me and my big mouth.'

Doreen shook her head. 'You weren't to know. She's been ill since May and in hospital since the beginning of the month. They tell me it won't be long now.'

Frankie didn't know what to say. She'd never really liked Mrs Toms but, for Doreen's sake, it was upsetting to think of her as being so ill.

'I wonder,' said Doreen, 'if you would come round to my place sometime. There's something I'd like to show you.'

'Yes, yes of course,' said Frankie. 'Do you want me to come now?'

'Come Sunday,' said Doreen. 'About ten.'

They parted and Frankie biked home. Poor Mrs Toms. And poor old Doreen. Whatever would she do now? Presumably she'd have to move when her mother died. She'd never manage to pay the rent by herself. Besides, no landlord worth his salt would leave a young unmarried girl in two rooms on her own. Frankie hoped one of the church people would take her in. After all, isn't that what was in the Bible? She frowned. Come at ten, Doreen had said. Wouldn't she be going to church at that time? Her heart sank. Oh no, she wasn't going to ask Frankie to go with her, was she?

*

Frankie felt a little nervous when Sunday morning came. She'd dressed with care. It probably wasn't a good idea to go round to Doreen's place dressed in old togs – not if there was a chance her friend would ask her to come to church. She didn't exactly put on her best clothes but she did have a freshly ironed long-sleeved blouse, her Fair Isle cardigan and a box pleat skirt. Aunt Bet had baked some Sussex Plum Heavies and she sent a jar of blackberry and apple jelly to go with them. Frankie arrived just after ten. When she opened the door, Doreen looked very tired. There were dark circles under her eyes and her face was very pale. She seemed surprised to see Frankie but quickly recovered. 'Come in, come in.'

Immediately behind the front door was the sitting room. It was a rather stark room with an old-fashioned brown sofa and one easy chair. The walls were dark and badly in need of a make-over. There were no pictures and the fireplace contained a vase of dried flowers which were clearly years old and rather tatty. Frankie shivered.

'This way,' said Doreen. Frankie followed her across the threadbare mat and into the kitchen. A wall of heat met them. The kitchen was clinically clean but very old-fashioned. Doreen had the oven on and the door open to warm the room. 'I'll make some tea,' she said bumping the oven door shut with her knee.

Frankie put her basket onto the kitchen table and took out Aunt Bet's cake tin. 'My aunt sent me with a gift,' she said, sitting down at the table.

Doreen looked inside the tin. 'How lovely!' she cried. 'I'll get us some plates.'

While she busied herself laying the table, Frankie said, 'How is your mother?'

Without faltering, Doreen said, 'She died early this morning.'

Frankie was horrified. 'Oh, Doreen, I'm so sorry. You should have said. I'll go if you like?'

'No!' cried Doreen, her exclamation making them both jump. 'Please don't. I want you to stay. I've never been allowed to have a friend in my house before.'

Frankie blinked in surprise.

The tea made, Doreen sat at the table. 'This looks lovely,' she said helping herself from the tin. 'I'm starving.'

Frankie couldn't help looking around. Compared to Aunt Bet's, the kitchen did seem awfully empty. There was nothing on the shelves but a door at the other end of the room made her think everything was in the pantry. Doreen was already eating. 'This is delicious. Come on, tuck in.'

Frankie had already had a hearty breakfast and wasn't particularly hungry so she took the smallest plum heavy and cut it in half. It crossed her mind that Doreen might suddenly break down, but so far there was no sign of it.

'I haven't seen you since Mum made me leave the florist,' she said, spitting a few crumbs. 'Are you still there?'

Frankie nodded. Despite her intention to stay for a year and then move on, she still worked at the shop. She was one of the chief florists now, sometimes taking charge of the really big occasions such as a wedding or a civic dinner.

'And Mrs Waite? Is she still there?'

Frankie nodded again. 'Still there.'

'I don't think she liked me much,' said Doreen. 'Although thinking about it, it was probably because of my mother. She always did rub people up the wrong way.' She stopped eating and, lifting her head up to the ceiling, added, 'I hope it was worth it, Mum.'

Frankie reached across the table for Doreen's hand and gave her a little squeeze.

'You know, when she died,' Doreen said matter-of-factly, 'I felt a sense of relief. Do you think that is wicked?'

'No, of course not,' Frankie said gently.

'Well, I don't care if it is,' Doreen said defiantly as she reached for another plum heavy. 'It was a happy release for Mum when it came and as for me, for the first time in my life, I can do what I want, when I want.'

Frankie watched her as she slapped the jelly onto the two halves then bit into the crumbly cake. 'Is there anyone you can stay with, Doreen?'

'Like who?' Doreen challenged. 'My mother fell out with my whole family and the neighbours stopped speaking to us years ago.'

Frankie sipped her tea. 'So what are you going to do now?'

'Apparently I have to register the death,' said Doreen, catching a stray crumb from the corner of her mouth, 'but I can't do that until tomorrow.'

'Would you like me to come with you?' Frankie asked. 'I can get the time off work.'

'I'll be fine,' Doreen said brightly. She blew out her cheeks and leaned back in her chair. 'That was scrummy. Thank you and please say thank you to your aunt.'

Frankie waved her hand dismissively. They sat in silence until Frankie became very aware of the ticking clock. 'What will you do afterwards? Once everything is settled, that is.'

Doreen blew out her cheeks again. 'Well, I can't stay here. My job won't cover the rent and everything else. I guess I'll have to look for a live-in job somewhere.'

It all sounded very bleak to Frankie.

'You know, there is one thing,' said Doreen. 'You remember the last time we met, I told you that my mother took something from your house the day she died?'

'You said it was some tarot cards,' said Frankie.

'That's right,' said Doreen.

'Did you actually see them?' Frankie asked. 'Only, my aunt was very surprised when I told her. She said my mother would never have something like that.'

Doreen shrugged and pulled the corners of her mouth down. 'My mother was convinced that was what was inside. I only saw the box itself. It was gold with a little yellow star on it.'

'That's right,' Frankie cried. Now she remembered the little box in question. She'd never seen her mother open it but it had stood on the mantelpiece next to the candle in a stick, kept there in case of a power cut.

'My mother wouldn't have the box in the house,' Doreen went on. 'So she buried it.'

'Buried it?' Frankie squeaked.

Doreen nodded. 'She did it that night when I was in bed. She never realised I was watching her from behind the bedroom curtains. I know exactly where it is.'

Frankie felt her jaw drop.

Doreen rose to her feet. 'Come on. One good turn deserves another. Let's go out and dig it up.'

Twenty minutes later, they found it. It was a little further along the flower bed than Doreen remembered, which was hardly surprising considering six years had passed since she'd watched her mother bury it. She handed it to Frankie. 'There you are,' she said triumphantly. 'At least I can put one wrong right. Your mother was very kind to me.'

Frankie gripped the tin and brushed off the excess dirt. The lid came off easily but there were no cards inside. As soon as she saw what was there, a tear sprang to Frankie's eye. She was looking at two buttons, the same size and colour as the ones on the bodice on the princess doll.

'Oh!' cried Doreen. 'I remember your mum made you that beautiful dolly for your birthday. Those buttons were on her jacket, weren't they?'

Frankie nodded.

'Do you still have it?' Doreen asked.

'Yes,' said Frankie, but she didn't have the heart to tell Doreen that when she'd started feeling so angry with her mother for pretending the princess story was true, she had shoved it in a bottom drawer.

# Fourteen

Frankie couldn't stop thinking about her friend Barbara. They had parted on bad terms and apart from a couple of times at the end of the summer when she'd seen her walking around the town on Conrad's arm, she hadn't seen her since. When she had called at Barbara's house a few weeks ago, she hadn't been able to get an answer, so Frankie wondered if she and her mother had moved somewhere safer. The summer season was over. Conrad had moved on. Had Barbara gone with him? Frankie had written to her a couple of times but she'd never had a reply so she decided to go back to her house once more.

Barbara lived with her mother in a small terraced house in Kingsland Road. It had a tiny front garden and a striped curtain in front of the front door to protect the paintwork from the sun. When Frankie knocked this time, Mrs Vickers opened the door. She was wearing a cross-over apron but Frankie could see that she'd put on a bit of weight since she last saw her. She was friendly enough when Frankie asked after Barbara but she didn't invite her in.

'Sorry, dear, Barbara isn't here,' said Mrs Vickers. 'She's gone to Lewisham to look after my sister.'

'Oh,' said Frankie, surprised. 'When will she be back?'

'She'll be gone a while, I'm afraid,' said Mrs Vickers. She began to close the door. 'I'll tell her you called.'

Puzzled, Frankie turned to go. As she shut the little gate, a movement at the upstairs window made her look up. There was no one there but the net curtain was moving. How odd.

\*

Doreen was still in her old home. Her mother's funeral, held in the meeting hall where they had worshipped, was a cold affair in more ways than one. For a start there was no heating at all so everyone shivered in the damp atmosphere even though they still wore their outdoor coats. The room itself was cheerless with bare walls and very little light; the windows so high up it was impossible to see out. When Frankie mentioned it to Doreen, her friend told her it had been built that way so that the worshippers wouldn't be distracted by the outside world while they said their prayers.

Frankie was made to sit with a small group of other people who were strangers to the assembly; people who were made up of Doreen's neighbours and the lady from the grocery shop. They were bunched together as 'unbelievers' which was hardly welcoming and made Frankie feel awkward and uncomfortable.

Nobody spoke to them. So apart from a limp lettuce handshake from a big woman with a sour expression at the door, she had no contact with the mourners. There was no eulogy and the sermon was sprinkled with liberal doses of hell, judgement and damnation. Doreen sat on the front row sandwiched between the leader and the big woman who turned out to be his wife. After the burial, they ate a few meagre sandwiches in the same hall, which by now had all the chairs pushed against the wall.

Doreen had been given notice to vacate the rooms she and her mother had shared and although she planned to join the armed forces, she hadn't done so yet. She was also under immense pressure from the deaconate and the leaders of her mother's church not to join up. War, they told her, was sin, and killing the enemy was the same as murder. It was common knowledge that women weren't to be sent to fight so although Doreen listened, she hadn't the strength to argue.

'It's not that I don't believe,' she told Frankie later, 'it's just that I want to have a life of my own.'

'And why shouldn't you?' Frankie said stoutly.

Now that she had nowhere to live, the members of the group wanted her to stay with the church leader and his wife but much to their disapproval, Aunt Bet had said she would take her in on a temporary basis.

'That girl,' the leader's wife had said to Doreen in ringing tones, 'is very worldly. She uses a man's name.' She curled her lip in disdain. 'Frankie. What sort of a name is that for a young girl? She wears lipstick and I've seen her in man's apparel.' She curled her lip and added disapprovingly, 'Trousers! You mark my words. That girl will lead you astray.'

When they'd gone, it was obvious from the look on her face that Doreen dreaded having to be with them.

*

Sidney Knight had had an answer to his prayer. Not that he ever actually prayed, but if he had done, this would have been a miracle. Another postal order had dropped onto the mat and with it a short note to apologise for the delay. It was much larger than usual; three figures, no less. With no race meetings in the foreseeable future, it would certainly come in handy, but then some do-gooder turned up at the door and asked him to take in lodgers. 'Part of the war effort,' she said, ticking his name off a list on her clipboard.

'I can't have anybody until the repairs are done,' he said.

The busy-body remained at the bottom of the stairs. By the expression on her face, he knew she could smell the stink so it came as no surprise when she said she'd come back when the guttering was fixed.

That weekend Sid blew the lot on the dog track.

*

When she moved in at the farm, Doreen had a camp bed in Frankie's room, but it was far from ideal. The room was far too small for two people. They were constantly stepping over one another's things, but Doreen assured everyone that it was sheer heaven.

In the end, it was Frankie who saved the day. They were having their tea break at her Red Cross class, when her partner Margery happened to mention that her evacuees were going back home to London.

'Their mother misses them,' she explained. 'And seeing as how Hitler hasn't bombed us yet, she thinks she may as well have her children with her.'

Mrs Kerridge called everybody back to the practice and Frankie put their empty teacups into the hatch. 'You'll miss them,' she said as she lay on the floor to begin their practising.

'I most certainly will,' Margery went on. 'It sounds silly but since they came it's made me realise just how lonely I've been.'

They were taking it in turns to practise the prone-pressure method of trying to rescue a person who had been involved in a drowning accident. Frankie lay on her tummy with her head on her forearms and closed her eyes while Margery applied pressure to the small of her back and counted up to eight. When she reached eight, Margery ran her fingers down Frankie's arms and pulled them forward as she continued counting to twelve. After that, she started all over again.

'Will you take another lodger?' Frankie asked as they swapped places.

Margery pulled a face. 'If I could find the right person I might.'

'How about a seventeen-year-old girl who has just lost her mum?' said Frankie, and noting the look of horror on Margery's face she added quickly, 'No, not me, my friend Doreen. She's trustworthy and honest and she'd be no trouble.'

'Come on, you two,' Mrs Kerridge interrupted. 'Stop chatting. You've got a drowning woman to save.'

As their instructor moved on to check up on the other students, Margery and Frankie exchanged a naughty grin.

'Tell her to come and see me,' Margery whispered.

And it didn't end there. Once Mrs Waite knew she was looking for work, she was only too pleased to offer Doreen her old job back. One of her florists had joined the WAAFs and another had moved to Scotland in the hope that it would be safer, so there was a vacant position for Doreen at the shop.

*

The one thing Frankie had never addressed during all those weeks was how she'd felt when Doreen returned her mother's box. She'd thanked her friend, but wouldn't be drawn into a conversation about it. She didn't even mention it to Aunt Bet when she got home, although she did take it to the bathroom with her and clean it off. Seeing the buttons again made her want to get the doll out of the bottom drawer but somehow she never found the courage to pull it open. She guessed that the buttons must have come from a card of six. Four were on the doll's bodice-cum-waistcoat and the two had been saved in the box as spares.

Frankie put the box into her underwear drawer and covered it over. She went to sleep watching the drawer but her emotions were completely shut down. She wasn't angry with her mother any more, but she still didn't like what she'd done. It felt too much like telling lies to just forget about it. She told herself she wouldn't have been so upset if it had been made clear that the princess story was made-up, but the fact that her mother let her go on believing it was true until she was ten years old was insulting. It was as bad as insisting that there really is a Father Christmas. She sighed. Perhaps she was still angry with her mother after all.

She felt nothing for a couple of nights but then an increasingly heavy feeling developed in her chest and it was hard to keep the tears at bay. Distant memories and feelings kept creeping back uninvited. The smell of her mother's hair after she'd washed it, the silkiness of her best blouse, the comfort of her arms when she pulled Frankie into a cuddle, the sound of her laughter, her silly jokes, 'What do elves learn at school? The elfa-bet'. For the first time in ages, Frankie was forced to admit that she still missed her mother dreadfully.

At the end of November, Alan came home on forty-eight hours leave before being sent to Hilsea Barracks, Portsmouth, and from there to the British Expeditionary Force in France. Uncle Lorry met him at the station and the family decided to make the most of their time with him. He spent the first day tinkering with his beloved bikes and then he went for a long ride.

The next day, even though it was still four weeks away, they ate Christmas dinner with all the trimmings and put on paper hats. Uncle Lorry carved the joint and afterwards everyone searched their Christmas pudding for the lucky sixpence. Doreen had joined them. She seemed in awe of the whole event.

'I've never had a Christmas like this before,' she whispered as she and Frankie were doing the washing up.

Aunt Bet was ensconced by the fireside, putting her feet up for a well-earned rest. Uncle Lorry and Alan had gone out for a walk while, surprisingly, Ronald had offered to do the drying up. He didn't say much but Frankie couldn't help noticing that he spent a long time looking at Doreen.

'Didn't you and your mum celebrate Christmas then?' As Frankie asked the question she could already guess the answer. What a miserable childhood poor Doreen had had. Although Frankie's had been marred by the loss of her mother at a much earlier age, there had been plenty of love and laughter along the way.

The family didn't exchange presents but they sent Alan on his way with some extras in his kitbag: some shaving soap from Frankie, a book from Ronald, a few quid from Uncle Lorry and a fruit cake from Aunt Bet. Then they all piled into Uncle Lorry's truck and set off for Worthing station.

'It'll all be over before Easter,' Alan assured his mother as he boarded the train but nobody really believed that, least of all Alan himself. When the war had started, everybody had said it would be all over by Christmas. Well, here they were with Christmas less than a month away and from what they'd heard, the Germans still posed a threat to the free world even though there had been relatively little fighting. Pathé News reels reported the sinking of British ships including the carrier HMS *Courageous*. The soldiers in France might only have to contend with minor skirmishes but they were patrolling two hundred miles of the border, a formidable task even for such highly regarded military men.

'Bye, son,' Aunt Bet said as Alan leaned out of the door to kiss her on the cheek. Her voice was thick with emotion. 'God keep you safe.'

The guard blew his whistle and everybody waved handkerchiefs until the train was out of sight. 'I'll write,' Frankie called after it.

\*

During the next few weeks, things remained very quiet. The assassination attempt on Hitler at the beginning of November had given everybody hope that his regime wouldn't last long but sadly it wasn't to be.

Newspapers reported the arrival of thousands of Canadian troops, including a large number to be based all along the South coast including Worthing. They were put to work building the sea defences and preparing even more gun placements. Barrage balloons floated over important buildings such as the gas works. Sandbags surrounded the town hall steps and the pillar boxes were changed from red to yellow as they were spruced up with a gas-sensitive paint. Everywhere had the feel of war but nothing much was happening. Everyone else called it the Phoney War. Uncle Lorry called it the Boring War.

\*

Christmas 1939 came and went. As they sang carols in church on Christmas morning, '*all glory be to God on high and to the earth be peace*' took on a resonance of its own. Never before had the country been more fervent in its prayers.

Frankie continued with her Red Cross activities and now that two of the older girls in the florist had joined the Wrens, she took on greater responsibility. People were still getting married or having funerals so although floral arrangements had suffered through lack of supply, the demand was still there. To help things along they now specialised in silk flowers as well.

Now that Doreen had somewhere to live, Frankie set about introducing her to a life outside the strict confines of her mother's diktat. While she was careful not to expose her friend to danger (in Frankie's opinion Doreen was so naive about some things), she wanted her to enjoy life. As a consequence they went to shows and the pictures, or they jumped on a bus and went to Brighton or Chichester, and sometimes they went to dances put on for the Canadian soldiers by the WI in villages including Tarring, Ferring and Lancing.

Doreen's wardrobe needed to be updated. All of her clothes were hopelessly old-fashioned and she only had dowdy colours such as muddy brown or washed-out blues. There was little money so the girls had to resort to making their own clothes. Once Aunt Bet had taught them both how to use the treadle sewing machine, they were away. As Doreen had dark hair, when they went to jumble sales they picked up anything in cobalt blue, turquoise, bottle green or a rich gold to turn it into something else. On the other hand, Frankie looked for mint greens or baby blues. She discovered that tomato red was far more flattering than a plum red on her and they had such fun choosing together that they became more like sisters.

As winter turned to spring, Ronald finally plucked up the courage to ask Doreen out. Frankie was pleased for them both. Ronald was such a caring chap, Frankie felt she didn't have to worry about Doreen being out of her depth when she was with him but of course that left Frankie, herself, on her own. She had been asked out a few times. They were nice people but that was as far as it went.

She still wrote to Alan every week. He didn't often send a reply and when he did, it was short and to the point. Easter was early, March 24th. On a postcard she received at the beginning of April he had written, *'Marched to church. Afterwards the French women gave us chocolate. Weather cold.'*

Then, in the spring of 1940, the Germans invaded Norway.

# Fifteen

**Broadwater, Sussex, March 1940**

Doreen had decided to join up. She was almost eighteen and she badly wanted to 'do her bit' but she found it difficult trying to decide which of the uniformed services to go for.

'I saw something in a magazine,' Frankie said. 'Stay here and I'll get it.'

She couldn't afford to buy magazines herself but one of the girls at work used to pass on the odd one. The article in the magazine turned out to be most helpful. Frankie and Doreen pored over it very carefully. Out of all the pictures, the girl in the Wrens uniform looked the most attractive. Navy blue, smart and with a straight jacket, it gave the wearer a nice shape. By contrast, the ATS girl looked frumpy.

'The WAAF uniform is a better colour,' Frankie remarked.

'Yes, but look at those huge pockets,' Doreen protested. 'My hips will look a mile wide in that.'

Ronald who was sitting at the table mending a watch, snorted. 'Does the future of this country really depend on you girls liking a uniform?'

Frankie and Doreen grinned at each other. 'Absolutely,' Frankie said teasingly. 'These things are really important.'

*

The invasion of Norway had precipitated a domino effect. France, Belgium and Luxemburg quickly followed. Aunt Bet was frantic with worry about Alan, who was now trapped in a rearguard action with the expeditionary forces. The government dithered and Chamberlain, although he had been warned for months that this would happen, behaved as if he was caught on the back foot. Everything looked very bleak until Churchill took over the reins of power. He didn't promise much but he was refreshingly honest. His speech to the Commons was widely reported in the newspapers and Uncle Lorry read it out at the dinner table.

'*You ask, what is our policy? . . . it is to wage war by sea, land and air . . . against a monstrous tyranny . . . I have nothing to offer but blood, toil, sweat and tears . . .*'

'So that's that then,' said Aunt Bet. 'Looks like we're in for the long haul.'

Things were looking grim but to celebrate Doreen's birthday, Ronald had promised to take them both out for tea. He had booked a table for three thirty in the Arcade Café. He glanced up at the clock. 'Better get ready, girls,' he said putting the watch workings on the tray and covering it with a cloth. 'The bus will be here any minute.'

Rationing had already begun to dominate their lives so all three of them were looking forward to an afternoon of indulgence. Bacon, butter and sugar had been rationed since January and meat had been rationed since March. The egg allowance was down to one a week per person so Aunt Bet had to sell most of her supply but the café had a reputation for delicious teas which, as yet, hadn't changed.

It was obvious that Ronald liked being with Doreen. They were fairly alike in many ways. Doreen enjoyed simple things, things which had been denied her for so long. She enjoyed swimming in the sea, going for long walks and to the pictures.

Since Aunt Bet had taught her how to use the treadle machine, she enjoyed dressmaking. Ronald was a quiet man. He found conversation a struggle. At one time it used to irritate Frankie, but now she realised that it was because he couldn't really hear what was being said. Doreen made him feel relaxed.

When they got to the Arcade Café, they all sat near the window. It was fun watching people walking by and it also meant that they didn't have to keep conversation going all the time. All at once, Doreen leaned back in her chair and pressed her head against the wall anxiously. Nothing was said, but they all noticed that across the road, the wife of the leader from her mother's church had just got off the bus. Frankie knew she was still desperate to persuade Doreen to stay with her and her husband, and just lately they had redoubled their efforts to get her back. The leader had only stopped coming to the farm when Uncle Lorry threatened him with the police. Then, as soon as Doreen moved out and went to live with Margery, they started going round there, even offering her the security of marriage with a widower in the congregation.

Frankie had laughed when Doreen told her. 'You're joking! It sounds like something out of a Victorian novel.'

But it had frightened Doreen. 'He's really old, Frankie,' she complained. 'He must be thirty-eight if he's a day, and he's got four children. I don't want to be tied to a man like that.'

In the end, Frankie went with her friend and they explained everything to Margery. The next time the leader turned up at the house, she threatened to set the dog on him. The dog was a daft old thing, half blind and with about as much energy as a limp lettuce, but that was enough to finally persuade the man to leave Doreen alone.

'It's all right,' said Frankie looking out of the window again. 'She's gone.'

Their tea came and Doreen elected to pour. They were about

half way through their meal when an old lady right at the back of the room stood up and shuffled her way towards them. She didn't say anything but she laid two white feathers on Ronald's plate. As she returned to her table, he pushed them aside in disgust and carried on eating.

'What did she do that for?' Frankie hissed. Doreen had gone bright pink. 'Ronald?' Frankie insisted.

'Forget it, Frankie,' Ronald said dismissively.

But Frankie continued to frown.

'They used to do that in the last war,' said Doreen, 'for people who hadn't joined up.'

Frankie could feel her temper rising. 'What right has she . . .?'

'Frankie,' said Ronald, 'just forget it.'

Doreen continued eating her cake but by now Frankie was so cross hers tasted no better than sawdust. She rose quickly to her feet, scraping her chair noisily across the floor as she went.

'Frankie, don't,' Ronald said helplessly.

The waiter, who must have seen what had happened, came hurrying over. 'Please, Miss,' he began, his hand held up in a defensive position. 'I don't want any trouble.'

But Frankie sailed past him and reaching the old woman's table she stuffed the feathers so hard into the sandwich on her plate that it was reduced to bits. 'How dare you,' she snarled. 'What right have you to judge him?'

'This country is fighting for the survival of France,' the woman retorted. 'We need every able-bodied man in uniform.'

Every eye in the cafe was on them as Frankie bent down and whispered right in the woman's ear. 'And he would go if he could, but the army doctor has refused him. So why don't you mind your own damned business?'

The woman's face was scarlet. 'Well, really!' And as she gathered her things to leave, Frankie swept back to her own table.

Doreen was staring at her, wide-eyed.

'What?' Frankie challenged.

'That's quite a temper you have,' Doreen remarked.

'I hate injustice and unfairness,' said Frankie, throwing herself back into her chair.

Ronald looked hurt and embarrassed. 'I know you mean well, Frankie,' he said quietly, 'but I don't need you to fight my battles.'

# Sixteen

**Somewhere in France, April 1940**

The French countryside looked a lot like home. Until he'd joined up, Alan had never been further than East Sussex one way and Hampshire the other, and that was only for a motorbike scramble, so he hadn't paid much attention to his surroundings. His mind would have been totally focussed on the course and coming first.

At one of their camps he'd remarked as much to his new pal, Ginger. 'This place reminds me of Arundel.'

'Hardly surprising, boi,' Ginger said sagely in his heavy Suffolk accent. 'We were invaded by the French back in 1066, remember?'

Alan vaguely remembered being told that although the castle at Arundel was a Victorian reproduction, the original building had been started quite soon after William the Conqueror won the Battle of Hastings. It stuck in his mind because construction began on Christmas Day a year later, but he couldn't recall the name of the first Earl of Arundel . . . Roger something, wasn't it? He grinned at his mate, 'Ah, 1066; the only date in history I remember.'

Their first few weeks in France were a doddle. Alan and Ginger had been thrown together as soon as they'd arrived.

They were about the same age, the only difference being that Ginger was already a married man. His wife was expecting a baby. Both men had grown up in the country; Alan in Sussex and Ginger in Suffolk. Both liked motorbikes and Ginger was impressed to hear of Alan's successes. 'I never met a champion afore,' he said admiringly.

They went back to the ports, unloaded supplies and equipment and relocated them to army dumps further up country. There was little or no action and strategically they were only there to reinforce and hold the lines.

Apart from being away from his family, Alan was enjoying his experience. Frankie wrote as often as twice a week sometimes, so he was up-to-date with all that was going on at home. When he wrote back, he wasn't allowed to say where he was or exactly what he was doing and some of his off-duty antics weren't the sort of thing he would share with close family. As a result, his replies were short and sweet and confined to the back of a postcard.

He'd been surprised to hear that Barbara Vickers had moved to Lewisham. Shame. She'd been a real hot tomato, the little minx, and he had some fond memories of fumbles and more in the barn or out in the open countryside on warm summer nights. Her mother had probably sent her away to protect her from the Canadian soldiers billeted all around the town. He grinned to himself. Perhaps it should be the other way around – that she'd been sent away to protect the soldiers. She was a bit of a goer, that one.

When the Germans broke through, Alan was reconnaissance rider for a large convoy of a hundred and fifty heavy-duty lorries and Ginger was one of the lead drivers. They were in the process of delivering a hundred tons of petrol and a hundred and thirty tons of rations from the railway to forward dumps. They had only just arrived at their destination when all hell broke loose.

They didn't engage and there were no casualties among them, although the Germans bombed the nearest town several times. After a couple of days, they were ordered to fall back. With Alan up front and Ginger in the first of thirteen lorries, they headed back towards the coast. It turned out to be a nightmare scenario. The roads were choked with terrified civilians fleeing the fighting and German planes machine-gunned anything that moved. It was imperative to keep going to reach the port signposted Dunkerque, so they travelled through the night without lights but eventually everybody was in need of rest.

Hiding the lorries was no easy task but they found a place where the road dipped between high banks, deep in the French countryside, surrounded by trees. They drove the lorries into the dark shadows under the trees and apart from a couple of chaps on guard, everyone had a bit of shut-eye. The next after-noon, with strict orders to keep his eyes peeled, Alan was sent to spy out the lie of the land. He hadn't gone far before he had to report back.

'There's a couple of Jerry tanks in the woods,' he said, willing his voice to sound calm and in control. 'The men are out of the vehicles and apart from one man on guard, they're all having a smoke or a kip on the grass.'

The sergeant gave the order to take the Lewis gun in a light lorry to try and flush them out. The rest of the men, rifles at the ready, advanced by the side of the road, using the high banks and the trees as cover. They soon spotted the Germans and opened fire, killing two of them. The rest hurried back to their tanks and went deeper into the woods. The men were just about to move into the wood after them when an enemy plane came along the road, flying low, its machine gun blazing. As it passed, everybody, soldiers and civilians, dived for cover and then they heard the sound of heavy gunfire coming from a position about half a mile up the road. They could smell smoke and, above the sound of the bullets and return fire, they could hear the cries of men. The corporal ran ahead and reported back that another convoy had been hit and was ablaze. Alan felt sick. This was nothing like what he'd seen at the pictures. His stomach heaved when he saw men covered in blood or with limbs blown off and still alive. A bit further up the road, the machine guns had mowed down fleeing women and children. He retched as he saw an hysterical mother trying to put the bits of her shattered child back together again. This was terrifying. It was hell on earth.

'But for the grace of God,' he whispered to himself. His heart was pumping as he and his mates were given the order to disperse. As they did so, they heard the tank burst out of the woods and head towards the remains of the convoy.

Alan and Ginger stuck together. He went back for his bike but the Jerry plane had rendered it useless. The bullet-riddled petrol tank was pouring fuel over the road and the back wheel was buckled beyond repair. 'Look out!' Ginger cried and at the same moment, the bike exploded into flames.

Alan had no time to register his shock because Ginger cried, 'Look out! There be another one, boi.'

Alan glanced behind him and spotted a tank only about thirty yards away and coming up the road towards them. The two men made a dash for the ditch and ran through the mud as fast as they could. Breathless and scared, they reached some sort of gate and made their way along the other side of the hedge until Ginger got a stitch and had to stop.

'Go on, go on, Alan,' he said urgently. 'No need for you to risk capture as well, boi.'

But Alan didn't want to risk going on alone. 'I'm not leaving you,' he said. 'We stick together.'

The tank rumbled past them, German troops with rifles

running alongside it. Alan and Ginger held their breath. The enemy were so close they could almost touch some of them, but they managed to stay hidden. They stayed under the hedge for a couple of hours and as the light was fading, they decided it was time to move on.

'Don't want to miss the eve'n performance,' Ginger joked.

Luckily for them, the night wasn't too dark and they managed to stay close to the road until they reached a farmhouse. Neither of them spoke French and the farmer couldn't speak English but somehow or other they managed to understand each other. The farmer's wife gave them a hot drink and some bread and cheese before her husband pointed them in the right direction for Dunkerque.

When they reached the beach about eleven hours later, tired and hungry, they had the most appalling shock. The sands were crowded with men – exhausted, injured, and looking like thousands and thousands of dejected black crows without hope. In front of them lay the Channel, glistening, cold and deep, and far out to sea, they spotted a Royal Navy ship. Clearly the water was too shallow for it to come any closer or it would run aground. The pier had been bombed so men waded in the water to meet a small craft ferrying them from the beach to the ship. It would take hours, days to get this many men onto the ship via such a small craft. With the enemy like a pharaoh's army behind them, they faced twenty-two miles of water between them and home, but this time there was no Moses to hold out his staff to make the waters part. They were well and truly trapped.

Alan and Ginger threw themselves onto the sand to rest. There was some chap asleep nearby but as Alan looked more closely he could see his tunic was covered in blood. The man was as dead as a doornail.

Alan would have wept if he had the energy, but he didn't.

At least they could lie down and recover for a while and then, he supposed, he would be a prisoner of war for the duration.

'I suppose we can thank God we're safe,' said Ginger.

But then they heard the drone of a German plane.


Uncle Lorry twiddled the knobs of the radio until a voice cut through the early morning stillness of the kitchen. The nine o'clock news last night had been grave. The British Expeditionary Force was in retreat.

Everyone stopped what they were doing to listen.

'*This is a BBC announcement read by Alan Howland. A number of appeals for recruits have been issued today. The Admiralty wants men experienced in marine internal combustion engine or service in the engine room of yachts and motorboats. Others who have had charge of motorboats and have good knowledge of costal navigation are also needed. Applications should be made to the nearest Registrar Royal Naval Reserve or to the Fishery Officer.*'

# *Seventeen*

**Broadwater, Sussex, May 1940**

The pain was indescribable. She couldn't believe it would be this bad. When it finished, Barbara relaxed her head on the pillow and wiped the dampness away from her face with her hand, letting out an involuntary sigh. She must look an absolute sight. Her hair was stuck to her forehead and she was all sweaty. Her mother leaned over her and gripped her shoulder.

'You're doing well,' she said curtly, 'but try not to make too much noise. We don't want next door running for the doctor just yet, do we.'

Barbara whimpered and then closed her eyes as another pain began to build.

Her mother pressed a clean folded handkerchief between her teeth. 'Here, bite down on this.'

Barbara barely heard her as her stomach muscles tightened again. This was worse than dying. She wanted to cry out, 'No, no, hang on a minute. Just let me get my breath,' but once the pains started, there was no stopping them. It was relentless, persistent, demanding, and intense. It grew in strength until it consumed every part of her. She couldn't move. She couldn't think. All she could do was grip onto the sheets and wait until it was gone. Just as she was beginning to feel that she could bear it no longer, the iron band across her belly began to fade. It faded but not altogether. And the worst of it was, even though it was gone, she knew all too well that any minute now it would start all over again.

At first, she'd thought it would be exciting to have a baby. Her baby . . . Conrad's baby would soon be in her arms. She could just imagine herself lying back on the bed looking all serene and beautiful like they do in the pictures. Her hair would be spread out on the pillow like luxurious velvet and her make-up perfect. When it was all over, he would come into the room and smile down at her. Then he would look into the crib, all white and frilly, and catch his breath when he saw his child for the first time.

'Darling,' he'd say, 'you are such a clever girl. I love you so much . . .'

In short, he'd be over the moon.

Oh God, the pain was coming back again. It had been like this for hours. It seemed a lifetime ago when Barbara woke up with a mild stomach ache. She'd called out to her mother as she'd tumbled out of bed. It was six-thirty in the morning.

'Thank God it's not the weekend,' her mother had murmured as she covered the bed with an old blanket and some towels before making Barbara lie down again. 'At least the neighbours are out at work all day.'

Through the thin walls of their two-up, two-down semi-detached cottage, they heard their next-door neighbour setting off for work at seven. After a short lull, their grandchildren would turn up, ready for school, and then their grandmother would set off with them, pushing her bicycle so that she could jump on it and head for the hospital where she worked as a ward cleaner, once the children were through the school gates. The postman knocked at nine fifteen with a parcel and the milkman left two pints on the doorstep at eleven. Apart from that, Barbara and her mother were alone all day. They didn't even respond when someone knocked on the back door at about one o'clock, but Mrs Vickers couldn't resist peeping out from the behind the curtain in the back bedroom. It was only Alice Davis come for a cup of tea and a natter. Thankfully she wandered off after about five minutes. Hiding Barbara's pregnancy for the past six months had been an enormous strain on them both. Thank goodness it was almost over.

The labour proceeded normally as Barbara's waters broke. Meanwhile, their neighbour rode up the garden path at about four and their grandchildren came back home from school at four-thirty. Their grandfather arrived back home at five. There was a sticky moment when her neighbour knocked on the wooden partition between their two sculleries for a chat while she was making the tea but Mrs Vickers ignored her. It was better if their nosey neighbour thought she was out for the day. She couldn't risk her wanting to come round for something. After that, whilst the appetising cooking smells wafted through the window, Barbara's labour pains continued.

It took a great deal of effort not to cry out but Barbara knew it was imperative that their neighbours didn't know what was going on next door.

In between her pains, Barbara couldn't help wondering why Conrad had never replied to her letters. She had been bitterly disappointed, there was no denying that, but she told herself it was probably because he was too busy doing his part to entertain the armed forces. Now that he was part of ENSA, Conrad would be keen to get a firm grip on his chosen career so she knew he wouldn't say no to any booking, no matter how far flung the post. As the months rolled by, she decided that he had replied but most likely the postal service was a bit naff. Or maybe he'd been moved on to God-knows-where before her letters had arrived. She gave up writing when she was seven months gone. She didn't want him arriving home to see her looking massive and with swollen ankles anyway. She would try again once the baby was born and while her labour progressed, she fantasised how it would be when he finally found out.

A little later, Barbara and her mother were relieved to hear the children's father arriving next door to collect them for the weekend. Once the children were gone, and their neighbours, still none the wiser about what was going on next door, set off for the workingmen's club for the evening, Mrs Vickers and Barbara could relax a little at last.

But in no time at all, it was eleven-thirty and the neighbours were back home, albeit a bit tipsy. Mrs Vickers watched from behind the curtain as they staggered up the garden path, hanging onto each other to stay upright.

'That's good,' her mother whispered as she came back from the window. 'With a bit of luck they'll both crash out like a light and sleep soundly.'

As the night wore on all Barbara wanted was for it to end but her labour went on and on. At one time she'd cried and, glancing anxiously at the dividing wall, her mother had pressed the pillow across her mouth.

'Nearly there,' Mrs Vickers whispered. 'Another twenty minutes and it'll be all over.'

Barbara groaned inwardly. Twenty minutes! That sounded like a lifetime. Twenty more minutes . . . Tearfully she moaned in anguish. 'I can't, I can't.'

Her mother wiped her face with a cold flannel. 'Don't be silly now. Come on, when the next pain comes, push.'

And so as the thin grey light of morning came, the baby's lusty cry filled the air.

'It's a boy,' Mrs Vickers said delightedly, 'and he's a sturdy little fellow.'

Turning her head away, Barbara wanted nothing more than to sleep. Mrs Vickers cleaned the baby up and wrapped the afterbirth in newspaper ready to put it on the fire in the range. It only remained to wash her daughter and make her comfortable. Once all that was done, Mrs Vickers felt free enough to start removing the last of the padding from around her own stomach. What a relief! Over the past few months, while Barbara hid upstairs pretending to be in Lewisham with her auntie, Mrs Vickers had added layer upon layer across her belly to keep up the appearance that she was expecting. They had concocted the plan almost as soon as Barbara realised she was in the family way. As luck would have it, the conception coincided with the last time her husband had come home on leave. She pretended to be excited. In truth, nobody envied a woman in her early forties having to start a family all over again but they admired her courage and her ability to stay cheerful. A few people asked her if Barbara would be coming home for the birth and tutted behind her back when she said the girl couldn't get away. Mrs Vickers knew what they were saying but she didn't mind. Once the baby was born Barbara could get on with her life with nobody any the wiser. The baby would stay in the family but it would be brought up as Barbara's little brother or sister.

Barbara looked exhausted.

'I'm going to knock on the wall for the neighbours now,' said her mother picking the baby up. 'You can stay here in bed. I'll tell everybody you're resting because you've been up all night.'

'Where are you taking him?' Barbara asked weakly.

'To my bedroom,' said her mother. 'It's got to look right.'

'Can I hold him?' asked Barbara.

'Best not to,' her mother said firmly. 'It will only encourage your milk to come in. Besides, you mustn't let yourself get too attached. From now on he's your little baby brother, remember?'

Barbara stared, aghast.

'It's for your own good, Barbara,' said her mother. 'It's what we agreed.'

Her daughter nodded dully. 'Can I give him a name?'

Mrs Vickers frowned. 'For goodness' sake,' she began irritably.

'It's just a name, Mum.'

Her mother sighed. 'Go on then.'

'Robert,' said Barbara, tears welling in her eyes. 'He's called Robert.'

Her mother pulled the corners of her mouth down disapprovingly. 'Oh no, he'll end up being called Bob. I think Derek would be much nicer.'

Barbara looked horrified.

'Anyway I'm taking Derek into my bedroom,' said her mother. 'He can sleep in the bottom drawer for now.'

Barbara watched her own bedroom door close and a few minutes later she heard her mother knocking on the wall. 'Mrs Reed. Mrs Reed, can you do a bit of shopping for me? I've had my baby.'

Barbara heard a muffled reply through the wall.

'Yes,' her mother went on. 'It came about six o'clock. A little boy. I've got my Barbara but she's exhausted, poor lamb. She's been up all night helping me.'

Mrs Reed said something else.

'Yes,' said Mrs Vickers. 'She came home last night. Yes, yes, it was a stroke of luck but she'll have to go back for a couple of days. My sister says Barbara has been a godsend.' There was a pause and then her mother added, 'Oh yes. The doctor is very pleased.'

Barbara turned her head towards the wall and allowed her tears to fall. When they'd planned all this she hadn't counted on being so upset. She'd just given birth to Conrad's baby and already she was being forced to give him up. She hadn't even

121

been allowed to see him properly and her mother was insisting on calling him Derek. What was even worse, from now on she had to treat her own child as if he were her brother. She swallowed the lump in her throat and wiped her wet cheeks with her hand. This was going to be so hard, much harder than she had imagined, but she supposed mum was right. It was the only way to protect her good name. No man wanted soiled goods and Barbara knew she couldn't bear it if everybody knew she'd just given birth to an illegitimate baby.

# *Eighteen*

## Broadwater, Sussex, June 1st 1940

These were very anxious days: days in which the whole nation listened to every news bulletin with bated breath for news of what was happening in Dunkirk. There were stories of men being machine-gunned from the air, drowning in the sea, and ending up too badly wounded to survive. It was also becoming more apparent that the whole army had gone into action with outdated weapons. Rifles originally issued in the Great War had been mothballed for years. The only good thing that could be said about them was that they were capable of killing the enemy. The army had no mortars or hand grenades and there was a shortage of spare parts for the anti-tank rifles. The revelation brought a rising tide of anger throughout the nation.

With news as bad as this, everybody was struggling to stay calm. Wherever Frankie went, apart from the weather, people could talk about nothing else. And why not? Most knew someone who was over in France, be it a husband, brother, father, nephew, grandchild, a work colleague, a friend, or a neighbour. It was a shared experience. At home, Aunt Bet said nothing but she was short-tempered. The old cockerel ended up in the cooking pot because he'd chased her and tried to give her a peck one time too often.

'He'll be as tough as old boots,' Uncle Lorry grumbled, and he was right.

As they all gathered around the wireless for the BBC's nine o'clock news broadcast a couple of days later, it was with a degree of relief that they heard about the evacuation. An armada of fishing boats, shrimpers, trawlers and pleasure boats were on their way. It almost sounded romantic except that the brave little ships were being targeted by the Luftwaffe as soon as they went to sea, although the RAF boys high above the clouds were doing their best to protect them.

By the time Alan and Ginger got on board a ship, they had been stuck on the beach for three days. It wasn't going to be possible to get the equipment back so the men had made an improvised pier using their lorries. Once they reached the end of the 'pier', it was just water. Alan and his mate had been standing in line for hours which was very cold and uncomfortable. The German planes kept coming back and every time they machine-gunned their bullets sent sprays of water into the air.

'I think I prefer the beach at Lowestoft to this, boi,' Ginger joked. 'The ice cream queues are a lot shorter.'

Alan knew he'd soiled himself but what could he do? Nobody spoke much but he guessed there was a lot of praying going on, even from chaps who didn't believe in God. Every now and then someone would get hit and fall into the deeper water and drown.

There was a destroyer tied to the mole. It was badly damaged but that didn't stop the gunners having a go with their anti-aircraft guns. They kept it up until finally a German bomber brought the gun down.

A ship called *The Curlew* moored alongside a couple of Thames barges which had run aground. Alan and Ginger made their way over the side and found a small space on the crowded deck. Once there was no more room, the little ship set off. Even when they were on the open sea, the danger still hadn't passed. The Germans were still shooting and they had to avoid the traffic jam as they were going in the opposite direction to the boats heading for Dunkirk and the men still waiting on the beach. It only took a minute or two before Alan's mate was asleep.

They arrived in Ramsgate at about four in the morning. As he'd been seasick half way across, Alan wasn't feeling so good. Neither of them had eaten for three or four days and after standing in the water for so long, Alan could hardly feel his feet. Some of the rescued men were in a distressed state. One chap had gone off his rocker and was in such a panic to get off the boat that one of the sergeants had to knock him out to gain control.

Alan had to haul Ginger off the boat, with his limp arm around Alan's shoulder and his head lolling. He didn't seem to be able to use his feet either.

'Come on, mate,' Alan encouraged. 'Nearly home. Forty-eight hours with your little missus and you'll be as right as rain.'

He ended up having to drag Ginger towards a line of St John ambulances waiting for them at the jetty. The WVS ladies were passing mugs of hot, dark, sweet tea around. It was only as the ambulance man took Ginger from him and Alan let go that he realized his pal had been bleeding. When he took his hand away from Ginger's waist, Alan's hand was covered in blood.

'This one's a goner,' he heard the ambulance man say.

Alan's mind went into freefall and everything went black.


'They say the troop train will be passing through Worthing tomorrow,' Uncle Lorry said.

Aunt Bet's face lit up. 'Does that mean Alan will be coming home?'

'Shouldn't think so, love,' said Uncle Lorry. 'He'll be sent back to the barracks first and then he can apply for leave.'

It went unsaid, but they were all thinking the same thing . . . if he's survived.

News filtered through to North Farm that Mrs Vickers had had a baby, a boy called Derek. As she hadn't heard from Barbara, Frankie decided to call round to see Mrs Vickers. The baby was a good excuse. He was a bonny little chap with a red screwed-up face and long fingers. For someone who had just given birth, Mrs Vickers was doing amazingly well.

'Barbara will be home again soon,' she explained when Frankie asked for her London address. 'My sister is a lot better now.'

Frankie felt a little awkward so she gave Derek a rattle and left.

*

Because petrol was rationed, the local florists had banded together to form an association. This meant that they took it in turns to collect their orders from their suppliers rather than doing it individually. This month it was Mrs Waite's turn so Frankie had to take the van to the station to collect everything. As it happened, she was on the platform waiting for the London train to pull in when the first of the troop trains went by. She was met by a heart-rending sight.

The train slowed, probably because it was going through a station, and Frankie was desperate for a sight of Alan. He had to be on the train, didn't he? His barracks was Hilsea and this was the Portsmouth train but instead of the usual proud smart soldiers, she was faced with the sight of bedraggled and exhausted men. They were in various states of dress or undress, unshaven, exhausted, pale or asleep. Men had their head on the tables, or they leaned their heads against the headrests with their mouths wide open. Some slept on each other's shoulders. She even caught a glimpse of some poor soul asleep on the floor. As the train picked up speed, the porter standing next to her mumbled, 'Poor blighters.'

Doreen had passed her medical to get into the Wrens but her lack of education let her down. She was bitterly disappointed but that was when Ronald stepped in. He promised to help her with her reading and mathematical skills and he set about devising a plan.

It was four days before the family heard what had happened to Alan. Apparently he had been rescued and was unharmed in body. He had, however, been admitted to hospital near Ramsgate. An old mate of Uncle Lorry lent them his car and the following Sunday Aunt Bet, Uncle Lorry, Ronald and Frankie set off to see him.

The hospital turned out to be in a country mansion which had been requisitioned by the government. The sweeping drive to the main entrance was certainly impressive and after the recent spell of bad weather, it was a real treat to see it bathed in sunshine. As they went up a flight of steps to the main entrance, they could see some patients in the grounds but there was no sign of Alan. There was a small desk to the left of the main doors and the receptionist took down their details. The family was told to wait in the waiting room and someone would come down to them. By now their anxiety levels were rising. Why all this fuss? They had expected to simply walk onto the ward.

After a few minutes a man in a white coat came down and introduced himself.

'Doctor Boucher,' he said extending his hand towards Uncle

Lorry. Then he motioned them all to sit down. He was a small man, balding and slightly stooped. He looked about fifty and he had a tired expression. 'Your son,' he continued, addressing Aunt Bet and Uncle Lorry, 'is not physically hurt but I'm afraid he's suffered a bit of a breakdown.'

Frankie blinked. A bit of a breakdown? What did that mean? She glanced over to Ronald but he wore a blank expression.

'It happens sometimes,' the doctor went on. 'A person can come through a great trauma and appear to be all right but then it really hits home and the body sort of shuts down.' He sat on a chair next to them. 'He looked pretty awful when he came in,' he sighed. 'Some of those lads had been on those beaches for as many as five nights. You can just imagine. No toilets, unwashed and wounded. The nurses had to cut their uniforms off them.'

'Is that what happened to our Alan?' Uncle Lorry asked.

Doctor Boucher nodded. 'Not only that but we believe his best friend died in his arms on the way back from France. The poor chap appears to have been shot, and your son blames himself that he didn't even notice.'

Aunt Bet put her hand over her mouth and let out a small whimper. Frankie leaned over and squeezed her other hand.

'It's the shock, you see,' the doctor continued. 'The shock and the guilt.'

'Guilt?' said Frankie. 'What has he got to feel guilty about?'

'Absolutely nothing,' Doctor Boucher agreed, 'but we find that a lot of our patients do. In Alan's case I would say he feels guilty because he had no idea his friend was so badly injured and because he survived and his friend didn't. They were all exhausted. From what I can gather, Alan didn't take his boots off for four days or more and he spent almost a day standing in the water waiting to be picked up so his feet are pretty bad as well.'

Aunt Bet swallowed hard. 'Will he recover?'

'Given time.'

Uncle Lorry looked around. A couple of patients shuffled past them; a nurse was with them but they seemed to be in a world of their own. One man was continually doing and undoing the buttons on his coat and the other was clenching and unclenching his fists. 'What sort of hospital is this?' he said cautiously.

'A mental hospital,' said the doctor.

Uncle Lorry leapt to his feet. 'You've put my son in a nut house!' he exclaimed.

Aunt Bet grabbed at his sleeve. 'It's all right, Lorry.'

'Oh, no, it's not, Bet!' Uncle Lorry shouted. 'None of my family has ever had anything wrong with their heads and I'm not having it. My boy locked up with a load of lunatics. No, it won't do.'

Doctor Boucher sighed. 'But he isn't locked up Mr Cavendish,' he said patiently as if he had seen this reaction a thousand times over. 'Right now he's too ill to take care of himself. We have given him a safe place where he can collect his thoughts and talk about what's happened to him, which will help him to come to terms with it.'

Uncle Lorry snorted.

'But you believe that he will get well?' Aunt Bet said cautiously.

'As I've said, given time . . .' said the doctor. He turned towards Uncle Lorry adding, '. . . and understanding, I see no reason at all why he might not return to society.'

'Can we see him?' Ronald asked.

'Of course,' said the doctor. 'I understand that you've come a long way so I'll make sure the ward sister knows and she'll relax the visiting hours. I have to caution you not to pressurise him or try to make him talk about Ginger.'

'Ginger?' said Aunt Bet.

The doctor rose to his feet. 'His friend.'

They all headed towards the door. 'Perhaps,' Doctor Boucher added as an afterthought, 'only two at the bedside. I don't want him overwhelmed.'

As he and Alan's parents left, he called over his shoulder to Ronald and Frankie, 'There's a small tea room on the side of the house. You're welcome to get some refreshments there.'

With a heavy heart, Frankie watched her aunt and uncle walk up the stairs then followed Ronald out of the building.

# *Nineteen*

On the way home, nobody spoke. Frankie spent all of her time biting back the tears. It was too awful to see Alan – big strapping Alan who had been more like an older brother to her – reduced to a shivering, hollow-eyed wreck of a man who, at times, didn't even seem to be aware that she was in the room.

She and Ronald had found the tea room and even had time to stroll in the grounds before Uncle Lorry came to find them. Alan's room, which was on the first floor, had three other beds in it but the other occupants weren't there. He looked up when she and Ronald walked into the room but didn't acknowledge them. He was sitting in a big chair by the window and Frankie's first impression was that he had diminished in size. Conversation was difficult and punctuated by long silences when she and Ronald couldn't think of anything else to say. They felt a sense of relief when the ward sister came to say that Alan needed a rest and that it was time for them to leave.

During the drive home, Uncle Lorry was angry. 'He's never going to get better in a place like that,' he grumbled. 'Fancy locking him up with a load of nutters. It isn't right.'

'I'm sure they're doing their best,' Aunt Bet ventured. 'You heard what the doctor said. To get better, he needs to talk about it.'

'Don't be daft,' Uncle Lorry snapped. 'He doesn't need to

talk. He just needs to get on with life. They're treating him like some hysterical woman.'

'It's the new way of doing things, Dad,' said Ronald.

'Load of tommyrot more like,' his father retorted. 'What he needs is to get back home to the farm where he belongs. That'll do him more good than all the talk in the world.'

Whilst Frankie understood her uncle's determination to get his son back home, she questioned the wisdom of removing him from hospital. Doctor Boucher seemed very caring and he understood Alan's mental state. Uncle Lorry's assertion that 'all the boy needed was to buck up and forget about it' was far too simplistic. Alan wasn't just miserable. He was damaged.

*

Back home, they were the ones who 'got on with it'. Aunt Bet began the first round of bottling fruit and making chutney. Uncle Lorry strode around the farm, biting people's heads off and making himself extra work so that he didn't have to come into the house apart from meal times. Ronald took on extra book-keeping jobs and continued to help Doreen with her studies. Frankie had never seen them kissing or anything but they seemed very close.

Frankie carried on too, but she was so frustrated. On the one hand, the government was saying that the country needed every able-bodied person to fight for freedom, yet on the other hand, they had imposed an age restriction. Like Doreen, she badly wanted to join up but the Wrens and the WAAFs only took women of eighteen and over. She wouldn't be eighteen for another year and the war would probably be over by then. At this stage of her life, the only services open to her were the land army or the Auxilary Territorial Service, the women's branch of the army which was known by its acronym of ATS. But this was June and she'd have to wait until September for her birthday before she could apply.

She'd fished out her birth certificate from the dresser drawer where Aunt Bet kept all the important papers. She studied it carefully, wondering if she could alter it in some way, but changing the word 'September' was impossible.

It wasn't until she was throwing out some waste at work that Frankie hit upon an idea. She had wrapped all the bits in a newspaper and as she was about to toss it into the bin, she caught sight of a headline. *Fire took everything.* Underneath was the story of a woman who had lost her home and everything in it when a chip pan caught fire. It was a light bulb moment for Frankie. What if she told the authorities that she'd suffered a house fire? She could say she was already eighteen but she couldn't prove it because she'd lost all of her papers in that fire. Of course the authorities might check up on her but with a war on, who would have time for that? And even if they did, by the time they found out, she would have been enlisted for some time and would most likely already be eighteen. They'd hardly chuck her out, would they?

On the way home that night she stopped by the ATS recruiting office which had been set up in a small room in the Old Town Hall. An enormous army sergeant took down her details, her name and address and her date of birth (the new one making her a year older).

'Well done, Miss,' he boomed as he rose to his feet. 'You'll be hearing from us soon.'

Frankie shook his spade-like hand and headed for the door. Outside on the step, she was tempted to do a little jig. All she had to do was pass the medical and she was in.

*

With the terrible events of Dunkirk behind them, everyone settled back to an uneasy peace and Barbara came home. Frankie called round to see her again but she wasn't very talkative. She'd found herself a job in a NAAFI canteen set up in Broadwater for the Canadian troops.

'She'll be like a kid in a sweet shop,' Aunt Bet muttered darkly when Frankie told her but Frankie wasn't so sure. These days Barbara seemed very subdued.

The whole country had expected the Germans to follow up their occupation of France with an invasion along the south coast but instead, Hitler turned his attention towards Russia.

'I reckon the Nazis think we'll be happy to settle for a peace treaty,' Ronald said.

'Churchill will never agree to that,' Uncle Lorry harrumphed.

Frankie had to agree. They had read of him saying as much in the House of Commons. 'The Battle of France is over. I expect the Battle of Britain to begin.' And he was right.

From July onwards, although the weather was glorious, the idyllic peace of the countryside was interrupted by the incessant drone of aircraft. Day after day they heard Hurricanes and Spitfires from Tangmere, Ford, Westhampnett and Shoreham heading over the Channel to intercept the German Luftwaffe. The boys in blue were doing their best to stave off the Nazis and many a day they heard a dog fight overhead.

Frankie had her medical and passed with flying colours but she didn't say anything to Aunt Bet and Uncle Lorry until an official-looking envelope dropped onto the mat one morning. Her aunt and uncle were still driving to Ramsgate every other weekend to see Alan but there was hope that he would be transferred to Graylingwell hospital's Summersdale block. Uncle Lorry was still upset that his son was classed as mentally frail but if he was in a more local hospital, such as the one in Chichester, he firmly believed it would be much easier to get Alan home.

To her enormous surprise, when she opened her letter, Frankie discovered she had to report to the ATS training camp the day after tomorrow.

'I wasn't expecting it to come so soon,' she confessed as she told Aunt Bet what she'd done.

There was a list of requirements with the letter but she was only allowed to take one small suitcase. Mrs Waite seemed a little shocked that Frankie was going so soon but she and the girls wished her luck. Doreen took the news stoically. Frankie knew she'd have mixed feelings: pleased for Frankie but disappointed that she still hadn't managed to get into the Wrens. They hugged and wished each other luck. 'You will write?' asked Doreen.

'Of course,' Frankie assured her, 'and you write back. I'll be good practice for you.'

The next day, Aunt Bet came with her to the station to see her off. Frankie was both nervous and excited. When the train arrived she climbed aboard and put her suitcase onto the overhead rack. Then she opened the window and leaned out.

'Take care, lovey,' said Aunt Bet, 'and don't forget to write.' There were tears in her eyes.

'I won't,' said Frankie. 'And thank you for all you've done for me.'

Aunt Bet looked such a forlorn figure as she waved goodbye from the platform. Frankie felt so sorry for her. Just that morning they had had a letter to say that Alan had been diagnosed with Battle Fatigue and would be in hospital for at least a few months. When he read it, Uncle Lorry had thrown the letter onto the kitchen table and stomped outside, slamming the door behind him. The one good thing was that Aunt Bet still had Ronald at home. With his ear trouble it wasn't likely that he would be going anywhere.

*

Frankie arrived at the barracks at four-thirty. She was directed to her hut by the soldier on the gate. There were several other girls already inside and as she came through the door, they introduced themselves. Almost as soon as she'd heard their names Frankie forgot them, but they had come from all over the country and, like her, with a single purpose – to help win the war.

Her bed was between a girl called Peggy and another called Arlene. Peggy was about her age but Arlene seemed quite a bit older. Peggy was from Powys in Wales and had two brothers, both in the army. Arlene had a cut-glass accent and her father was a Brigadier which was why she had chosen the ATS. She obviously moved in exalted circles but she didn't put on airs and graces.

Peggy kept looking up at the clock on the wall. 'I hope we get something to eat before we go to bed. I'm ravishing.'

Frankie guessed she hadn't intended to use the wrong word but didn't correct her. When Arlene caught her eye, they exchanged a wry smile.

After a meal at seven, they were told to have an early night but first they had to learn how to make up their beds with knife-edged corners and smooth sheets. For some girls it took several goes before they could get it right.

Lights out was at ten but that didn't stop the girls talking until someone opened the door at ten-thirty and barked for 'Silence!' Everyone settled down after that.

First thing in the morning after breakfast, they were told to report to the stores. On the way, they passed a sort of makeshift garden. Someone had planted anemones and grape irises in a large tyre. They looked very pretty and added a nice splash of colour to the grey surroundings. Peggy was thrilled. 'Oh look,' she cried. 'Enemas. I love enemas.'

When they reached the stores, everyone was issued with her uniform. Skirt, shirt, tie, cap and stockings came first.

'Blimey,' one girl gasped out loud. 'Look at these lovely thick brown lisle stockings. They're just the sort my granny likes to wear.'

The room was filled with giggles.

They were even kitted out with standard issue underwear in the form of a couple of suspender belts, brassieres and three pairs of knickers. If the stockings were awful, the knickers left the girls speechless. They were huge, stretching from the waist to the knee and so roomy that two people could have worn them together. The colour itself beggared belief. Khaki.

'Boomin' passion killers,' Peggy whispered. 'Don't you just love 'em.'

'And the colour of diarrhoea,' Arlene replied from a bit further up the queue. 'At least no one will notice how scared you are if the Germans come,' another girl called Joan quipped and everybody laughed.

Frankie was about to say something else about the infamous knickers but she was pushed along the line to collect a pair of black lace-up shoes, a gym kit, towels and her own personal mug and cutlery. Everybody was supplied with sanitary towels, the type known as bunnies because of their long loops, and a sanitary belt. Frankie staggered under the weight of her kit bag but she was subjected to another medical and the nit-nurse before she was allowed back to the hut to put everything in her locker. The most difficult part of the whole exercise was having to pack up her own clothes to send them back to Aunt Bet. From this moment on, it seemed that the army owned her body and soul.

*

The next four weeks were a challenge. The new recruits spent a lot of time marching on the parade ground. Frankie managed quite well but some of the girls were confused. More than once when the sergeant bellowed 'Right turn', she would find herself facing a girl who had turned left, but as the weeks went by, they smartened up and started to look like a proper army unit. Afternoons were spent having lectures on anything from the history of the British Army to the causes and prevention of venereal disease. For some, it came as a bit of a shock to talk so openly about such things. It soon became obvious that some of the girls had never even kissed a boy. Frankie had had the odd 'end of the dance' kiss, but she was fairly innocent as well. Of course, living on a farm, she had seen animals mating as they did it freely, but the terrible pictures of syphilitic sores and the ravages of gonorrhoea came as a real eye-opener.

'I'm never letting a man near me again,' Arlene declared as they made their way back to the hut.

# Twenty

**August 1940**

The days in training camp sped by, punctuated by kit inspections, polishing shoes, ablutions and having intelligence tests. One of Frankie's tests was to write an essay on her life before she'd joined the ATS. As she picked up the pen she toyed with the idea of writing something entitled 'My working day as a florist', but somehow she ended up writing about motorbike scrambling. The more she wrote, the more vivid the memories became. She could almost taste the earth splattered in her mouth as she tackled a deeply rutted and muddy hill, and in her imagination she could feel the thrill of staying on the bike after a jump onto firmer ground. As she wrote about it she experienced again the warm sense of pleasure she got from stripping down an engine, finding a fault and rebuilding it. The examiner called time and she realised she hadn't properly answered the question. She'd made no mention of losing her mother or going to live with Aunt Bet. She hadn't said anything about Uncle Lorry being in a reserved occupation and too old at fifty to be called up anyway or Ronald, refused call-up on health grounds, or even poor Alan, already mentally damaged by the war. She laid her pen down and sighed. What an idiot she'd been. She was bound to get a low mark. She'd probably end up in the laundry or something.

139

To mark the end of their four-week training period, the girls were asked to say which branch of the ATS most appealed to them. Some postings were more popular than others. One of her room-mates, Joan, hadn't done terribly well in any of the aptitude tests so she was quite happy to be enrolled as a mess orderly. Arlene was articulate and experienced in social etiquette so they wanted her in head office. Frankie and Peggy were to be sent to No.1 Motor Transport Training Centre in Camberley, Surrey. Peggy was to train as a driver and Frankie was to be a dispatch rider. Apparently the role of the ATS girl was to change. Now that so many men were called up, the army had decided to try an experiment. Women were to be trained to take over important non-combatant posts and they were the guinea pigs. Frankie was overjoyed as it turned out that her essay had alerted her superiors to the fact that she was already an accomplished motorbike rider.

On the last night of their four-week training period, there was a chance to let their hair down at a dance in a hall requisitioned by the Navy, Army and Air Force Institute, known more colloquially as the NAAFI. They had no other clothes because they'd had to send everything home when they joined up, so all the girls went in uniform. The dance band wasn't brilliant but they could hold a tune and the lads from some neighbouring barracks had turned up as well. Frankie met a nice chap and enjoyed quite a few dances with him interspersed by a drink or two from the bar.

The girls had agreed to stick together on one table, so everybody came back to the table when their dance was finished. Peggy was on her own for a while but then a good-looking, fair-haired chap asked her to dance. Frankie was thrilled for her.

Frankie excused herself from her partner and went back to the hut before the end of the dance. She was tired and wanted to get a bit of an early night although once the others came in, they'd probably want to talk for a while. She had the wash room to herself which was a luxury and as soon as she'd put her pyjamas on, she finished off a letter to Alan. He'd been in Ramsgate for seven weeks and then they'd moved him to Graylingwell, which was near Chichester. It wasn't as far for Aunt Bet and Uncle Lorry to go to see him but with the travel restrictions in place and petrol now off limits for private use except in dire emergences or for a restricted occupation, it didn't make it that much easier. In her letters, Aunt Bet told her that he was much the same as he'd been when they'd seen him, but when Frankie wrote to him she pretended that he was the same old Alan. In this letter, she told him about her new posting and although she couldn't mention that it was in Camberley, she told him it was a lot nearer to where he was and that she hoped to see him soon.

All at once the door burst open and Peggy came flying in. She was in quite a state and almost hysterical. She threw herself onto her bed and sobbed into the pillow. Frankie was appalled. Jumping out of bed, she padded over to her friend.

'Whatever happened?' she gasped.

Peggy turned her head to look at Frankie, her eyes red and blotchy and a watery snot dripping off the end of her nose. 'Oh Frankie,' she blubbed. 'I tried to stop him but he's done it.'

Frankie's mouth dropped open. 'What do you mean, he's done it?'

The last time she'd seen Peggy, she and the fair-haired chap were happily dancing. Peggy seemed relaxed enough and as far as Frankie could see, he'd seemed all right. What on earth had happened? What was she saying? Had the rotter forced himself on her?

Peggy reached in the drawer of her bedside locker and pulled out a huge handkerchief. 'He's done it,' she repeated. 'I felt him. I felt his . . . his, you know . . . his thingy.'

They could hear voices coming their way. The other girls were coming back from the dance. Peggy blew her nose noisily. 'What am I going to tell my mother? Oh Frankie, this is awful.'

In the event it was only Arlene and another girl who came into the hut. They gathered around Peggy trying to console her. 'I think you'd better tell us exactly what happened,' said Arlene. 'Start from the bit where you left the dance.'

Peggy took a deep breath. 'We went outside and he walked me as far as the perimeter fence,' she began. 'The guard said he couldn't go any further.'

'That's right,' said the other girl. 'The men aren't allowed near the women's billets.' She squeezed Peggy's hand. 'So what happened then?'

'We walked a little way beside the fence and then he asked me if he could kiss me,' Peggy said beginning to cry again. 'And then . . .' She gulped as she struggled for the words.

'And then?' Arlene cajoled gently. 'What happened then, darling?'

'He put his hands right down over my bottom and . . .' the words were rushing out now, 'he pulled me closer and when he kissed me he pulled me *really* close to him and I felt it move.' She put her hands up to her face and covered it in horror. 'You know, his what's-it . . . his do-da.' Her shoulders sagged. 'Oh lummy-charlie it was enormous!'

There was a quiet moment as the girls looked from one to the other. Frankie was biting her cheeks in an effort not to laugh out loud. Nobody knew what to say but it was obvious Peggy didn't understand the first thing about the facts of life.

Frankie put her arm around Peggy's shoulders. 'I don't know much about having sex,' she began. 'I've never done it, you see . . .'

'Well, I didn't want to,' Peggy wailed.

'I know people can do it with their clothes on,' Frankie said gently, 'but you've still got your great coat on.'

'And it's done up,' said one of the other girls.

Arlene spluttered and stood up from the bed.

There was a second or two of silence before Peggy gave them a grateful smile. 'Is that true?' She looked up at the other girl who nodded vigorously.

Peggy turned back to Frankie. 'So he didn't . . .?'

'No, of course he didn't,' said Arlene, walking away. 'Blinkin' men. That happened to me once. I thought it was his pencil.'

# Twenty-One

**ATS Training Camp, Camberley, Surrey, September 1940**

Frankie was given seven days leave before she had to report to Camberley and her first priority was to see Alan.

Graylingwell hospital in Chichester was, in fact, several buildings set in an impressive landscape of gardens with a sixty-acre market garden and two farms. Alan was due to be discharged the following week so when she arrived, he was working on one of the farms. He certainly looked a lot better than when she'd seen him the last time. Back then he was exhausted and couldn't concentrate on anything. He still looked a little strained and he sometimes had that far-away look in his eye but he greeted Frankie warmly.

He took her to the hospital shop which had a small area converted into a tea room. Alan explained that by working on the farm he had earned some tokens which he could only spend in the shop, so he insisted on buying Frankie tea and cake.

As they waited to be served, she noticed that he was still restless. He leg kept jigging up and down as he sat and he fiddled with the sugar server.

'I work with the pigs,' he announced. 'Got a good breeding system here.'

'That's good, 'Frankie said.

'We're self-sufficient,' he went on. The tone of his voice was flat and without enthusiasm. 'Pretty good when you think of the size of the place.'

Frankie nodded her approval. 'What do you think of my uniform then?' she said proudly.

Alan looked at her as if he'd only just noticed. 'ATS.'

'I'm off to Surrey in a few days,' she went on. 'I'm going to be a dispatch rider.'

He made no comment and the tea arrived. He took his mug and slurped loudly.

'Are you going back, Alan?' she asked cautiously.

'I am in the army.'

'Where will they send you?'

He shrugged. 'The Doc is trying to get me a desk job.'

'That sounds like a good idea.'

'I'm not a coward!' he snapped. His hand jerked and he slopped his tea onto the table.

'I never said you were,' Frankie said. She cut her cake in two and picked up one half to eat.

Alan had pushed the whole of his cake into his mouth in one go. 'They're discharging me on Friday,' he said splattering her face with crumbs.

'Will you get any leave?'

He shrugged again and then helped himself to the rest of her cake on her plate. She watched him wolf down the rest of his tea in one go, her heart broken. 'I've got to go,' he said banging his mug down and standing to his feet. The chair scraped along the wooden floor. 'Thanks for coming.'

She stared after him as he crashed out of the room, the door banging behind him. Whatever had happened to him? Where was the gentle fun-loving Alan she'd grown up with? When did he become so uncouth and bad-mannered? She felt something trickle down her cheek and realised she was crying.

A woman leaned over the table to take away his plate and mug. She gave Frankie a sympathetic smile. 'Don't worry, love,' she said. 'It'll all come right in the end.'

*

Back in Worthing there was a chance to catch up with her friends. Barbara was doing well although she did look a bit tired. It wasn't until she got home that Frankie realised that most of their conversation had been about her. She had chatted about Alan and the ATS. She felt bad now. She'd forgotten to ask about Barbara's aunt or how Barbara was getting on in the canteen. She should have asked if her friend was thinking about joining up as well but in her excitement everything else had gone out of her head.

The next day, she and Doreen went to the pictures. Doreen seemed different and yet the same. She looked very grown up and sophisticated with her hair swept up in a new style. The film was a pleasant distraction from everything around them (there were even sandbags against the cinema walls), but the Pathé News was an unpleasant reminder with footage of the bombardment across the English Channel which had followed in the weeks after Dunkirk. It was frightening to realise how close the Germans had come, and only a few miles from where she lived. Their guns, thought to be captured French railway guns, had a range of thirty miles but a combination of heavy smoke screens and RAF fighters in the skies resulted in little damage to the British shipping. As the news faded, there was a ripple of applause in the cinema.

When they came outside they stopped off at some tea rooms. 'How's work?' Frankie asked after they'd placed their order. She was determined not to make the same mistake with Doreen as she had with Barbara, only talking about herself.

'Not brilliant,' said Doreen. 'Mrs Waite is just about ticking over but I get the feeling it won't be for long. People don't have the money for luxuries like flowers We've been busy making up wreaths for the local funeral directors using silk and paper but once they have enough to keep going, I think the shop will close.'

'What will you do then?'

Doreen shrugged. 'I'm still applying for the services.'

'You still want to be a Wren.'

Doreen nodded. 'I do.'

'What about you and Ronald?'

'There is no me and Ronald,' Doreen smiled. 'I know what you're thinking but it's not going to happen.'

'Why not?' said Frankie. 'I've seen the way he looks at you and he's a nice person.'

Doreen seemed embarrassed. 'Surely you know,' she began.

'Know what?'

Doreen leaned forward and spoke in a confidential whisper. 'Ronald isn't interested in me,' she said. 'We had a long conversation soon after we met. I love him to bits but not in the way you're thinking about.'

Frankie was puzzled.

'Oh, Frankie,' said Doreen. 'Ronald bats for the other team.'

'What team?'

Doreen sighed. 'And I thought I was supposed to be the innocent one,' she teased. 'Your cousin likes girls, but only as friends.'

'Oh, I see,' said Frankie, although she didn't see at all.

# Twenty-Two

The billet at Camberley was luxurious compared to what Frankie was used to. Set in the lovely Surrey countryside, the building had been a boys' prep school before the war. As soon as she arrived, Frankie was given blankets, sheets, towels and soap and taken to her new sleeping quarters, a room which had once been the boys' dormitory. She made her bed just as she'd been taught and put a photograph of Aunt Bet and Uncle Lorry on the bedside locker.

She hadn't brought the doll but she had packed her mother's tin. It was empty. She left the two buttons on top of the chest of drawers in a little pot which had once been used for loose face powder. She had decided that the tin with the yellow star would be useful for her hair grips.

The girls who had joined her were a lot like the others. 'You won't believe the hassle I had in getting here,' one girl cried. 'Every train from here to kingdom come was chock-a-block with soldiers.'

'I guess they're getting ready for the invasion,' said Frankie.

'That's enough of that kind of talk,' the Squad Corporal interrupted and Frankie jumped.

The girls were all kitted out again. They had all the usual stuff including the passion killers, but this time they had smart uniform slacks as well and they were issued with grey dungarees to wear when they were doing vehicle maintenance classes.

'Shall we go for a walk around the grounds when we've done this?' Frankie suggested.

'Someone told me there's a tennis court behind that row of trees,' Peggy said.

'Tennis!' cried another girl. 'Oh, do let's have a game before we turn in.'

But back in the dorm they were all issued with white tape, some indelible ink and a pen with a scratchy nib.

'Mark all items of clothing with your name and number on the tape,' said the Squad Corporal, and as she handed round a small sewing kit, she added, 'You have all you need here in your housewife.'

Frankie groaned inwardly. Looking at the pile of clothes in front of her, she knew this was going to take ages. 'No stroll around the grounds or tennis tonight,' she said ruefully as the Squad Corporal left the room.

She was about half way through when the dinner gong sounded and her one consolation was that the meal was more generous than Aunt Bet could manage.

Later that night, as she lay in bed she could hear the incessant drone of aircraft. It was followed by loud bangs and rumbles. Some seemed awfully close. Had the Germans come at last? Eventually, unable to sleep, she got out of bed and looked through the window. In the distance she could see a red glow against the black sky. Frankie took in her breath. Whatever it was, it was big. Another girl came to join her. 'What is it?' she whispered.

'Looks like a big fire,' said Frankie. 'The Germans must be bombing a factory somewhere.'

'My God. That's not a factory,' the girl said. 'That's London. London is on fire.'

*

149

The six-week course went by very quickly even though the horrors of the nightly bombing of London disturbed everybody's peace of mind. The tuition was good but for Frankie it was a bit of a doddle. She already had plenty of experience in driving, riding a motorbike and vehicle maintenance. Of course, military ambulances and large lorries took a bit of getting used to, especially when she had to remember to double de-clutch when on the move, but having spent years helping her uncle and cousins, she adapted quite quickly. There were some things which were new to her. Map reading was one of them. This turned out to be a real challenge because all place names and sign posts had been removed at the beginning of the war. The government felt that should there be an invasion, the enemy would have as little help as possible. Frankie had to learn how to use a compass and the stars at night.

Proper sleep was a luxury when they could get it. In the main, their nights were filled with the sound of aircraft overhead, ack-ack guns and the bombs dropping over London. The city had had a pasting and it had been going on for weeks. It was hard to get any sleep. Frankie would lie on her bed wondering how many poor souls had been ushered into eternity tonight. If her nights were interrupted, her days were filled with drill, physical training, first aid classes (another easy one for Frankie), shoe cleaning, button polishing, and getting their inoculations up to date. There were compensations along the way. There were male officers and soldiers on site and the girls met both in the NAAFI canteen when they were off duty. It was an opportunity to play cards, or darts, have a drink and a chat or to have a bit of a sing-song whenever some local singer turned up to entertain them. On Saturdays there was usually a dance band and twice a month they held a talent show. Of course most of the acts were rather mediocre or rubbish but occasionally there was a flash of real talent. One, Lance Corporal Malcolm Hawke, was a fantastic trumpet player and everybody clapped like mad when he'd finished his performance.

While she was at Camberley, Frankie became best friends with Rita Bartlett, who came from the East End of London, and Lou Haynes, who lived in Potters Bar. Rita was a fun-loving girl who had an eye for the lads. A wicked flirt, she drew the cream of the gathering on dance nights. The men who flocked to her table looking for a twirl on the dance floor with Rita often had to make do with 'her friends' but Lou and Frankie weren't complaining. They made the most of it and had a good time.

Rita never lacked a beau and she took risks. They were supposed to be in bed by ten and lights out at ten-thirty but quite often, because Frankie's bed was right next to the window, she would hear a tap on the glass some time after midnight. It would be Rita, with one foot on the guttering over the porch and hanging onto the drainpipe down the wall, waiting for someone to open the window to let her in.

'Blimey,' she whispered one night when Frankie opened the window, 'I thought you was never coming, gal. It's bleedin' perishing out here and I been banging on the winder for hours.'

'Sorry,' said Frankie sleepily. Rita tumbled in and Frankie closed the window. 'Did you have a nice time?'

'He was all right,' she said with a non-committal shrug. 'I'll say one thing though; he was a great kisser.' She giggled.

'Shh,' a voice further down the dormitory complained. 'Some of us are trying to get some kip around here.'

'Sor . . . ree.'

'You're drunk,' said Frankie with a grin.

'Just a lickle bit,' Rita said as she finally wobbled to her feet. 'Now where's me bed?'

Frankie took her by the arm. 'Come on, I'll show you.'

As they made their way down the dorm, Rita bumped into

a couple of other beds and woke the girls in them before she reached her own. Frankie helped her off with her coat and Rita kicked her shoes under her locker. She'd undressed as far as her petticoat when the heard the sound of footsteps outside in the corridor.

'Quick,' Frankie hissed. 'Somebody's coming.'

Rita tumbled between the sheets but when the door burst open and the light went on, Frankie was still standing beside her bed. She stared ahead in a daze.

'What are you doing out of bed, Sherwood?'

It was the Sergeant, an absolute dragon of a woman who stood no nonsense. Several sleepy heads were roused from their pillows. Rita pretended to snore. Frankie was struck dumb.

'I said what are you doing . . .?'

Frankie still stood like a rabbit caught in the headlights.

'I say, Sarg,' Peggy called out in ringing tones, 'do be careful. I think she's been sleepwalking.'

The Sergeant looked at Frankie suspiciously. 'But her eyes are open.'

'That doesn't matter, Marm,' said Lou. She slipped out of her bed and came up to Frankie. 'Come on, love,' she said gently. 'Let's get you back to bed.'

Peggy came to join her and the pair of them helped Frankie back to her end of the room. 'You know, it's dangerous to wake sleepwalkers,' Lou went on as they tucked the sheets around Frankie.

The Sergeant, clearly not completely convinced, stood in the doorway, glaring.

As she padded back to her bed, Lou added, 'Anyway that's what my old man says and he's a doctor so he should know.'

The Sergeant snorted and snapped off the light. After she'd closed the door again there was a silence in the room for several minutes until Rita spoke out a muffled 'Thanks, girls.'

'Is your father really a doctor?' Frankie asked.

'Na,' said Lou. 'He's a coalman.'

And gradually the sound of people chuckling filled the darkness.

\*

Friday was always pay day. Everyone assembled on the parade ground in front of a trestle table. Two officers sat on one side and a wages clerk sat at one end of the table. As each girl's name was called, she had to break ranks, march smartly to the table, salute and give her name, rank and number. After she'd stood to attention, one of the officers handed out her wage which worked out at 7/6 (1/6 a day) and the wages clerk showed her where to sign for it. Another snap to attention and she'd march back into line. Afterwards, Frankie went back to her hut to write a letter to Aunt Bet. She'd been saving her money so she slipped a ten bob note between the pages. 'Now that Alan is home, treat him to a pint from me,' she wrote. 'Give him my love, won't you.' Aunt Bet hadn't said how he was in her last letter but Frankie hoped he was back to his normal self.

At last the six weeks were over and they had received new orders. Frankie was posted to Kent and Lou was coming too. Frankie had never been there but Lou had family nearby. Rita was going to Southampton. They commandeered the NAAFI for their farewell party and had a great time. Lance Corporal Warren – Bunny, to his friends – brought along a bottle of scotch. Frankie had never had it before but was willing to give it a try. It burned all the way down her throat, and she coughed until she had tears in her eyes.

'Have a bit more, love,' said Bunny when Frankie had finished coughing. He had sat next to her and put his arm around her in an intimate way. 'You'll soon get used to it.'

'Bugger off, Bunny,' Lou said protectively. 'She's had enough.'

They said their farewells, swapped addresses and then turned in for some sleep but once again it wasn't to be. Before long, they heard the rumble of aircraft engines as the Luftwaffe came over thick and fast once again. Frankie closed her eyes and willed herself to shut the noise out. She needed all the rest she could get. Tomorrow she would be going to her first posting. The time for play acting and exercises was over. She was now a fully trained member of the ATS and like thousands of others, she was part of the British fighting force with the sole aim of turning the tide and bringing the Nazis down.

# Twenty-Three

**Broadwater, Sussex, December 1940**

'Come on, son,' said Lorry. 'You've been sitting staring out of that window for long enough. Put your coat on and come down to the Wigmore Arms for a drink with Ronald and me.'

Alan rose wearily to his feet. He'd been home five days and already he was bored out of his skull. Life on the farm and indeed, life with the family had lost its appeal. Everything and everybody annoyed him. No, he didn't want to help clean out the pigs. No, mum could collect the eggs when she got back from the shops. Of course he hadn't seen the coalman or heard him shout. Too bad he'd driven away without making a delivery but what the heck, he'd be back tomorrow, wouldn't he? Why the hell didn't they all leave him alone? Every time his mother asked him, *do you want a cup of tea, would you like to read the paper, shall I put the wireless on for you, dear,* he wanted to scream 'For God's sake put a sock in it, will you?' He knew she meant well but it was more than anybody could take.

Any loud noise made him jump and then the pictures in his mind would start up all over again. That chap floating in the water with one side of his head nothing more than a bloody mush; the machine gunfire ripping alongside the long queue of men standing in the water (and he was one of them) until it picked out some poor sod, seemingly at random, and ended his life; the sea itself, full of pee and shit and blood as it lapped the shore. Every now and then the air had been pierced with the cries of someone in pain; some poor, horribly wounded soul blaspheming, or some poor kid weeping for his mother or sweetheart or wife as the last of his life ebbed from his body. If only it would all go away, if only he could switch it off.

And then there was Ginger. How could he have not known his best mate was dead? When had he been shot? He racked his brains trying to work out when it had happened. How come Ginger hadn't cried out? If only he'd made a noise, or said something, Alan would have realised. Someone suggested it was because Ginger knew there was nothing he could do, so he'd laid there and bled to death. But he could have done something, couldn't he? He could have stuffed something into the wound to stem the flow of blood or called for a medic and told him to hang on . . . anything. Alan hit his head with frustration in an effort to stop remembering but it was no use. The Doc had said he was all right but he didn't feel all right.

They walked to the pub in Leigh Road. Alan was aware that his father and brother were talking but he didn't join in. After a recommendation from a member of the Worthing office, Ronald had been asked to go to the Admiralty in London for some sort of interview. He didn't know what it was about but it was for some sort of hush-hush thing in Buckinghamshire.

'What time did you say the train is in the morning, son?' Lorry asked.

'Seven-fifteen,' said Ronald. 'I've got no idea what I'm getting into, but it might give me a chance to do my bit.'

'Your mother and I will miss you, lad,' said Lorry giving him a clap on the back, 'but you can go with our blessing.'

They'd reached the pub. The Wigmore Arms was a popular pub about half a mile from The Cricketers in the centre of the village. As the three of them walked in they were greeted warmly by the regulars and several men offered to buy Alan a drink. While his father and Ronald played darts and shove-halfpenny, he was content to tuck himself into a corner and drink. It was a pleasant evening until someone remarked about the length of time he'd been in hospital and asked him when he was going back. Alan immediately saw red.

'You suggesting I'm a shirker, pal?'

'No, no, not at all,' the man protested. 'I'm sure stopping at home for a bit of your mum's cooking is just what the doctor ordered.'

All at once, Alan was on his feet, pushing his chair over. Nobody actually saw what happened but the next thing they knew, the small round table full of empty glasses had been knocked over and the chap was sprawled across the floor. Lorry rushed to calm the situation but by then Alan had already punched two more men.

'Come on,' he goaded as he put his fists up. 'Want a fight, d'ya? Come on then. I'll knock the lot of you to kingdom come.'

The barman sent the potboy to fetch Constable Harris, then joined in with his regulars to get Alan out of the pub. It was not so easy as it looked. With the drink inside of him, Alan had gained the strength of ten men.

Lorry was mortified. As he attempted to restrain his son, Alan lashed out again and his father ended up on the floor. Alan was eventually ejected unceremoniously onto the street as Ronald helped his father to his feet. Lorry, his nose bloodied, apologised and offered to pay for any damage as the barman picked up a chair.

'We've known each other for years, Lorry,' said the barman. 'You're always welcome into my pub, but that son of yours . . .'

'I understand,' said Lorry, pressing his handkerchief to his nose to staunch the flow of blood. 'No need to say more.' The two men shook hands and Lorry went outside to find Alan and take him home.

Sadly they were too late. Another man lay on the ground and PC Harris had just arrested Alan for being drunk and disorderly.

'But he's got to be back in the barracks tomorrow,' Lorry protested.

'I can't help that,' said PC Harris, 'He'll be in the magistrate's court first thing in the morning.'

# Twenty-Four

**Deal, Kent, Summer 1942**

Two more Christmases came and went but the opportunity to celebrate was sparse. The war had been going for three years and little had changed. Starting in September 1940, the Germans kept up their relentless bombing night after night and although much was made of the raids in London, many other cities were the victims of the bombing too. Southampton suffered serious raids followed by Bristol, Coventry and Birmingham. In December it was the turn of Sheffield, Liverpool and Manchester, the latter even having a terrible raid on Christmas Eve.

'Call themselves Christians,' one of the girls complained. 'Bloody barbarians more like.'

The New Year brought more of the same, beginning with the bombing of Cardiff on January 2nd, and so it went on.

The Blitz on British cities lasted until May 1941 but the raids continued – the only change being the number of bombs being dropped. As time went on, the girls in Frankie's battery were informed that thirty-seven thousand tons had been dropped in the capital in 1940 and that became twenty-one thousand tons in 1941. As 1942 came round, there were fewer still, but it didn't feel much better. A bomb was a bomb and people still died.

All this time, Frankie and Lou had been billeted in the same house. Mrs Kane was a homely woman who spent a lot of her time helping her neighbours. She was the main carer for an old lady three doors down, taking her meals and doing her washing and shopping. She helped out at a Red Cross shop two days a week and did a shift at the local telephone exchange on Saturdays, but, amazingly, she still found time to look after her lodgers. If they were off duty in the evenings she would get out the playing cards or some sort of board game; anything to take their minds off what was happening overhead. Throughout the long winter months there was always a jigsaw puzzle waiting to be done on a table in the corner of her kitchen-cum-sitting room (the only room she heated), and there was another one in the Anderson shelter should they need to go there during the night.

Mrs Kane had been widowed in the Great War and had no children but she lived her life as if those around her were her family. Frankie and Lou considered themselves very lucky. Other girls were not so fortunate. They heard stories of bedrooms running with damp, sparse food, and lecherous relatives turning up in their bedrooms uninvited when they were trying to sleep.

Lou worked a twelve-hour shift on the battery and by the time she came off duty, she had no voice because she had to shout instructions to the gunners over the sound of the guns themselves.

Frankie's duties were entirely different. Sometimes she had to take dispatches from one gun site to another or to HQ, and at other times she was an outrider for a convoy taking much needed supplies to a barracks or port. When she was dispatch rider, it often entailed riding her bike across unfamiliar territory in the dead of night with only one inch of light on her headlamps. Coupled with that, there was usually an air raid in progress.

'I don't know how you cope with it,' said Lou. 'You must have nerves of steel. I'd be absolutely terrified.'

In truth, Frankie was scared but she had trained herself to concentrate on getting the job done rather than what was going on around her. This meant she could keep bad thoughts and panic at bay. The work was relentless and she was tired out but she kept going. She had a few narrow squeaks, and the worst was to come one evening in July 1942. Frankie was on her way to Divisional HQ when a bomb dropped in the next street. The blast between two houses blew her off the bike. For a couple of seconds, she lay in the road, completely stunned until the need to get vital information to the Port of Dover kicked in. Her leg was quite painful and when she looked down, there was blood. Limping heavily, she looked around for her machine. It was lying in the road. Ignoring the raid going on around her, she went back for it but the front wheel of the bike was completely misshapen. She couldn't ride it and besides, her head was spinning. It was imperative that she get the dispatches to HQ so there was nothing for it but to run the last half mile.

In the end, Frankie staggered rather than ran. The noise from the nearby battery was tremendous. It was where the country's only fourteen-inch guns were firing across the Channel. The guns, named 'Winnie' after the prime minister Winston Churchill and 'Pooh' after the story book character, were positioned three quarters of a mile from the sea, near the village of St Margaret's at Cliffe, just off the main road between Deal and Dover.

'Dispatches for Major Ryan,' she gasped as the sentry halted her at the gate.

The sentry let her through and escorted her to the office. Feeling cold and clammy although she probably looked flushed, Frankie couldn't stop shaking, only managing to say her name and hand over the documents before she finally collapsed. She was immediately bundled off to the sick bay but the nurse took one look at her leg and decided she needed to go to hospital. Frankie drifted in and out of consciousness until they took her in a St John ambulance to Deal and Walmer hospital. Only vaguely aware of what was happening, she eventually found herself between crisp and cool sheets for the first time in days. Someone gave her an injection and she slept. They woke her every now and then to take her temperature or offer her a bed pan but everything else was sleep, sleep, and yet more delicious sleep.

She woke to the sound of a trolley trundling through the ward and a voice saying, 'Cup of tea, Miss?'

Frankie hauled herself up the bed on her elbow. 'Ooh, yes please.' She glanced under the sheets. There seemed to be a thick bandage on her leg between her knee and her hip and the leg itself felt rather sore. 'What day is it?'

'Thursday,' said the ward orderly who had handed her the tea.

'How long have I been here?' Frankie asked the nurse when she came a little later on to take her pulse.

'Three days.'

Frankie was aghast. 'Three days?'

'You came off your motorbike and scraped the skin off your thigh. We had to clean it up in case any grit was in the wound but don't worry, it wasn't too bad after all.'

'I seem to have been sleeping a lot,' Frankie remarked.

'You were exhausted,' said the nurse. She was an older woman with flecks of grey in her hair and Frankie wondered vaguely if she had been retired and called in because they were short staffed. So many girls were joining the auxiliary services now.

'When can I go home?' Frankie asked.

'The consultant will be doing a ward round later on this morning,' said the nurse, scribbling something on Frankie's chart. 'They'll tell you then.'

'Does my aunt know I'm here?'

'Of course,' said the nurse. 'Don't you remember? She was here last night.'

As she hurried away Frankie frowned. Oh dear, poor Aunt Bet, to come all this way and she wasn't even awake!

The ward cleaners bustled around after breakfast making sure everything was straightened and spotless. Once the beds were made, each patient was expected to lie still and not disturb the bedclothes. At ten forty-five a bevy of doctors arrived through the doors. They worked their way around the ward, standing at the foot of each patient's bed until the consultant had looked at the notes and studied the patient's chart at the bottom of the bed. Every now and then, the consultant would bark a question at one of the junior doctors.

Frankie lay perfectly still as the consultant and his entourage moved towards her bed. At the same time there came the sound of hurrying footsteps as the ward doors burst open.

'Ah, Doctor Delaney,' said the consultant, as he pulled the curtains around her bed, 'so good you could make it.'

Frankie turned her head to glimpse the newcomer. Doctor Delaney was a man who stood out from the rest. He was about five foot eight inches tall and had close-cropped, black, curly hair which framed his flawless ebony coloured skin. He was also handsome – very handsome, with dark enquiring eyes and an enigmatic smile. Frankie had never seen a completely black man before and this one was absolutely stunning. She didn't mean to stare but there was something rather wonderful about him.

'I apologise, Mr Hill,' he said. His voice was deep and the colour of velvet; his accent was American. 'I went to the wrong end of the hospital.'

'When in doubt, Doctor Delaney,' Mr Hill said, 'just ask.' There was just the hint of a teasing smile on his lips. 'We Brits always know the way.'

'I'm sure you do, sir.'

Frankie was mesmerised.

'Miss Sherwood?'

Frankie started as she realised that Mr Hill had been speaking to her. 'Beg pardon?'

Mr Hill tutted. 'See the effect you have on my patients, Doctor Delaney? I asked you what sort of hours you work, Miss Sherwood.'

Frankie blushed a deep crimson. 'It varies, sir,' she began, 'but in view of the present crisis I've been working quite long hours. It can't be helped. There is a war on.'

'When you came in, young lady,' he said in what was obviously a mock-stern voice, 'you were exhausted and severely dehydrated. We may be at war but you must make sure that you drink plenty of fluids and that you look after yourself.'

Frankie lowered her eyes. 'Yes, sir.'

'What do you think of this girl, Doctor Delaney?' the consultant said addressing the black doctor again. 'Like millions of others, she's not just doing her bit. She's giving her all.'

'I have long been an admirer of the British woman, sir,' said the doctor.

'I'm sure you'll be interested to know, Miss Sherwood,' Mr Hill continued, 'that this man has brought blood plasma donated to the people of this country by the United States. Should you have needed a transfusion for that leg injury of yours, this man might have saved your life.'

Doctor Delaney waved his hand dismissively and Frankie didn't know what to say. Her face was pink and her heart thudded in her chest. The consultant put Frankie's chart back on the end of her bed. 'So, from now on,' he said firmly as he looked at her over the rim of his glasses, 'you're to look after yourself, Miss Sherwood. You've got a bit of an infection in that leg which will keep you in hospital for a while but as soon as we discharge you, I certainly don't want to see you back in here again.'

As Mr Hill and his posse moved on, Doctor Delaney pulled the bed curtains right back. 'Good luck, Miss Sherwood,' he said, giving her a lingering smile.

And Frankie's heart did a somersault.

# Twenty-Five

Patched up and back home, it was strange being back in her old room on North Farm. The days she'd spent here seemed a lifetime ago. When she got up the next morning, Frankie found the courage to open the bottom drawer. The princess doll was still there, just as she'd left it. A rush of feelings flooded through her: love and loss, pain, and joy. She'd forgotten how beautiful the doll was. Now that she was older, she could appreciate the fine stitching on the waistcoat and how dainty the buttons were. She lifted the skirt and was transported back nearly nine years to the day when she'd first set eyes on the doll's petticoat and pantaloons. She lifted her head and remembered her mother's enigmatic smile as she'd watched her. There was a pain in her chest now, a terrible longing and she was surprised to find that her cheeks were wet with tears.

'Oh, Mum,' she whispered and all at once she knew she'd spent too much time being angry with her. Now that she understood all the love which had been sewn into this doll, she wondered why she had been so cross all these years. Everything her mother had done for her was because Frankie was the centre of her life. Those stories . . . they weren't lies. Her mother had no intention of making a fool of her. She merely wanted to entertain her child. And now, because of what had happened to Alan and her own accident, Frankie could see that she'd rejected her mother because it was the only way she could deal with her pain and loss. Just like her poor cousin, she'd been lashing out at nothing. What an idiot she'd been.

Gazing out of the window and onto the farm, she thought of Doctor Delaney. How handsome he'd been. In her mind's eye, she could still see his lovely smile and hear his honeyed voice and she wished with all of her heart that she might see him again.

She heard Aunt Bet calling upstairs, 'Breakfast is ready, dear,' and she jumped. She had been hugging the princess very tightly as she sat on the bed rocking herself.

'Coming,' she called. Frankie had planned to take a walk up to Hillbarn but now she was consumed with a longing to see her old home again. It wasn't that far and although her leg was still stiff, the doctor had told her she could do mild exercise so she was sure she could walk that far. Placing the princess back in the drawer, Frankie pulled on her dressing gown and hurried downstairs.

Aunt Bet was happy to do whatever she wanted so, after breakfast, they strolled down to the village. Nothing much had changed in Broadwater although, less than three miles away, Worthing had experienced its own share of bomb damage and loss. Several houses had been destroyed in Haynes Road and nine people had died when a plane crash-landed in Lyndhurst Road. Mercifully it narrowly missed the hospital or the death toll might have been much higher. There were bomb craters on the Downs but it was comforting to see that, despite the war, life in Broadwater went on as usual. The new parade of shops built in 1934 was flourishing. Frankie couldn't really remember how things had looked before but of course Aunt Bet could. They linked arms as they walked along the road where she used to live and all at once they were standing right outside the gate.

'It's changed so much,' Frankie whispered.

'It looks a right mess,' said Aunt Bet disapprovingly.

Thick ivy branches covered the walls of the house. Old tin cans and beer bottles littered the area around the front door. The little garden in front was unkempt and overgrown with only a forlorn rose waving on a straggly bush under the window. Frankie swallowed hard. 'Mum planted that bush in memory of my father,' she said, her throat tight with emotion and Aunt Bet squeezed her arm sympathetically.

They heard a footfall behind them and a voice said, 'Excuse me, dear.'

They were standing in front of the gate, blocking the way for an old lady with a pram. 'Oh sorry,' said Frankie stepping aside.

The old woman looked up at her with rheumy eyes. 'Frankie?' she said. 'Is that you?' It was only then that Frankie realised it was Mrs Dickenson, her old neighbour. 'My, my,' Mrs Dickenson went on, 'haven't you've grown into a fine young woman.'

As soon as the older woman saw she was with Aunt Bet, Mrs Dickenson invited them both in for a cup of tea.

It seemed churlish to refuse so they followed her into the house. There was nothing in the pram apart from a little shopping so Frankie guessed that she used it to balance. Mrs Dickenson was beginning to look her age. Her legs were bandaged and she struggled to walk. The house smelled stale and it was dark in the hallway. A cat greeted them lovingly but Mrs Dickenson shooed him outside and shut the door.

'All on my own now, dear,' she said inviting them into the kitchen. She switched the gas on under the kettle and reached for the tea caddy. 'My old mother, God rest her soul, died back in '38 and the boys left home. Cyril got married and moved to Canada; Morris and Bert joined up when the war started. Morris is in North Africa, of all places, and Bert is in

Leeds.' She chuckled to herself. 'And here's me, never been any further than East Grinstead.' She put three cups and saucers onto the table. 'Just me and Puss left but as long as I can get about . . .' her voice trailed. 'Oh, it's good to see you, dear. In the ATS, so I see.'

Frankie nodded and told her a little of what she was doing. With the tea made, Mrs Dickenson sat at the table with them. 'And what of you, Mrs Cavendish? You and your family keeping well?'

Nodding, Aunt Bet told her about the rest of the family, mentioning that Alan had been at Dunkirk.

'That was a terrible business,' said Mrs Dickenson, 'and it was a terrible business what happened to your poor sister all them years ago. She was such a lovely lady.' She nodded towards the window. 'She made them curtains for me. Didn't charge me a penny piece for them either.'

Frankie glanced over at her aunt. 'I don't remember.'

''Course you don't, dear,' said Mrs Dickenson. 'You were only a little girl.' She pushed the cups of tea in front of them. 'I always thought there was something fishy about her death. I did try to tell the police but they insisted it was natural causes.'

Aunt Bet sniffed. 'I always wondered why someone turned the place over.'

Mrs Dickenson nodded in agreement. 'I heard somebody banging about – opening drawers and then there was a lot of bumping, like something being lumped upstairs but I didn't go round. I feel bad about it now but I was on me own and I thought it might be burglars.'

'I discovered a while ago that the person who was searching for something was Mrs Toms,' said Frankie.

'Mrs Toms?' Mrs Dickenson exclaimed. 'What, that religious nutter?'

As Frankie went on to tell Mrs Dickenson about the discovery she and Doreen had made in Mrs Toms' garden, the old woman's eyes grew larger. 'Well, I'll be damned. I wish I'd gone in there now. If I'd known it was only that awful woman I'd have given her a piece of my mind if nothing else.'

Aunt Bet covered the old lady's hand. 'Please don't blame yourself,' she said. 'You did the best you could.'

Mrs Dickenson gave her a watery smile. 'Then there was that foreign-looking chap who was knocking on her door. What was he doing there?'

Frankie frowned. 'Pardon? What foreign-looking chap?'

'Miss Paine saw him as well,' Mrs Dickenson went on. 'You remember her? She used to live the other side of you and your mum. She died a few months back. Anyway, he was wearing a funny shirt. Not like one I've seen before. It looked a bit like an old-fashioned night shirt, you know, with buttons up to the neck but no collar.'

'There was a lot of talk at the time about some Russian chap,' said Aunt Bet.

'The shirt sounds a bit like the sort of thing a Russian would wear,' said Frankie. She gave an involuntary shiver. He didn't sound like the sort of customer her mother usually had but there it was again. Russia. She recalled the story of the princess in London. But it was ridiculous. It was just a story. Wasn't it?

'My neighbour down the road swears she saw him too,' the old lady went on. 'She was waiting for the London train and she saw him get off the Littlehampton train on platform two.'

'So he must have travelled from London,' said Aunt Bet.

'I suppose he must.'

'Did you ever see him again?' asked Frankie.

Mrs Dickenson shook her head. The three of them sat in silence, each lost in her own thoughts. 'Of course you know who lives in your old place now, don't you?' Mrs Dickenson went on. 'Sidney Knight, your old landlord.'

'I know,' said Frankie. 'I came back when the war broke out and he shouted at me.'

'You never said,' Aunt Bet said.

'I shouldn't have been here.'

'What made you come?' Mrs Dickenson said.

'I wanted to smell Mum's roses.'

'He's let the place go to rack and ruin,' said Mrs Dickenson. 'The only time I've ever seen him do anything in the garden was to cut back that rose bush. Took it right to the ground, he did. Mind you, having said that it was a mass of blooms the next year.'

'Roses like a bit of pruning,' Aunt Bet remarked sagely.

'He never did anything else,' Mrs Dickenson muttered. 'There's a bloomin' tree growing out of the guttering round the back.'

'I thought he had one of those posh houses on High Salvington,' Aunt Bet exclaimed.

'He did, but he sold that soon after his dad died,' said Mrs Dickenson. 'Got a tidy sum for it too although I doubt there's much left. Sidney spends all of his money on sick horses.'

Puzzled, Frankie and her aunt glanced at each other. Mrs Dickenson cackled. 'They must be sick. They're nearly always last past the winning post.'

Frankie smiled.

'Of course, he's not here now,' Mrs Dickenson went on. 'He's having a holiday courtesy of His Majesty.'

Frankie raised her eyebrows. 'Eh?'

'She means he's in prison,' said Aunt Bet. 'What did he do?'

'Stole a charity box,' said Mrs Dickenson with a disgusted tone and the three of them tutted and shook their heads.

The tea was gone and Frankie and her aunt could see Mrs Dickenson was looking tired so they made their excuses.

'Before you go, my lass,' said Mrs Dickenson, handing her a pair of scissors, 'you go and cut that rose.'

171

'I can't,' said Frankie. 'It'd be stealing.'

'Who's to know?' said Mrs Dickenson. 'Besides, it's only dying on the twig, isn't it?'

Despite Aunt Bet's protestations that she would over-tire herself, they made their way back to the farm via Hillbarn with a couple of blooms from her mother's rose bush. The council had built that golf course her mother had talked about, but there was still plenty of space to walk. It was wonderful to enjoy the peace and quiet far away from the ravages of war. Back at the farm, Frankie put one of the roses between two sheets of paper and left it under a heavy book to dry out.

# Twenty-Six

**Central London, Thursday June 17th 1943**

Once Frankie was back on duty, the days seemed to merge into one another. There were periods of time when she and the other girls were stretched to the limit and the ravages of war had been relentless, but there were also periods of time when Frankie had been able to relax a little. Sometimes she wondered how they all kept going, but they did. She remembered the strict instructions Mr Hill had given her when she was in hospital and always made sure she kept a full water bottle, especially when she had to ride long distances with dispatches.

It had been almost a year since her collapse when Frankie was told to report to St George's hospital for a medical. Since her brief spell in hospital, the army wanted her to have yearly check-ups because they had given her a new experimental drug, something called penicillin, to combat the infection in her leg. St George's was one of the few hospitals which had remained in the capital. Places such as Charing Cross hospital and St Bart's had been relocated at the beginning of the war. She wasn't quite sure why she had been asked to attend, and she wasn't planning to go but Aunt Bet had persuaded her it would be no bad thing.

'The rest of us poor plebs,' she joked, 'have to pay for every darned thing. You get it for free. Make the most of it, girl. At least if there's something wrong with you they'll pick it up early.'

Her battery commander arranged for Frankie to spend two nights in digs in London so she travelled by train to the hospital. They took blood, her blood pressure, temperature and weighed her, then she saw the specialist. After a thorough examination, he declared her fit and she was free to go. It was a godsend because she had the rest of that day, and all of the next, before she had to catch the train back to Kent, so Frankie decided to make the most of it.

First she did a little window shopping in Oxford Street and Regent Street. She had a few coupons and although she couldn't afford anything, it was fun trying on dresses and hats at leisure. By five o'clock she was ready to catch the tube back to her digs. The train arrived and quite a lot of passengers got off but only a few got on. It was much less crowded now but Frankie had to stand. A man rose to his feet to offer her his seat. As she turned to thank him she blurted out 'Oh!' as she got the surprise of her life. It was Doctor Delaney, the American she had seen in the Deal and Walmer hospital.

He raised his hat and smiled. 'Nice to see you again. I trust you are well?'

Her heart was already fluttering. Fancy him remembering her. 'Yes, yes.' Her cheeks flushed. 'Er, I've just been to Charing Cross for a check-up.'

He seemed puzzled. 'Why would they send you to Charing Cross?'

Frankie shrugged and he laughed. The train jolted forward as she sat and he grabbed the strap above her head. As he swayed above her, Frankie could hardly breathe for the thought of him so close.

At the far end of the carriage she saw a man give a small boy aged about eight or nine a thick sandwich. The boy was obviously hungry because he could hardly get it down quick enough. She noticed the doctor's eye was drawn to them as well. The man and the child exchanged a grin then the man tousled his hair. Frankie guessed he must be the boy's father.

As the train rattled on, she saw the man move closer to another passenger. At first she thought it was just an accidental movement caused by a lurch of the train. But was it? Frankie was horrified to see the man slip the other passenger's wallet into his jacket pocket. Heavens above! He was a professional pickpocket.

What should she do? Frankie shifted her bottom to the edge of the seat as if to get up but at the same time she glanced up at the doctor. He shook his head slowly. She did wonder briefly why he'd done that and it dawned on her that if she drew attention to the incident on such a crowded train and people got angry in such a confined space, it could be dangerous. There was bound to be a kerfuffle, maybe a fight.

The thief may have noticed them looking because he decided to move further down the carriage. Tugging at his son's coat sleeve, he turned to leave but the boy began to choke. The man patted the boy's back. 'Choke up, chicken.' The boy was retching but still the sandwich was stuck. The man patted his back a little harder.

By now other passengers were beginning to take notice.

'Put him across my lap, Mister,' a large woman said.

The child was dumped across her knees and she began to pat his back vigorously. 'Johnny,' his father cried desperately as the boy continued to choke. 'Oh God, what can I do? Johnny, don't die. Breathe.'

The people around him were starting to panic. The boy was deathly white and breaking into a cold sweat.

'Hang 'im upside down,' someone shouted.

'Put yer finger in and get it out,' said another.

'Let me through,' Doctor Delaney interrupted. 'I'm a doctor.'

When he reached the boy, the child was already in a state of collapse. Frankie watched anxiously as he spun the lad around so that his back was against his stomach and grasping him firmly just above his waist, he jerked the boy hard. There was a retching sound but no more.

'What the 'ell is that black man doing,' the large lady cried. 'Make 'im stop. 'e'll hurt the little fellow.'

Before the boy's father could intervene, the doctor repeated the procedure and this time a large lump of soggy bread flew out from the boy's mouth and on to the carriage floor. The boy began to cry piteously. Frankie felt a wave of relief.

The atmosphere in the carriage completely changed. 'Well done.' 'Thank Gawd for that. I thought 'e was a goner.' 'You were amazing, doc.'

The boy's father was cradling his son. His eyes were filled with tears. He held out his hand towards the doctor. 'Bert Harper,' he said snatching off his cap and shaking the man's hand. 'I'm eternally indebted to you, sir.'

The doctor shook his head modestly.

'May I know your name, sir?'

'Delaney. Romare Delaney.'

Romare, thought Frankie, her admiration soaring. What a lovely name . . .

By now the boy was pink and breathing normally.

'I can never thank you enough, sir,' said Bert.

Romare looked directly into the man's eyes. 'I can't imagine how hard it must be to get off a train to find that something so important to you is missing.' And Frankie saw Bert's face pale.

The train was slowing again as Romare made his way back to his case on the floor. Frankie had tucked it closer to her leg to keep an eye on it when he went to help. People shook his hand or patted him on the back. As he reached his case, he smiled at Frankie as they both heard the pickpocket say, 'Excuse me, sir. I think you dropped your wallet.'

They looked back to see the bemused passenger thanking Bert profusely.

The train came to a halt and Frankie and the doctor stood to leave. Bert Harper and his son were just in front of them. The doors rumbled open and Romare stepped aside to let Frankie go first. As Romare stepped off the train, he and the boy's father exchanged a knowing smile. 'Thanks once again, Doc,' said Bert, as he and his son hurried off.

She and the doctor went up the escalator and reached the ticket barrier at the same time. Once through, he suddenly turned to Frankie. 'I know it's probably not what you English people do,' he began, 'but can I offer you a drink?'

Frankie was surprised – pleasantly so – but at the same time she was struck dumb.

'I'm sorry,' he said, raising his hat. 'Please excuse me.'

'No, no,' cried Frankie. 'I would love to have a drink.'

The station tea rooms was closing so he escorted her towards the pub across the street and they went into the lounge bar. Frankie asked for a sherry.

'Mr Hill, the consultant, said you had brought some donated blood to this country,' said Frankie, uncertain how to begin the conversation.

He put her sherry down on the table in front of her and nodded. 'That was my privilege, yes, but it wasn't just blood. It was blood plasma.'

Frankie was confused. 'So what's that?'

'Plasma is one of the components of blood. I've been working with a man called Doctor Drew. He's heading up an exciting programme which is saving a lot of lives.'

'But we already have donated blood here,' said Frankie.

'Doctor Drew has developed a way of separating plasma from blood cells,' Delaney continued. He drank from his beer glass then put it onto the small table in between them. 'Once separated, the plasma goes through a process to remove any contamination and it's tested for bacteria, before it's put into shipping containers.'

'Sounds complicated,' Frankie said.

Romare Delaney smiled. 'Doctor Drew's efforts mean that blood can be carried over long distances and still be safe to use.'

Frankie nodded, impressed. 'I see.'

'It also lasts a lot longer as well.'

They stopped talking to watch a pianist settle down at the piano and start to play. The landlord put a pint of brown ale on the upturned lid and the familiar notes of Artie Shaw's 'Stardust' filled the smoky blue air.

As it finished, Frankie leaned forward. 'So if there was a battle,' she said, suddenly very interested, 'your blood plasma should make it possible to save a lot more lives.'

'Sure,' said Doctor Delaney.

'We've been hearing a lot about the "Blood for Britain" campaign,' Frankie said tentatively.

'That's part of it,' said the doctor. 'We collected fifteen thousand units and I was given the opportunity to travel here by plane as a representative of the American Red Cross.'

'That's amazing,' Frankie gasped.

The pianist was playing 'You'll never know'.

Delaney smiled. 'And you? What have you been doing, Miss Sherwood?

'I'm a dispatch rider,' she said. 'I'm in the ATS which is part of the British army; and the name is Frankie.'

'Frankie,' he said, a smile tugging at his lips.

'Actually it's Frances Sherwood, but everyone calls me Frankie.'

'Then I'm delighted to meet you, Frankie Sherwood.' His

eyes lingered on hers, then he said, 'I don't get to see many dames doing your kind of job back home.'

I bet you don't, she thought. The war had changed a lot of attitudes towards women and their capabilities. 'Will you be over here for long?'

'Just a few months. At the moment I'm in no hurry to go back,' he confessed. 'Despite the war, I like it here. You Britishers are pretty nice people.'

Frankie laughed. 'I'm glad to hear it.' She paused. 'You haven't had any problems about your colour then?' The second the words were out of her mouth she regretted them. 'I'm sorry, sorry. I shouldn't have said . . .'

'No, no,' he said. 'That's fine and the answer is some, but not like it is back home.'

She looked away, embarrassed.

'Back in the States the Red Cross still excludes coloured Americans from giving blood, so although Doctor Drew and I are pioneers we can't donate our own blood.'

'But surely there's no difference,' Frankie protested. 'Blood is blood, isn't it?'

Doctor Delaney shrugged. 'They have the data.'

An angry heat swelled in Frankie's veins. 'So what happens if a coloured soldier needs this blood?' she said crossly.

'That's our next battle,' said Doctor Delaney with a concerned frown as they paused to applaud the piano player.

It was pleasant being in his company and when he offered to buy her a meal, Frankie didn't refuse. The pub only served sandwiches so they went in search of somewhere else before finding a small café about a quarter of a mile away.

They were about halfway through their meal when the air raid sirens went off.

'Sounds like the buggers have started again,' said the waiter. 'I thought we were done with all that.'

It was true. Since May 1941 the number of bombs dropped on the capital had diminished rapidly. There had been sporadic raids but London itself had enjoyed a period of calm. An ARP stuck his head through the open door. 'Come on, ladies and gents; let's be having you.' And that meant everyone, including the café owner, had to go to the nearest air raid shelter. As he was hustled towards the door, the doctor stuffed a couple of notes in the proprietor's hand. The man seemed surprised. 'Thanks, mate.'

They could hear the first of the bombs falling as they hurried down the stairs of the shelter but Frankie wasn't at all afraid, not with this lovely man beside her. She turned to give him a smile.

'You know, I'm getting used to air raid shelters and the bombs,' he said as they found a space to sit on the floor together. 'It's all very sad because I've even developed a taste for tea and warm beer.'

Frankie laughed.

Somewhere further down the platform, a lone harmonica was playing. Romare took off his coat to lay it on the tiled floor and when Frankie sat, he slid down beside her. Before long, the platform grew noisy as it filled up. People who had obviously done this many, many times before arrived with extra clothing, rolled mattresses, blankets and pillows. Families bagged places together and settled down with their flasks of tea and paper bags of sandwiches. A lady with a Red Cross badge on her coat offered them an army blanket to sit on and Romare took it gratefully. Where the wind whistled down from the tunnel it was cold. He put his coat back on and they sat on the blanket.

'Hey, you,' someone called out. 'You look like that Paul Robeson fella. Can you sing one of them spirituals?'

'Ooh, yes please, Mister,' a plump middle-aged woman cried after him. 'I love them songs.'

Romare shook his head in disbelief. 'I'm no concert singer,

Ma'am,' he apologised politely. 'My only singing back home is done in church or maybe my bath tub.'

She chuckled. 'But perhaps you might make an exception for us? It would help to sooth the kiddies to sleep.'

Romare shifted himself awkwardly. Frankie glared at the woman indignantly.

A modest man, Romare would have refused if it weren't for the little boy huddled close to his parents nearby. More to soothe the child than anything else, he allowed himself to be persuaded and rose to his feet. A moment later, the sound of his beautiful bass baritone voice drifted through the chilly station. The people on the platform were spell-bound.

*Oooh sometimes it causes me to tremble, tremble, tremble . . .*

Frankie relaxed and leaned against the wall. Closing her eyes, she drank in the moment. *Were you there when he rose up from the tomb . . .*

Romare glanced down at her and as his eye met hers; it was as if everyone else had faded away and he was singing only to her. As he finished his song, there was a round of enthusiastic applause.

'Sing us another one,' someone cried.

Romare gave them a slight bow. 'Last one, okay?'

For a second he paused, trying to think of something suitable and then he remembered a song his mother sang when he was a child and tired from working in the fields, so to the delight of his audience but mostly for her, he sang.

*Oh Shenandoah, I love your daughter*
*'way you rolling river,*
*for her I'd cross the foaming water . . .*
*'cross the wide Missouri . . .*

As his song drew to a close, there were tears in Frankie's eyes. The crowd applauded again and Romare lowered himself to the floor beside her.

'You have an amazing voice,' she said. 'Where did you learn to sing like that?'

Romare smiled; his eyes had a far-away look. 'In the cotton fields,' he said. 'We sang to move the day along.'

'Sounds like hard work,' she remarked. 'How old were you?'

'I worked in the fields from the age of eight,' he said. 'By the time I was nine I could pick a bag of cotton weighing a hundred pounds.'

Frankie took in a breath. 'So how did you move from the cotton fields to being a doctor?' she asked incredulously.

'I was lucky,' he said simply. 'My teacher, Thelma-Mae Thomson, gave me extra lessons and I won a scholarship.'

'You are amazing,' Frankie gasped.

'My friends and family were the amazing ones,' he said. 'I took on extra jobs, but the folks at church raised funds and took up a collection and my family scrimped and saved. My daddy even sold his old truck to get me the railroad fare and when I was seventeen I went to Washington DC to get me an education.'

Further down the platform, the harmonica player had moved on to the more popular music and an impromptu sing-song began. They didn't sing at the tops of their voices as in the concert halls but quietly, so that it sounded like a gentle hum. Everyone was aware that mothers were trying to get their children to sleep. Tunes such as 'Roll out the Barrel', 'We'll Meet Again' and 'Lili Marlene' drifted through the cold air and despite the distant thuds as the bombs fell, Frankie felt her head sagging towards his shoulder. It was hard to keep her eyes open.

# *Twenty-Seven*

**Lewes Prison, Friday June 18th 1943**

Sidney Knight felt awkward dressed in his own suit. It had been more than a year since he'd put it on and back then it had fitted quite well. Since he'd been in prison, he'd lost a lot of weight. The place was damp and he'd developed a bit of a cough.

'Stand in line,' the guard said gruffly.

Sidney shuffled towards the other prisoners waiting to be released. There were eight of them altogether. They'd been inside for different things – theft, wounding with intent, affray, fraud – and they'd all had different sentences – eighteen months, four years, two months, two years – but today they-shared a common release date. Sid had completed a two-year sentence with a year off for good behaviour. It was a stiff sentence for just a few quid but the judge had taken a dim view of stealing from the less fortunate.

The small door of the prison was opened and everyone filed outside. The other ex-cons had people to meet them. Sidney was on his own but he didn't mind. All he wanted was to get back home. He had to check nobody had been snooping around his place. Since he'd been inside he'd had had a couple of nightmares. In his dreams the girl had come to the house looking for her mother. In that strange way things work in dreams, he tried to tell her Moira wasn't there but she kept running up the stairs. He was right behind her but he couldn't catch her before she'd opened the attic door. Her terrified scream would wake him and he'd be in a cold sweat. Now that he was on the outside, he couldn't wait to check everything was all right.

Sidney had enough in his pocket for the train fare home and a beer once he got there but as he walked towards the station, he passed a billboard saying, *Ascot Gold Cup today.*

His heart fluttered. Which horse was the favourite? If Owen Tudor was running, he'd back it. The three-year-old had won the New Derby in 1941 and of the eleven times he'd raced, he'd come in first in five of them. Sidney had planned to go straight to the station but now he looked around for a bookie.

# Twenty-Eight

**London, Friday June 18th 1943**

Although exhausted from lack of proper sleep, when the ARP wardens deemed it safe to leave the shelter, Romare and Frankie walked to the top together. The streets were silent in the eerie half-light of morning, but the air smelled of smoke and dust, and cordite filled the air. Someone somewhere had had a pasting.

'I need to get back to St George's hospital in case I am needed,' he told her. 'You go home and get some sleep. Do you know Speakers' Corner? I'll do my best to meet you there at three or I'll get a message to you. Okay?'

'Okay,' she said smiling.

Frankie did as he said and slept until her alarm woke her at lunch time. Being a week day, the crowds at Speakers' Corner weren't too large and before long she spotted him coming towards her. He looked so handsome her heart skipped a beat.

They wandered around listening to the speakers for a while. There was nothing very inspiring, although some of the hecklers made their rhetoric amusing. In the distance, they saw the famous Tony Turner, a man dubbed the Thunderous Voice of Socialism. He was talking about equality for women in society, something which made Frankie prick up her ears. 'Listen to what I say,' he boomed, to which a heckler retorted, 'Whatever you say, keep your mouth shut.'

She and Romare turned towards Hyde Park and strolled along the pathways. It had changed since the onset of the war because some of the park was given over to allotments in an effort to help feed the nation. It struck Frankie as a miracle that the vegetables were still growing and nobody had stolen them.

'Tell me about your childhood,' Romare said. They walked side by side, their hands only touching briefly now and then. Each time she felt his fingers brush hers, Frankie's heart leapt. 'What does your father do?'

'My father died when I was a year old,' she began, 'and I lost my mother when I was ten.'

He looked at her, stricken. 'Oh gee honey, I'm so sorry.'

'It's all right,' she assured him with a shrug. 'It's just the way life turns out sometimes, isn't it?'

'What happened to your mom?'

So she told him. She told him about her birthday tea on Hillbarn and the doll her mother had made. She told him about coming home from school to find the ambulance outside the door. She told him about Aunt Bet and Uncle Lorry, and Alan and Ronald, taking her in. She told him about the scramble races and the florist shop and eventually joining up. 'I was always motorcycle mad,' she said. 'That's why I joined the ATS. When I heard that chap saying women should be able to do the same things as men he's quite right. Do you know once I came second in a race but I was disqualified just because I was a girl!'

They had reached the Serpentine and he stopped walking. Frankie felt her face flush.

'You're real fiery, ain't you,' he said, a small smile tugging at his lips.

186

'I'm sorry,' she said. 'I know I shouldn't go on like that. It's just that it makes me so cross, the unfairness of it all.'

'Don't apologise, honey,' he said. 'I like a woman with spunk.'

They resumed their walk. 'What about you?' she asked. 'You told me about your family and the church helping you but was it hard becoming a doctor?'

'For a black man like me? Yes. I went to the Howard HBCU.'

'HCB . . .?' she began.

'H-B-C-U,' he corrected. 'Historically Black College University.'

'So you had to go to a school just for black people?' Frankie squeaked.

'That's right,' he said.

Frankie felt her hackles rise again. 'But that's awful!'

Romare chuckled. 'That's the way it is in the States, honey. Black folks don't mix with white folks. If we were back home right now I'd be whipped for standing so close to you and I could never ask a white girl on a date.'

Frankie gaped in disbelief.

'Anyway, you asked about my schooling,' he went on. 'My Uncle Lemuel had a shop in Washington DC and I needed somewhere to live while I was doing my studies. All I had to do was help out in the store.'

'So how long were you there?'

'My uncle took sick so I had to take a back seat for a year,' said Romare. Frankie slipped her hand in his and gave it a squeeze. 'We all knew he wasn't going to survive. He had no family of his own, so during the Fall of 1934 my family joined us.'

'That was nice,' she said.

'Yup,' he said. 'After nearly half a century apart, my daddy and my uncle had a few precious months together before Uncle Lemuel died.'

The atmosphere had become tinged with sadness. 'But it wasn't all bad,' he added quickly. 'My uncle's two shops became four and daddy was very popular. As for me, I had time to devote myself to my studies.'

They were walking towards a WVS van which served teas. Romare bought them a cup each and they sat on a nearby bench to drink them.

'I have enjoyed my time with you, Frankie,' he said as they resumed their walk. 'Is it possible I could see you again?'

'I should like that, Romare,' she whispered. 'I should like that very much.'

# Twenty-Nine

**North Farm, September 1943**

September found Frankie home again with a magical seven-day pass. She was so exhausted, her first few hours were virtually 'wasted'. She woke at eight thirty, a lie-in as far as she was concerned. Normally she woke at 6am to the sound of the National Anthem being played over the tannoy system and the squad corporal bursting into the room to chivvy them all out of bed. After fifteen minutes of PE exercises outside, even in the dead of winter, it was back to the hut to get washed, dressed and tidy her bed before breakfast at eight. The army didn't give anyone time to think.

Behind the blackout curtain of her bedroom, her window was slightly ajar. Frankie lay in bed listening to the comforting sounds of the farm. The geese had gone but the chickens still scratched and clucked contentedly in the yard. She remembered dear old Loopy-Lu who had been such a comfort to her when she'd come here as a child. She'd lasted several years beyond normal chicken life but only because nobody had had the heart to serve her up for Sunday lunch, not even when she'd stopped laying. She'd always been fiercely independent and that was to be her undoing. Old and arthritic, she steadfastly refused to be locked into the hen house at night and the time came when she wasn't quite quick enough. One evening, the fox got her on her way to her favourite roosting place in the old tree behind the hen house. It was a sad end but Frankie was comforted by the fact that she had enjoyed her life and far outlived her sisters.

There were only three ducks left on the pond. One had been last year's Christmas dinner and the others had been picked off by gypsies or scared away by a stray bomb.

Today the sun was shining. She could see its borderline at the side of the curtain. It would have been wonderful to spend some time with Romare but he had been seconded to a hospital in Manchester. He'd also joined the American army and because he was already a doctor and they had a grave shortage of black doctors, he was given the honorary title of Lieutenant.

Something thudded onto the small paved area under her window and a few seconds later, she heard the ratchet of the mangle as Aunt Bet prepared her washing for the line. Frankie stretched and yawned luxuriantly. She supposed she'd better get up.

She heard a footfall and someone struck a match. Her aunt stopped turning the handle and said, 'You all right, son?'

For a second Frankie had forgotten that her cousin was home on leave too. He was on a six-day pass. It was purely coincidental but nice for Aunt Bet to have them both. Sadly, Alan hadn't been much company. The medics had declared him fit for duty but he was far from the man she knew. The trouble was, he looked perfectly well. He'd manage normal duties for a month or two then the same old trouble would start all over again. Morose and bad tempered, he'd already upset both his parents by the time Frankie arrived. She heard his grunted reply.

'Why don't you go for a walk or something, son,' Aunt Bet said. 'It'll do you good.'

'For God's sake, mother,' he snapped. 'Will you give it a bloody rest. Nag, nag, nag. You're driving me crazy.'

Frankie sat up as the door slammed and he went back in the

house. What could they do? The army had tried everything. The softly, softly approach, the hard work with no time to think approach, long periods in the glasshouse for insubordination, and punishment regimes – but he remained totally out of control.

Her eye drifted towards the drawer where she'd kept the princess doll hidden away for so long and a germ of an idea stole into her mind. When she arrived downstairs, she was wearing her old overalls.

Alan was sitting at the kitchen table smoking his third cigarette. He barely acknowledged her as she walked in. There was a basin of dripping in the middle of the kitchen table. Frankie picked it up and looked closely. There was still a wedge of beef jelly juices at the bottom.

'Ooh, delicious,' she said.

She made herself some tea and put a slice of bread under the grill. She made no attempt to engage in conversation with Alan. She could easily guess the reaction if she did. The smell of warm toast filled the kitchen. When it was done, she stuck the knife into the dripping, scooping some of the brown liquid onto her toast. One mouthful sent her into ecstasies of delight. She had been right. It was delicious.

When she'd finished, she cleared away her plate and cup and saucer and headed for the back door.

'Where are you off to?' Alan said at last.

'The barn,' she said as she began closing the door behind her. 'To look at the bikes.'

She'd only been in there about twenty minutes when he strolled through the door. She didn't acknowledge him but she couldn't resist a small smile. She'd known he wouldn't be able to leave her here alone. He'd have to stick his nose in. So far, so good. The plan was working.

\*

When Bet had finished putting the washing out, she came back to the house, calling as she went. The kitchen was empty. Upstairs, Frankie's bed was made and her room neat and tidy. Alan's room resembled a doss house. It took a while to create some semblance of order: making the bed, folding discarded clothes, emptying the ash tray and the overflowing chamber pot. She was really worried. What had happened to the cheerful chappie she'd always known? Alan was no shrinking violet. As a boy he'd got into any number of scrapes but they were mostly harmless pranks. The only really serious thing he'd got into trouble for was experimenting with an old stirrup pump he'd found somewhere. She hadn't been too pleased when he'd put one end into a muddy puddle and aimed the other end at the postman. The postman hadn't been too pleased either, but when the dust had settled Lorry had just laughed and said, 'Boys will be boys.' These days, Alan was in much deeper trouble. If he wasn't picking a fight, he was smashing glasses in a pub or losing a day's pay for refusing to obey an order. Her son had been locked up in more cells than she could remember. When would it all end? She had a terrible dread that by the time the war was over, her rudderless boy would be beyond salvation.

She heard the back door open and called out again. There was no answer so she hurried downstairs. The back door was closed again and Alan's army trousers were in a heap on the floor. The overalls he usually left on the hook behind the door had gone. Bet walked down the path towards the barn. She could hear voices.

'I've already removed all the spark plugs,' Frankie said. 'They're clean.'

'Then the carburettor must be clogged up with old petrol,' said Alan.

'Already sorted that too,' said Frankie.

'Did you look at the jets and gaskets?'

'Why do I need to do that?'

'You should remember that, you daft mare,' said Alan. 'I used to explain it to you often enough.'

Outside the door, Bet held her breath. He wasn't going to lose his temper with Frankie, was he? Frankie didn't reply.

'Sometimes the gaskets get brittle, remember?' said Alan, his tone a little less exasperated.

'Oh yes,' said Frankie. 'That's right. I might need to rebuild them.' Another pause.

'Well, go on then.'

'Okay, okay, keep your hair on.'

Bet turned around and made her way back to the house. God bless you, Frankie, she thought. I bet you knew what you were doing all along. This is the first time in a very long time that Alan has thrown himself into anything that isn't to do with drink and fighting.

Frankie was enjoying herself. She always liked to be around the bikes and this one, a Richman JAP Scrambler, had been a particularly enjoyable ride. Laid up for the duration, it was in a sorry state. The shiny chrome tank was covered in grime and pitted with rust. Alan was at the other end of the barn tinkering with one of his old machines. They worked together in companionable silence and she lost all track of time until she saw Aunt Bet slip in with a plate of doorstep sandwiches and two mugs of steaming tea.

'Thought you might be peckish,' she said as their eyes met.

As her aunt hurried off, Frankie pulled up an old wooden crate and an empty oil drum. Wiping her hands on an old rag, she called, 'Biggest is mine.'

Alan looked up and grinned. He always used to say that to her when she first came to live with them. He was only teasing of course and his father would give him a playful cuff on the shoulder as he said, 'You have whatever you likes, girlie. It's all the same.'

They ate in silence until Alan said, 'So how are you doing in the ATS?'

Frankie shrugged. 'All right, I guess.' Obviously the next thing was to ask him about the army but Frankie knew how touchy he was about that. 'I never did thank you for helping me as a child,' she said, keeping her eyes on her feet. 'I could never have got through it without you.'

He slurped his tea noisily.

'I blamed myself, you see.'

He nodded. 'I remember.'

There was a pause, then she said, 'And you're doing the same.'

'Frankie,' he said, 'don't.'

'He had a wife, didn't he? Why don't you go and see her?'

Alan looked up. 'And why would I want to do that?'

'It might help her.'

A frown crossed his brow and she could tell she'd taken him by surprise. He was expecting her to say, it might help *you*.

He looked away. 'She lives in Suffolk.'

'So?' Frankie challenged. 'I'll come with you if you like. You've got four days of leave left. I've got five.'

He rose to his feet, his back to her as he put the mug back onto the bench. 'I can't just drop in. She isn't on the phone.'

'I'll drop her a line and get it in tonight's post,' said Frankie. 'We can go the day after tomorrow.'

He walked back to the bike he was working on. 'Better get this finished then.'

*

The next day, Frankie took the opportunity to catch up with Barbara. Since she'd given up the NAAFI, she'd got a job at the telephone exchange at Goring. Her shifts meant that

Frankie was able to meet her in a small café along the Goring Road. Barbara had lost weight but she looked well. There was a lot of catching up to do and it seemed an age since they'd been together.

While they waited for the cottage pie they'd ordered, Barbara was fascinated to hear about Frankie's travels. 'I admire you so much,' she said. 'Once you made up your mind to something there was no stopping you.'

Embarrassed, Frankie said, 'I never got around to asking you, did your aunt recover?'

For a second Barbara hesitated then said, 'Oh yes, ages ago.'

Frankie smiled. 'How are your parents?'

'Okay,' Barbara answered with a shrug. 'I still live with mum and Derek. Dad joined up as soon as the war started. He only just got in. Another year and he would have been too old. He's in Italy somewhere. Mum hates it.'

Frankie nodded grimly. So many families had been ripped apart by the war.

Their meagre meals arrived with a plate of bread and butter. When the waitress left, Frankie said, 'Alan is back home on leave.'

'I heard he was ill,' said Barbara. 'Is he all right now?'

'Yes and no,' said Frankie. 'He's back in the army but he's not the Alan we knew. Whatever happened at Dunkirk changed him.'

'Poor Alan,' said Barbara. 'I'm sorry to hear that. I liked him. I liked him a lot.'

The mood had become sombre. 'I've met someone,' said Frankie recalling how excited Aunt Bet had been when she'd told her all about Romare the night she got back home. 'An American doctor.'

'Oh Frankie, that's wonderful. Are we going to meet him?'

'I don't know,' said Frankie suddenly feeling coy. 'It's early days yet. Have you got a new sweetheart?'

Barbara chuckled. 'I'm still Conrad's girl. I know you didn't like him much but he truly is the most wonderful man. He's with ENSA at the moment entertaining the troops but after the war he's going to Hollywood. He's going to be famous one day, I just know it.'

'He still writes then?'

Barbara looked a bit uncomfortable. 'They rush from place to place,' she said, 'and it's hard for the mail to get through. I write to him every week and I'm sure he'll drop me a line when he gets time.'

The waitress came back to clear away their empty plates. 'Pudding?'

Both girls shook their heads but opted for a cup of tea. 'Fancy coming to the pictures with me?' Frankie asked.

'I'll have to ask mum,' Barbara said dully. 'She needs a bit of help with our Derek. He can be a bit of a handful at times. Now tell me a bit more about this American doctor.'

# Thirty

The train was late. They'd set out in the early morning hoping to reach Suffolk by lunch time. The change from Victoria to Euston went well but the Cambridge train was delayed by a troop train. Alan became irritable and agitated. He was already chain smoking and Frankie had a dread that he would suddenly decide he would prefer to go back home. Their destination was a small market town about fourteen miles from Cambridge called Haverhill. They finally arrived just after two and, if she was honest, Frankie was relieved that the journey was over. Alan kept saying he needed a drink but the time of day meant all the pubs would be shut. They had an address and the locals were friendly enough but they struggled with the strong Suffolk accent when they asked for directions.

The house was a Victorian terrace and a middle-aged woman opened the door when they knocked. 'Oh come in, come in, my dears,' she cried. 'Carrie is waiting for you.'

They stepped straight into the sitting room of the cool cottage. The door was open and they saw an attractive young woman sitting at the kitchen table beyond. She had a pale face with neat brown hair rolled at the sides in the fashionable style being adopted all over the country. She was dressed in a plain white blouse with a pretty brooch at the neck and a floral skirt. She rose to greet them. She and Alan lingered over their introductory hand shake, then they all sat. The older woman, Mrs Dale – Carrie's mother – busied herself with the tea pot. While they made the usual chit-chat about the journey and where they'd come from Carrie pulled a tea towel from a plate of sandwiches in the middle of the table and invited them to help themselves. Frankie was very grateful. She was starving.

They drank tea and ate sandwiches until they were interrupted by the sound of a child crying. Carrie excused herself and left the room. While she was gone, Alan leaned towards her mother. 'I've no wish to offend you, Mrs Dale,' he began, 'but Ginger was a very special mate of mine and we made a pact, see? We promised each other if one of us copped it, the other one would look out for his family.'

'That's very nice of you, son,' she said, 'but there's no need.'

'All the same,' Alan insisted, 'I promised.'

The door opened and Carrie walked in carrying a little boy. He was a sturdy little fellow with bright ginger curls and a mass of ginger freckles on his cheeks. He rubbed his eyes sleepily. 'This is Billy,' she said. 'Say hello, Billy.'

Alan grinned. 'Well, I can see he's Ginger's all right.'

The little boy struggled to get down, and with one cautious eye on Alan, he reached for his toy box. Frankie was surprised to see her cousin kneel beside the lad and the two of them spent some time lining up his toy cars.

Eventually Carrie said, 'Can you tell me something about how Ginger died?'

For a second, Frankie froze. How was Alan going to cope with that? She decided he might do better if he spoke to Carrie alone. Alan nodded but before he began, Frankie interrupted. 'Mrs Dale, I couldn't help noticing your lovely garden . . .'

Mrs Dale looked from her daughter to Alan and back again. 'Shall we take Billy out for a breath of fresh air?' she suggested.

The garden wasn't that big but Billy couldn't wait to get in his pedal car. Frankie and Mrs Dale sat together on an old wooden seat. 'I'm so glad you came, my dear,' she said. 'It's been very hard for Carrie losing Ginger.' She jumped up when Billy got one wheel stuck at the edge of the path. 'She'd known him all of her life,' Mrs Dale went on as she sat back down. 'They grew up together; sat next to each other at school. There hadn't been a day they weren't with each other until this blessed war came along. She was broken-hearted when we got the telegram.'

'Alan felt the same,' Frankie confided. 'He had a breakdown and was in hospital for some time. I was only a kid when my mother died and I went to live with my aunt, his mother. He's been like a brother to me and it hurt so much when he seemed to lose his way.'

'I wasn't sure when he mentioned helping out,' said Mrs Dale. 'We don't want charity, you know.'

'I know,' said Frankie, 'but I think it would help Alan as much as you.' Mrs Dale looked as if she was considering the matter. 'You could always save it for Billy,' Frankie suggested. 'Keep it as a little nest egg for later on.'

Mrs. Dale smiled. 'All right. Then that's what we'll do.'

When they went back into the kitchen Alan and Carrie were holding hands over the table. It was obvious they'd both been crying but Frankie and Mrs Dale said nothing.

On the trains back to London and on to Worthing, Alan was very quiet but Frankie could see the visit had had a profound effect on him. He only smoked three cigarettes all the way.

*

When she got back to the farm there was a letter from Doreen on the mantelpiece. '*By the time you read this I shall be on board ship,*' she wrote. '*I can't tell you where but I shall be plotting like mad. It's wonderful to be a fully-fledged Wren, although I did get teased a lot. I can't tell you the number of times I was sent to find the keys for Davy Jones' locker or some red oil for the port lights, but I shan't be fooled again. When I get some leave we must get together again.'*

Frankie smiled to herself. Good old Doreen.

'Ooh, before I forget, Barbara came round,' said Aunt Bet. 'She'll meet you outside the Odeon at five-thirty tomorrow night.'

*

The last night of her leave had come around all too quickly so it was nice to be spending time with an old friend. She met Barbara outside the cinema and they saw *The Magnificent Ambersons*, a lavish tale of an American family spanning three generations. It was still early when they came out of the cinema so they went into a fish and chip shop nearby. Sitting on a bench overlooking the barbed-wired beach, they enjoyed their cod and chips out of newspaper and chatted about nothing in particular, although Frankie's mind drifted back to the film now and then. She wondered what Romare would have made of it.

'Frankie, I want to tell you something,' Barbara said as she came back to the bench having chucked the newspaper into a bin. 'But I have to know that you won't breathe a word to a living soul.'

'Of course.'

Barbara took a deep breath. 'Derek isn't my brother, he's my baby.'

Frankie gripped her friend's hand, which was resting in her lap. 'I know.'

Barbara's eyes grew wide. 'But how? Who told you?'

'Nobody,' said Frankie.

'Then how?' Barbara repeated. 'We've been so careful.'

'That time I came to see you,' said Frankie, 'when your mum said you'd gone to your auntie's, I saw the bedroom curtains moving. I guessed you were there.'

Barbara seemed anxious. 'You didn't tell anyone, did you?'

Frankie shook her head. 'No.'

Barbara looked down. 'Mum said she wanted me to have another chance. She said if I told anyone Derek was mine she'd have the baby adopted.'

'So she pretended she was the one who was pregnant and that you'd gone away,' said Frankie.

Barbara nodded. 'I spent six months hiding in my bedroom.'

'But it was a pretty wonderful thing to do,' Frankie remarked.

'Was it?' Barbara said darkly.

Frankie looked at her in surprise.

'Oh Frankie,' Barbara blurted out. 'I feel like she's stolen him from me. I'm not allowed to touch him or play with him in case I give the game away. She won't let me out at night because she says I can't be trusted. I'm only here now because she knows I'm with you.'

'I'm sorry,' Frankie gasped. 'I had no idea.'

'I can't tell anyone because she lied to the authorities as well. Derek's birth certificate says she's his mother. If I tell, she'll go to prison.'

Frankie didn't know what to say. 'But you couldn't support him on your own even if you could put it right.'

'But he's *my* baby!' Barbara cried desperately. She began to sob. Frankie put her arm around her friend's shoulders and drew her close. Why was Barbara telling her all this? Did Derek's birth somehow impact her own family? She thought back to that time when Barbara was going out with Alan before he joined up, and her blood ran cold.

'Tell me,' she began hesitantly, 'is the baby Alan's?'

'Of course not,' Barbara sniffed into her handkerchief. 'Alan and I were finished long before I fell pregnant.' She took a gulp of air. 'Derek is Conrad's baby.'

Frankie felt a wave of relief. 'And how does he feel about it? Have you told him?'

'I've written loads of times but like I said, he's all over the place and you know what the post is like these days.'

Or maybe he doesn't want to know, Frankie thought to herself. 'Well, you can't do much about it until Conrad comes home,' she said, fully aware that she was offering little comfort.

Barbara sat up and dried her eyes. 'I just had to tell someone or I'd burst.'

'Your secret is safe with me,' said Frankie.

# *Thirty-One*

## Winterbourne Whitechurch, Blandford, Dorset, Christmas 1943

The war dragged on right through 1943. There were moments when peace seemed just around the corner but it never came. Frankie, like so many others, heard of friends dying, or being maimed for life and others being taken prisoner. Arlene, the girl who had made them all laugh when she told them she'd confused a man's penis with his pencil, was killed when her battery took a direct hit and Peggy, the girl who had been so terrified of getting pregnant, left the service because she had to get married!

Frankie kept up her letter writing to Alan but he didn't reply often. However, she could tell by the tone of his letters that he was feeling a lot more settled. He hadn't been in trouble at all since they'd taken that trip to Suffolk. Ronald was enjoying his new life as well. He wrote of concerts and long discussions far into the night. He said nothing about his job and she didn't press him for information. She knew that when he'd gone to Bletchley Park, Ronald had signed the Official Secrets Act and was therefore bound by law not to discuss his work. Barbara wrote every now and then and Frankie tried to be as sympathetic as possible without actually saying anything. She didn't put it past Mrs Vickers to read her daughter's letters. Other than that, there was little Frankie could do. Mrs Vickers kept her daughter and grandson as far away from each other as possible and, to add insult to injury, when Barbara's father, who had escaped from a POW camp, arrived home, he was delighted to have a son at last. Conrad still hadn't been in touch and Frankie was of the opinion he never would be. The man was a complete rotter but the sad thing was, Barbara was the only one who couldn't see it.

The letters Frankie looked forward to most were the ones from Romare. They had corresponded regularly since their last meeting and she enjoyed his long, chatty missives. They'd managed a few dates as well. Nothing exciting, but it was so good just to be with him. They went to the pictures in Dover whenever he came down on the train, or to a show in London – a grateful patient paid for the seats – and a couple of times they'd managed a drive around Hastings and Eastbourne when a friend loaned him his car for the day. It always had to be last minute, but that made it all the more fun.

It didn't take long for Frankie to realise that she was falling in love and she was reasonably sure that Romare felt the same. She counted the days, sometimes the hours, before they would be together again and she made no secret of the fact that she wanted to be with him more. When they were apart, he was never far from her thoughts.

On leave, footloose and fancy-free, Doreen turned up to visit Frankie. The girls in Frankie's billet made room for her but they had to sneak her in past the landlady. Frankie was now based in the Blandford Forum area. As the troops massed all along the south coast ready for what was called 'the big push', she had been moved from Kent, to Poole in Dorset, and now on to Blandford. Her duties as dispatch rider took her as far west as Weymouth and she often escorted huge convoys of lorries from Southampton to places she'd never even heard of.

Doreen and Frankie had a lot of catching up to do and chatted far into the night.

'There's a dance at the village hall in Winterbourne Whitechurch tomorrow night,' Frankie told her. 'Fancy it?'

'Rather,' said Doreen.

It was wonderful to be able to dress up again. So many of her outings were in uniform but on this occasion Frankie got the glad rags out. They set out with a few other girls in an old jeep. The journey was only about five miles but it was freezing. They had their big coats on but the jeep was open to the elements. Still, nobody really cared. The hall was a new one, only finished in 1937, so it was light and airy. When they walked in, the place was heaving with American GIs. There was a small wooden stage at one end of the hall where the locals had made up a seven-piece band. They were brilliant and played all the modern tunes.

Despite the ambience of the place, the atmosphere in the hall was a little tense. It seemed that the white Americans objected to being in the same hall as the black GIs. They were refusing to mix with them and judging by the rude remarks they were making, they held their fellow countrymen in complete contempt. That didn't bode well with the organisers, probably because of the British sense of fair play and love of the under-dog. Added to that, the black soldiers were more popular with the local girls because they were much better dancers, especially when it came to the jitter-bug. Frankie admired the dance but ducked out of it, making the need to guard her non-alcoholic punch her excuse. On the other hand, Doreen was having a high old time. As Frankie watched her being flung in the air showing a mixture of suspenders and stocking top (oh, where did she get hold of them?) and the occasional glimpse of knicker, she wondered what the leaders of Doreen's mother's church would think of her now.

'Dance?'

Frankie looked up to see the three chevrons of a US staff sergeant on the sleeve of the man in front of her. She accepted his hand and he led her to the dance floor while the band played a more sedate fox trot.

Her partner was a big man with a shaved head on a thick weight lifter's neck. He had small eyes and large jowls. He was not very good-looking; in fact the only striking thing about him was a ring which he wore on his right hand; a snake with red ruby eyes eating its own tail. He said his name was Lyman Spinks and he came from New Orleans. Hardly letting her get a word in edgeways, he boasted that since being called up, he had risen quickly through the ranks because he was so good at his job. He told her he was in the military police and men feared him. When she managed to speak, she asked him how he liked England. He laughed and criticised the quaint things he'd come across. He hated warm beer, the outside toilets, the old-fashioned bathrooms and the lack of refrigerators. 'You Britishers,' he declared, 'are so backward compared to the United States of America.'

By the time they'd had been together for the required three dances, Frankie had decided she didn't much like Lyman Spinks. But as they cleared the floor, he followed her and asked her if she wanted a beer.

'I don't think you'll get one in here,' Frankie said pleasantly. 'They don't have a license but there's a pub just down the street.'

'What were you drinking then?'

'The ladies have made a fruit punch. It's very nice.'

He left her at the table and went off mumbling about stupid Victorian attitudes. Frankie suppressed a smile. A dark hand

and pink palm appeared in front of her and a familiar voice said, 'May I have this dance, Ma'am?'

Her heart skipped a beat as she looked up into his handsome ebony face with its coal black eyes. 'Romare!' she gasped. 'What on earth are you doing here?'

He laughed. 'It's a bit of a surprise for me too,' he said, 'but when I read in your letter that you were being posted here, I thought I'd surprise you. Dance?'

Lyman was nowhere to be seen. Besides, she didn't want to dance with him again, so she accepted and placed her hand in his. Romare was gentle and polite, complimenting her on her dress.

'What are you doing here anyway?' she asked.

'I've been posted to a stately home nearby,' he said. 'It's called Kingston Lacy and it's being set up as an American hospital.'

'And don't you look smart in your uniform,' she teased. The pair of them laughed with ease.

It was wonderful to have him hold her so close. She could feel his breath on the top of her head and his arm around her waist felt so strong and dependable. When the dance came to an end, he escorted her back to the table where a very angry-looking Lyman Spinks was waiting. As they approached he rose to his feet.

'What you doing here, boy?' he demanded. 'Who said you could dance with my girl?'

Frankie was horrified by the vitriol in his voice. 'Excuse me,' she said huffily, 'but one dance doesn't make me anybody's girl.'

'I went to get you a drink,' Lyman protested.

'And for that I'm grateful,' she said, sitting down, 'but that doesn't mean you own me.'

Doreen, hot and sweaty, threw herself into the seat next to Frankie. 'Phew, that was amazing,' she cried and, picking up the glass of punch Lyman had brought back for Frankie, she added, 'Is this for me? Oh thanks. I'm as dry as a biscuit.' And with that she downed it in one go.

Lyman leaned towards Romare. 'You can go now, boy. And keep your filthy black hands off white girls, d'you hear me?'

Romare pointed to the badge on his arm. 'I think I outrank you, soldier,' he said, his voice as cold as ice.

Lyman's face went the colour of puce and, as he squared up to Romare, one of the organisers came bounding over to the table. 'Now come along, lads,' he said firmly. 'None of that nonsense here, if you please. We're all in this together, aren't we?'

The two men separated but as a gesture of defiance, Lyman tossed the chair over as he turned to leave. Romare pulled up another chair and sat at the table. Frankie turned to her friend.

'Doreen, do you remember I wrote and told you about a man I'd just met? Well, this is him. Doreen, meet Romare, Romare, meet Doreen, one of my oldest friends.'

The pair of them shook hands but in no time at all, Doreen was back on the dance floor with another black man. They were so good at the jitter-bug that just before the interval, rather than share the floor with her, people peeled back to the edges of the room to watch her and her partner. When the music stopped everybody clapped and Doreen and her partner took a bow.

Frankie and Romare hardly noticed. They were busy catching up with each other. 'That Lyman Spinks seems a pretty nasty piece of work,' Frankie remarked. 'I can't believe he spoke to you like that.'

'Spinks and I go back a long way,' said Romare.

Frankie was surprised. 'You know him?'

'Sure,' said Romare. 'His family owned the cotton fields my family worked on as slaves.'

'Your family were slaves?' Frankie squeaked.

'Way back,' Romare said. 'As soon as my great-great-granddaddy was freed, the Spinks family made him a tenant. They gave him one mule and two acres of land.'

'My aunt and uncle have a smallholding,' said Frankie. 'I know how hard the work is.'

Romare nodded. 'By the time my grand-daddy worked the land they realised that they had swapped one form of slavery for another. They bought the seed and the fertiliser; they maintained the farm buildings and planted. When the crop matured, they harvested it but then the landlord took half.'

'What!' Frankie cried. 'You're joking.'

Romare's face had a far-away look. 'There was little to spare so the corn store offered them credit.'

'Don't tell me,' Frankie said crossly. 'The corn store belonged to Spinks.'

Romare nodded. 'For a long time it seemed like we'd never be free.'

'But you made it,' said Frankie, her admiration making her eyes sparkle.

'It was touch and go,' Romare admitted. 'When I left for Washington my daddy said "Be sure and hide your railroad ticket. You don't want old man Spinks taking it from you."'

Their gaze drifted towards a group of white Americans who seemed to be deep in conversation.

'Lyman's father?' Frankie asked.

Romare nodded again. 'When I got to the railroad station, Lyman's car drew up. I can see him now. "Where you goin', boy?" He knew where I was going. It was the talk of the town. The black folks were proud of me. "Did you heared that? Romare Delaney got a scholarship." But the white folks was

209

mad. "He aint nothin' but another uppity black-toed pigeon," they said. "Who does he think he is?"'

Romare stopped talking and lowered his head. 'I'm sorry. I'm spoiling your evening. I shouldn't rake all this up again.'

'No, no, it's okay,' said Frankie. She sensed that he needed to get this off his chest. 'Go on,' she encouraged.

'Spinks demanded to see my ticket,' said Romare with a shrug. '"You need a ticket to get on the train," he told me. "You got a ticket, boy?"'

'I hope you refused to show it to him,' said Frankie.

Romare laughed sardonically. 'I knew better than that. Even if I looked him in the eye I'd be frogmarched to the nearest police station. They'd lock me up on some trumped up charge and I'd miss my train.'

Frankie stared at him open-mouthed. 'So what did you do?'

'I gave him a ticket,' said Romare.

'And?' Frankie asked anxiously.

'He tore it up.'

'Oh Romare . . .' she whispered.

Romare leaned back in his chair. 'Don't you fret, little lady,' he said, a smile tugging at the corners of his mouth. 'As soon as he'd gone, I ran like hell to the depot.'

Puzzled, Frankie frowned.

'I had my ticket in my sock,' he grinned.

'But I thought you said . . .' Frankie began.

'A couple of weeks before, I'd picked up a railroad ticket on the floor in the corn store. Somebody dropped it. It was no good. That was the ticket Lyman tore up.'

They made eye contact and they laughed.

'There will now be an interval for twenty minutes,' the organiser called out, 'so get your raffle tickets now.'

Frankie explained what the raffle was and then noticed that Romare already had a strip of tickets in his top pocket. He raised an eyebrow and she laughed out loud. He was so easy to be with. 'There's a pair of stockings on the table,' she told him confidentially. 'I haven't had a new pair in ages.'

He nodded sagely. 'Your wish is my command, my lovely English rose,' he said, giving her a mock salute.

The line sounded a little corny but as their eyes met, she felt the colour rise to her cheeks. He had meant every word.

Doreen was back, this time with a man in tow. His skin glistened with perspiration. 'This is Henry,' she said. 'He's a terrific dancer. Sit down, Henry, and rest your bones.'

Henry snapped to attention. 'Sir, permission to sit, sir.'

Romare gave him a lazy smile. 'Sit, soldier,' he said. 'We're off duty now.'

Henry draped an arm around Doreen's shoulder and sat next to her.

The interval came to an end and the raffle started. Sadly none of their tickets came up but, as luck would have it, Spinks won the stockings. The night was almost over by the time they all went back to the dance floor and Frankie was already feeling anxious that she would soon have to say goodbye. Romare held her close for the last waltz, his mouth and warm breath close to her hairline. Her whole body tingled with desire and then the lights went up.

'That's it, folks,' the organiser called out. 'Thank you for coming and be careful to observe the blackout as you leave.'

Doreen and her partner were kissing on the dance floor. Reluctantly Frankie fetched their coats from the ladies' cloakroom and while Doreen went outside with Henry, Romare helped her put her coat on. 'I'm in this area for a while,' he said. 'If we can both get leave we could see each other again?'

'That would be lovely,' she said.

They were interrupted by a terrible scream outside. While

everybody looked around in stunned surprise, Doreen burst back through the doors. 'Oh please, they've stabbed him. You've got to come. There's so much blood. Please, please help him.'

# Thirty-Two

It was gone one in the morning before Frankie got back to her billet. Terrified that her landlady, Mrs Evans, would refuse to let her in, she had allowed Romare to accompany her to the door. He had insisted on bringing her home himself. They knocked on the door twice. Eventually Mrs Evans opened the door and stood with her arms folded over her ample bosom. One look at her angry expression told Frankie she wasn't going to believe anything she said.

'Mrs Evans . . .' she began.

'I run a respectable house,' Mrs Evans interrupted tartly. 'I don't hold with girls who stay out half the night with men, especially coloured men.'

'Ma'am,' Romare said quietly, 'I should hate for you to think ill of Miss Sherwood. My name is Doctor Delaney and Miss Sherwood was assisting me in an emergency at the hospital.'

'Well, I'll give you ten out of ten for originality, young man,' Mrs Evens sneered. 'I've never heard it called that before.'

'Miss Sherwood,' said Romare addressing Frankie, and ignoring her angry landlady, 'if you would like to get your dress professionally cleaned, you can send the bill to the hospital and I will personally see to it that you are reimbursed for any expense.' He saluted smartly adding, 'The United States of America is grateful for what you have done tonight to assist one of her citizens and so am I. Goodnight, Miss Sherwood, and goodnight to you too, Ma'am.' With that he walked swiftly to his jeep and drove off.

Frankie could tell that Mrs Evans had had the wind taken out of her sails but she still wasn't entirely convinced. The doorway was darkened because she had automatically drawn the blackout curtain before she'd stepped outside, but once Frankie was indoors she could see the state she was in. There were blood stains from just below her bust line down onto the skirt. Her hands had been washed (she'd done that in the ladies whilst she waited to hear what had happened to Henry) but there were still definite smears of blood on her upper arms.

'Good Lord!' Mrs Evans exclaimed. 'Whatever happened?'

'A man was attacked after the dance,' Frankie said quietly. She had become aware that the other girls were gathering on the landing upstairs.

'There's no hot water in the tank,' said Mrs Evans. 'You'd better come into the kitchen and get cleaned up.'

The other lodgers took that as an invitation to come downstairs and Frankie was surprised to see that Doreen was with them. 'Miss Toms is here just for the night,' said Mrs Evans, clearly having no idea that Doreen had already been kipping on the floor in Frankie's room for two nights. 'She missed her train.'

Everyone gathered around the table as Mrs Evans put the kettle on. 'So tell us what happened, dear,' she said, her tone of voice completely changed and far more sympathetic.

Frankie hesitated. It had been so terrible she struggled to find the words.

'We thought the poor man had been stabbed,' she said looking directly at Doreen, who had come back with the other girls while Frankie went with Henry and Romare to the hospital, 'but it was much worse than that.' She saw Doreen put her fingers to her lips, her eyes widen with apprehension.

Mrs Evans put a bowl of warm water onto the table. Frankie slipped out of her dress and stood in her petticoat. Pressing her hands under the water, she began to wash down her arms. All at once her eyes filled with tears. 'Oh Mrs Evans,' she said brokenly, 'they'd cut his thing off.'

She heard a sharp intake of breath from everyone in the room.

'Cut his thing off?' Mrs Evans repeated. 'But why?'

Frankie's voice was small. 'Because he'd danced with a white girl.'

Doreen cried out and ran from the room. One of the other girls followed her and the group could hear the sound of crying in the hallway. Mrs Evans stood with her back to everybody, her hands braced against the sink. 'Well, I don't hold with our girls going with coloureds, but nobody deserves that.'

Frankie continued to wash her arms as silent tears wet her own cheeks. Nobody spoke. They were all in shock. The kettle boiled and Mrs Evans made some tea. Frankie dried her arms and sat.

As she pushed cups of tea around the table Mrs Evans said, 'Will the poor man be all right?'

'Doctor Delaney said he'd have difficulty in spending a penny,' said Frankie, 'but the main problem is the loss of blood. He was haemorrhaging pretty badly when we found him.'

Doreen, puffy-eyed and as white as a sheet, came back into the room. 'Will he die?'

'At the moment he's holding his own,' said Frankie using the stock phrase so favoured by hospitals. Nobody knew what it meant but it gave people a vague understanding of the seriousness of the moment.

'I suppose it means he can't have children,' one of the other girls said.

Doreen made a small sound in her throat.

Frankie shook her head. 'I don't know. Doctor Delaney said he'd been quite damaged down there but I'm not exactly sure what that means.'

'So how come you were involved?' Mrs Evans asked.

'I was with him in the back of the jeep on the way to the hospital,' said Frankie. 'I just held him.' She closed her eyes remembering how Henry had wept and cried for his mother and howled in pain all the way to the American hospital in Kingston Lacy. It was an image she would carry in her head for a long time. 'He was in a lot of pain.'

'It's all my fault,' Doreen whispered.

'No!' Frankie said fiercely. 'Don't you dare think that. Henry was having a wonderful evening. It's the fault of small-minded racists. It's the fault of people who think that because they are white they are somehow superior. It's the fault of their parents for bringing them up that way. It's the fault of their jealousy and bigotry . . .' She choked on her words and then burst into tears. A couple of the girls comforted her as best they could.

After a few minutes Mrs Evans cleared her throat and said stiffly, 'Well, girls, I think you should all go back to bed. Some of you are on duty in the morning.'

Miserably they all filed out of the kitchen and made their way upstairs.

'Frankie,' said Mrs Evans as she walked out of the kitchen, 'I may not share the same views as you but I'm sorry for not quite believing you.'

Frankie acknowledged her apology with a nod of her head and made her weary way up to her room.

Doreen lay wide eyed on the floor between the two beds. As

Frankie undressed and climbed into her bed she whispered, 'I can't believe that happened.'

'I know,' Frankie whispered back.

'I couldn't do anything to help him,' said Doreen. 'That big man pulled my arm right back and I fell over. I saw the three of them grab Henry and then he screamed.' She began to cry again. 'I didn't realise, Frankie. I didn't know. I thought they'd just cut him.'

'There was nothing you could have done,' said Frankie.

Doreen blew her nose. 'Henry was a lovely man. Do you think I could go and see him in hospital?'

'I think you'd best stay out of it,' said Frankie's room-mate in the other bed. 'Those Yanks are big trouble.'

'But I'll have to tell the American military police what happened, won't I?' Doreen murmured.

'Please yourself,' said the girl, 'but you'll probably make things a whole lot worse for him.'

'Why do you say that?' Doreen gasped.

Frankie's tone was bitter. 'Because it was one of the snow-drops who did it.'

The heavy wooden doors swung open and two military policemen, one black, the other white, both wearing the army issue white helmets which had given them the nick-name of 'snowdrops', strolled down the centre of the hospital ward. Henry sank back against the pillow in a vain effort to make himself smaller. He was more comfortable now. The pain was less acute since the doctor had given him that shot. He could feel tears coming again as he remembered what they had done to him. What sort of a man was he now? A man with only half a pocket-rocket. And what about Erma? They'd already got three kids and she'd told him she don't want no more but what sort of a husband would he be from now on? What if

217

he couldn't get what was left up, and how could he satisfy her even if he could? How was he going to tell her? The snowdrops were coming his way and his blood ran cold when he saw that one of them was Sergeant Spinks. Dear God, he hadn't come to finish the job, had he? As they marched towards him, Henry was only too well aware that Spinks was a stickler for respect but he hadn't the strength to leap from his bed and stand to attention. Besides, the blood transfusion equipment was in the way. He pulled his body straight and stared up at the ceiling.

'At ease, soldier,' Spinks said in his distinctive southern drawl as he removed his helmet. 'We just come to ask you some questions about Saturday night. This here is First Sergeant Giles.'

Giles leaned over the bed and shook Henry's hand. 'I'm real sorry this happened to you, soldier,' he said.

Spinks pulled up a chair and sat. 'I hope I can rely on you to tell this officer the truth. We none of us want to waste time.'

Although he was more senior in rank, First Sergeant Giles, a black man, was left standing. He looked around for another chair and spotted one on the other side of the room.

'The First Sergeant is going to be taking some notes,' Spinks went on as the black officer walked out of ear shot. 'We aim to do all in our power to catch the bums that did this to you.'

As Spinks made eye contact with him, Henry's eyes grew wide and his heart was thumping in his chest. What was his game? Before the black officer returned, Spinks leaned close to Henry's ear and whispered, 'I hope you've learned your lesson, boy.' Henry trembled.

'So,' said Giles, sitting down and getting out his notebook, 'you were at the dance all evening.'

'Yes, sir.'

'Did you get involved in a fight or annoy someone?'

Spinks, who sat turning his ring on his finger, glanced up and Henry shook his head vigorously. 'No sir.'

'You went outside with a girl, is that right?'

'Yes, sir.'

Spinks tut-tutted as he took a silver case from his top pocket and took out a cigarette. He tapped it on the case then put it between his lips and lit it with his lighter.

Giles was still scribbling. 'And what was your intention?'

'Nothing, sir. Just a kiss goodnight, that's all. I is a married man.'

Spinks shook his head in a disapproving manner.

'Then what happened?'

By now Henry's eyes were as big as saucers. 'I ain't too sure, sir. All I knows is, somebody grabbed me from behind.' He turned his head away as if ashamed to voice what happened next. 'They pulled my pants down and then I felt them cut me . . . ' His eyes filled with tears then he blurted out, 'They cut my dick right off, sir.'

'Are you sure you didn't already have your pants down, soldier?' Spinks said lazily. 'Weren't you already having your way with that white woman?'

'No sir, no!' Henry panicked. 'I knowed she was a respectable girl.'

'Can you describe your assailants?' Giles asked.

Henry glanced at Spinks. The sergeant kept eye contact while he took a long drag on his cigarette. 'It was too dark, sir.'

'You said "they" pulled your pants down.'

'There was more than one, sir,' Henry said helplessly.

'Describe them.'

'Like I said, sir, it was too dark.'

'What about the girl? Could she identify who did this?'

'We've made extensive enquiries, sir,' said Spinks, 'but the girl cannot be found.'

'Was she a local girl?'

'Just some white trash whore,' said Spinks.

'She was a respectable woman,' Henry protested. 'She was in the Wrens.'

'Ha! What is it the Limeys call them? A sailor's nightshirt,' Spinks sniggered. Henry made to protest but he waved his hand dismissively. 'You were popular at the dance, weren't you?' Spinks went on. 'The crowd gave you a clap for your dancing. Maybe one of the other black boys was jealous.'

'No sir.'

'Maybe they all got together and decided to teach you a lesson.'

'No sir.'

'You know, Sir,' said Spinks looking at the First Sergeant. 'I think that's what happened. He got beat on by the coloureds.'

'No, no sir. It wasn't like that.'

Spinks leaned towards Henry. 'Soldier, I hope you're not suggesting a white man did this to you,' he said coldly.

'No sir,' cried Henry. 'Like I said, it was dark. It all happened too quick. I never saw who done this to me.'

# *Thirty-Three*

**North Farm, Broadwater, Sussex, April 1944**

Aunt Bet welcomed Romare into her home like a much-loved son. Frankie had told her some time before that he was black so she knew it wouldn't be a problem, but getting time off together had proved to be extremely difficult. Like hundreds of others caught up in this wartime situation, they had to settle for a snatched hour or two here and there and only when they could get their leave to coincide. They still managed to write to each other and occasionally they arranged to speak on the phone but they were both very busy.

Things were moving on apace all along the south of England and even Worthing itself resembled an army barracks. The Fourth Armoured Brigade had taken over the Eardley hotel and two hundred tanks lined the streets all around. The Fifteenth Scottish Infantry had commandeered the Beach Hotel, the Royal Scots Greys were in the Steyne, and Warnes Hotel was occupied by the Fourteenth Field Ambulance Regiment. It was said that more than two million troops waited on the coast from Kent to Dorset, so it was obvious that something big was about to happen.

Somehow or other, Romare had managed to get two whole days off and Frankie swapped with another girl to get a forty-eight-hour pass. The plan had been for Romare to meet the family.

Once on the farm, Romare was given Alan's room and Frankie found herself back in her old childhood bedroom for the first time in over a year. They were determined to make the most of every second they had.

'Anything you would particularly like to do?' Frankie asked him when he had unpacked.

'I should like to see the sea,' he replied with a smile.

They caught a bus down to the town but it was hugely altered. There were servicemen everywhere and hundreds of tanks lined the narrow East Worthing roads.

'We'll have to come back after the war so you can see Worthing at its best,' Frankie told him as they strolled near the front. She slipped her arm through his.

'I intend to,' he said with a grin. 'I shall walk my lovely wife right along here and when we reach the pier, I shall kiss her and tell her how much I love her.'

Frankie lifted her face to his and smiled. 'Lucky lady.'

'Lucky guy,' he said drawing her close and kissing her cheek.

'So what do you think of my Aunt Bet and Uncle Lorry?' she asked as they resumed their walk.

'They're really swell people,' he said. 'I can see why you speak so highly of them.'

'They opened their hearts and their home to me,' said Frankie. 'I can never repay them for what they did.'

'Frances,' he scolded gently, using the name she never owned, 'you can't repay love. You just return it.'

'Quite the philosopher, aren't you,' she teased.

'Honey,' he said in all seriousness, 'you act like you don't deserve to be loved.' He'd touched a raw nerve and she felt her face flush. 'Don't try and work it out. You *are* loved. Love is a gift. Just enjoy it. They did what they did because they love you.'

She could feel her eyes smarting.

'And I love you too, Frankie. I know we hardly know each other but I feel like I've known you all my life.' He turned to face her. 'It won't be easy, me being black and you being white. We'll never be allowed to live in peace in the Southern States. Washington is a lot more tolerant, but mixed marriages are still pretty rare.'

'It wouldn't bother me,' she said stoutly. 'We can always live over here.'

He smiled and, putting her hand back through his arm, they walked on. It was only as they walked in silence that Frankie began to understand how he might be feeling. She was confident that they'd be happy in this country but she had, in effect, asked him to sever his roots.

'Is it because of your family?' she said. 'Surely they'd want you to be happy. You told me how much they sacrificed to send you to college.'

She recalled the time when he'd shown her his photographs of a group of well dressed, happy people standing outside a drapery store. 'There's my mom and daddy,' he'd said. 'That's my sister Selma, who got married in '33, and my nephew, Jefferson, who is coming up for twelve.' He grinned. 'He's a good boy. Always in a hurry. He's going places, I reckon, and yes, he was on the way when she got married.'

'Naughty girl,' Frankie had teased.

Romare stopped walking and pulled her into his arms again. 'I do love you, Frankie,' he said quietly. 'You know that, don't you?' He dropped his head and kissed her cheek. As they walked on again, she had never felt so loved in her whole life – except maybe when her mother was still alive. That was a love that perhaps she had taken for granted. But now, after what he'd just told her, it dawned on her that she was loved by others too: not only Aunt Bet and Uncle Lorry but Alan and Ronald as well. She wiped a tear from her cheek with the palm of her hand.

'You okay, honey?'

'Yes.' Her voice was thick with emotion.

'Frankie,' he began again. 'I want to ask you something, but I'm real scared you might have to say no.'

'I don't think I would say no,' she said softly. They had stopped walking and were now standing facing each other. Romare chewed his bottom lip for a second, and then he spoke. 'Will you marry me?'

As she heard the words she'd so longed to hear, she thought to herself: every girl dreams of this kind of moment. There was no Hollywood music. All around them people were going about their daily business, but the place where they stood looking into each other's eyes felt almost like hallowed ground. She reached up with her fingers and brushed his lips. 'Oh yes, my darling. A thousand times yes.' And then he kissed her.

'You're crying again,' he said, stopping to look at her.

'Because I'm happy,' she said squeezing his arm and moving closer. 'Wonderfully, deliriously happy.'

The hours together sped by. Uncle Lorry took Romare for the obligatory pint at the local pub and while they were gone, Aunt Bet quizzed Frankie about her handsome doctor. 'What if he takes you back to America after the war?'

'He tells me he'd prefer to live in England,' said Frankie. 'Besides, even if the military send him back, he says he has enough money of his own to return whenever he wants.'

Aunt Bet nodded sagely. 'Are you sure about marrying him?'

'Positive,' Frankie said. She saw her aunt look away. 'I don't care what other people think and neither should you. We are just two people in love.'

Aunt Bet shook her head. 'If only life was as simple as that.'

The last thing Frankie wanted was to fall out with Aunt Bet

so as she put the dirty crockery into the washing up bowl, she changed the subject. 'Any news of Alan?'

'Oh Frankie, you'll never believe this but he's training to be a cook.'

'A cook!' Frankie exclaimed. She filled the washing up bowl with hot water and tossed in some soda crystals.

Aunt Bet nodded. 'When he went back this last time he got called into the office. He had a long talk with the officer in charge and the upshot of it was that Alan was sent to the cookhouse. He loves it!'

Frankie laughed out loud and then her face fell. 'Oh, dear, does that mean he'll be sent back to France when the big push comes?'

'I'm not sure,' said Aunt Bet, picking up the tea towel to dry the dishes, 'but an army marches on its stomach, so they say, so I imagine he'll be in some field kitchen away from the fighting.'

Frankie grinned. 'The thought of Alan in an apron. Is he still in touch with Carrie?'

Aunt Bet shrugged. 'I suppose so. She opened a Post Office Savings Book for the little lad and I know Alan pays in so much a week. I've no idea how long he'll keep it up but it will be a little something for the boy.'

When Romare and Uncle Lorry came back from the pub, they seemed on very amicable terms. That night Frankie went to bed happy. Things had turned out better than she expected and once this terrible war was over, she and Romare could start a new life together.

\*

Their final hours together went all too quickly. After breakfast, they caught the bus to Arundel. Romare was very impressed by the castle and the market square, calling it the stuff of fairy tales. They ate dinner in a small riverside café and caught the bus back to Worthing mid-afternoon. Frankie had loved every minute. They got off the bus in Broadwater because Frankie wanted to show Romare the house where she'd lived with her mother.

'It's very overgrown and run down,' she explained, 'but I want you to see the place where I grew up.'

She had mixed feelings as she walked along the street. Part of her was wishing that she could turn the clock back and she imagined what it would have been like to say, 'Mum, Dad, this is the man I love.'

Someone walking behind them seemed to be quickening his or her step and as Frankie glanced back her heart skipped a beat. It was Sidney Knight. He caught up with them just before they reached the gate.

'Like mother, like daughter,' he sneered. 'She was always one for the foreigners but at least her fancy man was white.'

Frankie's eyes blazed. 'How dare you!' she cried indignantly.

'Bloody Russian,' he said, pushing past. 'I soon put a stop to him.' He laughed sardonically. 'Got the shock of his life.'

'You can talk,' Frankie retorted. 'I remember how you used to harass my mother with your disgusting suggestions.'

He glared at her and quickly coming back to the gate, he spat at her. Romare lurched forward as Frankie was left with a large globule of beery spittle running down her cheek. Sidney only just managed to slam the front door before Romare reached it.

# Thirty-Four

**Broadwater, Sussex, April 1944**

Barbara Vickers lay on her bed and stared at the ceiling. Another tear trickled down her face and soaked into the pillow under her head. Her room was next door to the bathroom where she could hear Derek's happy chuckling as her mother blew raspberries on his tummy. He was a happy little boy but Barbara's heart was breaking. She wanted to barge through the door and shout, 'Stop doing that. He's *my* child. I should be the one making him laugh,' but of course she couldn't.

It had been bad enough when her father came home on leave. Watching him dangling Derek on his knee and making plans for 'his boy' when he got back from the war was agony. Dad was so happy about Derek, but it was a lie. Derek wasn't his son. He was his grandson. Barbara had been so stressed by the time Dad went back to the regiment that she was glad to see him go. She'd lost count of the number of times her mother had given her 'that' look; the look that said, *I'm doing this for your own good*; the look that said, *don't you dare tell anyone the truth, not even your father*.

What hurt the most was that her mother didn't want her to even touch Derek. 'You start cuddling him and you'll give the game away,' she'd said. 'It's best you let me do everything.'

Barbara had acquiesced but it was so, so difficult. It tore her apart. Every fibre of her being wanted to hold her son, to take him for walks, to read him a bedtime story, to blow raspberries on his tummy and make him laugh.

She turned on her side and looked at the picture in the frame on her bedside table. A man in a dark dinner jacket smiled at her from under the glass. It wasn't a real photograph, just the picture on the programme she'd bought when she'd gone to see his show at the Connaught Theatre. 'Oh, Conrad,' she whispered, 'why, oh why don't you write to me?'

Her Basildon Bond was still on the dresser. She would write to him one more time, only this time she would send him a picture of their beautiful son. She was positive that as soon as he saw how like him Derek was, he would want to see him. She imagined the scene. Tall, dark and handsome, he'd be so repentant. 'My darling,' he'd say, 'I'm so sorry I put you through all this. I've been foolish and cruel. Can you ever forgive me? Let me make amends with this fabulous fur coat just like the one Barbara Stanwyck wore in her latest film. Let me make amends with this engagement ring. Darling, please say you'll wear my wedding ring . . .'

With one eye still on her writing pad, she swung her legs over the bed and sat up. There was no time like the present. She'd write to Conrad now.

The words didn't come easily. She didn't want to come over as critical. After an hour and countless wasted pages she finally had the form of words she wanted.

*My darling Conrad,*

*I think of you all the time. It's a marvellous thing you are doing for the war and I feel sure you will be richly rewarded. I have enclosed a photograph of our son. As you will see, he was a beautiful baby and so like his handsome daddy. He's nearly four now and I'm sure that by the time you come home, he'll run into his daddy's arms. Take care sweetheart and I shall pray for you every night until you are home safe and sound.*

*All my love, Barbara*

She heard her mother going downstairs. In a moment or two, she would creep along the corridor to her mother's bedroom and kiss Derek goodnight just the way she had done ever since he was born.

\*

## Wareham, Dorset, June 1944

Romare knew he was going to France. The first casualties of the invasion would be brought back to Britain for treatment but it was imperative to set up field hospitals on French and Belgian soil as quickly as possible to give the injured the best possible chance. The United States would still be segregating its men so it fell on his shoulders to ensure that every coloured soldier had a fair chance of survival. Romare rose to the challenge with his usual passion.

Since his two-day stay in Broadwater, he'd realized just how much Frankie meant to him. He adored her and could hardly wait to make her his wife, but the final moments of his stay had given her a taste of what life might be like: a white girl married to a black man. When Sidney Knight spat on her, Frankie had been very upset and it was only because she'd begged him not to that Romare hadn't kicked the door down and floored the guy.

'I refuse to let that stupid ignoramus spoil our relationship,' she'd said robustly, but the need to protect her was almost overwhelming.

Since that time, he and Frankie could only manage to snatch an hour or two here or half an hour there to be together but they made the most of it. Then, miracle of miracles, he managed to get almost a whole day at the beginning of June. Rumour had it that D-Day, as it was now called, might be on June 5th. For that reason, he knew this would be the last opportunity for them to be together for a long time.

'Shall we do it now?' he'd written in a letter, 'or wait until I get back?'

'Now,' she'd replied. 'Now, now, now . . .'

So, having made all the arrangements, Romare asked Frankie to meet him in a market town called Wareham.

The weather wasn't that good: wet with a blustery wind. The clock on the turret of the red brick building was striking the hour as she rode her bike up South Street. He was waiting by the door, a small posy of flowers in his hand and a beaming smile on his face. When he took her in his arms, his kisses had never tasted so sweet.

'I can hardly believe this is happening.'

'It won't be easy. Are you sure, honey?'

Frankie frowned. 'Of course I am.'

She'd been over the moon when he'd said they should get married before he went to France but there was no time to arrange a proper wedding. She wrote and told Aunt Bet and Uncle Lorry but Wareham was miles away and it was difficult to find a civilian train these days.

He smiled mysteriously. 'There's a special surprise waiting inside.'

'What?' she said breathlessly.

'Wait and see,' he said.

Romare put his hand gently onto her back to encourage her through the doors and there in the foyer stood Aunt Bet, Uncle Lorry, and Barbara.

'I can't believe you've come all this way,' Frankie cried happily.

'I wouldn't miss the wedding of the year!' said Barbara with a chuckle.

'You look so happy,' said Aunt Bet, as she pinned a corsage onto Frankie's lapel. 'Your mum would have been so proud.'

There were several other weddings taking place: happy brides in gowns, other brides in uniforms like herself and a scattering of pregnant brides so Frankie and Romare had to wait for their turn until the registrar called their group into a small room.

'I wish your folks could have been here too,' she whispered for his ears only.

Her husband-to-be pulled her close. 'They would have been here if it weren't for this damned war,' he said. 'We mustn't let that spoil the happiest day of our lives.'

'I know,' she began, 'but . . .'

'No buts,' he said firmly.

Once inside the town hall, and now a married woman, Frankie hugged Aunt Bet and Uncle Lorry. 'I hope it's not too much of a shock for you seeing us here,' said Aunt Bet, wiping what she called 'a speck of dust' from her eye. 'He swore us to secrecy.'

'Good job I said yes then,' Frankie quipped and they all laughed.

Uncle Lorry took a couple of pictures with his box Brownie and then they all walked to the nearest pub for a few sandwiches and a celebratory drink.

*

A little while later, between the showers, the newly-weds went for a walk along the banks of the river Frome. It was a bit cold for the time of year but they hardly noticed.

231

'I have another surprise from you,' Romare said as he took some keys out of his pocket and jangled them in front of her face.

Frankie was puzzled. 'I don't understand.'

'A doctor friend of mine owns a house just off the high street,' he said lacing his fingers through hers. 'It's ours for today if you would like.'

'Oh Romare,' she whispered.

He kissed her tenderly. 'Are you ready for me, my lovely English rose?'

'Yes my darling,' she said breathily. 'I'm ready.'

Hand in hand they turned back towards the main shopping area but they hadn't gone far before a voice called out, 'Doctor Delaney? Is that you?'

Romare turned to see a man leaning out of the driver's window of an old van. Frankie recognized him at once. The man stopped the engine and jumped out onto the street in front of them. 'You don't remember me, do you?'

'Forgive me,' said Romare, 'but I don't.'

'Bert Harper. You saved my boy's life on the tube train that night,' said the man lifting a grimy hat towards Frankie. 'Afternoon, Miss,' and looking from one to the other he added, ''E was a ruddy marvel, 'e was. My little lad was choking on a bit 'f bread my 'ld mother gave 'im. Couldn't get 'is breath. I tell you, I was scared out 'f me wits I was. But the 'ld doc here, he grabbed him round the waist and give 'm such a jerk, the bit 'f bread flew right out of 's mouth, just like that.'

Frankie gazed admiringly towards her husband. 'I know. I was there.'

''Ere,' said Bert, 'let me buy you both a drink.'

'I'm afraid we're in a bit of a hurry right now, Bert,' said Romare.

'Whatever it is it can wait,' Bert insisted. 'I wants a chance

232

to say fank you.' He glanced up at the town hall clock which said one twenty-five. 'We've just got a moment before closing time.' And with that, he bundled them into the nearest pub.

They found a seat by the old fireplace and Bert headed towards the bar.

'I'm sorry, honey,' Romare said when he'd gone.

She clasped his hands. 'It's fine,' she said gently. 'How could you refuse? He was so excited to see you.'

Bert reappeared with two glasses of beer and a sherry on a tray. 'Your very good 'ealth, doc,' he said, raising his glass.

The men drank deeply. 'And how is your son now, Bert?' asked Romare.

'Doing fine,' Bert said proudly. 'Top of the class at school and the life and soul of the party at 'ome.'

Romare smiled. 'I'm glad.' He drank more beer. 'So what are you doing down here?'

'Came to see a man about a dog,' Bert said, thumbing his nose.

Romare seemed a little confused but didn't ask what he meant.

'You going over with the Big Push?' Bert went on.

'You know I can't answer that, Bert,' said Romare.

The man nodded. Frankie brushed some confetti from her sleeve.

'You been to a wedding?'

Romare nodded. 'Ours.'

For a split second, Bert seemed uncomfortable, then recovering himself quickly, he said, 'Well, it was grand seeing you again, Doc. All the best to you both and I'm glad I had the chance to buy you a drink.'

Romare held his glass up as a toast. 'Thank you and I wish you all the best as well.'

Frankie finished her sherry and Bert stood to his feet before shaking their hands again. 'Can I give you a lift somewhere?'

'We aren't going far,' said Romare. 'We've a little cottage just around the corner.'

The three of them parted with a final handshake on the street and set off in opposite directions. The cottage turned out to be a delightful grey stone building just off the main thoroughfare and down a small cul-de-sac. Romare opened the door and, to Frankie's amusement and delight, he lifted her into his arms to carry her inside. When he set her on her feet, they kissed with growing passion. Eventually they broke off and he took her by the hand and walked her upstairs. He undressed her gently, not rushing her. Finally she stood naked before him. He had been taking his own things off at the same time and at last he drew her gently towards him. She recalled Arlene's story about thinking she could feel the man's pencil. There could be no such mistake concerning her husband's body. She shivered. He had much more than a pencil.

'Are you sure about this, honey?'

She nodded. She had the impression that had she shaken her head and said 'no', although he would have been disappointed, he would have respected her wishes. His hand moved gently down from her waist to her hips until it rested for a moment between her legs. Her heart was pounding as she felt every cell in her body yielding to the most delicious feeling. A moment later, he lifted her onto the bed and lay beside her. When he finally mounted her, she was totally relaxed and happy. They made love until the room grew dark as dusk fell.

Bert wasn't a happy man. He'd come all this bleedin' way but the big Yank had nothing much to offer. He agreed to take some fags but what could he do with baseballs and American football shirts? Nobody this side of the ocean played those games. Besides, as soon as he got them out of the bag, the punters would know they was nicked.

'I saw you with some guy when I drove up,' the big man said.

'Doc Delaney,' said Bert getting out his money for the fags. 'Cracking bloke. He saved my boy's life, 'e did.' He treated the Big Yank to the story, this time embellished with plenty of wringing hands and desperate cries. 'Ruddy marvel 'e was.'

The big man curled his lip. 'He was with a white woman.'

'Just got married,' said Bert. He glanced up at the big man. 'You got a problem with that?'

'Just asking. Where did they go?'

Bert shrugged. 'A cottage, he said. Not too far away. I saw them turn down there, by the phone box.'

The transaction done, the two men parted. As he watched the big man get back into his jeep, Bert had an uneasy feeling that perhaps he shouldn't have told him so much about the Doc. He wasn't too sure about English girls marrying them himself but some of these Yanks could be really nasty to the coloureds.

# Thirty-Five

The day had passed all too quickly. They had made love, slept a little then made love again.

'Thank you for getting Aunt Bet and Uncle Lorry to come to our wedding,' Frankie whispered. 'And Barbara too.'

'It wouldn't have been the same without them,' said Romare. He was tracing the line of her jaw with his finger. It was a deliciously sexy feeling. 'Your aunt did try to get hold of Alan and Ronald but they couldn't make it.' He looked into her face. 'They wanted to,' he added, 'but . . .'

'I heard on the radio that all leave is cancelled,' she said. 'I'm just glad you were able to come. It would have been a funny wedding with no bridegroom.'

He grinned. 'And even worse without the bride.' They kissed again.

Afterwards, making use of the two dressing gowns they found hanging on the back of the bedroom door, they went downstairs. To their great surprise and delight, they found a prepared meal waiting for them in the kitchen. There was a note beside a water glass from Romare's doctor friend wishing them well and hoping they enjoyed their brief stay in his home. He must have arranged for his cleaning lady to leave the food for them earlier in the day. Romare was visibly moved by his kindness. He and Frankie ate their meal and talked of their future.

'It's not going to be easy for you when I'm posted, Frankie,' he began.

'I'll be fine,' she said, but she sighed. 'Oh, I wish your family could have been at our wedding.'

'I thought about sending them the fare but it's not safe at the moment,' he said. 'Time enough to meet up when the war is over.'

'Or we could go to visit them.'

He nodded. 'We'd better go before I have a family of my own.'

She blushed modestly and laughed.

The meal over, they had just over an hour before Romare had to be on his way.

'Where exactly are you going abroad?' she asked. 'Do I need to worry about you?'

He grasped her hand and kissed her fingers. 'You know I can't tell you but no, you don't need to worry about me. I shall be working in a safe place.'

She nodded grimly and clenched her lips together to stop them from trembling. She understood what he meant. He was going over to France and would be in some field hospital a few miles from the front. Safe, but not completely safe. Her eyes glistened with tears. He leaned forward and kissed her. 'I'll never stop thinking about you,' he assured her, 'and I will come back.'

She held his face in her hands. 'Every night I shall look up at the stars and send you my love.'

'And you'll hear me saying "Goodnight Sweetheart",' he whispered into her ear.

She smiled wanly and he rose to his feet but instead of clearing the table as they had planned, he led her back upstairs. They took off their dressing gowns but they did not make love. They lay in each other's arms, just looking at each other and sharing a kiss now and again.

'You have made me so happy,' he whispered. 'My lovely English rose.'

'And you have made me very happy too.'

Back in Worthing, things were not so good for Sidney Knight. He'd managed to get out of national conscription, but it had cost him dearly. The doctor who had written the false certificate to avoid a Compulsory Work Order had charged him an arm and a leg. The gee-gees still hadn't been kind to him. The Grand National hadn't run since 1940 and the racecourse had been turned into an Italian POW camp. What sacrilege! Sidney had to resort to illegal meetings and betting in pubs and clubs. It was a risky business with police raids and the threat of heavy fines if he was caught.

He got by but he was definitely on a downward slide. He did the occasional scam and sometimes he was asked to forge a signature. Lean pickings – but suddenly he had the most extraordinary stroke of luck. Whist doing house clearance on a bomb site for a local firm, there was an accident on the road outside. A child had run across in front of a Post Office van. The driver screeched to a stop but swerved at the same time, hitting the side of Sidney's lorry. Then the car following behind ran into the nearside of the GPO van. In the chaos which followed, Sidney and a passer-by managed to get the rear car away from the Post Office van so that they could open the buckled driver's door and get the occupant out. Sidney would be the first to admit he didn't have the stomach for blood and gore so he kept well away while the medics attended to the casualty. That's when everything changed. Everyone's attention was either on the child (not badly hurt but very noisy), the hysterical mother, the driver of the GPO van who was protesting his innocence, or the elderly driver who had run into the back of him. Nobody, except Sidney, had noticed that the back door of the GPO van had burst open and that there were several mail bags inside.

By the time everyone had either been taken to hospital or the police station, the incident was over. Someone else from the Post Office arrived to put the mail bags into another van before the one involved in the accident was towed away. The postman thanked him for his help and drove off leaving Sidney to drive his lorry home. What no-one knew was that Sidney had squirreled away two mail bags under an old army blanket in the back.

Romare glanced at the clock on the bedside table. 'Better go.'

Frankie's stomach fell away. So it was over. This beautiful time they'd shared had come to an end. She wanted to cling to him, beg him not to go, suggest they run away, but of course she wouldn't. He had a duty; in fact they both had a duty which had to come first. As he got up and went to the bathroom she lay on her side and looked around the room. She wanted to remember everything about this place. The wallpaper, the curtains, the bed covers, the funny old chair in front of the dressing table where she'd folded her clothes. The memory would have to sustain her for perhaps a very long time. This was the room where she'd lost her virginity . . . no, the room where she had surrendered her precious virginity to the only man she had ever loved. This was the room where she had become a woman for the first time. The décor might be a little old-fashioned, perhaps even dowdy, but to her it was a beautiful place.

He came back into the room and leaned over the bed to kiss her again. She responded, then, dressed only in her petticoat, headed for the bathroom. A shuffling noise downstairs made her turn her head and her heart almost stopped. There was someone at the bottom of the stairs. She knew instantly it was a man although she couldn't see his face. He was wearing some sort of white hood. As she took in her breath noisily, he looked up and their eyes met. There was an air of menace about him. Panicked, she screamed and ran back to the bedroom. 'Romare, there's man with a white bag on his head downstairs.'

He looked up startled, and at the same time they heard several heavy pairs of footsteps on the stairs and the landing. Romare only had enough time to pull her protectively behind him before three men burst into the bedroom. Frankie screamed.

All of them were wearing identical hoods, one of which looked suspiciously like an empty flour bag, over their heads. Only their eyes were visibly behind ragged eye holes cut into the fabric. The first man swung a heavy piece of wood at Romare who only just managed to duck out of the way.

'Jim Crow don't sleep with white women,' the man snarled and Frankie recognised his voice straight away. It was Lyman Spinks. 'You know the rules, boy.'

Now she could see that the wood he was holding was in fact a baseball bat. He swung it again and she heard it crack against Romare's jaw. Her husband reeled from the blow and with a terrible cry of pain, turned sharply away from the bat and caught his head on the leg of the iron bedpost before he slumped to the floor.

'Romare,' she cried helplessly. 'Oh God, what have you done? Romare, Romare!'

Spinks pulled her away roughly, his snake ring digging painfully into the flesh of her arm and at the same time, the other two hooded men stepped forward and grabbed Romare by the arms, hauled him to his feet and dragged him out of the room. Desperate to help him, Frankie tried to get past the bulk that was Spinks' body. 'No, no,' she was screaming. 'Stop it! What are you doing?'

Spinks flung her against the dressing table as casually as he would throw a garment onto a chair.

'You've no right to do this,' she shouted defiantly as she pulled herself to her feet.

'That dog raped you,' Spinks said coldly. 'Back home we have a way of dealing with rabid dogs.'

'He did not rape me!' Frankie shrieked. 'I was willing and furthermore . . .' She didn't get to finish her sentence.

'Willing?' he roared. 'You were willing?' His voice was filled with contempt and loathing. 'Woman, shut your Goddamn filthy mouth. You disgust me, you good-for-nothing whore.'

She saw him raise the baseball bat again and everything went black.

'Time, gentlemen, please.'

The landlord's call had everybody rushing to the bar for one last pint. Bert had enjoyed a great evening. He was slightly tipsy and he'd made a bob or two selling under the counter nylons at half a crown a pair. In fact he'd done so well, he didn't have more than a dozen pairs to take back home so the trip hadn't been such a waste of time after all. Fifteen minutes later as they all piled outside, it was eerily quiet. The tanks which had been lined up all along the streets when he went into the Duke of Wellington were gone.

'Looks like something's happening at last,' a voice said behind him.

Bert said his goodbyes and walked towards his van. He was driving steadily down the high street when he saw two men in peculiar hats bundle another man into the back of a jeep. Their victim was struggling to get away but one of the assailants punched him in the goolies which rendered him motionless.

Rather than simply drive on past, something made Bert slow to a halt. The blackout made it hard to see clearly but when a third man carrying some sort of weapon appeared, Bert knew something was up. Somebody settling an old score perhaps? A gangland feud? He decided to keep out of it until the third man pulled the white hood off his head and Bert recognised the Big Man. Bert's heart skipped a beat. What the hell was he doing? The jeep drove off at a pace and it was only as Bert followed them that he realised that this could be near the cottage where the doc was staying. His blood ran cold. The Big Man had asked him an awful lot about the doc. Had he unwittingly put him in danger?

The jeep headed out of town. Bert followed it at a distance. The combination of the dark night, the lack of decent head-lights, the booze and trying to concentrate was giving him a headache. The jeep slowed to a halt and stopped. Bert stopped too. For a second his heart was in his mouth in case they'd spotted him, but luckily they hadn't. A moment later, he saw them dragging someone into the woods. The bloke was still struggling but he was powerless against the three Yanks. Bert reversed into a gate entrance and parked his van. By now, the cold night air and his growing unease had made him stone cold sober. He made his way into the woods, guided by their voices and laid low about thirty yards away. In the gloom he could just make out the three men standing by a large oak tree. They were sharing a hip flask and laughing. Bert wanted to charge up to them and demand to know what they'd done with the other man but he didn't dare. He was no match for those boys. They were twice the size he was. They hung around for several minutes, maybe as much as ten or fifteen, then they all shook hands and headed back towards the road. A few minutes later, he heard the jeep turning around and driving off.

Bert ran towards the oak tree thinking they had probably tied the victim (was it the doc?) to the tree. Maybe this was some sort of a joke. After all, the doc had said he'd just got married. Perhaps they were his mates and they would be coming back for him in the morning, but when Bert walked around the other side of the huge oak, he could see that this was no joke. A man's body was hanging from a rope swung over a low bough. Bert reached into his pocket and got out a torch. Using a torch would break the rules of the blackout but he had to know who it was. The little beam of light confirmed his worst fears. With a cry of anguish he grabbed the man's legs and tried to lift him. He managed to take his weight for a minute or two but what good was that? How could he cut the rope? Bert looked around for something to use as a stand for the man's feet and saw a shape a few yards away. He ran over to it. It was a piece of tree trunk probably used by boy scouts sitting round a camp fire before the war. He rolled it to the body but when he got it directly under the feet, it was far too short.

Bert was sobbing now and he put his hands on the top of his head. 'Oh my gawd, oh gawd.' He couldn't help. He couldn't do anything. The doc's body swung gently around and now Bert could see his distorted face. The eyes bulged, his tongue, huge and dark, lolled out of his mouth. He could smell shit and realised that as he was dying the doc had filled his pants. All he had on was his underpants. The man was gone. Common sense told him he'd been gone when Bert ran up to him. He could just make out something white on the ground and he picked it up. It was a pillow case with slits cut into the fabric for eye holes. What the hell . . .?

Bert lingered for a moment, tears and snot running down his face and his heart pounding in his chest, but then he heard the engine of a jeep coming along the road. As it screeched to a halt, Bert dropped the pillow case and ran like hell. They must have spotted his van in the layby and now they were coming for him.

Even after five years on the job, Bob Barrett still took his job as an Air Raid Precaution warden very seriously. He had joined up in 1939 and taken advantage of all the training on offer.

Not that he'd had much opportunity to use it. There had been little bombing in the area, the only real danger coming from the odd bomb jettisoned in a field before the flight home. He had all the equipment too, but again, he'd never had cause to use the gas rattle or the ceiling pike. Bob had made a few enemies along the way. That was because he spent most of his time patrolling Wareham and the surrounding area on his bicycle making sure that everyone adhered to the blackout, and he wasn't afraid to report any abuse of the rules. As a result, some who had once been his friends had heavy fines imposed upon them for minor breaches.

As he approached the small cul-de-sac at the end of the street, Bob could hardly believe his eyes. The front door of the cottage was wide open, curtains drawn back and light was spilling right up the pathway. Surely this was an open invitation to the Germans to bomb his beloved market town. This was a flagrant breach of the blackout, a definite fine, maybe the risk of imprisonment for the perpetrator. As he hurried towards the front door he was already getting his notepad and pencil from his top pocket.

'Hey, you in there,' he shouted authoritatively. 'ARP. Put that light out.'

There was no response. Bob stepped into the hallway and closed the blackout curtain behind him. 'ARP,' he shouted again. 'You're showing a light.'

He couldn't hear a sound. Now he was anxious. He knew the man who owned the cottage sometimes loaned it to friends. Sometimes he came down for the weekend himself. Bob had never met him, but they said he was some high-powered doctor in London. So where was he? Cautiously Bob searched the downstairs rooms. There was evidence that two people had eaten a meal in the kitchen but there was no sign of them. After a moment of hesitation when he'd called out again, Bob made his way upstairs. He found no signs of a disturbance on the landing but when he walked into the bedroom there was a scantily clad girl lying on the floor.

'Are you all right, Miss?' His question was a bit lame because from the look of her, she was far from all right. She had an ugly bruise on the side of her face which looked as if someone had hit her very hard. There was blood on the mat beside the bed and although she was still breathing, the girl was out cold. Bob wasted no time in racing downstairs to use the telephone in the hallway to summon help.

Deep in the woods with the body of Doctor Delaney hanging on a tree not thirty yards away, Bert held his breath. As soon as he'd heard the jeep coming back, he'd jumped into a ditch on the other side of a small hedge. Pushing himself under the overhanging foliage he hoped he was well hidden. He heard the men walking around and every now and then he saw the flash of a torch but luckily, although they came very close, they didn't spot him.

'He probably didn't even come this way, boss,' one man said.

'He could have come into the wood to take a whizz,' the other suggested.

'Or maybe he's doing some dumb Dora someplace else.'

The Big Man snorted. 'She'd have to be dumb to lay down for him,' he said and his two henchmen laughed.

He could hear them moving around. 'What's that on the floor?' one of them said. Bert held his breath and his hand went to his pocket. His torch! He'd dropped his torch. His heart began to pound again. Should he stay still or make a run for it?

'You dumb bastard,' said the Big Man. 'It's your damned hood. Do you want to be caught? Pick it up.'

Bert heard the sound of a slap and one of the men said, 'Yes sir, boss; sure, boss,' in that clipped way all the Yanks addressed their commanders.

As they all walked away, a wave of relief flooded over him. They'd found the pillow case, that was all. Bert listened for them to start the engine and even though he heard the jeep drive off, he waited for some time before moving. He wanted to make sure that one of them wasn't hanging around to jump out from behind a tree to grab him. Wet from the ditch and emotional about the doc, he finally reached his car to find they had slashed all four tyres and the rest of his nylons were scattered to the four winds. There was nothing else for it but to walk back to Wareham.

# Thirty-Six

Inspector Gerry Collins flicked through the pages of his file. What a night! The whole scenario had begun when the air raid warden, Bob Barrett, had found an unconscious girl in the cottage. The door was wide open and the light was showing all the way down the driveway so Bob had gone inside, calling as he went, and eventually found her on the bedroom floor. It had been a bit of a shock. He'd phoned for help then run up the road to fetch Collins. She'd been attacked and was out cold, so he'd said. Collins threw on his clothes and ran all the way to the cottage. By now all the calling out and running about had attracted other people from their beds. Some were dressed, others wore dressing gowns. Together, they made the girl as comfortable as possible until St John Ambulance arrived. When they'd gone, Collins spent a little while looking around the cottage. There was a US uniform neatly folded on the chair behind the bedroom door but no sign of the owner. Her things were on the dressing table chair. Downstairs there were signs that two people had shared a meal and he found a posy of flowers in the sink but he couldn't find a suitcase. What were they doing there? It was obvious that they hadn't been there long but were they there legitimately or had they broken in? The cottage belonged to a London doctor who had inherited it from his mother when she died. That much he knew, but the identity of the girl and the whereabouts of the man whose uniform was on the chair remained a mystery.

Puzzled, he'd returned to the police house to find a message on the pad. His wife had taken down the details and then gone back to bed. Nobby Clark, the landlord of the Duke of Wellington, had telephoned to say that a travelling salesman had gone into the woods for a pee and found a body hanging from a tree. Collins went down there straight away. He found it easily, only a hundred yards or so from the road; an African dressed only in his underpants. The question was, how had he got up there? There was a log which he'd probably used to stand on, but why was he half naked? Was he connected with the girl in the cottage? From the moment he saw him, Inspector Collins knew this was going to be a long night.

*

In the morning, the hospital told him the girl in the cottage still hadn't come round and so although he hadn't been able to talk to her, he took the opportunity to take a look at her. A pretty girl; young, probably twenty or twenty-one, and wearing a bright gold wedding band. When she was found she was only wearing her petticoat so his greatest fear was that whoever had done this had attacked her in more ways than one. He still hadn't properly connected her with the man in the woods until he went to the pub and asked Nobby Clark about the phone call.

'Oh, that was Bert Harper,' he said. 'He was the fella who found the body in the woods.'

'And he's still here?'

'He's gone to the garage,' said Nobby. 'Somebody slashed his car tyres and they're fixing it up for him. Who was he then? The body. I hope it wasn't the black man we had in here yesterday.'

248

'Well, he did look African.'

Nobby shook his head sadly. 'If it's the same bloke, he'd only just got married.' The landlord frowned. 'So what do you think happened? Knocked her about a bit and then went out and hung himself?'

Collins shook his head. 'There were signs of a struggle,' he said grimly.

'The blighters,' Nobby muttered.

Collins frowned. 'Why do you say that?'

Nobby was wiping the bar with a tea towel that had seen better days. 'We had a little reception for them,' he went on. 'Her mum and dad and her sister were here. At least that's who I think it was. They were going to go straight back home but then the flap started and all trains were cancelled. Any road, there were some of them white Yanks in the bar. Trouble makers. I heard them ranting on about a black guy marrying a white girl. "That's enough of that," I says. "You leave them alone. It's none of your business."'

Collins raised an eye brow. 'What happened then?'

Nobby shrugged. 'They up and left.'

'You say her family was here,' said Collins. 'What happened to them?'

'They had their breakfast and left for the station,' Nobby said. He glanced up at the clock. 'About ten minutes ago.'

Later that afternoon, Frankie opened one eye. She felt dizzy and disorientated. Her stomach felt queasy. She closed her eye then tried again. She was in a small room. If the door would stop moving from side to side she might be able to work out where she was. Her jaw hurt, her mouth felt funny and her chin was all tingly. She made an involuntary sound and Aunt Bet's face appeared in front of her.

'Hello, lovey,' she said. 'So you've woken up at last.'

There was a movement on the other side of the bed and she saw Uncle Lorry getting to his feet. He patted her arm and then said emotionally, 'I'll get the nurse.'

Frankie tried to lift her arm but it seemed to be attached to something.

'Lie still, lovey,' said Aunt Bet. 'You've got a drip in your arm.'

Frankie stared at her in bewilderment. A nurse bustled into the room. 'Ah, you've come round,' she said, taking Frankie's wrist in her hand and looking at the fob watch on the top of her apron. Uncle Lorry came back into the room and sat again.

'You gave us all a nasty shock,' the nurse went on. 'We were a bit worried that you might have broken your jaw but the X-rays tell us you've just been badly bruised.'

Frankie tried to make sense of what she was saying. How did she almost break her jaw? She didn't remember doing that.

Pulling out the retractable back rest, the nurse helped her to sit up a bit and then offered her some water. Never had water tasted so wonderful, but Frankie could only manage a few sips before she sank back onto the pillows. 'What happened?' she whispered.

The nurse wrote something on the chart at the end of her bed then looked up at Aunt Bet. 'I'll leave you to explain that, shall I?' she said. 'Try not to upset her too much.'

Aunt Bet glanced at Uncle Lorry helplessly.

'Why are you both here?' Frankie said as the nurse left the room.

'We were just about to catch the train,' said Uncle Lorry, 'when a policeman came and told us you'd been hurt.'

'We came straight here,' Aunt Bet went on.

'But Barbara went on home,' said Uncle Lorry. 'She had to be back at work but we'll let her know how you are.'

'Somebody attacked you,' said Aunt Bet, tight-lipped.

Frankie's mind struggled to comprehend, then all at once

her heart constricted. 'Oh Aunt Bet . . . Romare . . .' she whispered as it all came tumbling back.

'Don't even say that man's name,' Aunt Bet said savagely. 'He had us all fooled.'

Frankie frowned. 'I don't understand.'

'How could he have done this to you?' Aunt Bet was on the verge of tears.

Frankie shook her head making it spin again. 'It wasn't him,' she said. She was beginning to feel a tightness in her chest.

But Aunt Bet wasn't listening. 'They found him in the woods,' she said squeezing the end of her nose with her handkerchief. 'And after what he did, I can't say I'm sorry.'

Frankie's eyes grew wide and she tried to get up. 'Is he here? Is he all right?'

'Hang on a minute, Bet,' said Uncle Lorry getting to his feet. 'It might not be what you think.'

'Is he badly hurt?' Frankie repeated desperately.

'He's dead,' Aunt Bet said coldly. 'Hung himself, didn't he.'

'Shut up, Bet! Stop jumping to conclusions, will you!'

'Don't you speak to me like that,' she began but then Frankie began a terrible howl that went on and on and filled the room. Aunt Bet clasped her handkerchief to her chest, her mouth open in shocked surprise. Uncle Lorry leaned over and stroked Frankie's hair murmuring, 'It's all right, lass. It's all right.'

Seconds later they heard the sound of running feet as the nursing staff came back into the room to see why Frankie was still screaming.

Back in his office, Inspector Collins tapped the end of his pencil on his desk. There were so many things about this case that didn't add up.

Why would a man on his honeymoon night take himself off

in just his underpants and hang himself in the woods? It was an absolute nonsense and yet that's what the Yanks were making out had happened. One look at the fellow's bare feet told him an entirely different story. His soles were pink and unmarked but the tops of his feet were deeply scratched and had bled. No, as far as Collins was concerned, the man had been dragged to the woods. And another thing; did they think he was an idiot or something? How did a barefoot, near-naked man walk nearly three miles (there was no evidence that he drove there) out of town with a bump on his head the size of a goose egg? That alone would probably have knocked him silly. And where did he get the rope?

He still hadn't got the girl's side of the story but when he'd turned up at the American base, they were less than helpful. There was only a skeleton staff remaining and they were busy packing up to follow the advance to France. Time was of the essence because they had to be across the channel.

'Just wrap it up and file it,' the Base Commander had said. 'We've more important things to think about. Today is D-Day. There's a war to be won. One dead deserter in a wood can keep.'

But that wasn't Inspector Collins' way. He felt his temperature rise. 'If we don't stick to the rule of law,' he'd said tartly, 'what's the point of winning a war? We'd be no better than the Nazis; one rule for them and another for everybody else.'

The commander's eyes had glazed. 'Look, buddy, I'm sorry. I haven't got time for this. He was only a black man. Nobody cares. It's your problem.'

Frankie told the inspector a whole different story. Just the same as Aunt Bet, Collins had toyed with the idea that Romare had in some way been responsible for what had happened and that, ashamed of his actions, he had ended his own life.

'Romare didn't hurt me,' Frankie told him quietly. 'Why would he? I am his wife.'

252

White-faced and crushed, she went on to explain to Collins and his sergeant how she'd seen a man with a pillow case on his head at the bottom of the stairs; how he and two others had burst into their bedroom and coshed her husband over the head before they carried him off; she told them how when she had tried to run after them, Lyman Spinks, a staff sergeant in the United States army, had hit her across the face with a baseball bat.

'How do you know if it was him if you couldn't see his face?'

'I recognised his voice,' she said, her voice beginning to waver, 'and when he grabbed me, his ring made this mark on my arm. He always wears a ring on the third finger of his right hand. It's very distinctive: a snake with ruby eyes eating its own tail.'

The two men took down the details.

Frankie's chin was trembling. 'How did you find my husband?'

'A tip off,' said Inspector Collins. 'Someone rang my home to say he'd gone into the woods for a pee and saw a body hanging from a tree. I caught up with him before he left Wareham. A man called Bert Harper. It seems he knew you both.'

Frankie closed her eyes and sighed. 'My husband saved his little boy's life.'

Collins nodded. 'That's what he said. I don't think he would have come back to report it otherwise. His statement tallies with yours. He said he'd seen Lyman Spinks coming out of the cottage.'

Frankie looked puzzled. 'He knew Spinks?'

'He's had dealings with him,' said Collins. 'He says it was business but, between you and me and the gate post, I think it was black market stuff. However, I'm going to let that go for now. I'm much more interested in finding out about your husband's death.'

Frankie's face clouded. 'His murder, you mean.' She sank back onto her pillows, exhausted.

'We'll be going now, Mrs Delaney,' said Inspector Collins. 'Your aunt has given us her address and I believe you will be going back to Worthing shortly. Please accept our condolences and we shall be in touch.' He put on his hat, lifted it to her, and left.

Sidney Knight had put the mail bags down in the basement. It took him a couple of days to pluck up the courage to open them. Stealing His Majesty's mail was a serious crime. You could get up to seven years in the clink for it. In the end he decided he might as well be hung for a sheep as for a lamb so he broke the seals. The first bag contained registered mail and that meant money. He made up his mind to open a few at a time. He didn't want any attention drawn to his spending. His maxim had always been don't be greedy or you'll get caught, so with the bags stashed behind the defunct boiler, he began his modest spending spree. He soon worked out that envelopes with what looked like birthday cards inside were usually signed 'Love Auntie Joyce' or 'Love Granny' and had a couple of quid inside, sometimes as much as five pounds. An hour later he was on the street corner waiting for the bookie to put half a crown each way on Romping Home, a dog which was racing that evening at Hackney Wick.

# Thirty-Seven

**Kingston Lacy, Dorset, June 5th 1944**

The United States army didn't take kindly to the two British police officers who kept coming back to the base to speak to Lyman Spinks about kidnap and murder. Inspector Collins patiently explained that it was simply to eliminate the man from their enquiries and eventually it was agreed that he could speak to the staff sergeant provided another officer was present. The inspector and his sergeant were surprised to be taken to Kingston Lacy and onto a hospital ward to interview their man. Lyman Spinks, grey faced and clearly far from well, had a cradle over his legs. His doctor instructed them to be brief. 'The staff sergeant is very weak.'

Inspector Collins was tempted to ask him what had happened – had he had an accident? – but that wasn't why he was here. When Collins explained his mission, Spinks was completely indifferent. 'We have a way of dealing with animals like him,' he drawled. 'That fornicator should have stuck to his own kind.'

'So you are saying that man was hung – lynched – because he was sleeping with a white English girl?'

Spinks pulled himself up the bed and the inspector noted the snake ring on his finger. 'He had no right to mess with that woman.'

'You do know they were married.'

Spinks stared at the inspector in shocked surprise. 'That's even worse,' he spat. 'You plummy bastards should do all in your power to uphold the purity of Anglo-Saxon blood and Christianity,' he said speaking in a kind of chant. 'I believe in one hundred per cent Americanism. By marrying that woman, that dog crossed a boundary.'

'So you admit to hanging Doctor Delaney,' said Collins' sergeant.

'I admit nothing,' Spinks said, sinking back onto his pillows and closing his eyes.

The doctor leaned over his patient. 'You really do need that transfusion, sir.'

Spinks' eyes flashed open. 'I thought I made myself clear on that one doctor,' he hissed. 'Do you have a written guarantee?'

The doctor shook his head, 'No sir, but . . .'

'Then there's nothing more to be said,' said Spinks. 'I have God on my side. I shall be fine.'

Inspector Collins took this as his cue to leave and, quite frankly, he had heard enough. This man was a monster and he was quite happy to name him as chief suspect. He'd have to interview him at length at a future date, a prospect which didn't exactly fill him with joy, but with Mrs Delaney's testimony and an eye witness statement to the kidnapping, it felt like an open and shut case.

As he walked through the swing doors, the ward sister, an English girl, invited them into her office for a cup of tea. Collins accepted the invitation gratefully.

'I shall have to come back at a later date,' he told her. 'There are still some lose ends to tie up.'

'I'm not sure that will be necessary,' she said placing a cup and saucer in front of him and another in front of the sergeant.

'Oh?'

'He's refusing treatment,' said the sister.

Collins was puzzled. He had Spinks down as the sort who would demand the best of everything.

'He needs a blood transfusion,' said the sister, 'but we cannot guarantee that only a white man has donated that blood.'

Inspector Collins spluttered into his cup. 'What!'

'Sergeant Spinks has strongly held beliefs,' the sister went on. 'It's not just Jim Crow he hates. He doesn't like Jews, Italians, Russians or Catholics either.'

'So you're saying he's refusing a blood transfusion on the grounds that one of them might have donated it?' the sergeant asked in disbelief.

'That's about the sum of it,' she said, sipping her tea. 'He's pulled out the tubes so many times we've given in to his wishes now.'

'But that's crazy,' cried Collins. 'Blood is blood, isn't it? Somebody should tell him it's not black or white, it all red.'

For a split second, the sister grinned, then, turning serious again, she added. 'I just wanted you to know he's getting weaker all the time. I honestly don't think he'll survive this.'

'What happened to him anyway?' said the sergeant.

'Between you and me,' she began, 'and if you say anything I shall deny I ever said it, he thought he was going to stay over here but then they told him he was being sent to France.' She put down her cup. 'Unfortunately there was an "accident" (she drew the inverted commas in the air) with his gun and he shot himself in the foot.' She drew breath and sighed. 'I'm sure the other men must have heard the shot but it was some time before they found him.'

Collins looked away. Bloody coward. Whenever men were sent abroad there was always a small number of them who had this type of 'accident' so that they didn't have to go to war.

'So you're saying he did it deliberately,' the sergeant said dryly. He glanced up. 'I suppose that's why nobody found him.'

'Did they save his foot?' Collins asked.

The sister shook her head. 'Sadly not. In fact, Doctor Delaney was the only one who would have tried to save it, but he wasn't here, was he?'

Collins nodded sagely. 'From what I've heard, Spinks probably would have refused to let the doctor touch him anyway.'

The sister raised her eyebrow. 'You're probably right. Before you go, I want you to know that Doctor Delaney was a wonderful man and here at Kingston Lacy we shall all miss him terribly.'

Inspector Collins stood to shake her hand. He was feeling very emotional. So, Spinks wouldn't be around much longer and, in all honesty, he wasn't sorry. He didn't really want to talk to him again. If he did so, he'd have a job keeping his hands to himself.

After a couple more days, Frankie was moved back to Worthing but she was only in the local hospital for a day before being transferred to the Catherine Marsh Convalescent Home along the seafront just past Beach House. Slightly old-fashioned and earmarked for closure, the home had been a feature on the Brighton Road since the turn of the century. Under the terms of her annual subscription, Aunt Bet was allowed to recommend up to two patients a year for a three-week stay for seven and six a week. The normal charge for non-subscribers was fifteen bob. Everybody agreed that a short period with a more relaxed regime might help Frankie to begin to come to terms with her loss.

She was struggling. Her thoughts ranged from happy memories to agonisingly painful ones. One minute she was reliving the moment she and Romare had met by the town hall door in Wareham and he'd handed her the posy which was to be her wedding bouquet. From there they had walked hand in hand into the foyer where Aunt Bet and Uncle Lorry were waiting for them. She'd been so excited to see them and Barbara. Fancy all three of them coming all that way for such a short period of time. Apparently Doreen had been invited as well but there was a bit of a flap going on and she'd been unable to get leave.

It had been a lovely wedding. She smiled to herself, remembering the moment he'd made his promises and put the ring on her finger. Everyone knew they only had a few hours before Romare and Frankie had to be back on duty so the wedding reception had been limited to a drink in the Duke of Wellington. Aunt Bet, Uncle Lorry and Barbara were going to catch the afternoon train back to Worthing but as it turned out, all civilian trains were cancelled until the next morning. No reason was given but nobody moaned about it. It was plain that something big was about to happen.

Reliving those sweet memories took her to the moment when she saw the hooded man at the bottom of the stairs. After that it all became jumbled. The baseball bat, the blood, the sound of Romare's feet flopping on each stair as they dragged his unconscious body downstairs, the venom in Lyman's voice, and then the ringing blow to her own head. She still had nightmares and at times the aching pain of loss in her chest rendered her unable to breathe. And she wept. She wept until she felt ill; she wept until her eyes were so swollen she could hardly see.

One of her first visitors to the convalescent home was Barbara. It was a lovely sunny day so they sat in the grounds overlooking the sea. Frankie had a rug over her knees and although she greeted her with welcoming smile, Barbara was quite shocked by her appearance. Frankie looked pale and drawn and she still had a huge bruise on her jaw. She had also lost a lot of weight.

It was difficult for Frankie to talk about Romare because it still made her cry and her greatest grief (something she mentioned several times) was the fact that she didn't have a photograph of him. 'They haven't sent on the stuff from my billet yet,' she said sadly. 'And the US army haven't given me Romare's things either.' Even after so short a time, it was becoming difficult to remember his face.

'As soon as I can, I want to get back to work,' she told Barbara.

'Will they have you back so soon?' Barbara asked.

'They'll need dispatch riders, especially in France,' said Frankie. 'And it'll give me something else to think about.'

It occurred to Frankie as they talked that Barbara had changed too. She was no longer the bubbly girl with a *joie de vivre* she'd once known. Frankie guessed it was because Barbara's mother was still refusing to let her have much hands-on contact with her baby. 'How is Derek?'

'He's doing well,' said Barbara, her eyes lighting up. 'Into all sorts of mischief. He's coming up for five now. Can you believe it?'

'Does your mother . . .?' But before Frankie had even finished the sentence, Barbara was shaking her head so she added, 'I'm sorry.'

'I wrote to him again,' she told Frankie.

'Who?'

'Conrad,' said Barbara, 'but this time, instead of using the ENSA PO Box I sent a letter to his agent. Oh Frankie, his agent told me he'll give Conrad my letter at the earliest opportunity.'

Frankie struggled to find the right thing to say. It was unbelievable that her friend still held a torch for that man after all this time. Conrad had never written to her and as far as Frankie was concerned, he was an absolute rotter. 'I hope for your sake he writes,' she said gently, 'but after all this time . . .'

'I won't give up,' Barbara interrupted vehemently, 'I won't.' There was an awkward silence, then she added, 'I'm sorry,

Frankie. I'm supposed to be cheering you up, not getting cross. Have they found the fellow that did this to you?'

'Just before I left Worthing hospital Inspector Collins came to see me,' said Frankie.

'The policeman from Wareham?'

Frankie nodded. 'It turns out that Lyman Spinks shot himself in the foot so he wouldn't have to go to war.'

'So that means . . .?'

'Inspector Collins says he made such a botched up job of it, he's going to die,' said Frankie matter-of-factly. 'In fact he may be dead already.'

'What about the other two?'

Frankie shrugged. 'Probably over in Normandy by now.'

A nurse walked towards them. 'How are we feeling today, Mrs Delaney? Are you ready for lunch?'

Frankie feigned eagerness. 'Yes, please, nurse. I'm famished.'

'All right then,' the nurse said cheerfully. 'I'll come back in a minute to fetch you.'

'I'll be fine,' said Frankie, getting to her feet. 'I'll follow you in.'

Frankie took Barbara's arm and they strolled back towards the house. 'They certainly look after you here,' said Barbara. 'What's the food like?'

'All right I suppose, although I still have most things mashed,' said Frankie. 'It doesn't matter anyway. I've lost my appetite.'

They parted with Frankie promising to keep in touch. 'Try not to be too upset about Derek,' she said, giving Barbara a hug. 'At least you'll get to see him grow up. Lots of girls have their babies taken away.'

Barbara nodded bravely. 'You take care,' she told Frankie. 'Things will get better, I promise.'

Frankie smiled grimly.

*

261

Across the Channel things were moving on swiftly. By the end of August Paris had been liberated and General de Gaulle's rallying cry, 'Paris outraged! Paris broken! Paris martyred! Paris liberated!' reverberated throughout the free world. But it wasn't all plain sailing. The people of Paris were in the middle of a severe food shortage. Hardly surprising when the railways had been destroyed and the Germans had stripped everything stock piled in warehouses before they left. A British convoy called *Vivres Pour Paris* and consisting of five hundred tons of food entered the French capital on August 29th and Alan was part of it.

He was coping fairly well now. He still had flashbacks and Ginger was never far from his mind, but since Carrie had asked him to be Billy's godparent, Alan had a better focus in life. He had already amassed quite a bit of his money for Billy's savings account. It comforted him to know that Ginger would have been surprised – pleasantly surprised.

With the Americans flying in supplies and the French themselves in the surrounding areas pitching in, the terrible shortages and the threat of starvation in the city were alleviated within ten days.

The French women were very attractive, especially one of them. She had been in the crowds lining the streets as Alan's convoy rolled through Paris. She had dashed towards his lorry and jumped onto the running board with a red rose in her hand. As driver, for a split second he'd panicked but then he'd turned his head to look into the most beautiful blue eyes he'd ever seen. When she jumped down from the running board, having given him the flower, he thought she was gone forever but to his utter joy, she was at a reception the people of Paris had put on for the Allies by way of a thank you. He couldn't take his eyes off her and when the chairs were pulled back for a dance, he was the first at her side.

She was young, perhaps seventeen or eighteen, with a fresh face. Her dark brown hair was softly pinned back and she wore only a faint trace of lipstick. Her name was Thérèse. She spoke no English and he spoke no French but through smiles and gesticulations they made themselves understood. He quickly became aware that they were being watched.

'Mon père,' she smiled when he pointed to the man, so as soon as the dance was over, Alan went over to him to shake his hand.

In the days that lay ahead, Alan began an awkward relationship with the family. Naturally, the father was very protective of his daughter and Alan appreciated that the man didn't want his daughter to be seduced by some fly-by-night chap who was here today and gone tomorrow, so he did his best to let the man know that his intentions were strictly honourable. For the first time in his life, Alan was smitten and when the war was over, he knew he would move heaven and earth to make Thérèse his wife.

# Thirty-Eight

**Wareham Cemetery, Conniger Lane, Wareham, Dorset**

A week and a half later, Frankie and her family went back to Dorset for Romare's funeral. It was a traumatic time for everyone. Normally the body of a deceased American soldier was interred in a British cemetery or repatriated back to the States but to all intents and purposes, the army – who promised that they had informed his parents of his death – had, in essence, washed its hands of him. That meant the arrangements and the expense were left to his wife of less than one day. The question mark the Americans left hanging over Romare's demise (they still insisted that he must have committed suicide) meant that he couldn't be buried in consecrated ground. With no inquest and no trial, it seemed the problem would never be resolved. The service was conducted in a non-conformist chapel and he was laid to rest in the local cemetery.

The weather on the day itself couldn't have been better. It was warm and sunny and they stood around the graveside under a clear blue sky. Frankie looked around. Several of the locals had turned up; some people Frankie had never seen before.

'*Forasmuch as it hath pleased Almighty God . . .*'

Frankie was only vaguely aware of the minister's monotone voice. She was listening to the sound of a blackbird singing his heart out and the humming of bees and the clicking of grass-hoppers in the long grass.

'*We therefore commit his body to the ground; earth to earth, ashes to ashes, dust to dust . . .*'

The clods of earth fell with a thump on the top of the coffin. Faint and sick to her stomach, Frankie threw a red rose into the hole. 'Goodnight sweetheart,' she whispered as she turned away. Her lovely husband was gone. Gone forever.

At the wake held in the Duke of Wellington, a man in a pinstriped suit introduced himself to Frankie. 'My name is Doctor Roger Trent-Ellis,' he began. 'I am so sorry for your loss. It's a shocking affair.'

'Thank you for coming,' Frankie murmured mechanically.

'Dr Delaney was very much in love with you,' he went on. 'It was my cottage you were staying in.'

'Oh,' Frankie said, giving him her full attention. 'Thank you so much for that. You gave us . . . me, some very happy memories.'

The man pressed something into Frankie's hand. When she looked down it was a long white envelope. 'A few of my colleagues and I have motored down from London,' he went on, closing her fingers around the envelope. 'Dr Delaney and I became good friends when we worked together in the same hospital. I was the person who sent his letter. We are all indebted to your husband and so my colleagues and I want you to have this.'

Frankie began to protest but he squeezed her hand. 'Please allow us to do this for him. You will never know how much we respected and admired him.'

When she finally got back to the farm, Frankie opened the envelope. Inside there was a card signed by loads and loads of people and enough money to pay for everything. It hadn't dawned on her until she was on the train that Doctor what-ever-his-name-was said he'd sent her Romare's letter. What letter? She'd never received a letter. That was upsetting enough but what was worse – now she couldn't remember the doctor's name and neither could anyone else.

*

The next few weeks were a nightmare. A yawning emptiness flooded her whole being from the moment she woke up in the morning. She knew Aunt Bet was very worried about her but she couldn't seem to function properly. Frankie wrote letters to Romare's family but since she didn't have their address, (oh why hadn't they thought of these things when he was alive?) she had to entrust them to the army base. The days without him seemed to grow longer and longer. She would find herself staring into space, forgetting what she was doing; her mind wandering off to God-knows-where. Her own doctor said she should try to get back to normal living so a month and three days after Romare had died, Frankie reported for duty. Friends and family tried to talk her out of it but she was anxious to carry on and, at the very least, it gave her something else to think about. The D-Day invasion had gone well and the Allies had secured a toe hold in France. ATS riders were in great demand. After a chat with her CO, Frankie was told to prepare for a posting to Belgium. As she had already been away from the unit for more than four weeks, her embarkation leave was reduced to three days, which she spent quietly with Aunt Bet and Uncle Lorry.

Frankie was to set sail from Poole. She and the other girls who would be in her battery were given some Belgian francs and as Army regulations required, she wrote her will. She hadn't got much but she left it all to Aunt Bet and Uncle Lorry with the Russian doll donated to The Red Cross to sell or dispose of as they saw fit. There were two sections at the back of her pay book called Diagnosis and Disposal. If she was killed, the army would record how she had died (that was diagnosis) and they would fill in what happened to her body or remains (that was disposal). It was a sobering thought but now that Romare was gone, it didn't hold much terror. The details in their pay books were censored in case they were captured by the enemy. It was only then that Frankie understood what it meant to be in a war zone.

The day they marched onto the quay, there were several ships waiting to set sail. They were told to stand easy to allow a group of injured GIs to embark their vessel. They were a sorry lot. Some had bandaged heads, some had missing limbs and there were a few stretcher cases. These were the men who had been in that first wave over in Normandy and now, severely injured, they were going home. Everyone on the quay had enormous respect for them. Frankie joined her friends in shaking a few hands and wishing them luck.

'Thank you for what you've done. We'll never forget you.'

About half the men had struggled aboard their ship when Frankie heard a voice some way behind her, which made her freeze.

'Mind my leg. Be careful. And get your hands off me, boy.'

It was him. Lyman Spinks. He hadn't died after all. He was on crutches and she looked down to see one trouser leg flapping. So, the inspector was right. When he'd come to Worthing to hear her side of the story, he'd hinted as much. Lyman Spinks had taken the coward's way out to avoided combat but he'd lost his leg in the process. Looking at him, all she felt was contempt. Served him bloody well right.

As he came nearer she felt her heart race and the anger rising in his chest. For two pins she wanted to kick him over the gang plank and into the water, or snatch one of his crutches

267

away and yet she knew that if she attacked him she would only descend to his level; the level of the thug and the bully. Romare had fought discrimination and unfairness with dignity. He'd gained a reputation and worked hard but he wasn't a mamby-pamby or a pushover. He held his head high and his attitude had a way of making people look at themselves and the way they behaved. Without making speeches or being obnoxious, he made them feel so ashamed that they treated him with respect.

Spinks was almost level with her now. God, she hated him. He had no right to be here. The man should be locked up. There should have been a trial. Why hadn't Inspector Collins charged him? But even as she asked herself the questions, she knew the answers. The inspector had tried hard enough but to the American authorities Romare was only a tiny cog in the wheel and there were far more important things to do. They weren't going to arrest Spinks because he was wealthy and came from an influential family. Money talks, she thought bitterly, and the tide of resentment swelled inside her until it almost made her retch.

A medic was helping Spinks because he was on crutches. Another medic hovered close by. Frankie guessed that Spinks had lost his temper with the poor man because he was black. Ungrateful pig.

'Hello,' she said sweetly. 'Fancy seeing you again.' She had the satisfaction of seeing his face blanch. 'I was so sorry to hear about your foot.'

Several other soldiers were looking her way. Frankie raised her voice slightly.

'You should have aimed your gun above your foot, staff sergeant. That way you would have done less damage. Oh but then everyone would have known this was a self-inflicted injury, wouldn't they? Silly me. I'm guessing you did it because you didn't want to go over to France.' She put her index finger onto her cheek and looked thoughtful. 'Or could it be because you murdered my husband,' her voice had become cold and harsh, 'and this was a good way of getting away with it?'

By now she had caused a stir. Any sympathy he might have had evaporated. She noticed that the black medic assigned to help him up the gangplank had moved back a step or two to help someone else coming up behind him. The injured soldiers nearest him had also moved away. Spinks lifted his crutch to push Frankie aside.

'Careful now,' she said innocently. 'I'm only a small woman and you are a very big man. My jaw has only just recovered from the last time you hit me.'

His eyes flashed. 'I don't know what you're talking about, Ma'am,' he snarled. 'I've never seen you in my life before.'

'Of course you haven't, Staff Sergeant Lyman Spinks,' she said pronouncing his name in deliberate and ringing tones. 'Of course you would say that, wouldn't you. But let me make one thing very clear. I don't know how I shall do it, but I am here to assure you that one day I shall see you get your comeuppance. Justice for my husband will be done.'

She looked around. 'This man was responsible for my husband's death,' she told the crowd. 'He had him lynched. Yes, hung from an English oak for no better reason than he was black and he married me.'

'Get away from me,' Spinks snarled. 'You've no proof of anything.'

She could hear a buzz of conversation going around. 'Hands up if any of you men have had a blood transfusion.'

A few hands went up cautiously, including a few black hands.

Frankie smiled. 'For everyone here who has had a blood transfusion,' she said addressing the black soldiers in particular, 'my husband is the reason you are alive today. He fought for your right to have blood plasma.'

Frankie could see several heads nodding in agreement. 'Doctor Romare Delaney believed that every man's life was precious, no matter what the colour of his skin.' She turned back to Spinks with a curl in her lip, 'And you hung him out of jealousy and spite.'

As Spinks lunged towards her, Frankie could feel someone tugging at her arm. One of the other girls, anxious that she might get hurt, was encouraging her back towards the others. 'Frankie,' she whispered. 'That's enough.'

Spinks barged his way to the gang plank. Frankie stood with her hands on her hips to watch every painful step as he struggled to the top. Once on board the ship, he leaned over the rail and spat in her direction.

Only then did Frankie turn on her heel and allow herself to be led away. She was exhausted and trembling but she held her head high. She hadn't gone many steps before she heard a ripple of applause coming from the ship and by the time she had reached the rest of the girls in her battery the sound of thunderous applause, whistling and calling resounded all around the quay.

# Thirty-Nine

Even as she heard the applause, Frankie struggled not to break down. Every cell in her body wanted to let out her grief and loss. It was Joan who had tugged at her arm, the girl who had been with Frankie at her first posting. She had opted to be a mess orderly because she struggled with the skills she needed to be in the battery. Nearly five years on, she had risen through the ranks. She led Frankie back to the others. No one said a word but every now and then she felt a pat on her back or an encouraging touch on her arm. There wasn't a dry eye on the dock and everyone admired what she had done. For Frankie it had been satisfying and yet nowhere near enough. Romare deserved more than that; much more. He deserved justice, a proper trial, a conviction, and due punishment, something which had eluded him simply because he was black. All she had managed for his killer was a little humiliation. It was a small comfort that perhaps the men who had clapped her would make Lyman's journey home one to remember. He didn't deserve to be with those men anyway. They had been wounded in the field of battle. He had taken the coward's way out.

They boarded their ship and Joan made it her job to make sure Frankie was comfortable. As for Frankie, she dared not cry. If she started, she knew it would be impossible to stop. So she breathed in hard and stuffed it all inside, telling herself that the war wasn't over yet and she still had a job to do.

'You all right?' Joan asked as the ship pulled away from its berth.

Frankie nodded and her old pal squeezed her shoulder.

*

The crossing to Ostend was pretty grim. The weather had deteriorated and the sea was choppy. Several of the girls were sick and before long the open areas of the deck reeked of vomit. Frankie spent most of the trip trying to clean Joan up and convince her that she wasn't going to die. It was with a great sense of relief that everyone saw the port finally come into view. A couple of army trucks were waiting for them on the dock side but they didn't drive very far. Their first night was spent in some sort of municipal building which, up until a few weeks ago, had been used by the Germans. The place had been stripped bare but the plumbing still worked and it didn't take the army long to get the place up and running as a billet, albeit a rather meagre one. The girls cleaned themselves up and some of those who had managed not to be sick washed the vomit-stained shirts of the others.

That night, Frankie lay on her bunk and stared at the ceiling. Her thoughts were still centered on Romare and what might have been, but in her heart of hearts she longed for more. If only she could get some semblance of justice for him and clear his name. How dare the authorities insist her husband had committed suicide just because he was a black man and it was expedient? Spinks was a monster but in a funny kind of way, he couldn't help it. He had been brought up to think of himself as superior. He had been taught to hate the black man, but why? A hundred years ago those poor African slaves had never

272

asked to come to the cotton plantations. They had been forced from their homelands in Africa and shipped across the ocean to a land which, to them, must have seemed like hell on earth. The story might have been played out in the southern states but the people of Britain and Europe didn't have clean hands either. True, there came a time when they had been among the first to understand how appallingly the Africans had been treated and they started the anti-slavery movement but the prejudice remained. The Negro might have secured his freedom a century ago but was he really free? Until the mindless prejudice ended, no one was free to be himself. But what could she *do* about it? She was one woman, a not very well educated woman at that, who had been briefly married to a wonderful man, a doctor who happened to be black. Nevertheless, lying on that bunk bed and looking up at that ceiling in Ostend, she decided that when the war was over, she would try and make his voice and the voices of other downtrodden human beings heard. She couldn't help her beloved, damn it, but she would always stick up for his people.

*

Frankie spent the next few days escorting the convoys as the girls were posted to their new batteries and taking messages to various senior command posts. Because girls were not allowed in combat areas, she ended up manning an ack-ack gun at an abandoned German barracks in the middle of the countryside. Frankie thought she would struggle to remember what she'd been taught all those years ago but a few hours into her shift it became second nature. They were a grand bunch. The people she was closest to were Joan, the girl who had helped her at the quay side, and Connie from Blackpool, who was engaged to be married to a lad who happened to be posted in the same area. The place where they ended up had few facilities and was surrounded by muddy fields.

'Hardly the Ritz, darling,' Connie said sniffily as they walked into their hut.

'Good job you didn't pack your tiara then, M'lady,' Joan said dryly.

They made the most of it but the nights were cold. Each girl had two blankets but they had to resort to putting their great coats on the beds as well. 'I could do with a man in this bed to keep me warm,' said Joan.

'I wouldn't have the energy,' somebody yawned further along the barracks.

They were lucky enough to be invited to dances put on mostly for the troops. The Belgian people always gave them a warm welcome and the girls certainly didn't lack an invitation to go onto the dance floor. Frankie was polite but she didn't really join in. The Allies might have pushed through but it soon became clear that Hitler wasn't about to give up. Every night, hundreds of V1 rockets targeting Antwerp and London flew overhead and it was the job of the ATS girls to shoot down as many as they could. It wasn't easy. Quite a lot of the rockets flew at a terrific speed, under the range of the ack-ack guns, and for a terrible moment it looked as if the enemy would once again gain the upper hand.

Frankie knew they were some distance away from the front but that didn't make it any the less scary. A couple of times when she'd been out dispatch riding she'd come across a big sign at the side of the road saying 'Road under shell fire'. She wasn't a coward but it began to trouble her because it was becoming increasingly difficult to ignore what was happening to her body. When she'd come over on the boat, she'd managed to avoid being sick but for a couple of weeks she had woken each morning feeling decidedly queasy. Now that her breasts had started tingling the truth of the matter dawned. It was two months since she'd arrived in Belgium and four and a half months since her wedding day. Her uniform was becoming difficult to do up at the waist and it certainly wasn't because of the food. She was pregnant.

She told the girls in her battery first. They were all thrilled for her but it meant facing yet another tearful goodbye.

'Keep in touch,' Joan said. 'We want to know all about your baby.'

'I will,' Frankie promised.

Almost immediately, Frankie's commanding officer made arrangements for her to be posted back to Britain and to be medically discharged from the service.

# Forty

**Broadwater, North Farm, Winter 1944**

It wasn't until she came home that Frankie realised just how exhausted she was. The first three days back at the farm, she slept a lot. Without the other girls around and orders to follow, she found herself mourning her loss more keenly. She wished Romare could have known about the baby. And how on earth, she wondered, was she going to bring up her baby alone? She was a widow but her husband had been in the US army. She was their responsibility except that he hadn't died in combat. As far as the Americans were concerned he had died in mysterious circumstances, possibly by his own hand. As far as the British were concerned, he had, as the saying goes, been murdered by a person or persons unknown. Inspector Collins had done his best, but without a trial and conviction she was caught between two stools and, as a result, she was always someone else's responsibility.

Aunt Bet had been surprised when Frankie explained her condition but in her usual way, she had taken it in her stride and was already borrowing knitting patterns and sewing a layette. 'I've got a little saved up,' Frankie murmured, 'but what am I going to do for money?'

'Something will turn up,' Aunt Bet said breezily – and something did.

As Romare's wife she had inherited his money. She'd known the paperwork was coming, but the process had been slow and it came as a surprise to find out now that he had a tidy sum in the bank. If she was careful, it would get her through the first years with the baby but of course she would have to find a job eventually. Aunt Bet told her she was sure that in a few years' time she would find a new husband. 'You're an attractive girl,' she said. 'I'm sure someone will snap you up before long.'

Frankie didn't argue but she certainly didn't want to be snapped up by anybody. She tried not to be morbid about it but there seemed to be a pattern here. The people she loved the most met an untimely and suspicious death, so she made up her mind that she would avoid falling for someone else. It was better that way.

She would have liked to contact Romare's family in America to tell them about the baby but the army had closed the book and wouldn't give her their contact details. Perhaps it was for the best. Prejudice worked on both sides. Maybe they hadn't wanted their son to marry a white girl. Someone from the London hospital had sent his effects but she couldn't find anything helpful. 'I feel dreadful just taking everything,' she confided in a letter to Doreen, 'but what can I do?'

Doreen was more pragmatic. 'For heaven's sake, Frankie! You're carrying his child,' she wrote back. 'He would have wanted you to have everything. He loved you to bits and I think he would have moved heaven and earth for his baby.'

*

Ronald wrote to say he was coming back to Worthing for a short while. Aunt Bet had only seen her second son two or three times since hostilities began and Frankie hadn't seen him at all! She'd kept in touch by letter of course but Ronald didn't have much leave from his hush-hush job and what little he did get, he spent in London. He was looking for a flat or a small house to rent, he wrote, but it was difficult to pick something suitable at a distance. What he needed was someone closer, on the ground, so he suggested that Frankie might like to help him out. He gave her an idea of what he could afford, which turned out to be quite a bit, and asked her to look around. At first Frankie, aware of the desperate housing shortage, didn't think she could find anything, but because Ronald was able to go to the upper end of the housing market Frankie discovered there was a much better choice. She found him a really nice flat right on the seafront. Stoke Abbott Court was an attractive 1930s purpose-built block of Art Deco flats with the beautiful curved surfaces which imitated the racing cars and the great ocean liners which were so much a feature of that bygone era. The letting agent eyed her swelling shape and was a little concerned that Frankie was planning to set up home herself, but having been assured that the flat was for someone else, someone high up in the secret service, the man almost bit her hand off to get the client.

When she got back home, Frankie reflected on how much she had enjoyed doing it and wrote back to Ronald saying as much. Before long, and to her absolute delight, another couple of requests came back by return of post and Frankie set off once more, this time with the promise of a small fee if she got the job done. Frankie was delighted. It might not be much but it made her feel like an independent woman again and it was good.

Christmas was a much happier time this year. The fighting was still grim in Europe but was there was a tangible sense that things really were coming to an end. The East Worthing canteen had already closed because there were very few soldiers hanging around the town now, and early in December, the home guard was stood down. Alan was still in Europe but for the first time in years, Aunt Bet and Uncle Lorry had Ronald and Frankie home for Christmas. Ronald brought a friend, Eric, to join them and the invitation included Barbara as well. Her mother had decided to take Derek to her mother's (Barbara's grandmother) for the season and the invitation was not extended to Barbara.

As Barbara was getting ready to go up to North Farm, the doorbell rang. When she opened the door she got the surprise of her life. It was Norman Miles, the chap she had gone out with a few times before she'd met Conrad.

'Oh!'

'I hope you don't mind,' he began. 'I've got three days leave and nowhere to go. I just had to see you again.'

She invited him in and while he drank a cup of tea, she explained where she was going. 'I'm sure you can join us if you like.'

'Oh no,' said Norman. 'I don't want to intrude.'

'Don't be daft,' Barbara said. 'If I go there and tell them I left you all on your own, they'd kill me. Come on. The more the merrier.'

Eric was a fresh-faced man with soft features and it was obvious that he and Ronald got on well. Aunt Bet excelled herself in the kitchen with roast goose and all the trimmings. Uncle Lorry had bagged a couple of pheasants, which were in the oven today but would be used for the cold meat buffet on Boxing Day. Aunt Bet's Christmas puddings, made two months before the event, smelled wonderful as they steamed in the copper. Most people made theirs with reconstituted eggs but Aunt Bet had her usual Christmas 'accident' as she put some new-laid eggs into a bowl. She must have dropped them a little too hard, she confessed, and of course the shell broke. 'It was sheer luck that I was making the pudding today,' she said, rolling her eyes innocently.

'Quite,' said Uncle Lorry.

'It would have been such a waste otherwise,' Frankie said with a grin.

'You say that every year, Mum,' said Ronald.

'Moi?' said Aunt Bet, and they all laughed.

Frankie had made paper hats and Eric had brought some real Christmas crackers, something they hadn't seen in a long time. Ronald had arrived with a couple of bottles of wine and he delighted Uncle Lorry by giving him a bottle of 1943 Gordon & MacPhail Glenlivet whiskey all to himself.

Barbara and Norman arrived just as Aunt Bet was dishing up the vegetables and within ten minutes of his arrival, they were sitting at the table. Norman hadn't come empty handed. He handed Aunt Bet a bottle of sherry and a tin of broken biscuits. While Aunt Bet clapped her hands he slipped a box of Cadbury's milk chocolates into Barbara's hands.

'Oh my,' cried Aunt Bet. 'This will be a Christmas to remember.'

Uncle Lorry was just about to start carving the goose when someone tapped on the window pane. It was Doreen, looking very smart in her Wrens uniform. Frankie was thrilled but for a second Aunt Bet worried that there wouldn't be enough food on the table. However, that didn't dampen the level of her welcome.

Doreen was all apologies when she saw that they were just about to eat. 'I'm so sorry,' she cried. 'We thought you would be done by now. Shall we come back when you've finished?'

'Absolutely not,' cried Aunt Bet. 'Have you eaten?'

Doreen shook her head.

'We?' said Roland, the only one to pick up what she'd said.

'Terry brought me,' said Doreen cautiously. 'He's still in the car.'

'Then bring him in, lass,' Uncle Lorry cried as he shunted yet another chair up to the table.

'Who's Terry?' asked Ronald.

Frankie shrugged.

When he arrived, Terry staggered in with a huge hamper. Frankie was impressed. Tall, fair-haired and with a real twinkle in his eye, he was a navy man, an officer, and a Lieutenant. He held out his hand for her to shake. 'Hello, nice to meet you. Terry Fielding.'

Frankie slipped her hand in his and he gave her a firm handshake. She smiled. Good old Doreen.

'Oh look at you!' Doreen cried as came back indoors and held Frankie at arm's length. 'You look wonderful.'

Frankie laughed. 'Don't. I'm like a house already.'

'Come on now,' Aunt Bet cajoled. 'Sit down, everybody. Everything is getting cold.'

The meal was amazing. The goose was cooked to perfection and the pheasants helped to make sure everyone had enough to eat, even though they had been intended for tomorrow. Aunt Bet watched her family and friends tuck in and smiled. Today, as well as the goose and the pheasants, the nine of them would enjoy roast potato, roast parsnip, carrots and cabbage, gravy and stuffing. Let tomorrow take care of itself.

The conversation was lively and enjoyable. Ronald and Eric were bound by a code of absolute secrecy but that didn't stop them talking about jolly japes, concerts and days out together on a tandem.

'There's a beautiful lake in the grounds,' Ronald said. 'It's too cold now, but in the summer a lot of us gather there for a drink and a chat.'

'And some of us,' said Eric, giving Ronald a knowing look, 'stay up half the night.'

'He's not going to let me forget that one,' Ronald said good-naturedly.

'Why's that?' Frankie asked.

'He missed an important briefing and someone pressed the panic button,' Eric went on. 'Had half of security combing the grounds for him. Couldn't find him for ages.'

Uncle Lorry raised an eyebrow. 'How many have you got working there then?'

Ronald shrugged. 'Eight thousand?'

'Ten,' said Eric.

'Good God,' said Uncle Lorry. 'I had no idea it was so big.'

Doreen told them that she was on a forty-eight-hour pass. She glanced at Terry and gave him a shy smile. The way he smiled back convinced Frankie that he adored her. 'We wanted you to be the first to know.'

'Know what?' said Norman.

'Terry and I are engaged.'

It was time to offer congratulations and top up their glasses.

'When's the big day?' Frankie wanted to know.

'We may wait until the weather is a bit warmer, or the war ends,' said Terry. 'Whichever comes first.'

'Make it after March,' said Frankie squeezing Doreen's hand. 'I might be a bit slimmer then.' Everybody laughed.

'You must all come to the wedding,' said Doreen as she looked around the table. 'You've been more like family to me than my own family.'

'Doreen has told me all about you and what you did for her,' said Terry. 'I can't tell you how grateful I am.'

'We could always make it a double wedding,' said Norman. He didn't seem to notice Barbara freeze. 'What do you say, Babs?'

Barbara had gone bright red. 'I'm not ready to get married just yet,' she said quietly.

'Shall I clear the dishes?' Frankie said quickly. It was an awkward moment but one which soon passed as Aunt Bet rose to her feet and took charge again. 'Pop them on the draining board for now, and Ronald, would you get the best dessert dishes from the cabinet in the sitting room? Lorry, you come and help me take the pudding out of the copper.'

Terry's hamper contained a couple of tins of sterilized cream so they had a choice of cream or custard. He also had a small box of liqueur chocolates, just enough to go round.

'I've decided to emigrate after the war,' Ronald told them as he tucked into his liquor. 'There's a real opportunity in Africa to make a good life.'

Aunt Bet froze for a second, then turning to her son with a bright smile said, 'What will you do?'

'D'you know what, mother?' Ronald added with a chuckle. 'I shall be a farmer. Eric here is an excellent stockman and we have already gone into business together.'

Now that she understood what Doreen meant by Ronald batting for the other team, Frankie guessed that they would be setting up a home together as well. Well, good luck to them. If their secret came out in this country, they risked shame and imprisonment. 'It sounds like a wonderful opportunity,' she said. Perhaps things would be better for them in Africa.

'You could always come and join us,' Ronald said to Frankie. 'Once we're settled and the baby is born.'

'Yes, why not!' cried Eric. 'I fancy being a proxy father.'

Frankie smiled, only to humour them really, but it was certainly worth thinking about.

After lunch, they ate cob nuts and sweets, listened to the King's speech and dozed. The women prepared a cold buffet tea, which nobody really wanted but ate anyway, and Barbara's

Norman got the evening going with some excellent party games. By the time the day was over, everybody agreed it had been the best Christmas ever. Despite her loss, Frankie had enjoyed her day as well, although more than once she'd wished Romare could have been here with her.

# *Forty-One*

Frankie's baby, a girl, was born on March 5th 1945. Her labour began on a Sunday evening soon after supper, but Frankie didn't say anything. Everybody went to bed and she woke Aunt Bet at two in the morning. Her pains were coming fairly frequently by then but Aunt Bet decided that they could wait until a decent hour before getting the midwife out of her bed. At seven Uncle Lorry biked over to Broadwater, his trousers on over his pyjama bottoms, and the midwife was with Frankie by seven thirty. The baby took her time. She didn't put in an appearance until two thirty that afternoon. Even as a new-born she was an attractive little girl. 'Monday's child is fair of face,' Aunt Bet said when she saw her. The baby had a lusty cry, dark curly hair and she weighed in at seven pounds three ounces. Her fingers were long and artistic looking and she had a healthy appetite. Frankie fed her herself.

The next few days were filled with joy but tinged with some sadness. The baby was lovely but her arrival meant that Frankie missed her husband again. 'Romare should have been here,' she told those who came to visit and no one knew how to answer.

In the last few weeks before her delivery, Frankie had done some serious thinking. She was determined to do her best for her baby and although she knew she was very welcome to stay on the farm, she wanted her own home and her independence. The problem was – how to get it? If she rented rooms, something which would be difficult for Aunt Bet to accept, she would have to have a male guarantor. She was sure Uncle Lorry would do that for her, but it still didn't feel like being able to stand on her own two feet. She had to find a way to support herself long-term but who would look after her daughter while she was at work? Frankie spent some time walking around the farm partly to get a bit of exercise, partly to be alone and have time to think and partly to look at the land itself. By the end of February she was making a plan.

On Sunday March 25th friends and family gathered for the baby's christening in the eleventh century St Mary the Virgin Church in Sompting, a lovely church which sported an unusual Saxon tower with a Rhenish helm and a four-sided pyramid at the top. The baby was as good as gold, staring up at the vicar's face with a curious expression throughout the ceremony. She didn't even murmur when he splashed the water on her head. Frankie called her Lillian Rose.

Most of them were there: Aunt Bet, Uncle Lorry, Barbara, Mrs Waite from the florist shop and Ronald. Alan was still somewhere in Europe, and Doreen lord-knows-where. Afterwards, they gathered back at the farm for a little party and once everyone had gone home, Frankie put her idea to Uncle Lorry.

'Seeing as how I've got that money from my husband's will, I'd like to buy a little land off you,' she began. 'You don't have to say anything now, but would you give it some thought?'

Times were difficult for Aunt Bet and Uncle Lorry. With Alan writing to say he had fallen for a French girl and that he wasn't coming back to the farm and Ronald talking about emigrating to Rhodesia, Bet and Lorry faced a rather bleak and lonely old age. But unless he had help with the day to day running of the farm, Uncle Lorry couldn't carry on indefinitely. The work was simply too much.

Her uncle looked at Frankie with a puzzled expression. 'What land?'

'The bit we used to use for the track,' she went on. 'You always said it wasn't much use for anything else, so I should like to buy it from you. I have looked into it and I can pay the market rate.'

He stared at her for a second. 'Are you planning to use it for scrambling again?'

Frankie shook her head. 'I thought about that but with petrol still on ration I don't think it would work,' she said. 'No, I should like to use the land for people on holiday.'

'Holiday?' said Uncle Lorry. 'What sort of holiday?'

'We all know the war is practically over,' Frankie went on, 'so there's every possibility that people will soon have the time to get away for a little break. The trouble is, money is scarce. I plan to use the land as a camp site.'

Uncle Lorry's expression became a little warmer.

'I've already looked into it,' Frankie went on, 'and once everything is back to normal, I'll be able to get army surplus tents and blankets at a knock-down price. I know someone who will put in a word for me, one of the quartermasters from my old barracks. It's all legit, nothing black market.'

'You've certainly been busy,' said Uncle Lorry.

Frankie grinned. 'What could be better for a holiday than a place in the country with lots of lovely walks for the whole family?'

'Sounds good to me,' he said, 'but you don't have to pay me, love. You can have the land with my blessing.'

'I want this to benefit us all,' she said, shaking her head. 'If I pay you, the land will always be mine and you'll have a bit to put by so that you can retire whenever you want to. It's much better this way.'

'So you'll hire out the tents?'

'I'll start with the tents but I plan to look out for some caravans as well.'

Uncle Lorry looked impressed. Aunt Bet came into the room with a tray of tea. 'What are you two cooking up?' she said good-naturedly. 'You look as thick as thieves.'

When they told her Frankie's plan, Aunt Bet was very enthusiastic although at first, just like her husband, she tried to talk Frankie out of buying the land. In the end she could see the benefit for them all. 'I could sell eggs at the gate,' she said.

'Better than that,' said Frankie. 'We could set up a shop in the old bike barn. I'll pay you rent or, if we do it together, we could share the profits fifty-fifty. It could be a nice little money spinner. If holiday-makers are staying for a week, they're bound to run out of things like soap, tea and bread.'

She could tell by the expressions on their faces that she had given these two dear people a new lease of life, and if they managed to get it to work, a future for her lovely daughter.

\*

It was May 8th. There were four of them sitting at the table in North Farm: Aunt Bet, Uncle Lorry, Frankie and Mr Webley, their solicitor. Now it was official. Frankie was a landowner, something which was unusual for a working class woman. They had just finished signing the last of the papers when Uncle Lorry glanced up at the clock.

'They said Churchill was going to make a speech this afternoon,' he said, switching on the radio and twiddling the knobs. After a minute or two, the announcer's voice rang out loud and clear.

'*The Prime Minister, Winston Churchill, has officially announced the end of the war with Germany. In a message broadcast to the nation from the Cabinet room at Number Ten, he said the ceasefire had been signed at 0241 yesterday at the American advance headquarters in Rheims.*'

Uncle Lorry switched off the wireless. It was finally over. It was an odd feeling. After all this time – six long years – peace had come and this was VE Day. They'd prayed for it, worked for it, sacrificed the best years of their lives, suffered for it and some had died for it. Now that it had come it almost seemed an anti-climax.

Mr Webley shuffled his papers. 'Have you got sons in the forces, Mr Cavendish?'

'One boy in France,' Uncle Lorry said stiffly. 'The other one is at Bletchley Park.' He paused. 'You?'

'My boy was killed at Dunkirk,' Mr Webley said soberly.

'I'm sorry for your loss,' said Uncle Lorry awkwardly.

They stood and shook hands. Frankie sighed. Peace was wonderful but it would be tinged with sadness for a lot of people, herself included. They walked Mr Webley to the door and as he got in his car, they could hear the church bells at St Botolph's in Heene in the distance.

'Lovely sound,' said Mr Webley closing the door. 'I wish you well.'

'You too, sir,' said Uncle Lorry with feeling.

As the day wore on the celebratory mood grew stronger. Frankie, Barbara, and Aunt Bet took the bus into Brighton with the baby for the afternoon. In the centre of the town there was a lot of flag waving and hordes of happy people walking through the streets. Frankie and Barbara were kissed by strangers as they headed for the pier. They bought ice creams and Barbara bought a Kiss Me Quick hat. They took turns in pushing the baby's canvas pram. Lillian Rose seemed unperturbed by the

289

noise and the jostling. Their celebrations were interrupted by rain but not even that could dampen their spirits. Just before they caught the bus back, Aunt Bet treated them to afternoon tea in a little tea room near the Pavilion.

'Have you given Norman's offer of marriage – as impetuous as it was – any thought?' Frankie asked Barbara when Aunt Bet left the table to go into the ladies.

Her friend shrugged.

'He's a lovely man,' said Frankie, 'and he obviously thinks the world of you.'

'I know,' said Barbara. 'but I keep thinking that now that the war's ended, Conrad will get in touch soon.'

Frankie was so frustrated but she resisted the temptation to have a go at her friend. How could she be so stubborn? 'I admire the fact that you've stayed so faithful,' Frankie said as gently as she could, 'but don't you think it's rather a long time since you heard from him?'

'He's been travelling all over the world, Frankie,' Barbara said defensively. 'He probably doesn't have time for letter writing. After all, he's famous now.'

'Yes, but where there's a will there's a way,' said Frankie with a sigh. 'I just don't want you to waste your whole life waiting for him. I know you won't want to hear this but for all you know, he may even have been killed in action.'

Barbara gave her a stricken look. 'His agent would have told me.'

Aunt Bet was coming back, threading her way through the tables. 'Promise me you'll think about it,' said Frankie.

Barbara pulled the corners of her mouth down and rolled her eyes.

'Ready to go home?' said Aunt Bet cheerfully and they both nodded.

*

Frankie spent every moment she could on her parcel of land, determined to get it ready for the Whitsun bank holiday. While Aunt Bet looked after Lillian, she cleared brambles, tidied the paths and worked out where to pitch the tents to the best advantage. For a while it would be a bit basic but at least she could open to the public. She'd advertised North Farm Camp Site in the paper and created a large roadside sign to put next to the gate. She had worked out a competitive rate and now she was cleaning out the bike barn so that she could put a few grocery items for sale in there. She'd have to start with only a small amount of stock but she could build on her success and eventually create a decent camp shop. Uncle Lorry had laid on a cold water tap and cleaned up the old toilet block.

On May 17th she pitched four tents and waited with bated breath. By the evening of May 18th she had rented out five pitches and three tents to eight sets of campers. North Farm Camp Site was open for business.

# Forty-Two

**Worthing, 1946**

Sidney Knight had been ill for some time but in denial. The cough he'd developed in prison some years before had become progressively worse. It began with a tightness in his chest soon after VJ Day, but rather than waste money with a doctor's appointment, he dosed himself up with cough mixture and Friar's Balsam and went to the race meetings as usual. At the beginning of 1946, he collapsed in the street and was taken to Worthing hospital. An X-ray and a doctor's examination changed his life in more ways than one.

'I'm sorry to have to tell you that you have lung cancer,' said the consultant. He was standing at the end of Sidney's bed with the clipboard in his hands and surrounded by a bevy of junior doctors. 'I'm afraid it is very advanced and there is little we can do. We will do all we can to make you as comfortable as possible.'

Sidney lay staring at the ceiling for some time after the doctor had gone. It was hard to take it in. 'There is little we can do . . .' He knew a bloke once who had a lung removed. Why didn't they do that? Sidney asked the nurse when she came round to take his temperature.

'I'm sorry, Mr Knight,' she said. 'Didn't you hear what Mr Hermes said? It's too late.'

After a couple of weeks in hospital, they moved him to a nursing home. Desperate to get back home, he tried to make his escape but collapsed before he made it to the front door. That was when Sidney finally understood that he was dying. A lapsed Catholic, he asked for a priest to hear his confession. When the priest came, Sidney hardly knew where to start. Maud Parks, a cleaner who had worked in the Home for more years than she cared to remember, was deeply shocked by what she'd overheard as she tidied the linen cupboard in the corridor. By the time the priest left the nursing home, Sidney felt a whole lot better but the priest was a man with a burden on his shoulders. The rules of the confessional meant he could say nothing even though he knew about the mail bags and the fact that Sidney had been stealing his ex-tenant's cheques for years. He also knew another secret – something truly terrible. All he could do was pray that in the course of time, the God who knows all things would make it known. Maud felt equally bound. If she spoke about what she'd heard, they'd sack her for sure.

Sidney Knight died in October 1946. He had no money in his bank account, his last few pounds being put on a dead-cert at Newmarket. The horse came in fourth but Sidney never knew. By the time the result was made public, he had lapsed into a coma. The priest came back to give him the last rites and he died later that night. With no relatives, the state gave him a pauper's funeral and the speculation about who would inherit his house began.

'Here they are!' Frankie's excited cry as she looked out of the kitchen window brought everyone running. A Ford Ten Model trundled up the driveway and came to a halt just inside the gate. Frankie was already rehearsing her knowledge of the car. It was in excellent condition, probably laid up throughout the war, 1172-cc with a side-valve Four, if she remembered correctly, and a three-speed gearbox. Standard colour black.

The others had raced her to the door. 'Come in, come in,' cried Aunt Bet. Barbara was already helping Thérèse out of the front passenger seat. Alan was on the pathway with Uncle Lorry pumping his hand. 'Good to have you home again, son.'

Alan had married Thérèse in France just before he'd been demobbed in September 1946. It was impossible for Alan's family to travel to France and Thérèse's father wasn't about to let her go without a wedding ring on her finger. They'd had a simple wedding. Food and luxuries were in very short supply, even more so than in England, but her family had given her a good send-off and now she was in Worthing, ready to begin a new life in England.

They all piled into the house, everybody talking at once. 'How was the crossing?' 'Have you eaten?' 'You must be tired after your journey.' 'This is my friend Doreen and her new husband Terry. You remember Doreen, don't you?' 'Put the kettle on, Mother. They must be parched.' 'Sit here, dear, and make yourself at home.' In the distance an infant wail told Frankie that Lillian Rose was awake after her afternoon nap. She hurried upstairs to change her nappy and bring her down.

The war had been over for eighteen months but still the vestiges remained. The shortages were just as acute and now bread was rationed, something which hadn't happened all through the hostilities. The summer had been a dismal one and the harvest poor. June had been wet, in July there were severe thunderstorms and August was unsettled. Fortunately the weather hadn't interfered too much with Frankie's camp site. The stoic British holiday-maker wasn't about to let a bit of rain put them off and the pitches were usually all taken. She hadn't been one to rest on her laurels either. Frankie had bought three caravans, the bike barn was now a well-stocked shop (as well stocked as dwindling supplies would allow), and Uncle Lorry had created a children's play area near the trees with a rope swing – a rope which swung out over the small pond – and a wooden seesaw. North Farm Camp Site was proving to be very popular.

Frankie had also looked at other sites. She had bought ten acres of land in Durrington at the knock-down price of five pounds an acre. The ground was cheap because it was water-logged and unsuitable for building or growing – or so they said. Frankie called upon the services of old John Appleyard, an old-fashioned water diviner who discovered the source of a spring using a stick of willow. Once she knew where the water was coming from, Frankie hired a builder to dig down and pipe the water into the nearby stream. The ground dried out and she had another place to set up a camp site. This one was within easy reach of Highdown Hill, Titnore Woods and Patching Woods, all local beauty spots and ideal for walkers.

The year had been busy in more ways than one. Doreen had married Terry in the spring; a lovely wedding held in the same Sompting church where Lillian Rose had been christened, followed by a reception in the village hall. Doreen had already been demobbed and Terry only had a month to go. They planned to set up home in a brand new house in Dominion Road and Terry had already got a job as a salesman in a local estate agents lined up.

Now that Alan was back home, he had got a job as chef in the Beach Hotel along Marine Parade. It was a prestigious hotel which had been trading since 1867 and had just been refurbished after the war. Despite the shortages, Alan had been taking lessons with his French family and was confident that his French cuisine would rival any hotel in Brighton. He and Thérèse had rooms in the basement.

When Frankie appeared at the kitchen door with Lillian Rose everyone went into a kind of meltdown. 'Is this Lillian?' 'Aaah, she's lovely.' 'Hello, sweetheart. Did you have a nice sleep?' 'Come to your granddad, darlin'.'

She was a pretty child with a coffee coloured skin and a happy disposition. She loved the attention, of course, but she wasn't spoiled. Uncle Lorry was her special favourite and she held out her arms to go to him. Frankie put her down and she tottered towards him. He swept her up on his lap and smothered her with kisses as she snuggled into him, her thumb in her mouth and from there she regarded the friends and strangers all around her.

'Ah, she is so beautiful,' said Thérèse, clapping her hands.

They had gathered at the farm because Barbara Vickers was finally getting married the next day. She had waited throughout the whole of 1945 for a letter from Conrad but it never came. Norman still adored her and after the turn of the year, he courted her more fervently. At Easter she finally consented to be his wife and he was over the moon. Frankie felt Barbara was still hoping for rescue but she was very unhappy at home and she saw Norman as a way of escape. It was hardly ideal but Norman seemed keen to take her on and he was confident that eventually she would forget Conrad.

This was also the last weekend before Ronald and his friend Eric left for Rhodesia. It was proving to be a popular destination for a lot of ex-RAF personnel because the country was in the middle of an economic boom. Ronald and Eric had bought two neighbouring farms, one tobacco and the other for much needed vegetables including potatoes and onions. The new vegetable dehydration system meant that Rhodesia could export such products to far flung places such as the British Isles and be confident that they would arrive in mint condition.

Aunt Bet was passing the teacups around as everyone caught up with what they'd been doing since they'd last met.

'Frankie has some news,' said Aunt Bet. 'Go on, love. Tell them.'

With every eye looking in her direction Frankie suddenly felt overwhelmed. 'I had a letter from the London hospital where Romare used to work,' she began hesitantly. 'They want to honour his memory. They're naming a ward after him.'

'That's fantastic,' said Alan.

'And they want her to go up and cut the ribbon,' Aunt Bet said proudly. She reached up to the mantelpiece where a grainy picture taken by Lorry's box Brownie on Frankie and Romare's wedding day stood in a silver frame. It was the only picture Frankie had of her husband. Aunt Bet handed it to Thérèse. 'That's him.'

Frankie could feel her eyes smarting. She mustn't cry now. This was a happy occasion: Alan and the lovely Thérèse here in Broadwater; Barbara's wedding tomorrow; no, she couldn't cry.

'Can anyone come?' asked Doreen. 'I'd like to see you do that.'

'We never met the chap,' said Alan, looking at his wife to acquiesce, 'but I think Thérèse and I would like to come with you too. When is it?'

'Why don't we all go?' said Terry. 'Make a day of it.'

Frankie could hardly see for the tears standing in her eyes. Apart from Doreen, only her aunt and uncle had met Romare but it seemed everyone wanted to honour her husband. 'Thank you,' she croaked. 'It's a week on Saturday.'

Doreen squeezed her hand. 'Then we're all coming for a jolly.'

'Who's coming for a jolly?' They were interrupted by Ronald as he walked in the door and once again the hugs and hand-shakes began.

*

A week later, they all waited outside the ward doors as Frankie wielded a large pair of scissors. 'I now declare Delaney Ward open.'

As she cut the red ribbon, a camera bulb flashed and everybody clapped. She was wearing a two-piece suit in red with a hand knitted, cream short-sleeved jumper underneath. Her hair had been washed and set in the local hairdresser's the day before (Doreen's treat) and she had on some brand new plain black court shoes. Lillian Rose was at home being looked after by Sally, a local girl they sometimes used as a baby sitter when Frankie was serving in the shop. Everyone thought the journey would be too tiring for an eighteen-month-old.

Frankie walked through the doors with the dignitaries and the ward sister. It was a men's ward with fourteen beds. A nurse's station stood in the middle of the room and as they all came in, three nurses stood to attention. The poor patients seemed held down by their starched sheets and Frankie remembered how that felt. The room itself was light and airy and Frankie walked the length of the ward, smiling as she went. It was all rather surreal but at the same time, she was delighted that Romare was being given some vestige of respect and honour after all this time.

There was a small reception in a room near the main body of the hospital and Frankie and her family were treated as the guests of honour. She met up again with the doctor who had given her the money at Romare's funeral. She had forgotten that his name was Trent-Ellis but this was Frankie's opportunity to thank him. Even as she began he waved his hand away. 'We all wished we could have done a lot more,' he said. 'Did they ever catch his killers?'

Frankie shook her head. 'I'm afraid not.'

'Shocking,' Doctor Trent-Ellis muttered. He took Frankie's arm and led her to the buffet table. 'Please, do help yourself, Mrs Delaney.'

'When we were at my husband's funeral,' Frankie said quickly before he disappeared again, 'you told me you'd sent me a letter.'

'That's right,' he said. 'Romare knew he was going to France so he wrote you a letter that I was to give you in the case of his being killed in action. I know his death wasn't quite like that, but I reasoned that he would still have wanted you to have it.'

'Doctor Trent-Ellis, I never received that letter,' said Frankie.

The doctor looked surprised. 'You didn't?' he said. 'But I definitely sent it.'

'Can you remember the address?' Frankie asked. 'I moved around quite a lot back then. I was a dispatch rider, you see. Perhaps it went to one of my old billets.'

Doctor Trent-Ellis shook his head. 'It wasn't a billet,' he began. 'Oh dear, it's a long time ago and I hardly noticed.' He thought for a moment. 'It was a farm. Yes, that's it. A farm.'

Frankie's blood ran cold. 'North Farm?'

'Yes, that's it. Now let me see, Broad river I think.'

'Broadwater,' said Frankie.

'Yes,' said Doctor Trent-Ellis with a broad grin. 'Do you know it?'

Frankie nodded. 'It's my home,' she said quietly.

They regarded each other for a moment or two as the full import of what she was saying dawned on them both. 'You should have got the letter,' the doctor said.

'I never did.'

'I'm so sorry,' he said apologetically, then rather awkwardly, he repeated, 'Please, help yourself to something to eat.'

Frankie did as she was bidden but she'd lost her appetite.

# Forty-Three

**Broadwater, North Farm, 1947**

They were saying it was the worst winter for more than fifty years and Frankie could well believe it. The snow began in January and a month later it was still falling. North Farm was all but cut off by a huge snow drift anything up to four feet deep in places.

Uncle Lorry was frustrated because he knew there was a shortage of root vegetables in the town but he couldn't get anything out of the ground. He'd tried a pick axe and managed to dig enough for Bet's stew pot but it was too much like hard work to do it on a larger scale. They said on the wireless – the broadcasts were severely restricted because of the power cuts – that in some places farmers were using pneumatic drills to get their crops out of the ground.

Although Uncle Lorry and Aunt Bet kept their chickens indoors, several of them died, freezing to death overnight. Frankie did her best to keep Lillian Rose warm and with no income coming in, her small savings kept the family afloat.

Down in Broadwater, Sidney Knight's neighbours, desperate for fuel, had finally broken into his coal hole. The small garden at the back of the property was hideously overgrown. They'd had to beat back brambles and overgrown Buddleia and dig their way through a snow drift to make their way in.

Gwen Fielding had been the one who had mentioned the coal hole. 'He always kept it filled,' she'd said. 'And nobody's been in that place since he died. There must be a stack of the stuff down there.'

'We can't just take it, can we?' said Maureen Bishop. 'That would be stealing, wouldn't it?'

'Who from?' Gwen retorted. 'The man's dead.'

'His relatives perhaps,' Bill Bishop suggested.

'Look,' said Gwen. 'He's been gone for months. Nobody ever came to his place when he was alive and nobody's been there since he died. I'm guessing he didn't make a will and they can't find any relatives. The whole place is going to rack and ruin while here we're sitting here freezing to death for lack of a fire. I say we have a legitimate reason to go in there and get that coal.'

Put like that, no one was likely to argue so the small deputation, armed with buckets and shovels, made their way around the back of the house and eventually climbed in.

It smelled very damp and they could hear scuffling. Clearly the only occupants were rats and mice. To their absolute delight the coal hole was quite full so they agreed to make several trips, and involve a couple of other needy neighbours. It was after the third visit that Bill spotted something at the back near the wall. At first he panicked, thinking they'd uncovered a body. On closer inspection and under the light from several torches, they could see the bulky object was, in fact, a mail bag. Not only that, but there were two of them.

'Good God,' cried Bill. 'There was that Post Office robbery, wasn't there?'

'That was years ago,' said Isaac Fielding.

'I reckon that's where they come from,' said Bill. 'We'd better get the police.'

'Don't be daft,' said Gwen. 'What are you going to say when they ask you what you were doing in Sidney's cellar?'

It was a valid point and everyone was stumped. 'We ought to tell them somehow,' said Maureen. 'Some of this mail could be important.'

Everyone agreed with her, but they were all too scared to risk being caught.

Some days it looked as if things would improve and the services began again, but more often than not, as quickly as a thaw had begun, the weather conditions deteriorated rapidly. The snow came down with a vengeance early one Sunday evening in February. On his way to feed the animals Uncle Lorry spotted a broken down bus on the road to Sompting village. Thinking he saw movement inside, he struggled down the path and found five passengers, three children, a woman and an old man, huddled together as they tried to keep warm. The driver had set out for Broadwater to seek help.

'He left about an hour ago,' said the middle-aged woman, cuddling a small child.

'I doubt he'll persuade anyone to turn out in this weather,' said the old man. 'There was another chap, but he's just gone to see if there's a pub hereabouts that'll take us in for the night.'

It was obvious they couldn't stay there much longer so Lorry encouraged them to come up to the farm. They left a note for the driver and the man who had gone to look for accommodation and set off. The three children were crying with the cold by the time they all reached the back door.

Aunt Bet welcomed them in a way that soon had everyone feeling a lot more cheerful. Frankie recognised the woman with the small child. Margery had been Doreen's landlady and the child was her neighbour's little daughter. 'Her mummy is in Southlands hospital,' she explained, 'and I'm looking after

Vera until she's well again. The child misses her so much I thought we'd take advantage of the better weather and go over to see her.' Margery threw back her head and laughed. 'More fool me, eh.'

Frankie gave her a quick hug. 'You always did have a big heart.'

The other two children had been to Lancing to visit their grandmother. Aged eight and ten, they'd been trusted to catch the bus on their own.

'Is your mother on the phone?' Frankie asked. She could imagine that the poor woman being demented with worry. The boy, Brian, shook his head.

'But Mrs Cowley next-door has one,' said Sally, his sister.

Fortunately the telephone was still working and ten minutes later, they had put their mother's mind at rest. 'Your father says he will be up first thing in the morning to fetch you,' Frankie told them as she put the receiver down.

The old man sat hunched over the fire while the three women busied themselves doing their best to make everyone feel better. Frankie filled hot-water bottles and distributed blankets and Margery made the tea. Uncle Lorry stoked up the fire with their precious fuel to warm the room while Aunt Bet padded out their meal with more potatoes and a couple of swedes Uncle Lorry had pick-axed out of the ground.

Once she was warm, Vera wanted to play with Lillian and Uncle Lorry showed the other children a collection of Alan's old comics and his train set. It didn't take long for the unpleasant feelings of cold and misery to vanish.

By the time the man who had gone looking for accommodation arrived, they were all sitting down to a piping hot bowl of stew.

As he came in, he took off his gloves and blew on his hands. 'Couldn't find anywhere,' he said. 'The pub down the road is

303

all closed up. There's a note on the door saying they've got no coal and they've gone to relatives.'

He was a tall man, about Frankie's age or maybe slightly older, muscular and with a warm smile. His good looks were slightly impaired by a deep scar on the right side of his cheek. It was not unlike the scar on Basil Radford's cheek. The actor who had starred in one of Frankie's favourite films, *The Lady Vanishes*, had sustained his wound in the trenches but this chap was far too young to have been in the Great War. As the man introduced himself to everyone as Edward Hammond, 'just call me Ed,' she wondered how he had got his wound.

The children were all exhausted so it didn't take long to persuade them to go to bed. Vera and Sally were given Frankie's bed, and Brian was given a make-shift bed on the landing. Margery and Frankie were to share Alan and Ronald's room, while the old man was given the sofa. Ed insisted he'd be fine on the floor of the sitting room.

Gradually the others went to bed, but Frankie stayed in the kitchen for a while chatting to Ed. He seemed a nice chap. He'd spent most of the war in Italy, sometimes in the thick of a terrible battle, part of the time as a POW, and after the fall of Mussolini, he'd been posted to Germany.

'I'd most likely still be there if it weren't for me war wound,' he quipped.

'Looks as if it was pretty painful,' said Frankie.

'When it happened it made me eyes water for a bit,' he joked, 'but I was lucky. The doc reckoned another millimetre and the bullet would have taken half my face away. One good thing, it got me an early discharge.' He put his hand to his face as if he was in terrible agony and then grinned. Although slightly embarrassed, Frankie smiled.

'What about you?' he asked.

Normally when anyone asked her what she'd done in the

war, Frankie was frugal with information. She would tell them about her dispatch rider days but only say, 'My husband was killed.' She'd been talking for about twenty minutes when she realised she had told Ed everything. He listened intently but unlike when he'd told her of his own experiences, he made no flippant remarks or jokes.

The clock struck midnight. 'I suppose I'd better let you go,' he said. 'I've enjoyed talking to you. Perhaps we could do it again some time?'

Frankie hesitated. She had enjoyed talking to him as well but she wasn't ready for anything else. He must have seen something in her expression because he raised his hand defensively and said, 'A cup of tea and a chat somewhere, that's all. Promise.'

She nodded shyly. 'That would be nice,' she said, and she meant it.

*

As it turned out, Frankie enjoyed being with Ed. He seemed to sense that she didn't want to be hurried into any sort of relationship and yet as the weeks went by, she looked forward to his coming to the farm more and more. He took her to places she'd never been before. They enjoyed a meal out in some posh place far out in the country, or, more often than not, they'd simply go to the pictures. Later in the year they travelled to Brighton where he took her to the Theatre Royal to see *Charley's Aunt*.

'They're offering a tour of backstage if you're interested,' Ed said as they arrived.

'I've never been backstage before,' said Frankie. The play was great fun. Afterwards, those who had paid a bit extra waited in the foyer for their guide. It was fascinating.

'Built in 1807,' the guide told them, 'the theatre is one of the surviving "hemp houses" where every piece of scenery is raised and lowered into position by teams of men pulling on ropes.'

They were given a short demonstration and Frankie marvelled at their skill. As they stood with their heads craned back, Ed slipped his hand over hers and laced their fingers. It gave Frankie a delicious tingling feeling.

'I'm sure I'd pull the wrong rope,' she whispered.

'I'm sure you would,' Ed agreed and the room was filled with his deep-throated chuckle.

Ed had had his share of heartache too. His fiancée had been killed when the house where she was staying received a direct hit. 'I was in Italy at the time,' he said, 'trying to get leave so that we could get married, but it wasn't to be.'

'Oh that's so sad,' said Frankie. 'Sometimes the army can be so mean.'

'It wasn't their fault,' he said. 'My group was overrun and we were taken prisoner.'

It would be two long years before he was released and by that time, Jenny was long gone.

Now that he was back in civvy street, Ed was a jeweller by trade. His family owned a jeweller's shop in South Street in Worthing so she had to get used to him travelling to Amsterdam quite frequently to visit some dealer with uncut diamonds for sale. Increasingly, as time went by, she missed him. She missed his throaty laughter and his sense of fun. She missed his cosy bear hugs and lately, his more passionate kisses. He was a big man with coal dark hair and blue-grey eyes who seemed to get better looking every time she saw him. In fact she hardly noticed his scar anymore.

Lillian adored him. Calling him Uncle Ed, she would run to him on her chubby little legs and he would swing her high above his head. Frankie loved hearing her excited squeal and her chuckle of laughter as he tickled her tummy but sometimes it brought a pang of regret. Romare should have been doing that. Poor little lamb. She would grow up without ever knowing her father. The fact that children who had lost their fathers in the war were two a penny didn't help. Frankie would feel her eyes smarting because this was *her* child and *her* husband. She knew she would have to let go soon, but she wasn't ready yet. As 1947 turned into 1948, she looked forward to the day when Ed would ask her to marry him, but at the same time, she dreaded it.

# *Forty-Four*

**Broadwater Green, Worthing, 1950**

Barbara Miles stood in front of the hall mirror and patted her hair. Opening her handbag, she drew out her new Helena Rubinstein lipstick. According to the latest glossy magazines, deep red was to be the colour of the fifties and now, at last, she could afford to be at the forefront of fashion. She leaned forward and applied the vivid shade, pressed her lips together and then opened her mouth to get rid of any overspill at the corners with her finger.

She paused for a moment beside her marital bed. When she'd married Norman at the tail end of 1946, she had thought she was in for a life of drudgery but things had turned out very differently. She smoothed down the already smooth counterpane and thought of her nights sharing this bed with Norman. She had been surprised to find that he was such a gentle lover, so much so that it didn't take long for her to yearn for his touch. Her husband's love making was so unlike Conrad's hasty fumblings. Conrad had only ever made love to her in a bed once and that was in some seedy bedsit someone had lent him for the evening. Most of the time they were outside and he was in a hurry. They'd almost been caught out by a man walking his dog in Steyne Gardens once. It seemed funny at the time but the whole incident filled her with horror now. What on earth had she been thinking? Norman was so much nicer. Thank God he'd waited for her. She glanced around, admiring the pale pink curtains and cream walls. Who would have thought she would be lucky enough to have such a lovely home and be as well off as this? Shortly after his appointment to the finance department in the council, Norman had risen quickly through the ranks and was now deputy head of department.

She chewed her lip anxiously. How ironic. Now that she had the letter in her hand, all of this could be in danger. As she hurried down the stairs she could feel that unsettled feeling coming back into her stomach again. Behind her, Barbara heard Alice, her daily woman, coming downstairs with the Hoover and as she turned towards her, she was rewarded by Alice's admiring glance. Barbara smiled uncertainly.

'You can go as soon as you've tidied the kitchen, Alice,' she said pleasantly. 'Your money is on the table.'

'Thank you, Mrs Miles,' Alice murmured.

Outside a taxi tooted and Alice leaned the Hoover against the wall to open the door. Barbara walked through calling, 'See you on Thursday, Alice, and thank you.' The taxi driver had come around the side of the vehicle and as he opened the door, Barbara stepped inside. 'Goring-by-Sea Post Office, please.'

Sitting in the back seat of the taxi, Barbara opened her handbag to check that she had remembered to put in the letter. She ran her fingers over the buff coloured envelope. She didn't get it out. Since it had arrived a week ago, she'd read it so many times she knew it off by heart.

*Dear Mrs Miles*

*As you may have seen in the national newspapers, certain mailbags dating from 1944 have recently come into our possession. These bags include a letter addressed to you in your maiden name and the contents have been made known to a third party. We wish to return your property but would respectfully request that you attend the General Post Office building at the above address on Tuesday May 11th 1950 at 11.30am to that end.*

Barbara frowned anxiously. That letter could only have come from one person. Conrad.

It only took about fifteen minutes to get to the Post Office. She paid the taxi driver and ran up the steps. At the top, a large man, obviously a bit drunk, bumped into her.

'Sorry, lady,' he said lifting a rather greasy looking hat. She could smell his whiskey-soaked breath. Barbara shuddered inwardly and, ignoring his apology, put her nose in the air and walked on.

She turned just inside the door and was slightly alarmed to see that the man had followed her. Clutching her handbag closer, in her anxiety to get right away from him she bumped into someone else and apologised profusely. To her immense surprise, it was Frankie. Her short bobbed fair hair was styled attractively and she was smartly dressed in woodland green cigarette pants with a high waist band. She looked amazing. Her short jacket was rust coloured and the open neck print blouse underneath mirrored both colours. There was a kerchief knotted at her neck and she carried a small tan shoulder bag.

'Barbara!' she cried. 'What are you doing here?'

'I've come to fetch a letter,' said Barbara.

'Me too!' cried Frankie.

The drunk wobbled towards them. Barbara linked her arm through Frankie's and both women turned their attention in the direction of the Post Office cashiers. Having shown her the letter, they were both ushered into a small corridor where a row of green chairs stood against the wall. Several other people were already waiting. Frankie and Barbara sat on the end of the row.

'You look as white as a sheet,' Frankie remarked.

'It's that letter,' said Barbara speaking in hushed tones. 'I think it must be from Conrad.'

'Blimey,' said Frankie. 'After all this time?'

'Oh Frankie, I wanted him to write for so long but I don't think I could cope with it right now. Norman and I are happy.'

'Hang on a minute,' Frankie said in a low voice. 'They told me the letters dated from 1944. You had Derek years before that.' She put a comforting hand on her friend's arm. 'Don't go jumping the gun.'

Barbara looked down. 'But I wrote to him one last time in 1944.'

'I'm sure you're worrying about nothing.' Frankie said with an encouraging smile. 'By the way, how is your mother?'

Barbara shook her head. 'Not too well, I'm afraid.' She paused then added, 'I may have to look after Derek if she gets any worse.'

'I'm sorry,' said Frankie.

Barbara sighed and laid her hand across her stomach. 'Oh Frankie,' she said her eyes glistening with excitement, 'I want you to be the first to know. I think I'm having another baby.'

'That's wonderful!' Frankie cried. 'What does Norman think of that?'

'He doesn't know yet,' Barbara said. 'I've only missed my country cousins twice but I'm already beginning to feel queasy in the morning.'

Frankie leaned over and squeezed Barbara's clasped hands resting on her lap. 'I'm so thrilled for you.'

They fell silent for a moment.

'How is Lillian?'

'Doing well,' said Frankie her smile warming again. 'She's already five, would you believe?'

'And what about Ed? Has he asked you to marry him yet?'

311

Frankie nodded. 'Quite a few times.'

'Oh Frankie,' said Barbara squeezing her hand, 'You can't keep putting him off forever.'

'I know,' Frankie said miserably, 'I love him and I know he's wonderful but something holds me back.'

'It's Romare, isn't it?' said Barbara. 'Don't be silly, darling. He would have wanted you and Lillian to be happy.'

Frankie nodded.

They looked up as a woman wearing a dark brown coat who sat further along the row was called into a room and they watched her go until the door was shut.

'I wonder what this is all about?' Frankie mused. 'They told me they've found a letter of mine. I'm hoping it's from Romare. Apparently he wrote one to be sent to me in the event of his death but I never got it.'

'Someone told me it's something to do with that robbery in 1944,' said Barbara. 'I read about it in the paper. Some men clearing a house found some mail bags in the attic.'

'Basement,' the woman sitting next to them corrected. 'They found the mail bags in the coal hole down in the basement.' She frowned. 'My neighbour says they found something else in the attic.'

'Have they arrested the robber?' Frankie asked.

'He died years ago,' said the woman. 'The house was derelict for ages and then somebody bought it. That's when they found the mail bags. Been there for years, so I'm told.'

'Why didn't they just post them on?' said Frankie.

'Search me,' said the woman.

The door opened and the woman in the dark brown coat came out. The colour in her cheeks was high but she was dry-eyed. They watched her as she stood in the corridor for a few seconds and then she tore an envelope into several pieces before dropping it into a waste paper basket and walked away.

Barbara could feel that sense of foreboding descending again.

The door to the same room opened again and Barbara's name was called.

She stood up shakily. 'Frankie, there's a kiosk at the end of Sea Lane. I'll meet you there afterwards, okay?'

Frankie nodded and Barbara walked towards the door. At the same time, a policeman came out of another room further along the corridor and called Frankie's name. Barbara turned and gave her friend an anxious look.

The kiosk at the end of Sea Lane was little more than a wooden hut with some public toilets attached. As Frankie crossed the road she spotted Barbara a little further along sitting on a wooden seat overlooking the sea. She was leaning forward and her shoulders were shaking so Frankie guessed she was crying.

A moment later she was sitting beside her old friend. 'All right?'

It was obvious Barbara wasn't all right but it announced her arrival. Frankie's old friend lifted her tear-stained face and blew her nose. Frankie tried to work out what had happened. Had Conrad sent a letter asking her to marry him? If he had Barbara would be in an absolute spin. She'd married Norman on the rebound, that was true, but would she divorce him? Would he even let her go now she was pregnant? Frankie moved closer and put her arm around Barbara's shoulders.

'Was the letter from Conrad?' she asked gently.

Barbara nodded.

Frankie struggled to find the right words. 'I . . .'

'It was awful,' Barbara blurted out. 'I can't believe I've been such an idiot.'

Frankie frowned. 'So he didn't want to marry you?' she said cautiously.

'He never did,' said Barbara. 'Look.'

Frankie stared at the screwed up piece of paper in Barbara's hand as she held it out to her. 'Are you sure you want me to read it?' she began. 'After all, it's very personal.'

Barbara scoffed. 'Oh yes,' she said, her voice brittle. 'It's personal all right but you can read it. I want you to.'

Reluctantly Frankie took it from her.

*For God's sake Barbara stop sending me these bloody letters. What we had was nothing more than a bit of fun, that's all. I never promised you anything and if you've got yourself in the family way, that's your look out. You're nothing more than a silly little tart with stars in your eyes. I've told my agent if you send any more letters he's to put them in the bin. Now leave me alone and grow up! Conrad*

Frankie handed it back to her. What a nasty piece of work Conrad Merriman had been. She knew he was selfish and unthinking but to write a letter like that when a young girl had written to tell him she'd had his baby was nauseatingly nasty, spiteful and cruel. 'Barbara, Norman is worth ten thousand of him.'

'I know,' Barbara wept. 'Oh Frankie, I've been an utter chump, haven't I?'

Frankie resisted the temptation to agree. 'You were young,' she said. 'He filled your head with dreams of Hollywood and all that. You're not to blame.'

'Well, I think I am,' Barbara said firmly. 'I've been an absolute idiot.' She blew her nose again. 'Well, I'm a changed woman. From now on, I shall live my life as a devoted wife.'

'I never liked to mention it,' Frankie confessed, 'but I saw an article in *Picturegoer* not so long ago saying that Conrad had got married just after the war. Apparently they kept it secret because he didn't want his fans to know. I should have told you; sorry. I wasn't sure whether it was true.'

Barbara sighed. 'That explains a lot.'

They both fell silent, each lost for a moment in her own thoughts. 'What did they mean when they said your letter had been seen by a third party?' Frankie asked.

Barbara shrugged. 'I don't know. I forgot to ask them. When they gave it to me it had been opened. The police think the thief was looking for money, but perhaps someone else read it before they told the police but I'm only guessing. What about you?'

'I knew him.'

'Who?'

'The thief. He was my old landlord and he was living in my mother's place,' said Frankie. 'And it doesn't end there. That woman was right. When the police searched the whole house, they found a body in the attic.'

'Good heavens!' cried Barbara. 'Whose?'

Frankie shrugged. 'I have no idea.'

'Was it one of his lodgers?'

'He never had any,' said Frankie. 'Not since my mother died anyway. Perhaps because he didn't want anyone finding the body.'

'But that's awful,' said Barbara.

'Oh God,' said Frankie, leaning forward and putting her head in her hands. 'You don't think he had something to do with my mum's death, do you?'

'He could have done, I suppose,' said Barbara putting her arm around Frankie. 'You always said he was a nasty piece of work.'

'I know,' said Frankie with a nod. 'It seems he'd been stealing money that rightfully belonged to my mother for years.'

'Oh Frankie.'

'The thing that puzzles me,' said Frankie, 'is that I haven't the vaguest clue where that money was coming from.'

*

In the church of St Mary of the Angels, a lone priest knelt before the high altar. He was deep in prayer. No one could hear the words he said, but he said them from a heart overflowing with gratitude. A prayer he had prayed every week since 1946 when he'd heard the confession of a dying man in Worthing hospital had been answered at last. The body had been found.

# *Forty-Five*

Frankie had to wait until Lillian was in bed before she could share what had happened that day. She still lived at North Farm. A couple of years ago, when she was at last in a position to buy a place of her own, Aunt Bet began having trouble with her arthritis. Sometimes her fingers were so stiff she could hardly move them, especially when the weather was damp. Frankie didn't say anything to her because she was such a dear she would have insisted Frankie go, but she'd made up her mind to stay at the farm and take on some of the heavier work. Uncle Lorry was slowing up as well so he had let the big greenhouse go and they had fewer chickens and geese than they'd had in the old days. He was happy to potter about the camp site making sure the visitors had everything they needed and chatting to anyone who had a moment to stop and listen.

Frankie had three other camps dotted around the area now and they brought in a good income. She'd got hold of a few more 1930s caravans and done them up so that people who didn't fancy camping in tents could have a few more home comforts instead. She knew this frugal type of holiday experience wouldn't last. The good times were just around the corner, so they said, and with that in mind she had scrimped and scraped to buy a couple of parcels of land in the area. Housing was a top priority now that the war had ended so there was talk of large scale building in and around Worthing, Durrington and Broadwater. If she didn't have the wherewithal to build houses, she could sell her land to the highest bidder when the time came. Frankie was determined to provide as best she could for her daughter.

Ed usually came round most evenings and today was no exception. After she'd read Lillian a bedtime story, Frankie joined everyone at the kitchen table over a cup of tea and they listened wide-eyed as she told them about Sidney Knight, the body in the attic and the stolen money.

'Have you any idea who that person might be?' Frankie asked Aunt Bet.

'None at all, my dear. Your mother had no men friends as far as I know and she certainly had no time for Sidney Knight.'

'I never liked him either,' Frankie observed. 'I've no idea who the person in the attic is but I remember when Romare was alive we walked round to see my old home. Sidney came up behind us and he said something really weird.'

Aunt Bet frowned. 'What was that, lovey?

'It's a long time ago,' said Frankie trying to recall his exact words, 'but it was something like, "I put a stop to that Russian."'

'Did you tell the police?' Ed wanted to know and Frankie nodded.

'Never liked that Sidney Knight,' said Uncle Lorry. 'He was a lazy sod and a terrible gambler. Ended up in prison more than once.'

'The thing that puzzles me is the money,' said Frankie. 'Everybody told me my mother lived hand to mouth.'

'So she did,' Aunt Bet said stoutly.

'Then what was all this about?' She took some things from a buff coloured envelope and handed them around. The police had kept most of the evidence (as they called it) but they had let Frankie keep a couple of envelopes and her mother's old

Post Office Savings book. A cheque for fifty pounds had been paid into it in 1932. The family looked over the entry in bewilderment. 'There were other cheques,' Frankie went on. 'They did get less over the years but they were still coming.'

'So what happened to them?' Ed asked.

'It looks like Sidney created a false name and had them paid into his own account,' Frankie went on. 'He called himself Mr Sherwood-Knight and altered the name on the cheques.'

'Good God!' Uncle Lorry exclaimed.

'I seem to remember that when old Mr Knight died, Sidney was quite well off,' said Aunt Bet.

'He was,' said Frankie. 'There was another house and money in his father's bank account but the police reckon that over the years he gambled it all away.'

'Frankie,' said Ed. 'Did your mother have anything of value? Anything at all?'

Frankie shook her head. 'All she left me was the doll she made for my birthday.'

'Can I see it?'

Frankie looked puzzled. 'Why? What could that have to do with all this?'

'I don't know,' said Ed, 'but she obviously had something which was still bringing in money. Perhaps I'm barking up the wrong tree but I wonder if that doll might give us some sort of clue.'

Frankie rose to her feet with a sigh. 'I put it in the loft years ago,' she said, 'when Lillian was born. I thought she might damage it so I put it up there to give to her when she's older. It might take me a while to find.'

'Do you want me to help?' Ed suggested.

Frankie nodded. 'It might be quicker with two of us.'

They found torches and pulled the loft ladder down. It was hot and musty up there but once they'd switched on the electric light bulb Uncle Lorry had put up there just after the war, it was a lot easier to see what they were doing. Frankie soon found the box with the doll inside but before she went back down, Ed took the opportunity to take her in his arms and kiss her. Frankie yielded herself but it didn't take long for the old feelings of disquiet to crowd in. 'We'd better not keep them waiting too long,' she quipped light-heartedly, 'or they'll both be up here wondering what we're doing.'

They made their way downstairs. Back at the kitchen table, Frankie got the doll out of the box. Despite the fact that she was wrapped in blue tissue paper, her petticoat had little brown spots on it and Frankie's heart lurched with disappointment as she saw it.

'I'd forgotten how pretty she was,' said Aunt Bet.

'But look at all those horrible brown spots,' Frankie wailed.

'A drop of lemon juice or some white vinegar will soon cure that,' said Aunt Bet.

Frankie smoothed the crumpled dress down and stroked the doll's hair. Ed was looking in the box again and lifting the last of the tissue paper out, he picked up a small book. 'What's this?' he said.

'My mother used to tell me stories,' said Frankie. 'I thought they were real but then I found that book and realised they were all made up.'

Ed was thumbing through the pages. 'Have you ever read it?'

Frankie shook her head. 'Not really.'

'You should have done,' he said. 'I think your mother wrote it.'

Frankie frowned. 'Don't be daft,' she said good naturedly. 'It says on the front *by Daisy Alexander*.'

Ed held the book open on a page near the front where the publisher's name and other information was listed. He pointed to a line in minuscule print which said '*Daisy Alexander is the pseudonym of Moira Sherwood*'. Frankie's mouth dropped open.

'That's where the money was coming from, Frankie!' he said. 'Your mother was a children's author.'

'What!' cried Aunt Bet, taking the book from them and looking for herself. 'I don't believe it. She always told a good story, but I had no idea she'd actually got a story published. Well, I never.'

Frankie gasped and her eyes filled with tears. 'I was so upset when I found this book,' she said, her voice thick with emotion. 'In my heart I called her a cheat and a liar.' Her lip trembled. 'I didn't know. I didn't understand.'

Aunt Bet rubbed her niece's forearm. 'Don't take on so, lovey,' she said gently. 'She had us all fooled and it's all water under the bridge now.'

'But I feel so terrible,' Frankie said. 'How could I have been so stupid?'

'It's all right, my dear,' said Aunt Bet. 'It's just between ourselves. Your mother never knew what you were thinking and it was only natural.'

Ed, who had been looking closely at the doll, suddenly got up from the table and went to his jacket hanging on the hook by the door. He came back with his jeweller's loupe and picked up the doll again.

'What is it?' Frankie asked.

Ed held up the doll and examined the buttons on the bodice. 'You won't believe this,' he said with a smile, 'but these aren't glass buttons. They've got diamond chips around the edge and the little red stone in the middle is a ruby. They're not worth a fortune but they will bring you a tidy sum. Have you got any more?'

When he looked up, all three of them were staring at him open-mouthed. Eventually Frankie jumped up. 'There are two more,' she said. 'I put them in an old trinket box on my dressing table.' She left the table and ran upstairs. A couple of minutes later, she reappeared with two tiny and very dusty buttons.

Ed examined them. 'Would you like me to get them properly valued?'

Frankie nodded vigorously and then she put her hand over her mouth and burst out laughing. A moment later, they were all laughing.

'I'll make some more tea,' said Aunt Bet getting to her feet.

'Tea?' Uncle Lorry scornfully. 'This calls for a celebration.' And he reached into the bottom of the kitchen cupboard for the whiskey bottle and some sherry.

*

Frankie felt slightly mellow as she climbed into bed and pulled up the bedclothes but she didn't turn off the light. Not just yet. The one thing she hadn't told any of them, not Aunt Bet, Uncle Lorry, Ed or Barbara was that she had been given something else that day. As soon as she saw it, her heart had leapt in her chest and it had been hard not to cry out or indicate how much it meant to her. She had recognised the handwriting instantly even after all these years. It was Romare's letter and she wanted to read and savour it privately. She leaned back against her propped pillows and slipped a paper knife under the opening at the back. Her eyes were already filled with tears and she could almost hear his voice. Her thoughts went back to the first time she'd seen him when he'd run into the ward as Mr Hills was doing his rounds. She had loved him from that moment.

The paper was thin. Air mail paper.

> *My darling*
> *The fact that you are reading these words can only mean one thing – that I am no longer on God's earth. It is what it is. I can only imagine the heartache you must be feeling right now and my only comfort is that it will not be long,*

*even if you live to be a hundred, before we shall be together for all eternity. I write this because I want you to know how wonderful it has been to have your love and later on today to be your husband and lover, your friend and confidant. You have enriched my life in so many ways and my heart is full. My lovely English Rose, you mean more to me than life itself and although right now you are grieving I don't want you stay in that sad place. It pleases me to think of you being happy with someone else. You are not a person to stay alone, to grow old in widow's weeds. Promise me that you will embrace life in all its fullness. Find a new love. Be happy. Whatever has become of me, I am not unhappy. I have had the greatest gift of all. I have been loved unconditionally by a wonderful person – and that person is you my darling. Put this sadness behind you and go out into a new morning, a new beginning with a new love.*

*Thank you my precious girl and may God bless you always. Goodnight sweetheart.*

*All my love,*
*Romare*

Frankie read and re-read the letter several times before she was ready to lay down. She had always known Romare was someone special and now she had it in writing. As she pushed the letter back into the envelope something stopped it going back in. She looked inside. There was a small photograph blocking the way. She pulled it out and the tears flowed. There he was; her lovely husband of just one day, smiling up at her. He looked so young, so handsome. She turned the photograph over and through her tears she could just pick out an address. At the top he had written, *My mother's address. If you have a moment please write to her.*

# Forty-Six

**Worthing hospital, August 1950**

Barbara had been called to the hospital. Her mother was dying. Mrs Vickers lay on her pillows, pale and sickly looking, her eyes hollow and dark rimmed. Incapable of speech now, she breathed noisily through her mouth. Barbara held her mother's hand, the most intimate thing she had done in many a long year. As she waited for the inevitable, Barbara reflected on the course of her life and what her mother had done. Since receiving Conrad's letter she was finally able to look at the whole thing with different eyes. For years, she hadn't been sure that Mrs Vickers pretending to be the one who was pregnant was done out of love. Knowing how paranoid her mother was about scandal, it seemed more like an act of self-preservation, but having said that, it had given Barbara a chance to find the security of marriage and a life of her own. Perhaps Norman would never have asked her to marry him, had he known the truth about Derek. Without her mother she would have been labelled at best 'easy' and at worse a 'tart', and Derek would have been consigned to a children's home with only a vague hope of adoption.

When the nurse came around the screen to check her mother's condition, Mrs Vickers let out a long sigh. The nurse waited a moment or two, and then looked at Barbara with a sad expression and said, 'I'm afraid she's gone.'

Derek was all alone in the waiting room. Barbara's heart constricted as he lifted his tear-stained face towards her. He was ten years old, a bright child with his father's good looks. Barbara's own father had walked out on her mother soon after the war. Barbara guessed he must have realised Derek wasn't his child and the fact that her mother had no time for anyone else other than the child probably drove the final nail in the coffin of their marriage. Barbara hadn't seen him from that day until this but she had heard on the grapevine that he had a new wife and family.

Barbara sidled up to her son and put his arm around his shoulders.

'Is Mummy going to die?' he asked.

'I'm afraid she's already gone,' Barbara said gently, even though when he called his grandmother mummy it had cut her like a knife.

They sat together for some time and then he said, 'Will I come and live with you now?'

She hadn't asked Norman and the birth of their own baby was only a couple of months away but Barbara was confident enough to say, 'Of course you will.' And she felt the boy relax in her arms.

'You keep looking at me in a funny way.'

Ed had taken Frankie and Lillian to Devil's Dyke for the day. Although late in the year, it was gloriously sunny. They had loaded his car with a picnic hamper and a rug. Lillian had brought her little friend Susan along so while the girls ran around or played with a bat and ball, the adults had time to relax and enjoy some peace and quiet.

Frankie grinned. 'I was thinking just how lucky I am.'

When Ed had picked them up he had told her that the little buttons were in fact melee diamonds. 'They're very small,' he had said, 'maybe only two or two point five carats but the clarity is good with very little natural colour showing through.'

'So what does that mean?' Frankie asked.

'I shall have to put them through a diamond sifter to be really accurate,' he went on, 'but I think I can safely say you could get several hundred pounds should you want to sell them.'

Frankie's eyes had grown large. 'Would I have enough to travel a long way?'

Ed had looked a little puzzled but he said, 'Yes. Would Australia and back be far enough?'

'I don't think I want to go that far but I might like to go to America.' She watched his face fall then added, 'I never told you but I was given something else that day I went to the Post Office.' She reached into her handbag and drew out Romare's letter. 'It's the very last letter my husband ever wrote. I'd like you to read it because it directly affects you as well.'

As he took it, she rose to her feet and called the girls. 'Who wants an ice cream?'

Ten minutes later, Frankie rejoined Ed on the picnic rug. The girls were sitting on a bench next to the ice cream van with their sixpenny wafers. Ed handed the letter back.

'I've been a bit of an idiot,' Frankie began.

'No, not at all,' Ed interrupted.

'Oh I have,' Frankie insisted. 'Let me tell you, please.'

He nodded.

Frankie was staring at the blanket as she spoke. 'I realised after I'd read his letter that I was scared,' she went on. 'I adored my mother and she died. I adored my husband and he died. There was always a finger of suspicion over my mother's death and I know for sure that poor Romare was murdered. I think I've always been terrified that if I fell in love again history would repeat itself.' She looked up at him. 'I tried very hard not to love you. That's why I always pushed you away.'

'Oh Frankie,' he said softly.

'I don't know why you've hung around all this time,' she continued, 'but if the offer is still there, I should love to be your wife, Ed. Apart from my daughter, you mean more to me than anyone else in the world.'

The next moment she was in his arms and he was kissing her tenderly, lovingly, hungrily. He only stopped when they heard a little voice say, 'Ugh, what are you doing?' and they looked up to see Lillian, her face covered in ice cream, standing above them. Frankie and Ed burst out laughing. Frankie sat up and reached in her handbag for a handkerchief to clean her daughter up. 'I was telling Uncle Ed how much I love him.'

'Your mummy and I are going to get married,' said Ed.

Lillian stared at him steadily and for a moment Frankie's heart sank.

'Uncle Ed will be your daddy,' she ventured.

Lillian looked from one to the other, her expression unchanged. 'Does that mean I can be your bridesmaid?'

Frankie laughed again and said, 'We'd love you to be our bridesmaid.'

After a service in Broadwater parish church, they buried Mrs Vickers in the cemetery at Durrington. It was a dull day with drizzly patches. After the burial they met in Barbara's beautiful home in Ardsheal Road for the wake. There were only a few mourners: Aunt Bet and Uncle Lorry, Frankie and Ed, Barbara herself, and Norman. Alice, Barbara's daily woman, waited on them and they spent a pleasant hour eating dainty sandwiches in the sitting room overlooking the rain-swept garden. They shared their memories of Mrs Vickers but the sad thoughts soon passed as they talked about the future and especially Frankie's forthcoming marriage. Barbara was very excited for them. 'Wait until I've had the baby, won't you,' she teased. 'I don't want to look like a beached whale in the wedding photographs.'

'It won't be until after Christmas,' said Frankie. 'Ed has business in Germany.'

'Weird, isn't it,' Aunt Bet remarked. 'Five minutes ago we were at war with them and now you're doing business with them.' And everyone nodded sagely.

As they parted, Frankie and Barbara were alone in the hallway.

'Will you tell Derek that you're his mother now that his grandmother has gone?' Frankie whispered when she and Barbara were out of earshot of everyone.

Barbara shook her head. 'It doesn't matter now,' she said. 'And anyway, Norman has suggested that we might adopt him.'

'Oh Barbara,' said Frankie, grasping her hands in delight.

'I told Norman everything after I got that awful letter. It was such a weight off my shoulders.'

'And was he all right about it?'

Barbara smiled. 'He said he'd guessed Derek was my child.'

Frankie took in her breath. 'Never!'

Barbara nodded. 'Apparently it was the way I looked at him that gave me away.'

'And now he's willing to adopt him,' said Frankie. Barbara nodded again. 'Oh how wonderful,' Frankie went on. 'What a lovely man he is. What does Derek think? Have you asked him?'

'Actually he's very excited about it.'

Frankie gave her friend a hug and whispered into her hair, 'See? You've got your boy back after all,' and they parted after giving each other a knowing smile.

*

About a week later, Frankie was over at the caravan site near Highdown Hill when a police car pulled up outside her office. She had been cleaning out the static caravans ready for a new influx of visitors due to arrive later in the afternoon. It always amazed her how different people were. Some visitors left their caravan looking like a pig sty whilst others had obviously taken a lot of trouble to make sure their accommodation was left as they had found it. She had a 'full house' this weekend but this would probably be the last lot. It was already late October and the weather was definitely much cooler, especially in the evenings. Rather than lazing in deck chairs in the sun, the few visitors she had now enjoyed brisk walks on the hill to admire the autumn colours.

'Your aunt told us you'd be here,' said the man, who had introduced himself as Detective Inspector Wallis, a thick-set man with a mass of untidy hair and wearing a raincoat. He and his colleague, Sergeant Heaton, tall and very thin, shook hands with her.

Frankie invited them into the office. 'It's about the body in the attic of Sidney Knight's house,' DI Wallis began as they all sat. 'We have identified the man in question. His name was Ivan Yelchin. Does that name mean anything to you?'

Frankie shook her head thoughtfully.

'He's not a relative of yours?'

'I shouldn't think so,' said Frankie.

Sergeant Heaton leaned forward in his chair. 'Perhaps he was a friend of your mother's?'

Again Frankie shook her head. 'Don't forget I was only ten when my mother died, but I think I would have remembered someone with a name like that. Have you any idea why he was there?'

DI Wallis shook his head. 'We can only hazard a guess. Why he died is a mystery but we believe that Sidney Knight had something to do with it.'

'Is that because of what I told you?'

DI Wallis nodded.

'According to the neighbours he never invited people in,' said Sergeant Heaton, counting out the reasons on his fingers, 'he refused to get the guttering repaired even though it was obvious it was damaging the property and, considering he was always short of money, even though he could have rented rooms out, he never did. In short, we believe he was hiding something.'

'Like a dead body,' said Frankie.

'Exactly,' said DI Wallis. 'We've also had a report from a cleaner in Worthing hospital. She overheard a dying man saying his confession to the priest. There's no-one to corroborate her story and of course the priest is bound by the rules of the confessional but it seems that she heard Mr Knight confessed to killing a Russian.'

Frankie was puzzled. 'But why?'

'The cleaner said he told his priest he attacked the man out of jealousy.'

Frankie took in a breath. 'Did Sidney Knight murder my mother as well?'

'We don't think so,' said DI Wallis. 'According to what the cleaner overheard, Mr Yelchin had been to your mother's house earlier that day and left his hat. When he came back, your mother had had a heart attack and Mr Knight was rummaging through her things. There was a fight and it appears that Mr Yelchin was killed.'

'How come nobody reported Mr Yelchin missing?' asked Frankie.

'They may well have done,' said the DI. 'We know that he came from London and, from what we can gather, he was a bit of a loner so perhaps he didn't tell anyone he was coming to Worthing. If that was the case, when he went missing it would be a bit like looking for a needle in a haystack.' He paused for a moment before adding. 'We have no reason to suspect anyone else was involved, so we are closing the case.'

'The same goes for the Post Office robbery,' said Sergeant Heaton. 'We are aware that you and several other people have lost a considerable amount of money, but with no one to prosecute, there is little point in continuing our investigations.'

'I can only suggest that you make a claim against the Post Office,' the DI went on, 'but I imagine that with the passage of time and the lack of any real evidence, it will be hard to get any reparation for your loss.'

Frankie told them she was grateful that they had taken the trouble to come and tell her and they left. It was only as she was booking in one of the weekenders that something occurred to her and she couldn't wait to get home and check it out.

That evening, alone in her bedroom, Frankie got her mother's book out and fitted the final piece of the jigsaw into place. Opening the book to the same page where Ed had found her mother's name, she found two things she'd never noticed in the small print before. One line said, 'an autobiographic tale' and at the very top she read, 'Yelchin publications', followed by a London address. So her mother had been telling the truth – and Ivan Yelchin had been her publisher.

# *Forty-Seven*

**Broadwater, North Farm, April 1951**

Frankie and Ed's wedding was scheduled for early April. Easter Sunday was March 25th, and Lillian would be starting school next term so it seemed the ideal time. About a week before, Barbara came up to the farm and asked to speak to Frankie on her own and they went for a walk. The weather was cold and crisp but dry. Already small signs of spring were appearing. Catkins danced on the trees and the occasional primrose nestling under the roots of larger trees looked almost ready to flower.

'I need to ask you a favour,' Barbara began. She looked upset and Frankie noticed there were dark circles under her eyes, as if she hadn't slept. She had a scarf around her chin but her face was deathly pale.

'Yes, of course. What is it?'

'Promise me you won't breathe a word of what I told you about Derek,' she said urgently.

'Barbara, you know I never would do that,' said Frankie. 'You look really worried. What on earth has happened?'

Her friend's eyes filled with tears. 'I've had a letter from Conrad's lawyer. It seems that he and his wife can't have children and he wants his son back.'

Frankie's jaw dropped. 'Can he do that?'

'I suppose so,' Barbara said helplessly. 'He says he'll take me to court. Oh Frankie, we don't have the money for lawyers and all that. I don't know what to do. How can we compete with a big Hollywood star who has all the money in the world? Like he says, our son would lack nothing in life.' She put her hand over her face and wept into her glove.

'Bloody cheek!' Frankie cried.

Barbara fished in her pocket for a handkerchief and blew her nose. 'I just get my boy back and now it looks as if I shall lose him again.'

'What does Norman say?'

Barbara looked uncomfortable.

'You haven't told him, have you?' said Frankie.

'What's the point? What can he do?'

'Barbara, you can't keep something like this away from him,' said Frankie. 'He'll be terribly hurt.'

Barbara nodded miserably and the pair linked arms and walked on.

'Hang on a minute,' said Frankie. 'Didn't you once tell me that your mother made a false declaration on Derek's birth certificate?'

Barbara nodded miserably.

'Then where's the proof?' Frankie demanded.

They stopped walking and Barbara gave her a quizzical look. 'I don't understand.'

'If your mum registered her name and your dad's on his birth certificate, where's the proof that Derek is your baby?'

Barbara's eyes grew wide.

'Did you see a doctor when you were pregnant?'

'No.'

'A midwife?'

'No. You know I was in hiding for six months,' said Barbara.

'What about your mum?'

'Well, of course not!' said Barbara.

'But she went about her daily life, shopping, meeting friends, going to church?'

'Yes,' said Barbara.

'And everyone thought she was pregnant.'

'Yes,' said Barbara. 'That was the whole idea.'

'Then I'll ask you again, where's the proof Derek is your child?'

'But what about all those letters I wrote to Conrad? He's only got to produce them in court . . .'

'Judging by the vitriol in that last letter,' said Frankie, 'do you really think he kept them? All you have to say is that back then you were a silly schoolgirl with a crush who would do anything to marry a famous film star.'

Barbara's face broke into a wide grin. 'Frankie Sherwood,' she gasped. 'You're a ruddy marvel!'

*

Shortly after she'd found their address on the back of his photograph, Frankie had begun a correspondence with Romare's mother and it was obvious that the Americans were dying to meet her and especially their little granddaughter. She and Ed were soon to be married but as for their honeymoon, they decided to put it off until later in the year.

The war had been over for six years but the country was still struggling to get back on its feet. For any normal working class family a trip to the States would be prohibitive but now that Ed had got a good price for the buttons and he had put a large chunk of his own savings into the pot, it was perfectly possible to go. They decided to go over to New York on the *Queen Mary* and Mr and Mrs Delaney would meet them to drive them down to Washington DC. It promised to be a very exciting time and Lillian spent hours drawing and painting pictures for her granny and granddad.

Aunt Bet and Uncle Lorry set out to see them off at Southampton. The ship itself was huge and the dock crowded with passengers, crew, and other relatives and friends come to see their loved ones set sail. The whole dockyard was festooned with party streamers and at one end a brass band played. Although Lillian couldn't possible have any concept of what was happening, she was very excited.

'Goodbye, darling, and have a wonderful time,' said Aunt Bet, doing her best to hold the struggling child long enough to give her a kiss.

'We'll say our goodbyes here,' said Frankie. 'I don't want you both hanging around for ages and getting tired.'

'Oh, don't you worry about that,' said Aunt Bet. 'Lorry said he is taking me for an afternoon tea.'

Uncle Lorry seemed surprised. 'Did I?' he said uncertainly. 'I don't remember that.'

'That's because you're getting forgetful in your old age,' said Aunt Bet giving Frankie a playful wink. 'Take care now, my dear, and safe journey.'

Frankie could see the unshed tears in her eyes. 'Bye, Aunt Bet, and see you soon.'

They were travelling Tourist Class so they headed for the bow of the ship and took the forward stairs, down into the depths. The climb on the stair was quite steep and Ed explained that if they had a storm they shouldn't be scared if it was a little choppy. 'You'll soon get used to it,' he said confidently.

As it turned out, the cabin – or berth, as they called it – was rather snug but it was nicely decorated and the shared bathroom was only three doors down the corridor. After a little exploration, they discovered a shop nearby with a hairdresser's and barber's sharing the same space. They were also glad to find a kiosk next door which sold just about everything and anything they might need.

The days passed by very quickly. They ate delicious 'home cooked' meals, strolled along the decks, went to the cinema, played games and swam in one of the two swimming pools. Ed and Frankie felt as though they were living in the lap of luxury and enjoyed every minute. Four and a half days later they sailed into Upper New York Bay, past the Statue of Liberty and into the harbour.

*

Eldrick Delaney was easy to find. Frankie and Romare's mother had arranged that he would be wearing a tan coloured jacket and carrying a newspaper but when it came to it, Frankie could see his son in the way he stood and the way he looked. The resemblance was almost shocking as she found herself looking at an older version of the man she had loved all those years ago. Apart from his steely grey hair, Eldrick was Romare all over again. He greeted them with a wide smile and hearty handshakes, then he bent to look at his granddaughter.

'Well, my, my . . . nobody told me you was so beautiful,' he said. 'You know who I is? I's your granddaddy.'

'Pleased to meet you,' said Lillian bobbing a curtsey, although where she'd got that idea Frankie hadn't a clue. It didn't matter. Eldrick loved the gesture and roared with laughter.

They loaded his car with everything and then set off. Ed sat in the front passenger seat and Frankie was in the back with Lillian.

'It is far to go?' she asked.

'Quite a while I reckons,' Eldrick said with a chuckle.

Frankie settled back with her daughter. He'd said it as if it were a five-minute drive. Frankie had no idea it was so far from the terminal. As it turned out she enjoyed the ride. Lillian was sleepy so she put her arm around her daughter and it wasn't long before her head lolled on Frankie's breast. The men were talking so Frankie watched the world go by. How extraordinary to see the sort of neighbourhood and open countryside she had only seen on the cinema screen. Things were so much more advanced than back home. Wide streets, tree lined avenues, traffic lights suspended over the road and unmanned railway gates. They also went through mile after mile of beautiful countryside which, apart from the very wide open spaces, reminded her of home. But not everything was beautiful. The car went through some very run down areas too, past dark alleys full of ill-kept people milling about. They caught sight of an altercation between a street vendor and the driver of a large car which, even as they sped by, looked as if it was going to get ugly.

It seemed like no time at all before Eldrick called out, 'Here we is. We's arrived, little missy.'

Lillian yawned and stretched and Frankie and Ed exchanged a small smile. The welcome they had was almost overwhelming. It seemed that everyone wanted to pump Ed's hand or to kiss Lillian's cheek. Frankie was swept into everybody's arms and because they were all talking at once, she only caught a few names which hung in the air because she'd perhaps turn her head just as the person was being introduced and miss the face the name belonged to. 'This is Selma . . . Abe . . . Constance . . . I's Forrest.'

Somehow or other she was propelled towards a flight of steps leading to a white front door. The house was surprisingly attractive. She had heard stories of GI brides coming to the States after the war and ending up in one-room shacks miles from anywhere, but these people were obviously well off.

An attractive woman in her mid-fifties or early sixties greeted her and invited her inside. She wore a smart day dress in a lovely peacock blue and had matching jewellery. Her greying hair was beautifully coiffured in a uniquely African style.

'Come you on in,' she cried. 'I's Romare's mother. Cecelia my name. Come on in and welcome.' She held out her arms and Frankie went into her warm embrace.

In the moments which followed, Frankie and Ed were shown to their room and invited to 'wash up'. Dinner, they were told, would be on the table in twenty minutes.

'Well, they certainly gave you a warm welcome,' said Ed when they were alone.

Frankie hurriedly washed Lillian's face with a flannel and brushed her hair tidy again. As soon as her mother finished, the little girl hurried downstairs. Ed was about to follow her when Frankie caught his arm.

'I'm worried that you will find all this a bit hard to swallow,' she said. 'They'll be making a fuss of us because of my first husband.'

'I knew what I was letting myself in for when we came,' Ed said gathering her into his arms. 'I want this to be special for you and Lillian, so it's okay.'

They kissed tenderly. 'You're a remarkable man, Edward Hammond,' said Frankie looking up at him with a smile. 'And I do love you.'

'I think I'll get that in writing,' he quipped.

*

There were eleven at the table. Ed, Lillian, and Frankie, of course; Cecelia and Eldrick were joined by Constance, Cecelia's sister, Abe, her husband, Selma, their daughter, and Forrest, her husband. Selma had two children, a girl about Lillian's age called Shanice and a boy who was a couple of years younger called Darnell.

'My other son Jefferson should be here as well,' Selma explained, 'but he gone to Kannapolis for the union. He back tomorrow.'

Frankie nodded. She remembered the name. Romare had doted on him but she had no idea he had such a big family. She had already warmed to them. They were all so friendly.

The meal was delicious but rather strange to her palate. Brunswick stew which, according to Cecelia, consisted of lima beans, vegetables, corn, okra (a vegetable which looked a bit like a skinny courgette), and smoke pulled pork, which they ate with warm crusty bread and a fresh salad. It was followed by banana pudding which seemed to be layers of sweet vanilla custard, broken biscuits and bananas topped with meringue. Lillian enjoyed some home-made pink lemonade, which was very cold because it had been in their refrigerator, and the adults drank something called sun tea.

'I expect you wanna see the sights,' said Forrest.

'We got a lot planned,' said Constance, 'but some places, you have to go alone. They for whites only.'

Frankie glanced at Ed. 'I'm sure we'd much prefer to stay with all of you.'

Her statement was honest and heartfelt but the fact that this was a mixed race family in an America which was segregated had already brought an awkwardness into their being together.

*

The next few days passed quickly. Frankie, Ed, and Lillian wandered through Georgetown and along the waterfront of the Potomac river; they took Lillian and the other children to the park and enjoyed meeting other friends of the family. They also spent time looking through old photograph albums and hearing some of the family stories.

'I remembers the time Romare's cousin pushed him in the

water butt,' Cecelia said with a chuckle. 'The boy knowed he was in trouble so he knocks on the door and runs away. I opens the door and there's Romare standin' there, hair all plastered to his face, water coming out of his pockets and soaked to the skin.' Then she began to laugh. 'I tell you, that boy was always gettin' Romare into trouble.'

'What happened to him?'

'The Klan got him,' she said, her face clouding. 'They done to him what they done to my boy.'

*

As the week went on, Frankie was aware that there was an undercurrent in the home and it seemed to be something to do with the mysterious Jefferson who still hadn't turned up. They had woken one morning to the sound of Selma's voice on the telephone.

'He all right?' She took in her breath noisily. 'Where he gone?' There was a pause, 'He safe there?' Another pause. 'You sure? Oh God. Tell him to stay until the heat die down.'

Frankie and Ed looked at each other. 'Something's wrong, Ed.'

'I know, but they obviously don't want to talk about it.'

Throughout the day, Frankie tried to ask about Jefferson but people avoided the issue by changing the subject. Eventually late that afternoon, she and Cecelia were alone in the kitchen preparing the evening meal.

Frankie had been given some celery, onions and green peppers to cut up. 'Cecelia, I want you to tell me what's going on,' she said boldly. 'Where is Jefferson?'

'Don't you bother your pretty head about dat,' she said.

Frankie caught her hand. 'Cecelia, I want to know.'

Cecelia reached for a skillet and put it on the hob. 'It complicated.'

'I still want to know,' Frankie said doggedly.

Her ex-mother-in-law sighed. 'Romare fight his battle in England, Jefferson fight here but it the same fight.'

'Against racial discrimination?' said Frankie.

Cecelia nodded as she put some butter in the skillet. 'Jefferson live in Kannapolis,' she said. 'He work for Cannon Manufacturing. They the largest factory making sheets and towels in these parts, maybe in the whole world. Jefferson only got low pay but he union man.'

'So he's fighting for workers' rights?' said Frankie, trying to fill in the blanks. 'Romare always thought a lot of his nephew.'

'After the war,' Cecelia went on, 'they try to bring unions to Carolina but it ain't working. Jim Crow laws don't let white and black folks mix. The white boss stop them working together. Here, honey, put your vegetables in the butter.'

'So what you're saying is that the unions want to create better working conditions for the factory worker,' said Frankie as she pushed the chopped onions, celery and peppers into the pan. 'But because of segregation . . .'

'The union-shop say no discrimination,' Cecelia banged the wooden spoon on the side of the pan as she interrupted Frankie, then she stirred the vegetables and turned down the heat.

Frankie frowned. She could understand the fact that there were two opposing beliefs but surely with discussion and compromise everything would work out. Romare's mother moved back to the table where she crushed some biscuits into an oven proof dish.

'See, child,' Cecelia went on, 'we got a Cold War now and they accuse union leaders of being communist. If you communist you ostracised. You can't work. You can't shop at the store. Ain't nobody gonna help you cause they be called a communist too. They don't have to prove you communist. They just says you communist. How you gonna prove you ain't?'

By now, tears were running down the older woman's cheeks.

341

Frankie reached for her arm and gave her a comforting squeeze. The biscuits crushed, she gave Frankie some tomatoes. 'Layer these on top, will you, honey?'

Frankie began cutting again and while she did, Cecelia mixed some grated cheese, mayonnaise, sour cream, and seasoning in a bowl.

'What's this dish called?' Frankie asked as she watched Cecelia cover the biscuits with the tender vegetables from the skillet.

'Lowcountry Tomato Pie,' said Cecelia, putting the skillet onto a heat pad and reaching for the bowl. 'Everybody against them,' said Cecelia, beginning again. 'The mayor, the police, the president of the Chamber of Commerce.' She began putting the cheese mixture over the top. 'They set the whole town against them. They even controlled the churches.'

'Is that why you're so worried about Jefferson?'

Cecelia nodded. 'He got beat on but he got away,' she said. 'He in hiding right now but I knows they just biding their time and when they gets him . . .' She wrung her hands helplessly.

'Is there any way we can get him out of there?' said Frankie.

'Eldrick and me thought of that but everybody too scared,' she said, shaking her head. 'And Eldrick too old.'

The preparation finished, Cecelia opened the oven door.

'That looks delicious,' Frankie said making a mental note to try the recipe on the family when she got back home. 'Perhaps if somebody approached the leader . . .'

Cecelia smiled grimly. 'You won't want to mess with this man. He member of the Klan. When they came back from the war, he beat up on coloured men even though some of them got commendations for bravery. Nobody done touch him. He war hero.'

'Who is he?'

Cecelia came back to the table and picked up the bowl to put it in the sink. 'Him name Lyman Spinks.'

# Forty-Eight

Frankie and Ed talked far into the night.

'I agree that someone should try and rescue this boy, but why you?'

Frankie snuggled into the crook of his arm and put her hand on his chest. They were in shadows, the only light in the room coming from the moon shining through the lace curtains. Lillian was in the same room so they were whispering in case they woke her up. 'Spinks will be expecting someone from their own community to fetch him,' said Frankie. 'The last thing he'll be looking for would be an English woman.'

'I can see that,' said Ed uncertainly, 'but what if he recognises you? Won't you then become a target?'

'But he's not going to, is he? He has no idea we're here. We'll get Cecelia to arrange for Jefferson to be at a certain place; I drive straight there, pick him up and go.'

'I don't like it,' said Ed.

'Ed, I need to do this,' Frankie insisted. 'When Romare died I knew I could do nothing to help him but I made a promise in my heart that I would help his people. He doted on that boy. This is my one chance, maybe my only chance to honour that promise.'

'But where's it going to end, Frankie? We're three and a half

343

thousand miles from home and now you want to go on some risky rescue mission.'

Frankie raised herself up on her elbow and looked at him. 'Look, I know I haven't been very fair to you,' she admitted, 'and I'm sorry. You've been amazingly patient with me and I promise this will be the very last time I'll want to fight for somebody's cause. Please, Ed, please let me do this one thing for the sake of Lillian's father.'

'And what if something happens,' he said stubbornly. 'What if you don't come back? What happens to Lillian then?'

Frankie lay back down and stared at the ceiling. She remained silent for several seconds and then she said, 'I'm sorry but I can't turn away, Ed. I just can't.'

She heard him sigh. 'Then you're not going on your own, Frankie. I'm coming with you.'

She raised herself up again. 'No, I need you to stay here for Lillian.'

'I won't be thwarted this time Frankie,' he said. 'If you're going, we're in this together. I'm coming with you and that's that.'

*

The family had reservations about the idea too, but in the end they were persuaded. After the usual enormous Southern breakfast, Eldrick filled the car and, with Ed at the wheel, they set off. Lillian was quite happy to be left on her own because Selma had promised to take her to the zoo.

After all of her training with the ATS, Frankie was an excellent map reader. Two hours later, they reached a place called Richmond where Ed stopped for a comfort break. They set off again about half an hour later. After driving for another hour and a half, they reached La Crosse. This time they stopped for a meal in a diner where the waitress was so fascinated by the way Ed spoke that she made him repeat everything he said twice.

'Do you know Winston Churchill?'

Ed shook his head. 'I'm afraid not.'

'Gee,' she blurted out, 'say that again. "I'm afraid not . . ."' She looked around at her other customers, 'Don't you just love that English accent?'

'Two coffees please,' Ed said patiently. 'And two cinnamon buns.'

'You want coffee? Oh my mistake. I thought you Britishers only drank tea.'

Frankie was struggling not to giggle. The waitress served them and then turned her attention to some lorry drivers who had made their way into the diner.

'We got an English couple in here,' she announced as they placed their order at the bar. Everybody turned around to look at Ed and Frankie.

'My brother was in England in the war,' one of them said. 'What part you from?'

'The south of England,' said Frankie. 'Kent and Dorset.'

'I was sent to Italy,' said Ed.

'Me too,' said the lorry driver. 'Ah, those Italian chicks . . .' he turned back to the bar. 'Sweet memories.'

'What you doing in these parts?' his companion asked. He was an older man dressed in a checked shirt and a grubby jacket with a zip up the front.

'Just touring,' said Ed rather too quickly. 'We like to get off the beaten track and see the real America.'

The man gave him a long stare until the waitress put a plate of food onto the counter and then he turned away and began to eat.

After about an hour's rest, Ed and Frankie set out for Greensboro. The journey took about fifty minutes. Strangely enough as they pulled out of the car park, one of the lorries seemed to be going the same way.

Cecelia had told them that Jefferson was hiding on a farm between Greensboro and Kannapolis. The landmark was a water tower on a hill. They crossed a railway line and began to look for a dirt road on the right which apparently led straight to the farm. As they turned right, Frankie was relieved to see the lorry that had been following them go straight on. Everything was going perfectly.

A few yards from the road, the land looked barren and dry. A few rather scrawny animals fed on the parched grass and a dog on a long leash barked furiously as they approached the house. Frankie had a feeling that the family on the farm must be poor. Their home was little more than a one-room shack with a small veranda at the front. Two people sat there on wooden chairs. As Ed and Frankie drove up towards them, they stood up and hurried inside the house. By the time Ed got out of the car, the man had returned with a shotgun in his hands.

'Git off my land,' he snapped. 'Go on, git.'

Ed raised his hand. 'Whoa,' he cried. 'You should be expecting us. Cecelia sent us.'

The man lowered the shotgun and his face broke into a warm smile. 'Hey Martha, get on out here. The English have arrived.'

*

The couple prevailed on them to stay for something to eat and drink but Frankie and Ed decided they should return to Washington as soon as possible. As instructed, they gave the man and woman an envelope from Eldrick, which Ed guessed must be a monetary gift, and shook hands. After that they were taken across the fields. Jefferson was in a small room at the base of the

346

water tower. He scrambled to his feet as they walked in but he didn't look well. His face was bloodied and one eye was so swollen he couldn't open it. His right hand was roughly bandaged but from the way he held it, Frankie guessed someone had stamped on it or at the very least broken a finger. The man helped Ed get him into the car. They laid him on the back seat, covered him with a blanket to make him comfortable and said their goodbyes.

'If I tell you to hide,' said Ed, 'get down on the floor and cover yourself right over.'

Jefferson nodded miserably. 'Yes sir, boss.'

'I'm not your boss,' Ed said patiently. 'The name is Ed.'

While he'd been sorting Jefferson out, Frankie had slipped into the driver's seat. 'Come on, Frankie,' said Ed, coming around the car. 'I'll drive.'

'You've been driving all day,' said Frankie. 'You're tired.' She started the engine.

Her husband was annoyed but there was little he could do and he didn't like the idea of hanging around in this God-forsaken place, so the sooner they got underway the better.

The dirt track was the only way into the farm and they were both relieved when they caught sight of the road. As Frankie nosed the car to the left to get onto the highway, a large open car, at a glance a 1948 Mercury 8, with two passengers seated and a third riding on the folded down soft top at the back, turned at speed into the dirt road. On the back seat, Jefferson whimpered.

'My God,' said Ed as the car sped by. 'That was close. That idiot almost had you.'

'More than that,' said Frankie, her heart beginning to thump in her chest. 'That was Lyman Spinks.'

'Pull over and I'll drive,' Ed said authoritatively.

'No time,' said Frankie glancing into the rear view mirror as the car swerved recklessly back onto the highway in a hail of small stones and grass. 'He's right behind us.'

Ed turned sharply and sure enough the Mercury was speeding towards them and gaining ground. Frankie pressed the accelerator hard.

'Get down on the floor,' Ed barked at Jefferson.

The man was weeping now. 'Oh God, they's gonna kill me.'

'No, they won't,' said Ed. 'Not if we can help it.'

Frankie turned her head. 'In this together,' she repeated.

Ed grinned. 'In this together,' he said. 'Your driving had better be good.'

'It is,' said Frankie but she was aware that the Mercury, a much more powerful car, was still gaining ground.

It came up behind and hit her. The jolt pushed them hard into their seats and then propelled them forward. Frankie hit the steering wheel, a painful jerk which, for a second, took her breath away but she held her nerve and toed the accelerator again. Jefferson was thrown against the back of their seats and Ed hit his head on the dashboard before rolling down into the passenger foot well with a groan.

'Are you all right?' Frankie asked anxiously. Somehow she had managed to keep going although her speed had been reduced. 'Ed?' she said anxiously. 'Are you okay?'

When her husband lifted his head, there was blood trickling down his forehead.

He moaned slightly. 'Yes. Are you?'

Ignoring the pain in her chest where she'd hit the steering wheel, she nodded. 'What about our friend?'

Ed heaved himself onto his seat and looked behind. Jefferson was still on the floor but sobbing like a baby and shaking like a leaf.

That was when they heard the shot. The back pillion passenger had aimed the shotgun at them, probably hoping to blow out a tyre. The move made the driver of the Mercury lose a little ground for a while but with a more powerful engine than Frankie had, the gap between them soon became smaller.

They roared on but now the driver of the Mercury was trying to overtake. Frankie knew if he got ahead of her he would most likely slew the car across her path and they would have no escape. As the car came alongside she could see Lyman Spinks quite clearly. He raised himself in the passenger seat and undid his flies.

'Hey babe,' he shouted as he rubbed himself vigorously, 'when we stop the car I'll give you a taste of a real man.'

The man with the shotgun was aiming it right at Ed but as luck would have it, the driver of the Mercury suddenly swerved sharply to ram the side of Frankie's car just as he was about to fire and he lost his balance. With a scream of terror, he did a backward summersault over the boot of the car and disappeared into the road. The gun went off as he fell.

Frankie felt sick but they dared not stop. The Mercury slowed for a second or two, then picked up speed again.

'Good God, they're not even going to stop and see if he's all right,' Ed gasped incredulously.

The Mercury had almost gained enough ground to pull in front of them when a large truck appeared on the opposite side of the road, headlights flashing and horn blaring. It was travelling so fast, that there was every possibility of a head on collision if the Mercury stuck to its present course. Their aggressors had no option but to pull back.

Up ahead, Frankie could see the railway line but this time a train was coming. Unlike English railway crossings there was nobody in a signal box raising and lowering the barriers. Everything was all done automatically and as far as she could see, there were no actual gates or bars. Her heart sank as she heard a warning bell and the lights began to flash.

'You'll have to slow down, Frankie,' said Ed. 'You've got no choice. The train is coming.'

All her past motorbike scrambling skills kicked in and

Frankie did a quick speed guesstimation. How fast was the train going? How long before the train reached the crossing? How long would it take her to get there? The train driver blew his whistle as she sped on but she kept going.

'Frankie!' Ed screeched. He tried to snatch the wheel but she buffeted his hand away. 'For God's sake stop! You're going to kill us all.'

She knew then that she had no choice. Even if she took her foot off the accelerator immediately, the time it would take to slow down would probably mean they'd plough into the side of the train anyway. The Mercury 8 was right up behind them hell bent on ramming into the back of her, so she had to keep going. Pressing her foot down hard, she raced to get to the crossing before the train. Beside her, she heard Ed take in his breath noisily.

They only just cleared the crossing right in front of the oncoming train but as they hit the rails, the front wheels of the car left the road and for a few seconds they were planing. Frankie landed with a crash onto the grass verge on the other side of the tack and struggled to keep control. She dared not let the car roll or go down the ditch. The wheels spun madly as she hit the ground. Had the Mercury 8 managed to get across as well?

The train driver blew his whistle a third time and she heard her husband let out an anguished cry. It was only then that their car stopped moving. They were facing in the opposite direction. Frankie caught a glimpse of the Mercury 8 still heading towards them then she turned her head away. There was a loud bang and a couple of seconds later, Ed scrambled out of the car to be sick. Jefferson sat up and began to laugh and shout. 'You done it! You done it!'

Frankie, shaking and crying, looked up again. The train was still travelling but it was slowing down. Of the Mercury 8 and its two passengers, there was no sign.

*

When Frankie and Ed got back to Washington with Jefferson, they had an ecstatic welcome. Frankie was still in a state of shock and spent a couple of days huddled in a corner while her brain tried to come to terms with what had happened. Whilst she was glad to have rescued the boy, she was ashamed that she had put all of their lives in such mortal danger. She had to stop being so gung-ho about everything. Parenthood brought with it responsibility, she told herself. If things hadn't turned out the way they had, Lillian might be an orphan.

When the family talked things over, she wondered how Spinks could have known she was in the area.

'I don't necessarily think he knew *you* were coming for Jefferson,' said Ed, 'but I remember that chap in the diner who asked us why were in the area. He gave me a funny look, didn't he?'

'Oh yes,' said Frankie. 'It must have been his lorry that followed us.'

'And when we went down some obscure dirt track,' Ed went on, 'he put two and two together.'

'Lyman Spinks recognised me when the Mercury turned into the lane,' said Frankie. 'That's certainly the moment I recognised him.'

Jefferson had spent a couple of days in hospital. There wasn't a lot wrong with him apart from some nasty bruises, a broken finger and a small fracture in his cheek bone but he was still traumatised by the whole thing. The doctor told Selma time would heal all and by the end of the second week, he was beginning to improve. Everybody knew it wouldn't be long before he picked up the threads of his struggle to put an end to racist Jim Crow practices as well.

# Forty-Nine

The day of Derek's adoption and Barbara and Norman's baby girl's christening was bright and sunny. Frankie looked around Barbara's lovely garden and smiled. It was so peaceful here. All that had happened in America seemed a million miles away now. The thought of that perilous journey cast a shadow across her mind and she shuddered. One slip, one mistake and everything could have turned out so differently. Somebody up there must have been watching over them that day.

She missed Romare's family. It had been particularly hard for Cecelia and Eldrick to say goodbye to Lillian but there was always the hope that one day they might get together again. Right now, her only feeling was that it was good to be back home.

'All that business with Conrad Merriman?' Frankie had whispered into her friend's ear when she and Barbara were alone.

'Oh, I never told you,' said Barbara. 'Norman wrote a reply telling him I'd made it all up and I had a letter from his lawyer telling me he would not be pursuing the matter any further.'

'Will you ever tell Derek?'

'Possibly when he's much older,' Barbara told her. 'It would have to be my word only, because of that false declaration Mum made on his birth certificate. As you said, there's no way it can be proved.'

'But now the adoption has gone through, you really are his mother,' said Frankie.

Barbara smiled. 'It took me a very long time to realise what I had got,' she said. 'I kept saying I wanted to be loved and now I can see that even though I didn't like it, what Mum did was first and foremost because she loved me. And as for Norman . . . just look at him, the silly man. Daft as a brush.'

She was smiling contentedly and they watched as Norman walked around the garden showing baby Wendy, not even three months old, all the flowers and telling her their Latin names. After a minute or two, Barbara excused herself to go and join him.

Frankie took a moment to look around at all the people who meant so much to her. Barbara and Norman, of course, and Derek, pleased as punch and so smartly dressed in his first ever suit with long trousers. He was beaming like a Cheshire cat so no one could doubt how happy he was to be Derek Hammond. Then there were Aunt Bet and Uncle Lorry sitting together on the big swing seat. Aunt Bet was giggling like a schoolgirl as Uncle Lorry pushed it higher with his feet. Older and less able to do what they wanted to do, they were looking forward to retirement in a lovely little bungalow in Goring-by-Sea. What a debt of love she owed them, but even as the thought crossed her mind, she could hear the voice of her long-dead first husband saying, 'Love is a gift.'

Doreen and her husband Terry were laughing with Frankie's cousin Alan and Thérèse, his lovely French wife. They were probably talking about babies. Both women were expecting again and their other children ran around the garden enjoying themselves. Frankie sighed happily. There were times in life when you felt nothing could be better, and this was one of them.

Alice, Barbara's maid, wandered around the garden with a tray of drinks and for the first time since she'd got here, Frankie frowned. She became aware of someone standing beside her and turned.

'You look miles away,' said Ed.

'I was just thinking about something young Alice said,' Frankie replied. 'Did you know that the Worthing town councillors want to tone down the music in the dances in the Assembly Hall?'

'No,' he said feigning surprise. 'I didn't.'

'It's hardly fair, is it?' said Frankie. 'Young people enjoy jazz and rock 'n' roll and why shouldn't they?'

'Why indeed,' said Ed with a grin.

Frankie slipped her arm through his. 'Sorry, I'm getting my gander up again, aren't I, and I promised you rescuing Jefferson would be the last time.'

'You carry on, my darling,' Ed teased. 'You wouldn't be you without a little of your gander up about something.'

She nudged his arm playfully. 'I'm a lucky girl to be loved by you.'

He brushed her ear with his lips in that deliciously sexy way she loved and whispered, 'My darling, the pleasure is all mine.'

# Acknowledgements

I grew up in a time when people kept secrets. Adopted from birth, I was sixteen before I discovered that my natural father was an American GI and eighteen before I knew he was black. I had two siblings, who shared the same mother but we all had different fathers. It was 2013 before I found my brother and by that time my sister had died.

Writing this story has been my first venture into the world of the black American GI. I have always known that life was hard for them but I never realised just how difficult it must have been. They were patriotic people who loved their country but were held back by prejudice and in some cases spite. Linda Hervieux's book *Forgotten* and Graham Smith's *When Jim Crow Met John Bull* helped me understand the unfairness of it all. The characters in my book are totally fictitious but I have tried to express the frustrations and pain they must have felt.

Doctor Drew is real. He helped to plan a safe way of processing and storing large quantities of blood plasma, ensuring its contamination-free arrival in Britain and Europe. There is no doubt that he saved many hundreds if not thousands of lives during WW2. Although he was known as the 'father of the blood bank', the Red Cross in America excluded African Americans from giving blood so Drew himself could not be part of the very programme he had devised.

On a personal note, I am grateful to the Avon team for their encouragement and help to make this book the best it could be. Thank you to my agent Juliet Burton who is always so patient with me and I would never have managed it without the love and support of my long-suffering husband who is still waiting for his tea!

Keep reading to discover recipes inspired by the book and to read a special short story from Pam Weaver.

# Cecelia's Brunswick Stew

## You need:

- 4 oz butter
- 3 cloves garlic (minced)
- 1 large onion (finely chopped)
- 1 (15 oz) can tomatoes
- 8 oz chicken stock
- 12 oz barbecue sauce
- 2 tablespoons Worcestershire sauce
- 1 tablespoon brown sugar
- ¼ teaspoon cayenne pepper
- 1½ pounds smoked pulled pork (or chicken)
- 8 oz sweetcorn
- 8 oz butter beans
- Salt and pepper, to taste

## Method

1. Melt butter in a large Dutch oven (or cast iron cooking pot) over medium-high heat. Once melted, add the garlic and onions and sauté until soft for about 5 minutes.

2. Stir in the tomatoes, chicken stock, barbecue sauce, Worcestershire sauce, brown sugar, cayenne, smoked pork, butter beans, sweetcorn and salt and pepper.

3. Bring the mixture to the boil, then reduce to a simmer and cook over medium-low heat for 1½ hours, stirring occasionally.

# Cecelia's Lowcountry Tomato pie

## You need:

- 2 oz butter
- 5 oz chopped celery
- 1 onion (chopped)
- 1 green pepper
- Dumpling mix
- 2 tomatoes (thinly sliced)
- 8 oz Cheddar cheese
- 8 oz low-fat mayonnaise
- 8 oz sour cream
- 1 teaspoon garlic & herb seasoning

## Method

1. Preheat oven to 350°F (175°C). Lightly grease a medium baking dish.

2. Melt butter in a frying pan over medium heat. Put in celery, onion, and green pepper and sauté until tender.

3. Prepare dumpling mix and press into the prepared baking dish to form a crust. Layer with the tomatoes. Top with the sautéed vegetables.

4. In a medium bowl, mix Cheddar cheese, mayonnaise, sour cream, and seasoning blend. Spread evenly over the vegetables.

5. Bake 45 minutes in the preheated oven, until bubbly and lightly browned.

## Aunt Bet's Sussex Plum Heavies

Sussex Plum Heavies were a home-made scone which was eaten by farmers, shepherds and woodsmen. They were made with plain flour which was why they were called 'heavies'.

**You need:**

- 8 oz plain flour
- 2 oz lard
- 1 teacup of milk and water
- 1 oz sugar
- A few currants

**Method**

Rub lard into the flour until it resembles breadcrumbs. Add dried fruit then the liquid. Knead into a dough and roll or press into rounds. Bake in a hot oven for about 12 minutes.

An original recipe from the *Western Times* – Friday 17 December 1943

# The Silver Jubilee Quilt

'What did they say?'

Susan's husband, Jack, pulled a bottle of wine out of the kitchen cupboard. She watched as he poured himself a glass and downed it in one go, ignoring her. He poured another glass.

'This is 1977, not the Dark Ages,' she cried. 'They shouldn't be treating you like this.' Susan could feel the tension building inside her. Hurt and almost in tears, she said, 'I'm in this too, you know.' She really wanted to shout: *For heaven's sake Jack, pull yourself together and tell me what they said*, but she didn't. With his back still towards her, he braced himself against the worktop and stared down at his feet.

'Jack,' she said, coming towards him and laying her hand on his back, 'Darling . . .'

He jerked himself away from her. 'I have just endured nearly two bloody hours of police questioning,' he said through gritted teeth, 'and I don't want to come home to another grilling.'

Trying to help, she touched his arm but he snatched it away and his sudden move knocked the glass over. Wine spilled across the work surface and trickled down the drawers.

'That's all I need!' he spat.

'It's all right,' she said. 'It was an accident.'

Susan picked up a dish cloth and threw it over the spreading liquid.

'I'm going out,' he said in a more measured tone. 'I may be late. Don't wait up.' And with that, he strode out of the room.

As she mopped up the wine and wiped the drawers clean, she heard the front door slam. Susan slumped onto a kitchen chair and stared somewhere in front of her, her eyes unfocussed. Her chest felt as if it had a lead weight inside. She wanted to cry but she couldn't. Right now she was all out of tears. She knew where her husband was going – to the pub, and he'd be there until chucking out time. Why couldn't he see that drinking himself into oblivion wasn't going to solve anything? What made intelligent, articulated men so bloody stupid? She'd tried everything to help: being reasonable, indignation at the unfairness of it all, sympathy, understanding, encouraging him to talk, but it was no use. Jack was stuck and because he was stuck, so was she.

She wished her parents were here. She could have talked to her mum, but she and her dad were abroad. If all this hadn't have happened, Susan and Jack might have been on holiday with them.

'Oh Mum, what am I going to do?' she said aloud as the realisation of the situation she and Jack were in flooded over her again.

She didn't want to write and tell them what was going on. It would take far too long and a long distance transatlantic trunk call would be prohibitively expensive, especially when money was so tight. Besides, what could her parents do from such a distance except worry about her? It might spoil their holiday. No, she couldn't tell them until they came back at the end of May.

Jack wanted them to keep their heads down so as not to draw attention to themselves but she couldn't stay indoors all the time, could she? Why should she anyway? She had nothing to hide. Come to that, neither did he. A wave of nausea swept over her. Now she understood what it meant when people said they were sick with worry.

She heard the sound of something being pushed through the letter box. She didn't rush to the hall to see what it was. It was probably the Tupperware brochure. She'd have to stop buying that stuff anyway. Jack was suspended on half pay and there was no telling how long that would last. If he lost his job altogether they would have to move as well. Her wage from the nursery would hardly cover the bills, let alone an eight thousand pound mortgage.

She took a deep breath. *Stop this*, she told herself. *You'll only make yourself even more depressed.* She glanced up at the clock and rose to her feet. Today was her quilting day and she wasn't going to miss that. Wiping her cheeks with the flat of her hand, Susan fished under the pile of papers and other junk on the kitchen table. She was looking for the tin box of old newspaper cuttings.

It was underneath the *Worthing Herald* which was folded open to reveal the advertisement she'd spotted about two months ago. Distracted from her search for the cutting, she re-read the piece in the *Herald*. *In just a few weeks*, it said, *it will be the Queen's Silver Jubilee.* Twenty-five years ago, when Susan was just two years old, Queen Elizabeth II had come to the throne. A jubilee felt like a milestone and something worth celebrating, which was why the article had resonated with her so strongly. She read it again.

*Be a part of creating a quilt to depict village life. If you know the old village of Goring well, the Hon. Mrs Valerie Melcham is looking for women to take part in creating a quilt in honour of the occasion. Work will take place in the Old Manor House on Thursday evening with the aim of hanging the finished quilt in St Mary's church, Goring.*

Of course, Goring was now part of the urban sprawl that was Worthing but she'd been born and brought up in the village when it was still a village. By the time Susan had reached her teens, thanks to her mother, she'd been a reasonable seamstress.

She still enjoyed making her own clothes so when she saw the article about the quilt, she was keen to join in. Right now she could do with a bit of a distraction and some female company. The girls at work were nice enough but being part of a team looking after sixty under-fives at the nursery left little time for conversation. Besides, because of what had happened to Jack it felt like she was treading on egg shells. She and Jack hadn't been married that long, and it was embarrassing to admit everything was going so wrong so soon. At the quilting club, she could be sparing with her confidences while she did something relaxing and yet challenging and fun.

Susan pushed the jubilee quilt article aside. That wasn't what she was looking for. Delving deeper, she tugged at a flimsy cutting she'd left in the box a while ago and smoothed it out. Yes, this should do it. This should expose a fraud.

On her way out, Susan picked up the Avon catalogue from the front door mat and tossed it into the wastepaper basket.

*

Valerie Melcham stared across the dining room table and sighed. How many times had she sat here eating her evening meal all alone? Nigel had telephoned about twenty minutes ago. 'Shan't be in for dinner tonight. Something has come up.'

She could just imagine what that meant. Probably some long-legged dizzy young girl in the office had caught his eye. Miserably, Valerie looked down at her wedding ring. Her nails might be beautifully and expensively manicured but the skin on her hands was beginning to show signs of her age. Not that she was that old. What was it she'd recently read in her copy of *Tatler*? '*The forties are the new twenties.*' How different it all seemed thirty years ago when she'd met Nigel. Back then she'd been the pretty young thing and he'd been attentive and loving. She snorted. Oh, the irony of it all. He'd even been considered a 'good catch'.

She didn't know why it had all gone pear-shaped, but once the boys had come along, the distance between them had grown. She had tried, oh God she'd tried, but after only four more years she knew their marriage was a farce. He made no secret of the fact that he preferred younger women. They'd rowed and Nigel had said some terrible things. Eventually he'd confessed that all he'd wanted was sons to carry on the family name. He didn't want her, he said. He didn't love her. Never had. His torrent of words had hurt, but as resilient as she was, Valerie devoted her life to bringing up the boys and the renovation of the Old Manor House; not an easy task with a husband who squandered their money on fripperies. How many affairs he'd had, she couldn't recall, but now that she was older she was simply grateful that he no longer wanted to share her bed. She sighed. If only Ashley was here . . .

Valerie glanced at her watch. The ladies would be arriving within the hour to begin the quilt once more. She hoped there would be a good response from the advertisement in the *Worthing Herald*. The girl who turned up a couple of weeks ago was an absolute godsend but time was of the essence. They needed to get the quilt finished and there was only five weeks to go. Putting her napkin down beside her empty plate, she rose to her feet. When she'd started the project, Valerie had no idea how enormously satisfying it would be. Never one to do things by halves, she had consulted the experts at The Victoria and Albert Museum and the Royal School of Needlework for advice. The needlewomen working on the quilt may only be amateurs but she wanted them to create something which would last, something they could be proud of, something they could show their children and grandchildren. 'It doesn't need to be complicated,' she'd told the experts with a wry smile, 'just fabulous.'

\*

As Susan stepped over the red rope and onto the faded Georgian carpet, the last of the Saturday visitors to the Old Manor House gasped in shocked surprise. The security guard spun around.

'Not on the carpet, Miss,' he said with a smile.

'Whoops, sorry Stan,' she apologised teasingly. 'I forgot.'

He was a nice man, mid-fifties, a bit portly but she knew from the banter they often shared together that he enjoyed a bit of fun. He was a widower and she guessed that since his wife died he'd been a bit lonely. Conscious that by this time every eye in the room was upon her, Susan obediently followed him onto the wooden surround. He opened the big double door marked 'Private'.

'Please don't tell anyone I trod on the carpet,' Susan cried in a plaintive voice. 'I promise I won't do it again.'

As the door closed on the gaping visitors, Stan whispered out of the corner of his mouth, 'One of these days you'll get me shot, young lady.'

She grinned mischievously. 'How's the garden?'

'My Molly was the gardener,' he said sadly as they walked through the maze of corridors. 'I gets confused. I don't know me antirrhinums from me chrysanthemums.'

'Why not have a chat with Hazel?' Susan suggested. 'She's a keen gardener.'

Stan chewed his bottom lip thoughtfully so she knew he was tempted. There was a slight pause before he said, 'Na, you're alright.'

\*

Susan gave Iris Wilson a sceptical look as soon as she came into the sewing room. Should she come right out with it now?

'Ah, Susan, here at last,' Iris warbled. 'I was beginning to wonder if you were going to make it this week.'

Iris looked her up and down, but if she was surprised by the way Susan was dressed, she was much too polite to show it. They couldn't have been more different but they got on fairly well considering that they were poles apart. Iris, a lively sixty-year-old with tight white curls in her grey pleated skirt, powder blue blouse, hand-knitted cardigan and sensible shoes, while Susan, twenty-six, with shoulder length blonde hair cut in a Farrah Fawcett style, was more at home with her pale orange lipstick and blue eye shadow. Today she was dressed in an ankle-length purple print peasant dress under her long, flowing, multi-coloured coat. Susan was young enough to be Iris's daughter, she thought to herself as she studied the older woman's face . . . or was she?

Throwing her coat over the back of the chair, Susan was just about to sit down when Iris said, 'We've got to work on the quilt a bit further along the line.'

'But I haven't quite finished my square yet,' Susan protested mildly.

'I know,' said Iris, 'but Mrs Melcham thinks we should tidy up the bit June Carter was doing.' She came closer to speak more confidentially. 'Her stitching wasn't very good and now that she's left the group, we can make an improvement on it.'

When Susan had first arrived, the others had explained what they were doing and why. 'Every part of the patchwork needs to be part of the same story,' said Valerie. 'You have to ask yourself, what is my square telling people about my life in the village?'

'Well, I grew up in the village,' Susan had told them. 'I spent a lot of time playing by myself down by the sea. How about I do the old pond that used to be on the green?'

'What do you think, Hazel?' Valerie asked.

'Sounds perfect to me.' Hazel had said. 'I remember that old pond. It looks a lot tidier since the council grassed it over but it did have its own charm.'

'It would certainly be a talking point,' Iris agreed.

'Then that's what you can do!' Valerie had cried enthusiastically. 'The rag bag is over there.' She bustled away as someone required her in another part of the room. 'Remember, Susan,' she had called over her shoulder, 'it's important that you keep your own style and interpretation in the quilt, but at the same time, you must maintain the overall balance of the piece.'

Susan had worked quickly and her interpretation of the sea shore and the pond at Goring was now virtually finished. She'd put a child beside it (herself), a frog sitting on a stone and a newt in a jam jar. All she had to do to complete the square was to put a little piece of gauze on the end of the rod to represent a fishing net, but that would have to wait.

Taking her coat off the back of the chair, Susan moved further up the line.

'Hazel has gone over to Mrs Melcham's kitchen to get some milk for the tea,' said Iris, turning around to check that Susan was following her. She gave Susan a concerned look. 'Are you all right dear? You look a bit pale.'

'I'm fine,' Susan said dismissively. She was reluctant to admit it but she still felt a little queasy. *I only feel like this because I rushed up the hill*, she told herself.

Down the centre of the enormously long table, the material which was to become the Goring jubilee quilt lay in pieces along its entire length. Several women, all with long-term connections to the village, sat opposite each other working as though they were on a factory production line. As each person sewed her uniquely individual appliqué and embroidery square, the room was a hive of activity. As she followed Iris right down the line, Susan gasped. This was the first time she'd seen the whole thing laid out. They still had a long way to go, but already it held the promise of being truly magnificent.

Although Susan had only recently joined the group, the others had been gathering here for the past four months and already time was ticking by. The Silver Jubilee of Queen Elizabeth II was only weeks away and there was still an awful lot to do. Even though Mrs Melcham had changed the original weekly attendance to twice a week, everybody was working flat out. Each square represented some aspect of village life – past and present – and the people who lived there, while the middle section would be a beautifully embroidered map of the surrounding area, depicting the history of Goring. Once finished, the Silver Jubilee quilt was to have pride of place in St Mary's church, hanging from ceiling to floor in time for the special jubilee service on June 7th.

Susan's gaze fell onto Iris's back. What was it about this woman that made her feel uneasy? She looked the part but something wasn't quite right. Iris pulled a chair from under the end of the table and motioned to Susan to sit down. For the first time, Susan noticed her hands and a single breath escaped from her lips. That was it! Now that she'd seen them close up, Iris's hands were a dead giveaway.

'Oh hello Susan.'

Hazel Radcliffe, late forties and the local librarian, appeared with a bottle of milk and put it onto the draining board. She picked up the kettle, shook it, filled it from the tap over the sink and switched it on.

Susan smiled. 'Looks like I'm working down your end tonight,' she said.

'That's nice,' said a woman who was collecting bits and pieces from the material box. 'I'm Jenny Bartlett. I think I know you; I used to go to school with your mother.'

'Did you really?' Susan gasped.

Jenny nodded. 'Frankie Sherwood, isn't it? I'm afraid we rather lost touch. I went to her birthday party when she was ten. I left Worthing just after the war. My mother married a Canadian. I only came back a couple of years ago. I liked your mum. How is she?'

'Fine,' said Susan making herself comfortable. 'On holiday with my dad at the moment.'

They were interrupted by Hazel. 'I remember your mother

for practically saving the village school single-handed. If she hadn't started the petition and organised all those sit-ins, well, I'm not sure that we would still have a school in Goring by now.'

'Why was that?' Jenny asked.

'The powers-that-be,' said Hazel, now in full flow, 'wanted to send all the children to Ferring.' She reached into a workbox just in front of her to find a silk thread. 'It would have been such a pity if they'd closed us down. It would've taken the heart out of the village and most likely I would have been out of a job.'

Jenny retreated to the other end of the table. Susan took a deep breath as another wave of nausea swept over her. What was wrong with her today?

'I'm glad you're helping us,' Hazel said. 'Your stitching is really quite neat.'

'You mean you're surprised someone who looks as wacky as me could sew?' Susan teased.

'Yes,' said Hazel, completely unfazed.

Susan grinned. She liked Hazel. Her open honesty was blunt but with Hazel, what you saw was what you got.

'I was talking to Stan on the way in,' Susan said matter-of-factly. 'He could do with some help with his garden.'

Hazel's face coloured but she made no comment. 'This is June Carter's square,' she said pointing it out. 'I'm sorry she's not coming back but her stitching is terribly wonky.'

Susan studied June's square and then looked at Hazel's next to it. The older woman's style was completely different but that would only add to the diversity of the quilt. Susan recognised Periwinkle Cottage, Hazel's little home by the shops. She had even depicted herself working in the garden. The Hall stood in the distance. Today Hazel was unpicking some half-finished lettering.

'What does that say?' Susan began, but Hazel put her hand over the script. 'It doesn't really matter now. I've decided to change it.'

The kettle began to boil and Iris set about making some tea. And that was another thing, Susan thought to herself. She didn't seem to do much sewing. Iris was always the one running errands or brewing up.

'Your husband doesn't mind you spending so much time here?' said Hazel, deliberately changing the subject.

'No,' said Susan, pushing aside the acidic thought that Jack didn't give a stuff about her these days. She looked around for some scissors. They were going to have to unpick quite a bit of June's work. Iris came round with the teas. June was one of those people who had been brilliant in her younger days but now that she was in her late eighties, her skills, like her eyesight, were not quite as good. Nobody liked to offend her so it came as something of a relief when she announced to the group that her impending cataract operation meant that she would have to stop coming.

Susan looked for the starting point of June's work and eventually found it. As she cut the cotton and carefully pulled the thread, she was thinking about Jack. She had hoped that things would have worked out a little better by now but everything was just as bad. When the police took him to the station that first time for questioning, it didn't seem so terrible. There had been a discrepancy in the books, they said, and naturally, as he worked in the finance department, they wanted to talk to Jack about it. She trusted her husband implicitly. There had to be a logical explanation but when he came back home, he was in a state of panic.

'It's like they're accusing *me*!' he'd cried. 'They're implying that I must have been embezzling the money!'

She had immediately sprung to his defence. 'But that's ridiculous! Why would they say that? Have you done something you shouldn't have?'

'Of course I haven't,' he'd retorted, completely misunderstanding what she was saying. 'Well, I must say, it comes to

371

something when even my own wife insinuates that I could be a thief!'

'I didn't say that,' she protested but he wasn't listening and that had been just the start of their troubles. He'd never been charged but he was still suspended from work and the police were still investigating. It didn't help that every now and then they'd ask him to come back to the station for more questioning. Jack got so stressed every time – and then he'd started drinking.

Hazel glanced over Susan's shoulder to look at June's work. 'Oh dear, it really is a mess, isn't it?'

'I honestly think she couldn't see properly,' said Susan. 'Maybe we should have said something before.'

'You're probably right,' said Iris, putting a cup of tea on the windowsill behind them.

Just then, the door flew open and Iris was immediately thrown into a flat spin as the Hon. Mrs Valerie Melcham – *do call me Valerie*, the owner of the Old Manor House walked in. She was an attractive woman of indeterminate age, well groomed, well dressed and with an imposing personality.

Valerie normally sat in between Hazel and June to sew her own square. With minuscule, neat stitching, she was working on the family coat of arms but as usual, before she sat down, she walked around the room chatting amiably with the other women, thanking them for coming, offering help and advice where needed and doing a check of everybody's work. Susan glanced up as Iris followed Valerie like a twittering bird.

'Why does Iris always have to treat Valerie as if she's royalty?' Susan whispered between her teeth to Hazel.

'You remember your place, my girl,' Hazel muttered. 'And don't forget to curtsey when she comes to join us.'

At first shocked, all at once Susan got the joke and elbowed her in the ribs. 'You're wicked.'

Hazel grinned as Valerie and Iris headed their way. The four of them were from different generations and different social backgrounds, but they all got on very well. Valerie may have held the rest of group on a tight rein, but she was a little more relaxed with the people in her own circle.

'What were you two giggling about?' she asked, sitting down.

'Nothing,' said Hazel innocently in a voice which had suddenly become high-pitched as she stifled a laugh and dived under the table to retrieve some dropped pins.

*

As Valerie settled down in front of her own square, she watched Susan turning over the materials. How she envied her. Young and beautiful, she didn't have a care in the world. Most girls her age would have laughed at the thought of making a quilt but Susan didn't seem to care what people thought of her. Valerie loved her colourful clothes, her fantastic hair, her boundless energy and her quick, neat stitching. Susan refused to be bound by convention and respectability. How unlike herself. Valerie shivered involuntarily. This stifling, suffocating life of hers was becoming more and more unbearable, with it's never-ending demands on her time. This was the only place where she could relax and be her real self.

She knew people envied her lifestyle but what did they know of boring dinner parties or having to 'put on a show' for some fete or gala? She would have done it all gladly had she got a loving husband. Oh, he could put on the charm when he wanted to and everyone thought he was wonderful. She could see him now, laughing and joking, the life and soul of the party but at the same time his hand would be under the table secretly stroking some woman's thigh whilst he played the part of good ol' pal with her partner. She shook herself. When did she become so bitter, so filled with contempt? It wasn't a pretty virtue and when she had these thoughts she didn't like herself very much.

Her mind drifted back to last Christmas Eve and her lips curled into a secret smile as she relived that bitterly cold walk up to

Highdown with Ashley. What fun it had been, sticking her tongue out like a five-year-old to catch the falling snowflakes and pelting each other with snowballs as they ran back down to the car. She'd met up with Ashley last summer and they'd enjoyed some lovely days out. By Christmas last year they had become lovers and by the New Year she knew Ashley was someone very special.

Valerie shifted her position and found herself staring right into Hazel's face. Thank God the woman couldn't read her thoughts. Embarrassed, Valerie looked away quickly.

\*

On the opposite side of the table, Hazel caught her breath silently. Was it possible Valerie had read her thoughts? She hoped not.

She'd been eager to sign up to make the quilt if only to get a glimpse of the inside of the Old Manor House. After all, she'd grown up with stories of the opulence and splendour of the place. She remembered walking past the gates with her mother when she was knee high to a grasshopper.

'You should have been brought up there,' her mother used to say, 'but hypocrisy and snobbery kept you this side of the gates.'

It was the usual family skeleton. Hazel had been born illegitimate, at a time when that sort of thing brought shame. Her mother had been a fourteen-year-old maid working in the Old Manor House at the beginning of the 1930s when young Thomas Melcham was fresh out of boarding school. His parents had gone to the South of France for the summer but he'd persuaded them that he needed to have some extra tuition to prepare himself for university. Of course, he had no intention of working during the summer. Good-looking and lazy, he spent his time binge drinking and having wild parties with the locals. No respectable upper-class girl would risk her reputation by keeping company with him, but with his eighteen-year-old hormones raging, he'd found an outlet in young Mildred Radcliffe.

Hazel had heard the story so many times. Without going into intimate detail, her mother told her how exciting it was to hear Thomas's footsteps coming up the back staircase. He'd arrive, candle in hand and a bottle of wine tucked under his arm, just to spend a few hours with her. He looked so handsome in his nightshirt and, watching her mother's eyes glow as she told the story, there could be no doubt that he was a wonderful lover. He'd filled her little maid's head with promises that because he loved her so passionately, one day they would run away together. She believed every word but of course, when the inevitable happened, he'd left her to her own fate. In this day and age, it was the stuff of Mills and Boon books, but in real life there was a far from a happy ending. Thrown out of her job, losing the roof over her head and being sacked without a reference, Mildred was forced to go to the workhouse to have her child.

Although by the 1930s only a few workhouses remained, there was one at East Preston. Mildred had ended up there for the birth of her baby. When she was older, Hazel had been back there to see the place where she had been born and where she'd spent the first six years of her life. She only remembered a few things, like playing hopscotch in the winter and the vile-tasting stew they had every other Tuesday. Hazel had no idea what it was but she'd hated it. The workhouse itself was a forbidding building set behind a high flint wall and with a single tower in the middle. An infirmary and nurses' home had been added in 1906, but by the time Hazel went back to see it, the workhouse itself had been taken over by Sussex County Council. Nevertheless, it still sent a shiver down her spine.

Her mother had been forced to leave Hazel behind in the nursery when she finally got out of the place. Mildred's mother, Hazel's grandmother, wouldn't allow her back home because she had brought shame on the family so Mildred had taken another live-in job, this time with a crotchety old woman. Funnily enough, that had been the silver lining to her cloud. She worked for the old woman for several years and to her immense surprise, when she died, her employer had left her enough money in her will for Mildred to get a rundown place of her own. Hazel was seven years old when she went to live in their two-up, two-down cottage and her mother worked as a ward orderly in Worthing Hospital to support them.

Mildred called herself Mrs Radcliffe and Hazel was told to pretend that her father had died, but that didn't stop her from carrying the pain of being known as Melcham's bastard all her life. It left her bitter and angry. It also blighted her own relationships with men. Although she liked Stan the security guard, she wouldn't encourage him. She simply didn't trust anybody.

Hazel steadily unpicked the stitches she had completed only last week. This had been part of her revenge on behalf of her mother. She'd selected the Bible verse carefully. Exodus 20 verse 5: *Punishing the children for the sins of the father.* She knew people would ask her about it, and then she'd tell them about those dreadful Melchams and the sufferings Thomas had wrought.

The one thing she hadn't bargained for when she devised this mild plot was her growing friendship with Valerie. Hazel really liked her. As they'd worked together on the quilt, they'd enjoyed a good laugh and a joke. It slowly began to change Hazel's perspective on the past. Her mother was long gone. What did it matter what happened nearly fifty years ago? The past is the past. Hazel had to get rid of this stitching before Valerie saw the quotation. She glanced up again and as she did, she and Valerie exchanged a shy smile. Yes, working on this quilt had given Hazel something she hadn't bargained for . . . a warm friendship.

*

At last, Susan had decided what to create in the space that had been June's square. June, a stalwart of the community, had been a teacher in the primary school during the forties and fifties so

Susan planned to create a playground with children skipping and playing football. She searched for some material which would be suitable and found a little piece of pink and white gingham cotton and some soft leather. Ideal, she thought, for a dress and a pair of old fashioned boy's shorts, or maybe the football itself. She delved back into the box; that piece of brown cloth would be ideal for a wall or part of the playground.

'That looks promising,' Hazel said softly as Susan came back to the table. 'How is your Jack?'

Susan felt herself stiffen. 'Fine.' *About as fine as he could ever be*, she thought to herself, *while he's still traumatised by the events of the past few weeks*. Suppressing another wave of nausea, she vaguely wondered why the pieces of coloured cloth in front of her had begun to swim.

'Are you all right, Susan?' Valerie's voice suddenly sounded far away.

Susan nodded, but as she stood to her feet to look in the material box again, she could feel herself losing control of her legs.

'Look out!' cried Hazel. 'She's going to fall.'

Susan made a grab at the back of the chair but all too quickly, the floor came rushing up to meet her.

*

When Susan opened her eyes again, she was lying on a sofa and Valerie was holding a damp flannel against her forehead. Iris was patting her hand in an irritating way.

'She's coming round now,' said Iris.

Susan swallowed. 'Where am I?'

'In my flat,' said Valerie.

'You fainted,' Hazel explained. 'We got the security guard to bring you in here.'

'I've sent for the doctor,' said Valerie.

377

'There's no need,' Susan said as she tried to sit up. Her head was swimming again. 'I'm okay.'

'I'd prefer to get you checked over,' Valerie said as she put a light restraining touch on her arm.

Susan relaxed back onto the cushion under her head and chewed at her bottom lip anxiously. She dreaded what the doctor would say. She laid both hands over her gently rounded stomach. It couldn't be . . . could it? No, no, not now. The timing was all wrong.

There was a light knock on the door and Stan, the security guard, ushered a smartly dressed man into the room. 'Doctor Crawford,' he announced.

'Thank you Stan,' said Valerie. She stood, and looking down at Susan she added, 'Hazel, Iris and I will leave you to it.' Stan held the door open as they all left the room, but not before Susan saw him giving Hazel a friendly wink. The door closed and Susan looked up at the doctor, who was putting his bag onto the floor next to her.

'Well now, young lady,' he said amiably. 'Let's see what the problem is.'

When the doctor had gone, the others came back. They could see Susan was looking a bit tearful so Valerie said, 'I'll tell you what, you stay here for a moment and relax while we do a bit of clearing up and I say goodnight to the others. They're anxious about you and will want to know how you are. We won't be long, I promise.'

*

While Valerie was seeing the last of the team off the premises, Iris and Hazel put everything away. The quilt itself stayed on the table but Hazel covered it over with a dust sheet and Stan was there to lend a hand.

'I can give you a lift home when you're ready,' he told Hazel.

Hazel felt her cheeks go pink. 'There's no need,' she said stiffly. 'I'm used to the walk.'

'Oh, well,' Stan said amiably, 'if you change your mind, I've still got some sorting out to do . . .' And Hazel thought he looked a little crestfallen as he left the room.

Iris began to clean the sink area and Hazel took the partly used milk bottle back to the Manor House kitchen. In the hallway she paused in front of the family portraits. There were three of them: Lt. Col. Archibald Melcham 1805-1846, Rev. Richard Melcham 1832-1899 and Thomas Melcham 1912-1970. Hazel caught her breath. There he was. Her father. He wasn't very good-looking. Heavily built, he had a bulbous nose and a languid expression. She could see nothing of the handsome young man her mother had described so vividly. The portrait must have been done towards his later life and judging by the dates, he was only fifty-eight when he died and funnily enough that was the same year her mother passed away. An odd coincidence.

Lost in her own thoughts, Hazel didn't hear Valerie coming up behind her. 'My husband's father,' she said matter-of-factly.

Hazel was just about to say, 'and mine . . .' when Valerie added, 'Odious man. I couldn't stand him; a notorious womaniser and a drunk.'

Hazel was stunned. All her life, her mother had felt cheated out of a wonderful life in this house, but now it seemed that she had had a lucky escape.

'I pitied the poor woman he married,' Valerie said as they both headed for the sitting room where Susan lay on the couch. 'He led her a dog's life. Still, you just can't always tell how a person is going to turn out, can you?'

*

'There's no need to worry,' said Susan when they all came back into the room. She seemed a little more composed than before.

Her eyes were dry and she was sitting up. 'The doctor only confirmed what I already suspected.'

They all stared at her with blank expressions.

'I'm pregnant.'

Hazel clasped her hands together over her chest. 'Oh, how wonderful!'

Valerie beamed. 'A baby! Oh my dear . . .' But as she looked at Susan's face, her voice trailed. 'But you don't seem very happy about it. Is something wrong?'

Susan burst into tears. After a minute or two, she could feel Valerie's arm around her shoulder. 'Can I . . . can we do anything to help?' she asked with genuine concern.

Iris pushed a tissue into her hand and Susan blew her nose noisily. 'I'm scared of what Jack is going to say.'

'Oh dear,' said Hazel sitting the other side of her. 'Does that mean he's not the fa—?'

'Of course he is!' Susan cried indignantly. She wiped her eyes. 'It's just that . . .' She hesitated, unsure of how much to tell them.

'We don't want to pry,' said Valerie, glancing at the others, 'but I think I can speak for Hazel, Iris and me when I say that anything you say in this room will be held in the strictest confidence.'

'Absolutely,' said Hazel, and Iris nodded enthusiastically.

And a moment later Susan found herself spilling everything out, telling them things she'd never voiced before, not even to her own mother. She told them about Jack's suspension from work, his frustrations and just how much of a failure he felt. She told them that he wouldn't talk to her and that he was drinking far too much. She said he was a good man but this awful business had frightened him so badly that he couldn't see a way out.

'He's been asked to attend the police station three times now,' Susan went on, her tears flowing again. 'They've never charged him or anything but the strain is becoming too much to bear. My husband is a changed man.'

'You poor girl,' said Valerie. 'He's innocent of course.'

'Without a doubt,' said Susan, 'but Jack is convinced that they're making him the scapegoat.'

Iris patted her hand again. 'Why don't I go and make us a nice cup of tea?'

Valerie nodded and Iris left the room.

'What if they charge him and he ends up in court?' Susan cried helplessly. 'What if they find him guilty?' She gulped for air. 'And now that I'm expecting a baby it only makes things ten times worse.'

'My dear, I agree you have a problem,' said Valerie 'but you've got an awful lot of 'what-ifs' there. It may not be the total disaster you fear.'

'I wish I could believe you,' said Susan, pinching the end of her nose with the soggy tissue.

Iris came back in with the tea. As she set the tray down on the coffee table, Valerie stood up and went to the drinks trolley. 'Tea by all means,' she said, 'but who would like something stronger?'

Susan settled for the tea, but Hazel asked for a gin and tonic and Iris said she fancied a sherry. Valerie poured herself a stiff brandy. 'Cheers, everyone,' she said, raising her glass.

'Cheers.'

'Well now, my dear,' Valerie said coming back to Susan, 'let's all put our heads together and see if we can't help this girl, shall we?'

'I don't think you understand,' Susan said miserably.

'I think we understand better than you think,' said Valerie.

'If he gets sacked, we'll lose everything,' Susan went on. 'And now a baby . . .'

'I'm sure it'll be fine,' said Iris. 'He loves you, doesn't he?'

Susan nodded. 'I just wish he hadn't started drinking . . .'

'I'm sure when you tell him he'll be thrilled,' said Iris. 'From what you've said, all he really cares about is you.'

A small sound emitted from Valerie's lips. In her head she was hearing someone else saying the very same words to her: 'All I really care about is you.' Not Nigel, of course. Her husband would never say a thing like that. They were Ashley's words.

381

In the short silence that followed, each woman was left with her own private thoughts.

As Valerie sipped her brandy she was reflecting over her life with Nigel. It was hard to believe that they'd been married for twenty-eight years. The boys were all grown up now. One was a dentist, living in the States; the other a solicitor who had married a lovely girl and lived less than five miles away. What would they think if they knew her guilty secret? To them, she had always been a pillar of society, a woman who never put a foot wrong, totally reliable, unchanging, upright and honest. What would they say if they knew about Ashley?

She had met Ashley at her son's wedding. A distant relative of her new daughter-in-law. As always, Valerie felt her heart quicken just at the thought of him. What had begun as a light-hearted flirtation had eventually become a stomach-churning need. It had taken her a long time to break the rules but she didn't regret it. Not now. He meant too much to her. This wasn't some hole-and-corner affair, some sordid sexual scandal in hotel rooms far from home. This was beautiful, wonderful, passionate and meaningful.

The first time he'd told her he loved her, she'd wept for joy. He was so caring and considerate. He'd thought of everything. The flowers, the candlelit dinner, the soft music. But a couple of weeks ago he'd dropped a bombshell.

'The firm is moving to New York,' he'd told her. 'Come with me.'

'I can't,' she'd sighed.

'But I have to go and I can't bear to be without you. Please my darling, come with me and let me make you happy for the rest of your life,' he'd pleaded.

With a heavy heart, Valerie had tried to explain. People expected . . . it was her duty . . . her husband needed to keep up appearances . . .

'You funny old-fashioned thing,' he'd smiled. 'Don't you deserve some happiness too?'

She'd almost said yes then, but it was too hard, too much against everything she'd been brought up to believe. She simply couldn't do it. Amazingly, he didn't get angry, or shout at her. He'd simply held her in his arms and told her he would wait for her. In that moment, and for the first time in her life, Valerie had felt truly loved. He didn't want her for any other reason than that he loved her.

Still thinking about Ashley, she turned towards Susan and smiled.

'Excuse me,' Valerie said. 'I have to make a phone call.'

*

'You know, I used to dream about living here,' Hazel suddenly said to Susan as Iris left the room with the tea tray.

'I'm not sure I'd like it,' whispered Susan. 'I love old things, but being stuck in this great barn of a place must be like living in a museum. Would you really give up your lovely cottage to live here?'

Hazel looked around the room. 'It looks beautiful,' she nodded, 'but you're right, my place is much cosier.'

Susan stood shakily to her feet. 'I'm dying for the loo.'

'Shall I come with you?' Hazel asked. 'You still look very pale.'

'I'll be fine,' said Susan shaking her head. 'Just point me in the right direction.'

The toilet was down the hall and to the left. Susan could see Valerie on the telephone in a small office opposite the sitting room but it wasn't until she came out of the toilet that she noticed a shadow by the kitchen door. Iris was listening in to Valerie's conversation behind the door. Puzzled, but not exactly surprised, Susan made her way back to the sitting room.

*

A few minutes later, Valerie came into the room. 'Susan, I've just phoned my son. He's a solicitor. Do you think your Jack might agree to speak to him?'

Susan's jaw dropped.

'Close your mouth, Susan,' giggled Hazel.

'That's very kind of you but I don't think we can afford . . .'

Valerie waved her hand dismissively. 'My son says he'll do it as a favour to me; first appointment, no charge.'

Susan's eyes filled with tears. 'That's very generous,' she began.

'Good, then that's settled,' said Valerie. She crossed the room to her writing bureau and pulled out his business card.

The door burst open and Iris came back into the room. 'Have I missed something?' she asked cheerfully.

'Valerie's son is a solicitor,' said Hazel, 'and he's going to make sure Susan's husband is being treated fairly by his employers.'

'That's good,' said Iris sitting back down.

Susan frowned. 'Oh, that reminds me,' she said, fishing around in her handbag. 'Iris, you remember last time we were together we talked about the typhoid epidemic in Worthing?'

Iris frowned. 'Did we?'

'Yes,' said Susan. 'I mentioned it because Maude has depicted it so beautifully on her square and you said you'd been there at the time.'

Iris nodded. 'Oh yes, yes of course I did.'

'Well I found a newspaper cutting all about it,' Susan said innocently.

She handed the flimsy brown piece of paper to Iris and the older woman stared down at it. The picture was of a man drawing water from a tanker parked on a street corner and the caption underneath went on to say that a hundred and eighty-six people had died during the epidemic.

'I remember it so well,' Iris said in a sad voice. 'It was shocking, absolutely shocking.'

Susan gave her a long stare.

'What?' Iris said accusingly.

'I don't think so Iris,' said Susan. 'That took place eighty-four years ago and if you were old enough to remember it, you must be well over one hundred years old.'

As the others turned towards her, Iris's face flamed.

'I think you've got all dressed up and come here for some other reason,' Susan went on.

'I don't know what you mean,' Iris said haughtily.

'What on earth are you saying, Susan?' Valerie blurted out.

'For a start,' Susan continued, 'I don't think that's her own hair. It's a wig and her hands give her away.'

'What's wrong with her hands?' Hazel asked.

'Do they look like an older woman's hands?' Susan asked. Iris quickly put her hands behind her back. 'In fact, I'd hazard a guess that Iris is no more than twenty-something. Am I right Iris?'

Iris lowered herself onto a chair and slumped forward. She put her hand to her forehead and as she rubbed it, the whole of her hair moved.

'It is a wig!' cried Valerie. She hesitated before adding, 'But I don't understand.'

'She was listening in on your phone call,' Susan went on.

'Okay, okay,' Iris cried, her voice completely changed. She pulled off the grey wig to reveal her own flattened down blonde hair, and began to scratch her head vigorously. 'I knew I wouldn't be any good it this. I should never have allowed my brother to talk me into it.'

'So what exactly is going on?' Hazel said sternly.

'My brother is a private investigator,' Iris began. 'Your husband,' she added, looking directly at Valerie, 'wants a divorce. He feels sure you're having an affair and I was sent here to see if I could find any evidence.'

'Well that's rich coming from him,' Valerie cried indignantly. 'I've lost count of number of flings he's had over the years.'

'I'm sorry,' said Iris, looking contrite. 'I feel dreadful now. When I came the first time, you were so nice to me that I tried to get out of it, but my brother kept on and on. I won't let it happen again. I hated doing it. It's a sordid and deceitful business.'

'The stupid thing is,' Valerie said with a grimace, 'I've always put up with his infidelities to spare his good name. How ironic is that? And now I find out that he's planning to throw *me* to the wolves.' She paused. 'So who exactly are you?'

'My real name is Deidre Abbott,' said Iris, 'and I'm at drama school training to be an actress.' She looked around helplessly. 'Not very good, am I? The story of my life I guess,' she added without bitterness. 'I never was much good at anything.'

'I wouldn't say that,' said Valerie. 'You certainly had me fooled.'

'And me,' said Hazel.

'And I only twigged because of your lovely hands,' said Susan, anxious to be generous. 'No wrinkles, you see.'

Deidre smiled wanly.

'I've got a skeleton in my cupboard too,' Hazel suddenly announced. Every head turned in her direction as she took a deep breath. 'My mother used to work in this house.'

Valerie beamed. 'Did she really?'

Hazel nodded. 'She was a kitchen maid at the beginning of the thirties but she got the sack.'

'Got the sack?' Deidre echoed. 'But why?'

'I think I can guess,' said Valerie, lowering her voice. 'If she was here in the thirties she would have known my husband's father, Thomas.'

'She did,' said Hazel, her gaze on Valerie's face. 'And she had a baby – and that baby was me.'

'So Thomas was your father?' said Valerie incredulously. 'No wonder you were looking so intently at his portrait.' She suddenly looked stricken. 'Oh Hazel, I'm sorry I said all those things about him. If I had known I never would have mentioned it.'

386

'No, no,' said Hazel raising her hand. 'It's fine. You only told the truth.'

'And what might that be?' Deidre wanted to know.

'That he was a complete rotter,' said Hazel. 'My mother was only a child, fourteen, and she was utterly taken in by his charms.'

'Hazel, I'm truly sorry,' Valerie repeated.

'Don't be,' said Hazel. 'Talking about it has been immensely freeing. All my life, my mother passed her bitterness over to me. Now that I know the truth, I don't like the man but I understand what happened.' She held out her hand and Valerie came towards her, but instead of simply shaking it, she put out her arms and embraced Hazel.

They all sat down again and Valerie offered them all another drink but it was politely refused.

There was a knock on the door and Stan walked in. 'All the visitors have gone, madam,' he said to Valerie. 'Is there anything else I can do for you?'

Valerie glanced up at the clock. 'Anybody fancy putting in one more hour's work?'

The others nodded enthusiastically and Stan held the door open for them. As they filed out of the room, his attention was suddenly caught by Iris's apparently altered appearance and his mouth dropped open.

'Don't worry, Stan,' said Hazel giving his arm a gentle squeeze. 'I'll explain everything when you drop me home.' She hesitated for a second. 'The offer of a lift is still there, isn't it?'

'You bet,' he beamed.

Back in the sewing room, Deidre pulled back the white sheet.

Susan leaned over Hazel's patchwork. 'What *does* that writing say?'

'Better you don't know,' said Hazel. 'It doesn't belong there now.'

'So what will you put in its place?'

Hazel looked thoughtful. 'This quilt is supposed to be about life in the village at the time of the Queen's jubilee,' she said. 'Well, I live in Periwinkle Cottage, so it has to periwinkles.'

'There's some lovely kingfisher blue in the material box,' Susan suggested.

'I'm changing something in mine too,' said Valerie. She laid a piece of blue material onto the sky above the outline of the house, under the Melcham coat of arms. 'There's no life in this picture. It's cold as stone. I shall have a swallow flying over it.'

'Mmm,' Hazel agreed. 'A hovering bird will make all the difference.'

'Not hovering,' Valerie added mysteriously. 'My bird is flying away to freedom.' She sat down and smiled at Susan. 'Have you made up your mind about what else to put in front of the school?'

Susan held up a piece of soft black shiny material. 'How about a woman with a pram?' she said. 'A few more babies like mine will give this village a real future.'

Valerie began stitching.

'You're not going to start that bird now, are you?' Hazel asked.

'I'm going to *finish* it now,' said Valerie. 'I shan't be here much longer. I have a plane to catch. I'm going to New York.'

'What, leaving the village?' cried Susan. 'But I thought you loved it here.'

'I do,' Valerie said giving her an enigmatic smile. 'But today all of you have helped me to realise, I love someone else much, much more.'

*

The day of the Queen's Silver Jubilee dawned bright and sunny after a night of heavy rain. The celebrations began the evening before with the queen herself lighting a beacon at Windsor Castle. As soon as that was done, a chain of beacons from John o'Groats to Lands' End lit the night sky right across the country. By

Worthing pier the mayor and councillors, together with a small crowd of people, gathered to light their beacon.

On the day itself, a million people lined the streets in London to watch the royal procession to St Paul's Cathedral where nearly three thousand guests, including heads of state from all over the world, had gathered for a service of thanksgiving. Millions more watched it on television. Afterwards, up and down the country roads were closed while friends and neighbours held street parties where excited boys and girls in fancy dress took part in a competition for the most original costume.

The celebrations in Goring were a little more modest. They began in St Mary's with a church service and the dedication of the Goring Silver Jubilee quilt. A reporter hovered around talking to local dignitaries and officials as choir boys sang. Among the congregation were the women who had worked on the quilt including Deidre, Hazel and Susan. They sat together. Most of the guests were in the older age bracket and included Susan's parents. The quilt itself was magnificent. Everybody said so.

Afterwards, as they gathered for wine, cheese and biscuits in the church hall, the three women were joined by the men in their lives. Everyone was anxious to catch up with each other's news.

'Which bit did you sew?' Susan's father asked.

Susan pointed to her own square and then to the square which June Carter had started. 'I also helped to sew the loops onto the edge which was quite tricky,' she said. 'It was so heavy it slid off the table as we machined it so we had to ask Stan the security guard to hold it for us.'

'Incredible, darling,' said Jack. He leaned forward and whispered in her ear. 'You're amazing.'

'It must be in the blood,' her mother cooed. 'Your grandmother was a beautiful seamstress.'

For Susan that was high praise indeed.

The reporter and his photographer came round and Deidre, Hazel and Susan stood together for a picture.

'Is your husband alright now?' Hazel asked as Jack went to the table to fetch some orange juice.

Susan nodded. 'He was exonerated and the real culprit was arrested. It seems the bloke was doing his best to put the blame on Jack. He almost succeeded but they sussed him out and now he's going to stand trial at Lewes.'

'It must be a huge relief for you both,' said Hazel.

'We couldn't have done it without Valerie's help,' said Susan, stroking her rounded bump. 'Her solicitor son was marvellous.'

'What about you, Deidre?' Hazel asked. 'What are you going to do now that you have finished at drama school?'

Deidre slipped her arm through the tall, good-looking man standing next to her. 'Well, Rex and I are getting married in September,' she said. 'Rex is my agent.' She gazed lovingly up into his face.

'Congratulations,' cried Hazel and Susan.

'And I have a job now,' Deidre went on. 'I do commercials.' She held up her glove covered hands and began to sing, '*Hands that do dishes can be soft as your face . . .* Someone else is in front of the camera but those hands are mine!' And everybody laughed.

'She has to protect them to keep them looking good,' said Rex by way of explanation.

Deidre smiled inwardly. She wished her old high school teacher could see her now. How she would love to see him eat his words.

'You'll never amount to anything in this life Deidre Abbott,' he'd said one day. 'You were born thick, and you'll stay thick. Nobody's ever going to want the likes of you batting on their team.' *Well just look at me now*, she thought as she raised her eyebrow. *And I'll show you my bank account if you like.*

'Has anyone heard from Valerie?' Susan asked.

'She's in New York,' said Hazel. 'She's divorcing her husband on the grounds of adultery and I imagine she'll be re-married before the year is out.'

'Good,' said Susan. 'She deserves a little happiness. 'What about you Hazel? Are you feeling better about things?'

Just then Stan the security guard came up to them and handed Hazel a glass of wine. She gazed up at him with a radiant smile. 'Thank you, darling,' she cooed, and although she didn't answer the question, Susan guessed that everything in her garden was rosy too.

A woman tapped her on her shoulder and Susan spun around. 'Oh mum,' she called out. 'Look who's here.'

'Jenny Ruddock!' Susan's mother cried. 'I haven't seen you since my tenth birthday.'

'I'm Jenny Bartlett now,' said her old friend. 'It's good to see you, Frankie.'

The two women embraced each other warmly.

'I remember that lovely Russian doll your mother made,' said Jenny, stepping back. 'I was so jealous and then she told us the remarkable story that went with it, as I recall. Do you still have it?'

'It's still in the family,' said Frankie.

'Have you heard the story?' Jenny asked Susan.

'Of course,' Susan said. 'I grew up with it.'

Jenny slipped her arm through Frankie's and led her towards the reporter. 'This is my son,' she said. 'You really must tell him all about it.'

## The End

You can read Frankie's story
about her Russian doll in
*Goodnight Sweetheart.*

An unexpected letter will change
her life forever…

THE *SUNDAY TIMES* BESTSELLER

Pam Weaver

Can she keep
her family safe?

A
Mother's
Gift

A dramatic story filled with family, scandal and friendships
that bring hope in the darkness.

It's 1939 and the threat of
war hangs over Britain…

When war arrives, hope and friendship
will see them through…

A Sister's
Courage

MOLLY GREEN

An inspiring wartime story of friendship, bravery and love.

**Disowned and desperate.**
**But can she change her fate?**

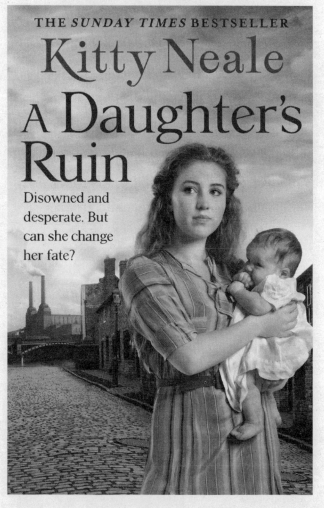

THE *SUNDAY TIMES* BESTSELLER

# Kitty Neale

# A Daughter's Ruin

Disowned and
desperate. But
can she change
her fate?

A heart-wrenching tale, perfect for fans of Dilly Court,
Katie Flynn and Rosie Goodwin.